# THE PATH

between pillars and growing divisions
in the town of Port Bedford
around which these adventures revolve
and which inspires some painful reflections
by the daughter of lesser relations
in the most privileged family of that town

## A NOVEL BY
## ERIK KONGSHAUG

D1547863

BLINKING YELLOW BOOKS

*Taos, New Mexico*

## ACKNOWLEDGEMENTS

The author would like to thank Heidi Tinsman, Seth Rolland, Debbie McCann, Martha Kongshaug, Beth Enson, Robert Westbrook & Phyllis Hotch for all their editorial support and input, and Robert Todd, Robert McCann & Gina Azzari for their artistic contributions.

The publishers gratefully acknowledge the assistance of Gina Azzari, Phyllis Hotch, Robert McCann & Seth Rolland in the production of this book.

### ISBN 1-883968-07-0

COVER DRAWING: "Back to Herself," by Robert Todd
PHOTOGRAPHS OF CANDY: Robert McCann
AUTHOR PHOTO: Heidi Tinsman
PRODUCTION: Stone Soup Graphics

Blinking Yellow Books is a non-profit publishing house, for the benefit of writers.
Contact us at:
Post Office Box 1860
Ranchos de Taos, New Mexico 87557

First printing: 1998

To H.T.—with love, passion and admiration

"I saw a yellow one lately, a little green. It was decayed at the edges. It was blown by the wind. When I was ten years old I used to shut my eyes in the winter on purpose and fancy a green leaf, bright, with veins on it, and the sun shining. I used to open my eyes and not believe them, because it was very nice, and I used to shut them again."

- Kirillov, in Dostoevsky's *The Possessed*

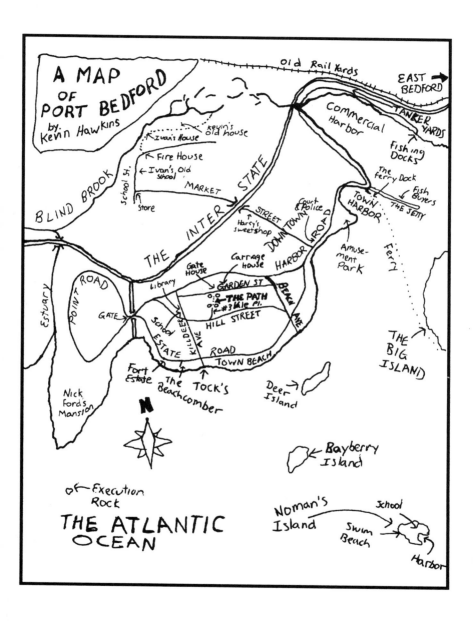

from Kate's diary,
June Twenty-first, 1976:

*I was walking home at night because I had to.*

*I was walking home at night because the library branch on Killdeer had to close.*

*I didn't see when a black shape rose up in the path, because the moon made shadows under the hedges.*

*I saw the man in the moon.*

*I tried to say Oh hi Nick but his face was pale and trembly so I stopped.*

*I stopped walking home.*

*I didn't want to look at him.*

*It wasn't me.*

# CHAPTER ONE

"Fifth grade!" shouted Kevin Hawkins—smallish, blondish, round-faced—with his left fist up in a gesture he had learned from Tock the candystand man. He was shouting to Kate and Johnny Harrigan, who spilled out together through the crumbling pillars of the old overgrown footpath, and onto the junky pavement of Kevin's dead-end street, like emeralds fallen from the sun-filled leaves overhead.

They were twins, but you couldn't imagine two more different twins in your life.

Kate was thin, taller than Kevin was, with stick-like arms and legs that were stronger than you might think. She wore glasses, little round gold ones and her hair was so blonde it was white.

Johnny was as big as a teenager, freckled everywhere, with hair that looked just exactly like a gray-black steel scrubbing pad. He had a So? on his face.

"I mean, hell and fuck," said Kevin to amend his enthusiasm as they came closer, "Not like fifth grade is that big a deal." Johnny let out a big laugh and poked Kevin in the belly.

"It grows on you," he said. "Fuck. I barely made it this year." The two of them went to private school and had already been fifth graders for weeks. "Better head to Tock's later to celebrate, though." He gave Kevin a shove so he almost fell down. All three started to run like cars out of control back to Kevin's house, giggling and tagging each other with no rules at all to the game.

Then another boy, on a bike, came to a skid like a fishhook in the salty sunshine—dropping down a big battered bag off his handle-bars right on Johnny's bare feet almost. Now Johnny had an angry Who's this? on his face.

Ivan had ridden all way from the other side of Port Bedford. It was a long way from there near the big harbor where Kevin used to live, past the tankers and fishbuyers, the ferryboats to the islands, past the abandoned amusement park where the wooden rollercoaster was rotting, past the gate to the Point, on Estate Road beyond Garden Street where all the real mansions were and where the road was blocked by a striped wooden gate that went up and down to keep you from going on, past the town park and beach, to here on Vale Place where Kevin lived now with his big sister, Deirdre. So that was why Ivan's face was all sweaty and blotchy red like someone had punched him.

Until five days ago, when Ivan showed up like a ghost at his school with a lost, hard look on his face, it'd been a while since Kevin had seen him. He was larger now than he used to be and more muscular too and he had this tough-guy squinty stare he didn't used to have, even when he wasn't trying. And his hair, always dirty and stringy brown, was longer too: almost down to his shoulders. He wore a black pocket t-shirt and long pants in spite of the heat and looked a lot more like the troublemaker that everybody heard he was, even though Kevin knew how smart he was: not just smart, like Kevin, but book-smart-without-trying, like Kate.

"It's hot," Ivan said, answering Kevin's silent question about his face, "and my bag doesn't balance so good."

"Hey, Ivan."

"Thanks."

Kevin cared a lot what Johnny and especially Kate would think about Ivan. He wanted to be extra careful not to say anything stupid.

This important moment, the very beginning of summer, it was hard for Kevin to believe he was even standing here, ready to bring his two worlds, old and new, together into one.

Johnny stood with both hands out, like he was holding up the world until someone provided him with an explanation. Kate squatted down behind a curtain of hair, digging at a hole in the pavement with a rock. They were sizing up Ivan in their different ways—Johnny staring straight into his eyes and Kate not looking at him at all.

"This is my old friend, Ivan," said Kevin. "He's coming to stay at my sister's with me." But it came out nervous and not like he'd planned it, so his eyebrows felt heavy. He was worried that Ivan might make things cloudy.

"Who?"

"Ivan Otrusky.  He's from across town where I used to live. Before my sister got her own place here.  Him and me were little together."

"Are you strong?" said Johnny.

"Stronger than me, maybe," Kevin answered for his friend. "But not as strong as you."

Johnny nodded seriously, like that was okay.

"We were best friends when we lived with our moms."

"Guess I can trust him," said Kate, "if he was best friends with you."

Ivan hadn't been bothered by them talking about him right in front of him like that.

It seemed to impress Johnny: "That's excellent, because, guess what, we can go to our house and hang out there—it's a really cool house. Our parents just took off for some weekend party or something and they'll be no one except maybe for Nick Ford that rents the Gatehouse by the road."

"Except he won't," said Kate very seriously. "Because he has another house somewhere else and he never will come back."

"Sure he might," said Johnny.   "He comes back sometimes, when he feels like it. It's his office I think. People come there sometimes with appointments and I show them the right house. There's no sign or anything."

"He won't," said Kate.

"I thought we were going to Tock's," said Kevin. He felt funny about going over to their fancy house on Garden Street, even if their parents weren't there. He had never been inside it before, as a matter of fact, even though it was just on the other side of the path. Like he would get it dirty or something. It always felt easier to wait outside.

"I better drop off my stuff first," said Ivan. "Didi home?"

"Probably not," said Kevin. "I think she said she was taking off somewhere."

"I hope she's there," said Kate.

"What's Tock's?" said Ivan

"He's a who. Runs a candystand on the water. C'mon you guys, let's dump off Ivan's stuff and go to your house if we're going. I want to get to Tock's before the workers get off."

Kevin lived at number 3 Vale Place now—a run down paint-coming-off white flat-roofed place. His sister Deirdre, or Didi as Ivan had called her, left cigarette butts and coffee cups and ashtrays all over the front porch all the time and there was a lot of junk in the yard. The door was closed. "I told you, she's not here," said Kevin. "Just dump your bag on the porch, Ivan, and let's go."

"How come she's not here?" said Kate. "I wanted to say hi and stuff."

"You know. I don't know. She had to leave. She's just always busy. Maybe we'll catch her later before she goes to the bar."

Ivan dumped his bike in the yard and walked up the three steps to the little porch and set down his bag. "Hey Cool," he said, holding up a piece of notebook paper that had been carefully weighted down on the porch rail with a pack of Juicy Fruit gum. It said, 'Hi Ivan,' then a heart, then 'Didi.' Ivan passed out the gum and soon they were all chomping. Kevin and Ivan took off their sneakers, knotting  the laces so they hung from their belt loops—the way Johnny and Kate had theirs—to start toughening up the soles of their feet for the summer.

The only thing Kevin's neighborhood lacked was other kids Kevin liked. There were no other good kids his age on Vale and if Kevin hadn't met Kate and Johnny, he would've been stuck with just his annoying neighbor, Bobby Carroll, who didn't appreciate Tock at all and was afraid of him. Without the path, Kevin's neighborhood and the pretty boring neighborhood of Kate and Johnny Harrigan would have been completely separate, and Kevin couldn't have possibly met them or have made friends. For grown-ups they were two whole different places.

Kevin heard the sound of clinking metal. The neighbor kid, Bobby, was using the oil can on his bike next door, whirring the sprocket so much with the wind and the cicada sound that Kevin felt dizzy and shut his eyes, but they were all red inside so he opened them again quick.

"You okay?" Ivan asked.

"Never mind. Let's go to your guys' house if we're going," he said to Johnny and Kate.

The neighbor kid was staring at Ivan with a half-afraid, half-hard look as they passed his driveway, until Ivan stopped and stared him back, which made Bobby Carroll look back down and start oiling his bicycle again. So they walked on.

"You know Bobby?" Kevin asked.

"No. Maybe he knows me. Who knows? A lot of kids think they do."

"He's sort of a jerk, but sometimes I have to stay over there when Deirdre's at work."

"So, why are your parents gone?" said Ivan to Kate. She shrugged.

"They're definitely not coming back, right?" said Johnny.

"Definitely. Dad's already at the weekend place and Mom's driving straight up after some meeting she has downtown." The three of them went on, but Kevin hesitated.

By the time he caught up, they had stopped. Kevin caught a whiff of cigarette smoke and heard the loud voices of bigger kids. Johnny was talking back to them, all out of breath but not sounding scared. He was so strong by himself that he was probably just mad at being outflanked. "If all four of us go, they'll let us by. Besides, they like you, Kevin, don't they?"

"I guess so." They knew his sister, Deirdre, from the Beachcomber where she worked. She let them drink there sometimes even though they weren't all eighteen.

"Think you can handle it, Ivan?" said Johnny, appraising him professionally. Ivan shrugged. "I think you can," Johnny decided.

Three big kids were camped around the pillars, like zombies. Pitching rocks and staring, and not doing anything at all. Kate was the first one to try walking through the pillars where they stood to get to the path.

"Hey, it's the little bookworm," said one, stepping in her way.

"Serious," said another. She told me some word the other day that, no shit, was like right out of a dictionary. Hey, what was that word you said?"

"Ominous," Kate said.

"Yeah. Check it out. And what does it mean?"

"Shadowy."

The third guy's voice was like stones cracking against pavement, "Hey, Nick was asking about you."

"Yeah?" said Johnny, pretending like they said it to him.

"Not you, Rover. Hey, I hear you kids been hanging around the Candyman. I'd watch it if I was you."

Only Ivan seemed completely unintimidated, turning to Kevin as if the older kids weren't even there. "So this guy Nick is the Candyman? His name is Tock, though, right?"

The third older kid guffawed.

"Leave 'em," said the second one, maybe because he remembered that Kate was smart. "These kids are okay. Calvin, right?"

"Kevin."

"Summer vacation for you kids now, right? Good times. What're you going to do? Go away to summer camp, I guess." He laughed like an ogre. "Just out on the streets like the rest of us, huh? Hey, I'll give you a ride in the Jalopy some time. Be cool."

"Thank you," said Kevin and they all filed by, eyes to the ground except Ivan to whom they seemed to give a bit of distance. It was a relief to enter the cool green shade of the path.

This municipal footpath was Kevin's one fragile connection to Kate and Johnny. Otherwise their street was in a whole separate neighborhood from his. Without it, they would have never come to his neighborhood. They would have had to go three blocks down on Beach, two over on Estate Rd., before they would even be near Tock's candy-stand which, so far as Kevin was concerned, was the whole heart of where he lived (that and the Beachcomber bar where his sister worked) and then it would take about another whole five minutes to get back again to Kevin's street from there. Instead, they practically lived right next to him.

Johnny started galloping up and down the hard dirt track where both ends were hidden from view and the world was nothing but a vaulted hall of green. He always made a lot of noise in here. Even more than just because he was big—like the world had to make room for him. His face round and smooth and evenly freckled even on his ears; it should have been a happy face, and Johnny was certainly smiling a row of wide flat teeth as he bombed back towards them and slapped his hands onto Kevin's shoulders to break his momentum. But it was a sad face, Kevin thought, no matter how big and loud he was on the outside. Johnny winked as he skirted deftly around Kevin and offered Kevin his tremendous back. "Hop on." he said snorting like a horse. Kevin jumped on.

"So let's ride," shouted Johnny. "There's cookie roll at our house. A war-horse needs plenty of fuel," he said

"Giddy up!" shouted Kevin, all the way to where he could start to see Garden Street; then he slid off and turned back for Kate and Ivan. Johnny galloped on ahead riderless.

As they caught up to Kevin in the middle of the path, Ivan was saying to Kate, "This is a cool place." You couldn't see either end and the birds were whacking around for mulberries. "It looks like the Secret Garden."

"It *is* secret," she said, but she looked at Kevin, not at Ivan because she could tell he was listening. Kate always knew who was listening and she knew how much Kevin loved secrets.

Johnny was way ahead already, so it was just the three of them. They could hear him whacking mulberry bushes and yelling, "Make way for the explorers!" Kevin had no idea what the game was, so it'd have been dumb to catch up.

"Is it a bad secret?" said Ivan. She smiled at him,

"Kevin was right, you're a nice guy, Ivan," she said. "Let's go."

Across the street from the well-kept pillars at the other end of the path, Kate and Johnny's house came into view so big that it had its own name—the Carriage House.

It was about as different from 3 Vale Place as you could get—rising above the Gatehouse, which stood shut up with the curtains drawn in front of it, like a mystery with five round turrets and steep crazy roofs it would be great to get on somehow.

Bees were buzzing in the flower borders of the long front walk that they followed in single file. Kate unlocked the door with a key from her shorts' pocket.

"There's no one here but me and Johnny, just like I promised. They won't be back until tomorrow. And he's not there either," she said looking over her shoulder at the Gatehouse.  So Kevin went in, even though he still didn't want to. He had an almost superstitious feeling that it would endanger the fragile friendship he'd created.

Their kitchen was blindingly white—white tile floors, white counters, table top and walls—and everything, from the pots to the oven, seemed to have shiny chrome handles.

A pale green book named The Secret Garden lay upside down on the kitchen table.

"Ivan reads a lot too," said Kevin, just to say something. Kate always had a book; that was why she wore glasses.  She looked like a little grandmother sometimes.

"You're staying with Kevin and Deirdre, huh?"

Kevin looked up even though she was talking to Ivan, not him: a reflex from hearing his name spoken.

"I guess for a little while, if it's okay," Ivan said.

"Deirdre's nice.  I like her."

"Yeah.  I think so too." Ivan scratched his arm muscle and slid some of his hair back behind his ear. "She used to look out for Kev and me when we were little.  Kevin and me used to run around in that salt marsh, you know, behind the firehouse and the warehouses?"

Kate put some of her hair back behind her ear too, "There's a lot of good places here. We'll show them to you. But first..." she pulled a roll of chocolate chip cookie dough out of the refrigerator, couldn't find a knife and started to slice it with a spoon. The lumps looked funny on the cookie sheet, and she laughed as she stuck it in the oven, then turned it to bake.

Kevin was just starting to feel halfway comfortable when the brief acceleration of a big car, pulling itself up the short cement ramp into the driveway, disrupted his mood. The engine stayed idling for a minute, filling the kitchen with white noise. Kate was frozen up against the oven by the time it shut off. Clicking metal, inside and out—the oven heating up, the engine cooling down.

"Fuck," Johnny hissed to her, "I thought you said..."

"She's not supposed to be here," Kate hissed back.

The sounds of quick heels on the flagstone walk. Kevin had a bad feeling.

"C'mon, let's leave out the back," he whispered to Ivan.

Johnny, meanwhile, had pulled himself up onto the kitchen sink to peer out the window,

"She's walking over to the Gatehouse;" he whispered, "why's she doing that?"

Through the open window, they could hear knocking on the door of the smaller house and a low woman's voice calling in a loud whisper, "Nick?" then, after a silence, "Damnit." Now the steps were coming towards them.

"The whole house smells like cookies," said Kate in despair.

The sound of keys, a moment of hesitation and Johnny and Kate's elegant mother, whom Kevin had actually only seen once before from a distance, stepped in the hall and said softly, "Is that you? Why are you in here?"

Johnny slid down off the sink, looked at the others uncertainly, and said, "Sorry."

Mrs. Harrigan rushed into the kitchen with a lovely look on her face, stopped suddenly and took a sharp breath when she saw the four of them, standing guiltily around the large kitchen floor.

After just a split second, she looked like what everyone's mom should be. She was tall and pretty and dressed nice and smelling of perfume. She hardly seemed to notice them after that.

"Oh," she said. "I just forgot something at the house, Kate...jewelry..." Her nostrils flared slightly, "Cookies? How lovely, why..." she put down her hand bag on the table, looked at her watch, but pretended not to, and slipped on a cheery flower-printed apron that hung by the stove. "Let me," she said. It sounded to Kevin like she was talking to herself. She didn't even seem to register that Ivan and Kevin were in the room. "Where were they...yes." She flung open a high cabinet and pulled out some paper cups and plates. She opened the refrigerator, counted heads and poured four milks, then put on a hot mitt and pulled the cookies out of the oven. They were still doughy and had barely started to brown, but she shoveled them onto the plate with a spatula, flicked off the oven, covered them with cellophane and thrust them into Kate's astonished hands. The cellophane beaded up like a window in the rain. "Now each of you take a cup and, well, there you are." Kevin stood mutely with his cup, wondering what to do next. "Run along," she said cheerily. She looked at her watch one more time. "I'll lock up and we'll see each other tomorrow night." Kevin wondered why he had been so afraid of meeting her all this time; she was like the perfect mom. "Kate, you have your keys? Lovely. Run along now. Out, out, out."

from Kate's diary,
June Twenty-second, 1976:


*But it was me when I saw through the window.*

*I saw them because Johnny was at wrestling and I was by myself in the yard throwing his GI Joe doll to see what way its arms and legs and neck was when it landed.*

*Their arms and legs and necks was twisting too and I knew I wasn't supposed to see that but I couldn't help it because I was there in the tree.*

*He picked up his big blue chin through the window and saw me in the tree and saw that I saw him too. His eyes were shiny black and his face was red and his teeth were hungry white.*

*My mom didn't see because she was on her back.*

# CHAPTER   TWO

Tock's was at the dead end of Killdeer, on the far side of Estate Rd., where no one went. Didi said she had no idea how he stayed in business. The street was chained off, condemned, ending at a falling down sea wall, beyond which the gray ocean extended to the horizon. Kevin had never been on the sea, though fishing boats and freighters and even tankers were plentiful in Port Bedford. Just somehow, the opportunity had never come up.

To the left was the municipal beach beneath an overlooking park. It cost five dollars to get in and had its own concession stands inside. On the other side there was a big fence that extended out even past the sea wall, a sheer drop of over thirty feet, hanging over nothing, to keep people from walking along the top of the sea wall to the natural rocky cliff of the coast farther up, where they could climb down to the water. They were in the process of replacing the old sea wall with a new one. To protect  the big new construction site. Sections of the brand new sea wall were already in place beyond the fence, made out of smooth cement. The remains of the old pebbly concrete one, broken up in big chunks, lay still in ruins on the water-line at its feet. Cranes still hung around behind the fence between knocked down trees, their yellow tops visible from almost anywhere in town.

They were building a fancy cluster of houses there too, called Ocean Spray, which was going to be like a separate community with a wall around it. There used to be a beautiful secret forest here called the Fort Estate,  because kids made forts back there.  And when Kevin first moved here, it ran half way up the Point. Only Deirdre, his big sister, said it was really called the Ford Estate, because somebody named Ford used to own it in the old times. Just like she said that the Forty-five Oat Flakes cereal he ate every morning were really Fortified not Forty-five. But it didn't matter anyhow, because it was all fenced up and they'd already torn down almost all the trees. To make room for one more walled off place where he wasn't allowed.

So far, though, the chained off end of Killdeer Avenue remained as falling down as ever. People from the municipal beach on the other side never came up here because the street was too broken down looking.

His whole name was Tom Tock. He had curly black hair and a long moustache. And a big tattoo of a swordfish showing on his muscly, olive-mocha colored arm.

The truth was Kevin liked to hang around Tock so much recently because he somehow reminded Kevin of his father. It all depended on what kind of mood they were in. His dad used to have a moustache too. Kevin hadn't seen his dad now in about three years.

"I'm a fifth grader now!" shouted Kevin, an incredibly bold move without sizing up Tock's mood beforehand. He just felt sure somehow Tock would appreciate his being done with school for the year.

"Do you know what that means?" Tock settled down on his elbows, lit one of his short cigarettes, ready to draw out all about Kevin's good feeling, like his dad used to do in the good days.

"This is a special occasion."

"What's so damn special about fifth grade," said Tock like maybe his mood might be changing.

But Kevin persisted. "I'm free!" he said.

"Free for what?" said Tock.

"Free for the summer."

"All right, boy. All right I'll buy that."

"Buy what?" said Kevin smiling.

"Buy nothing," said Tock. "You're free remember? Candy costs money." Tock never gave stuff away, but there was no harm in trying if he was in a good mood.

"What's fifth grade gonna be like?" said Kevin hanging off the counter by his fingertips.

"Ah, now that was a time," said Tock, his big fingers pulling down the corner of his moustache with his orange stained fingers.

"Like what?"

"Like a lot of things."

"Like what?"

"Like when I saw about differences, how 'bout that? And the differences between differences."

Kevin laughed, "Sounds like you were pretty confused."

"Not like you, eh?" said Tock.

"No really," said Kevin realizing that he might be already becoming a bother. "Like what?"

Tock lit another cigarette. It was okay. "That was the summer my uncle from East Bedford hired me on to his fishing boat. I'll tell you about it sometime. It could be, now it just could be the summer, Kevin, when you become a man. "

The word had a big sound. Then Kevin thought about becoming his dad and he wasn't so sure. A fisherman he liked that better. "I'm gonna be a fisherman too, Tock, just like you." Tock had a soft laugh for that, and a sad look to his heavy browed eyes.

"I'm no fisherman now, Kevin, not unless you call this stand a boat. Don't let 'em take nothing from you. That's the main thing."

"Hey Tock," said Johnny and Kate, one after the other. Ivan just smiled at him and sort of put his hand up.

"What's up, you guys, on a beautiful sunny day?" said Tock, tossing his closed jack knife in a spin and catching it. Then he put it in the pocket of his white cook shirt. His jack knife had a bone handle that looked like it was made out of fingerprints and it was huge as a dinosaur bone. Jack knives were big on all their minds this summer. Johnny said that the guy who had his office next to their house had one made out of solid pearls. Kevin just had a stupid one for camping so he never carried it around, but Ivan had a great one.

"This is Ivan," he said to Tock, "He's our new friend." Tock was an important person for Ivan to know.

"Ivan, eh? The Mad Russian." They all laughed at that. Ivan was skinny, even though he had muscles, and quiet most of the time. And Ivan laughed too.

"Really, I hardly ever get mad," and they all laughed even harder.

"So what made you throw your lot in with these tough guys, eh? The lady excluded, of course," Tock bowed a little, sweeping out his hand.

"I'm just as tough as anybody when I want to be." Kate had a quiet voice. Johnny made as if he were about to laugh and winked at Kevin. She looked at Johnny, in a stern way that made him blush and look at the ground, and then at Ivan who didn't laugh at all and stood there with the same wondering-what's-going-on face he'd had all day so far, and she smiled at him. Johnny looked up then, he'd stopped laughing, looked at his sister with a pained flabby expression, like his feelings were hurt.

"We're not so tough and she's pretty tough," said Kevin.

"Looks like it," said Tock shaking his head and laughing at some secret joke he had. He lit a cigarette and asked Kate what she wanted, "Guess you're the main man today."

"I didn't say that. I'll take three Atomic Fireballs." She laid a quarter flat down on the counter.

"Yes, ma'am."

Kevin decided on Jawbreakers and a box of Lemonheads for himself. Johnny got some purple gum. Ivan didn't get anything,

"Aren't you going to get nothing, Ivan?"

"I'm not hungry."

"Here," Tock threw him an Atomic Fireball. "Welcome to the neighborhood."

Tock never did something like that.

Maybe that's why Johnny broke away suddenly and sat down on the curb leaning over his knobby knees. He stuck half the log of purple gum in his mouth and chomped until everything around him had a purple smell. His lower jaw, pressed to his knees, made his head bob up and down as he chewed.

"What's the matter, Johnny?"

"Nothing.  Forget it." said Johnny. "You wouldn't understand." as if none of them were standing there, in a special circle around him. "It's about something I'm thinking about. About things," he added as if that were sufficient to explain why it was too profound for them to grasp.

Kate said, "What? I was just smiling."

"You can do whatever you want," was his answer, but it was snappy like he was hurt.

"You want a Lemonhead?" said Kevin.

It was quitting time now at the construction site and a bunch of the workers, mostly Portuguese and Spanish men from East Bedford, were walking over to the stand.

"I got a little business going on, kids. I'll catch you another time okay? Tell you lots. Whatever you want to know."

The conversation was over as quickly as it had begun. Tock was like that. And he had sent Kevin away before now when the construction workers came, on break or after work to buy coffee and donuts and talk with Tock. There was always something angry and serious about everyone's faces, like they were doing something dangerous. From far away it looked like they were just buying coffee maybe, but, if he didn't think so already, Kevin could have told that Tock was a pretty important person by the way the others looked at him. Of course Tock probably sold a lot of coffee too. But Kevin imagined they all used to be fishermen too, like Tock, and they had to meet to do the secret things fishermen need to do to still be fishermen. Tock always made sure Kevin was at the other side of the street though before he'd let them start talking.

They wandered over to the end of the old chainlink fence above the sea wall. Maybe after this summer Kevin would be old enough, and Tock might let him be a fisherman too. And Ivan was here, and Kate. Johnny was still moping though, and that spoiled his mood a little.

"So, you want that Lemonhead, or what?" said Kevin sternly. Johnny stuck the huge wad of his purple gum halfway out his mouth, so it stunk up everything. Johnny knew how much Kevin hated the smell of purple. "Don't listen to what the big kids say about Tock," said Kevin. "They're just jealous is all."

"It's not Tock I care about," said Johnny shaking his head dismissively. "I already told you you wouldn't understand."

"Why are you being such a drag all of a sudden?" Kate said. "Come on, let's do something," she added, one cheek bulging so the words came out garbly.

"All right. I've got something we can do. Enough of this sissy stuff. Let's see who's made of what, " Johnny said with an eye on Ivan. "Let's climb down the sea wall and go swimming." Johnny looked up and glared at everybody.

The only way out to the sea wall was out around that chainlink fence that had no wall under it. It kept going for a couple feet after the street ended. You'd have to climb with nothing under you but sharp rocks, a very long way down. The water down there was swirling around, and getting swallowed, and getting spit up from the big black holes between pieces of the old sea wall.

They waited a long time, just in case Johnny wanted to take it back. Johnny didn't look in a hurry now either.

"I bet there are caves down there," he said finally. "Maybe there would be a place where only we could go. And I could try out my new fishing rod. Look at this old rusty fence." Johnny rattled it with all his ten fingers, letting himself drop backwards over and over. Pieces of brown fell down all around.

"Well, if any one of us is gonna break it," Kevin said, "it'll be you, Johnny."

"All right, I'll go first."

"We can't swim down there," Kate suggested hopefully. "I don't have my bathing suit."

"We'll just look."

"Oh." She looked down over the wall. "In that case, all right then."

Everybody else was quiet.

"I'll go," said Ivan. "I don't care."

"Me first," said Johnny and stuck his toes in a hole, and the fence shook and swayed and jangled. His face was red and shiny. Drops dripped from the big smooth place of his double chin. But he got around and lowered himself down on the top rock. He was in the

Fort Estate where no kid had been for a year.

"It's not so bad," he said up though the fence.

Kate said, "I guess I'm next." She grabbed the fence and started to go around, and she was almost out to the end where she had to make the turn-around to the other side.

"What's wrong?" asked Kevin.

"My foot is stuck." Her voice was hard to hear in the wind. She was yanking and twisting her leg and you could already see it got scraped on the rust. She was looking to the side back at them on top of the wall, then looking down to Johnny, through the fence way down below on the rocks. Way too far to be any help. Her eyes were big, even though she'd taken off her glasses. "I'm stuck," she said and her mouth was very small; some of her hair was stuck in it. "This was a stupid idea, Johnny," she yelled and started wriggling her leg like she wanted to twist it off.

"Take your shoe off."

It was Ivan's voice. He was leaning over the top of the sea wall towards the fence, held up by only his hands. His feet were just hanging from the wall a little bit off the street. Kate reached down and slipped her heel from the dirty blue sneaker and wrapped the lace a couple times around her finger so she could hold on again. She smiled at Ivan again.

"Thanks."

Her barefoot leg  wobbled every time she stuck her toes in a new place. But she got around. And lowered herself onto the top rock of the crumbled old Fort Estate sea wall.

"Made it!" she shouted back up. Johnny gave her a little charley horse punch and turned away.

Ivan got around okay and then it was Kevin's turn. The wind made him feel like a ghost when there was nothing underneath him. And the rusty pipes of the fence made groan noises, like maybe this wasn't such a good idea. His heart was still racing after his feet found the safety of a large flat rock.

Safe, they climbed around on the old concrete for a while before discovering it at last: the perfect cave. Between two big pieces and one on top was a secret entrance underneath the rocks. Lots of smaller pieces inside you couldn't see at first. The darkness was cold and salty and still, even though it was windy and hot outside. Everything was gray, with just the one place where day came in, and all you could see was the water and the sky and a big tanker going in slow-motion on the line between them. Inside, was room for them all. One by one they crawled in and found a special rock to sit on. Their faces looked speckley. Kevin could see all the little every-colored molecules jumping in their skin. He smelled the water in the black spaces where he couldn't see. He heard it slosh and smack like lips.

Kevin whispered, "This is going to be a good summer."

"No one can know about this place, but the four of us," said Johnny. "Do we swear?" And they all did.

But Kevin's foot was starting to get wet. Water burst up all around them. They were half soaked by the time they'd scrambled out of the cave, laughing and whooping and fluttering water off of themselves with their hands. The tide was coming in. So they half wound up swimming after all.

from Kate's diary,
June Twenty-third, 1976:


*I met a new boy today whose name is Ivan. He is a friend of Kevin who's come to stay with him for the summer. I like his eyes which are sea color.*

*We had fun today but now it's dark. And the Gatehouse is dark and my parents too till tomorrow night. Me and Johnny have all the lights on to scare away robbers.*

*He has his office in the Gatehouse since before me and Johnny were alive.*

*It was a accident I saw him with his moonface in the daytime. I wasn't supposed to be home but I was.*

*I was supposed to go to the library and I didn't but then I went right away and I never told anyone so my mom didn't even know.*

*Only he knew so I was scared to come home.*

*But he was waiting for me on the path.*

*I wouldn't of told anyways but he made my mouth full of glue so I know I can never say.*

*He made me take off my pants too for him to see if I was hiding anything. I wasn't so Leave me alone.*

*He was scared for what he did though so Here Take this is a present for you.*

*It looked like a moonbone. I didn't want but he made me Take this and don't say anything.*

*I never did say not a word but yesterday he lied on me to my mom.*

*I thought if I didn't say he would never come back but I was wrong because he did anyways.*

*My mom and dad were just getting ready and me and Johnny were late for goodbye dinner and they were mad.*

*He busted right in the middle of kitchen dinner and said Sorry to interrupt but Carol I seem to have mislaid my penny knife you know* the one I wouldn't mention but I'm sentimental because I've had it since we were kids This is awkward but I think Kate must of taken it.

I didn't even cry when she spanked me in front of him and everybody. I stared straight at him while she did it and he was scared of me and couldn't look me back. Johnny looked away too. It was because he was sad for me I think but far away like he was wrestling inside and all tangled up.

I'm glad that only Johnny is here now. He's gone to his home and my parents are gone to their party and Johnny is snoring in his room.

I snuck out in the yard in my bare feet to put his stupid penny knife back through the mailslot of the dark Gatehouse. I opened up the blade first and dropped it so it stuck into the floor inside.

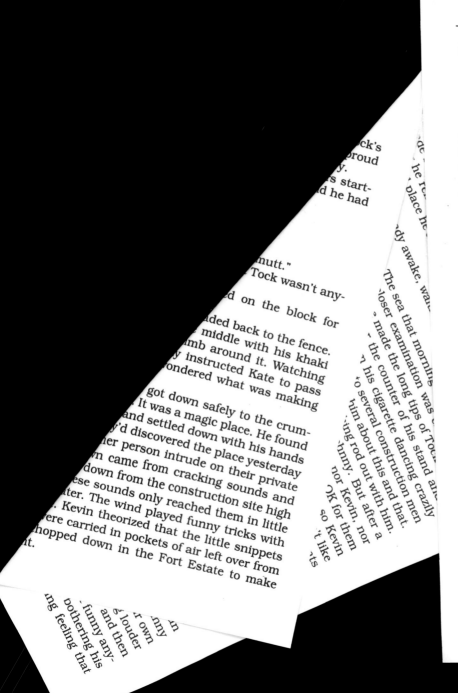

# CHAPTER THREE

Didi was working that night so Kevin and Ivan made peanut-butter sandwiches for dinner. And Ivan fell asleep in front of the tv before it even got dark. They hadn't talked about it, and Kevin didn't even want to imagine what he'd had to go through to get all his stuff out of his house, but Ivan's face had the exhausted look of a boy who'd taken everything  he could take. Watching him snoring softly on the couch, Kevin tried to remember how it was when he lived next to him.  He tried to remember but it was red and dizzy in there and all he could picture was the school they went to and not much even about that place, except lots of air in the lunch room moving around that smelled like hot paper bags.  And all the talking being like one noise, and Ivan and him eating lunch.

By around eleven, when the boring talk shows started to come on, Kevin started to drift off himself, curled up in Deirdre's big plaid chair, thinking about everything, wondering where Ivan would be a fifth grader, or if he ever would.

Ivan had been pulled out of the other public school across town. It was only at the last minute they decided to let him finish up the year at Kevin's school; the paperwork was still a little tangled. But Ivan thought the exams were easy and probably he did way better than Kevin, even though he hadn't been in the classes all year. Kevin's big sister Deirdre (he, like Ivan, usually called her Didi) was an adult and he lived with her. She went over to Ivan's school week before last and told them Ivan was living over here on this side of town now, which was sort of a lie at the time.

Now his thoughts drifted back to Kate and Johnny Harrigan. Everybody called them twins, but you couldn't imagine two more different twins in your life. They were totally different. Kate was much more like Kevin even though she was a girl; there was no competition between her and Kevin. The one time they decided to find out who was stronger with an arm wrestle, they had to call it after about half an hour on account of laughter. Johnny was real competitive, though: Not about school which pretty much bewildered him, but about sports of any kind. He was a competitive wrestler, best in his school and he had all kinds of trophies and ribbons for it. Mostly Kevin liked him because he was never afraid of anything or anyone, and because

he was generous with his fearlessness, always making sure
wink or a joke or his belly-shaking laugh that Kevin and Kate
when he was with them, no matter where they found th
That could be a big plus in Kevin's neighborhood sometim
and Kevin were mostly big on little things, Kevin thought,
big on big things, things that mattered in the world, li
Kevin couldn't imagine what it would be like to be so h
weight to carry always. Because that's how Johnny fel
n't afraid of anything it was true, but on the other
always careful not hurt his feelings. Because it mad
able if you said something mean to him by accide
would fall like a leaky balloon.

Kate was Kevin's real friend though who
some with alarming bits of information, like how
real birthdays five days apart.

Ivan of course was a whole different s
Kevin's friend since before Kevin could reme
that Kevin had seen Ivan from the outside
him, he'd just always known him. Kevin k
course, but like from the inside so it was
back out to think about it.

Kevin was worried about Ivan mee
didn't tell Kate and Johnny was that I
but that now he lived mostly in the
Kevin's old house and was mean to
sometimes when he came home, a
kind of big trouble with the law.
her own place she still took car
Ivan's father really lived at the fi
handle being his mom.  Only I
didn't tell them also how he figur
friends over here, he owed it to Ivan to giv
nor how he finally asked Deirdre about it the o
was in a pretty good mood.  She had said:

"What the hell, I practically raised him anyhow."  Sh
with Mrs. Carroll, the neighbor kid's mother, after that, who said s
could maybe help out when Deirdre was at work and stuff, but
wouldn't promise.

When the wind finally woke Kevin, it was morning.  He suddenly remembered it was summer; before he'd even opened his eyes,
his face was pressed to the little 'x's of the metal-smelling screen. The
leaves on the trees in his street were so big with blowing and with

Johnny and Ivan weren't really getting along very well.
Out of the blue, Johnny interrupted the construction workers'
conversation and asked Tock what he was, anyway.
"I don't know, what are you?" said Tock, suddenly steely-eyed.
"I don't know. I'm American I guess," Tock answered with his coffee-toothed smile.
"Not me," Tock what are you then?"
"What are you then?"
"I'm a mongrel."
"Is that like you're from Mongolia?" said Kevin, sensing To
dangerous mood and trying to shut Johnny up. He was pretty
of himself for pulling that country out of the hat of his memo
ed to laugh too. For Tock it soon turned to a coughing fit a
Tock burst out laughing: then the construction worke
to light another cigarette.
"Know what a mutt is?" Tock said to Johnny.
"Sure I do."
"I dunno, a dog I guess."
"Well, what's a mutt?"
That made Tock laugh again. "A mongrel is a
"You're a dog?" Johnny was laughing too, bu
more. "Stronger and smarter than any purebr
sure," Tock said.
Tock ignored them after that, so they he
Johnny strapped his fishing rod to his hug
army belt so his hands would be free to c
him down his bucket on a rope, Kevin
him act like such a jerk.
Johnny, now safely below, as he haughti
But Kevin brushed it off once he
bling remains of the old sea wall again
a comfortable looking nook in a rock
behind his head. Not once since the
had they seen or even heard anoth
world.  The only signs of the to
stuffy white dust smells wafting
above and out of view.  And th
packages between slaps of w
sound from the world abov
of words and work noises
places where a tree got
room for a new apartme

Normally Johnny would have laughed at a comment like that from Kevin, but this morning he just looked back blankly, like he hadn't even heard.

Kevin shrugged it off and leaned back to listen and smell behind his closed eyes, red and warm and floating. Today was another day of sunny and blue and it was summer at last. And, when he opened his eyes, he looked from his sun-filled cranny to an empty heaven, to a gray gull stuck to his piece of the sky, immobile against the wind and only twitching its wings sometimes to disturb the stillness, like Tock's moustache.

Farther out, where the tankers traveled, the horizon was murky. The sea mixed with the sky out there to make a blue so blue it was dark. But the horizon was far away and it was still a perfect day where he was. The sky wasn't worried where he was. Though the slow ticking of Johnny's fishing reel came to a gradual sleepy silence.

"This is bogus," said Johnny.

"What is?" said Kate

"This," said Johnny, kicking a loose piece of concrete angrily. "Hanging around down here or at Tock's stupid candy stand like a bunch of little kids. We could be out there like real people, sailing." Kevin sat up when he heard that,

"Sailing? Like on the ocean?"

Kate was looking at Johnny with a terrible scowl.

"Shut up, Johnny Harrigan," she said.

"Harrigan ha!" he said. "No one knows who I am. Maybe I'm the son of a sea pirate!" He jumped up onto a slab of old sea wall that jutted out over the water like a bowsprit and lifted his fishing rod to his shoulder aiming its tip down to the water like a harpoon. The tip of the rod was wiggling on its own. Ivan laughed. He had a very adult laugh. Only his crossed legs were showing, the rest of him was in the shadow between two rocks.

"Yo. Long Johnny Silver. Looks like you got a fish."

"I know that," said Johnny lowering the rod and busying himself pulling, then carefully reeling, then pulling again.

It was a flounder. Big enough to eat probably. Johnny pulled it off the hook. "Fill up the bucket with sea water," said Johnny to Kate.

"Fill it up yourself," said Kate. But, since Johnny had his hands full, Kevin grabbed the bucket and scooped it full of water. Johnny dumped in the fish.

He put down the rod carefully on a flat rock, "First fish of the summer." He let out a laugh. It was infectious, a real Johnny laugh and soon they were all laughing, even Kate.

"I like fishing better than sailing," said Ivan getting up to examine the fish in the bucket.

"Ever been sailing before?" said Johnny.

"No," said Ivan, embarrassed.

"Well," said Johnny.

"Neither have you, Johnny," said Kate.

"And whose fault is that?" said Johnny.

Kate was silent, her mouth a straight line.

Ivan looked at. Kevin and Kevin shrugged his shoulders. Ivan climbed out to the edge of the jutting rock and looked down the coast,

What's that way?" he said.

"Bedford Point, I guess," said Johnny. Suddenly a new dare loomed large over all of them. Of course it was Bedford Point, after the Fort Estate. That was the forbidden part of town, barred from the rest by a manned gate and a sign saying Private Road—Violators will be prosecuted. Even Ivan knew what Bedford Point was. Entrance was unimaginable.

But staring at the fence of the Fort Estate and the way it curved with the coast and disappeared from sight, the reality suddenly took shape in Kevin's mind. The Point was only protected from within. But now, just by accident, they might have stumbled onto a path along its unguarded edges.

"I don't know," Johnny said. "Not because I wouldn't," he added quickly, "but it might storm today."

"Then why'd you want to go sailing?" said Kate sharply.

"There's not a single cloud," said Ivan. "What more do you want? You were the one who said you were bored, not me. I'd be happy just to sit here all day."

Kevin looked out to where the sky was worried. Johnny was right, he had a good sense of the weather.

"Are you daring me, Otrusky?" Johnny's voice came back incredulous. "You think I'll chicken out because of some haze way out on the ocean? Think again, Otrusky," he said, casting his line into a swell with a plop. The first flounder of the summer flapped once in the bucket like it wanted to warn the others. Its eyes mushed together sideways and its mouth tried to speak.

"You won't leave your fish probably," said Ivan casually, dismissively.

Johnny looked at him and still looking, picked up the bucket. He had a dare in his eyes. Ivan shook his head, saying with his eyes that Johnny would never. But the water flew out in one big piece with the fish inside of it not understanding it was free until a second after it hit the ocean. It lay stunned then suddenly realized where it was and sprung back to life, a white spot growing smaller and dimmer until it disappeared into the cinnamon depths.

"What about it?" answered Johnny, dreamily. He stood at the water's edge, lost in the fish.

"Look," said Kevin, pretending he didn't see how worried the sky was. "Everything is blue all the way to infinity." In fact, Kevin's anticipation for this adventure was filling him with euphoria and, now that it had become a real possibility due to Ivan's innocent question, he was almost afraid what would happen if he disappointed it.

"We'll get in trouble, " said Kate. It was a simple statement of fact.

"Only if we get caught," said Ivan. His smile was sly and full of mischief. He crept out farther and farther on the jutting rock and now was leaning out way over the edge, looking for the fish maybe. A big wave was coming in just then and crashed under the rock so the spray flew up all around him and almost knocked him off. They all laughed as he spider-crawled back, a band of hair stuck wet across his eyes like a blindfold. "If we stay on the rocks they can't touch us." He pushed it back, blinking salt. "As long as it's low tide we can stay on the rocks. But that's why we have to go now and today. High tide's getting earlier and earlier, you know."

"And what if there's patrol dogs, like I heard?" said Kate. "And hired guards with shotguns filled with rock salt?"

"And what if there are machine guns, and H-bombs why not?" said Johnny—he was a bit of a military buff.

"Low tide does belong to everybody, I guess." said Kate.

"It's fair if we don't cross the tide line," said Johnny "that's the law isn't it Kate?"

"That's right," she decided.

"Me and Kev used to do it all the time over in the saltmarshes. We'd walk around on the mudflats in the harbor and no one could stop us."

"You should know, Otrusky," said Johnny. "You're the expert on trouble I hear."

"What d'ya mean by that?" said Ivan.

"I mean all this is your idea, isn't it? You put me up to it by acting so cool like that. We never did stuff like this before. You just got here and you're already getting us into trouble."

The line between the sky and the sea looked more and more murky and worried until Kevin's ears felt red.

"It's not true," muttered Ivan, "I haven't never hurt nobody ever. I don't care if we don't. You just said you were bored, that's all." His eyes looked angry. "Look," he said, "I don't know what Kevin told you about my dad..." Ivan had pale eyes looking out to the sea.    His mouth was a worried line.

"I didn't say nothing, Ivan," said Kevin quickly.

"What about him? What about your father?" said Johnny, there was a strange gleam in his eye. "I knew there was something funny about you, but I couldn't put my finger on it. Bet you don't know who your father is. That's it isn't it?" He stood up pointing at Ivan like he'd found him out, "That's it, isn't it? I know what you are, you've been trying to hide it." Ivan stood up, his face crazily lined with drying salt. "You're a bastard," said Johnny quietly, "aren't you?"

"Johnny!" shouted Kate. "What's wrong with you?"

"Did he just call me a bastard?" said Ivan to Kevin. It was confusing because Johnny had said a curse word at Ivan, but the way he said it, it didn't sound exactly like a curse. Kevin looked desperately to Kate. They had to break this up right away.

"He didn't mean it that way, Ivan." said Kate and put two hands on his shoulders so he sat back down on the rock. She looked sideways and worried back at Johnny. "Alls bastard really means is someone who doesn't know exactly who his father is maybe."

Ivan nodded his head up tough, like it was no big deal. "I knew that," he said.

"Are you?" said Johnny. His voice sounded more curious than anything else.

Ivan laughed. "I wish I was," he said. "I didn't want Kevin to say, but I'll tell you." He was looking at Kate not Johnny. "Because you're my friends now." He hesitated, looking into Johnny's eyes, then Kate's, sizing them up. "My dad is bad news, very. But there's something I haven't even told you yet, Kev. They just caught him for robbing a store night before last and he'll probably be in jail a long time. I'll be big by the time he gets out. So if he tries to touch me then, I'll kill him. And that," shouted Ivan jumping up and roaring like a bear with his arms over his head, "is why this is going to be a great summer."

Johnny's face was flushed and thoughtful; he was looking at his own shoes. "Wow," he said, "That's really messed."

Kate's stare was intense, straight into Ivan's eyes and Ivan was staring back. "I think I like you, Ivan," she said.

For himself, Kevin was amazed at the news. It must have happened while Ivan was home for the last time to get his bags. Kevin remembered now how flushed Ivan had been yesterday morning when he showed up on his bike.

A sudden flood of relief swept over Kevin. He put a hand on his friend's shoulder. "Good," he said. He didn't have to keep Ivan's secret from Kate and Johnny anymore. Ivan was right. It was going to be a great summer.

The four of them sat in silence now. The rocks around them had grown the sad faces of giants. And the faces of Kevin's friends were each looking inside. Kevin was looking inside too, thinking about things in his own family. But really he was looking out at the strip of blue-dark that was getting thicker and murkier on the horizon. And now he didn't care anymore.

"Let's go," he said. "Quick, before anymore of the tide comes in." He started making his way from rock to rock down the coast line and the others followed leaping across black spaces between the broken barnacled surfaces, rhythmlessly like a group of small frogs.

After a half an hour of tough going, and of his eyes focused on the next step before him, Kevin paused and looked up around him, stretching the tight muscles in his back. The yellow tips of the cranes in the construction site were behind his right shoulder now, peaking out high and tiny over green clouds of the Fort Estate trees still waiting to be cut down. They blurred in the sunshine.

Now a brand new steel chain link fence started up, coiled on top with barbed wire. It ran along the top of the rocks beside him, out the coast as far as he could see, still barring the way to the interior of the Point. And though the sun was shining, and though the fence had no rust to be seen, it glowered dull like a muddy puddle and didn't shine. When he turned to look out at the sea, he discovered that the murk on the horizon had grown half way up the sky. He was no longer even sure if the blue right over his head wasn't secretly a dark cloud, even though the sun still shone sullenly through. And the low tide coastline was getting thinner all the time. Johnny and Kate and Ivan were no longer following the path he picked among the boulders, but each had chosen their own. They spread from high to low, from the water's edge to the fence. And when his eye followed the fence it went on and on, disappearing finally and dimly where the coast curved inward far ahead. At least he thought it might be far. It was becoming hard to tell. He wished they could get off the shore.

Some time later, though the curve in the coast seemed no closer, he looked behind again. Kate and Ivan and Johnny had gathered behind him more closely and were following the path he picked. Then he looked further over his shoulder one last time. The way they'd come was just a very thin strip now for a few yards and behind that was nothing but a wall of white.

That's how the fog came—in a creeping wall that overtook them quickly from behind. It stole the sun and put a pale thing in its place. His hair started dripping, though it wasn't raining and when he turned to look behind him again, the bright red stripes of Kate's shirt in the rear had turned to dark, shapeless, colorless smears.

Without anyone saying a word, they stopped together and huddled onto the large flat shape of a rock at the water's edge. It was maybe two in the afternoon. Two muffled tones pierced the uncertain quiet.

"That's the foghorn from Execution Rock."

"Now what?" Kate's voice fell down from her mouth like a soft heavy thing. It made the water lap below them, black and slick. Then the foghorn again.

"Well we can't go back," said Ivan peering out to where they'd been. "Look. Everything's gone."

"We can't climb over barbed wire either," said Kate and the fog horn sunk them lower. "Unless..." she said, peering up into the dark of the land.

"What?!"

"Wait right here," she said.

"Kate..." The name fell dead sounding from Kevin's mouth because she was gone.

"Just stay there, you guys," her voice called back from above them. "I think this is the end of the fence. I'll find out."

Faces close together, the three boys stared at each other across pulled-up knees, and waited.

"It's getting cold," said Ivan.

"Should we go after her?"

"She'll be back."

"KATE!" shouted Johnny. Then they all started shouting like a panic took them. No sound, but the distant bark of a dog. Then after a moment Kevin thought he heard some clattering from the rocks above.

"Quiet!" said Kate's voice at last. "I'm coming back down."

There was a dark shape and then she was back in the circle holding a pale flower in her hand, "See."

"Where'd you get that?"

"Up there. I followed the fence a little ways and it turned a corner and ended. There's a garden and a big lawn I think. The fog's not so thick up there but I still couldn't see much. Come on," she said. "Let's go home." Kevin felt chilly inside and wished he were safe on a blanket in a boiler room somewhere.

Together they scaled the rocks and stood all four on the edge of a great lawn that disappeared in the distance. High strange sorrowful noises drifted towards them, until he realized it was from a hi fi somewhere.

"There must be a house over there," he whispered.

"Do you think..." A long low growl interrupted the question. It filled up the fog. It made the lawn grow up all around him until it felt like blades of grass were tickling the inside of Kevin's throat. "Bomb it for the road on the count of three," Johnny whispered. "One, two...GO!" The blades of grass inside him shrieked like a whistle to the thump of his feet as he ran. Nearby, to the right, the growl opened into a deep bellowing bark. The thump inside of him was losing to the dull gallop nearing in the blind white. It lunged and he heard cloth tear and a whimper from Ivan just behind.

"Ivan?"

"Keep running!" It went on forever, like in a nightmare. The yard was bigger than all the fields of his school put together. Bits of the others appeared and receded from the blindness, but he was alone with the thumping inside him. He could no longer hear the dog, but a black shape like an inkspot was growing out of the fog to his left until it became a house, larger than any he'd even imagined. Until thousands of doors and windows shone back the fog.

Johnny was beside him suddenly and their feet touched gravel at the same time. He watched Johnny stoop down for rocks and whip them behind him. The dog yelped and veered away.

He decided that the dark line ahead must be the pavement of Estate Rd. and he made for it with all his wind. But suddenly it shrunk instead of growing; he stuck out his hands and stopped himself short against a cold wall of stone. It surrounded the whole property and was too high to climb. Ivan reached it last and turned his back against it.

The dog's face emerged slowly, big and dark and drooping like an old man's face, but pulled back in three circles of skin around a yellow circle of teeth. The bulk of its body stuck high up in the air behind it. The low growl made Kevin dizzy.

Then it stopped, and the face withdrew its teeth. The hard voice of a man shouted a name then;

"Who's out there?" The dog started to growl again.

"We're just kids," Kevin shouted.

"Yeah," shouted Johnny," so tell your stupid dog to leave us alone."

"Serban!" the voice grew closer. The dog disappeared back into the fog, then quickly reappeared at the side of a large dark shape.

It was a huge man in a bathrobe, with a large long face beneath a gray businessman's hat.

"Nick?!" Johnny said, wonder in his voice.

"Yeah?" the voice said, uncertain.

"I," Johnny stammered. It was hard for Kevin to tell in the fog, but it looked like Johnny might be blushing. Not like he was scared, but like, like Kevin didn't know what. "I was just thinking about you," Johnny got out at last.

"What's this...why," the man stepped towards Kate who quickly slid between Ivan's back and the wall. "I see," said the man with a funny sound in his voice. Ivan was crying and breathing jumpy.

"My arm is bit," he said and produced four dark stained fingers from where he'd been holding it.

"All right. All right. All right." Each time the man's voice got higher and tighter and by the last one he sounded like just another kid. "Come inside and we'll get this taken care of," he said like a grown up again. Somehow, though his face was blue with a heavy beard, Kevin thought his face looked just like a kid who was scared. But then it suddenly twisted. When nobody moved, he yelled "COME" so furiously that the dog got panicked too and started circling his feet. "Please," he said more quietly and turned back towards the house. In spite of himself, Kevin followed, with a hung head like the dog, and so did the others. Except Kate wouldn't move. The man looked back and stopped. "I'm not going to hurt you for Godssake," he said, looking at her coldly, but then more and more upset. "I'm just going to call your parents, and get this all straightened out. That's all. Now come on all of you. I don't have all day." And with that, he grabbed Ivan's shoulder and guided him towards the black shape of his house.

"It'll be okay," Johnny whispered to Kevin at the rear. "He's like a friend of mine. You'll see." When they got closer, he saw the house had turrets, exactly like Johnny and Kate's house. And it was made out of the same dark shingles. But it was twenty times larger at least.

The man waited for them by a small screen door. His eyes were black.

"It was sunny this morning," he said as if talking to himself, holding the door open and looking down, so they each had to go under his arm, like London Bridge. Kevin was glad to know Johnny wasn't afraid of him.

"How many rooms in this place, Nick?" says Johnny looking up happily. The man half smiled,

"Too many. Where is your..." He peered back into the fog. "She's still standing there at the wall. John, go and fetch her. And come right back."

"Okay, Nick." Johnny jogged back into the fog while the rest of them waited silently at the threshold. He reemerged dragging Kate by one arm, unswayed by her reluctance. "C'mon Kate. What's the matter? It's just Nick from the Gate House. He's not mad or anything." Johnny was forcing her without even noticing. At last out in the open, she gave up and allowed herself to be led by Johnny underneath the man's arm.

They had entered into a kitchen. And somehow the man had managed to still hold Ivan by the shoulder, which he turned with his large hand to look at the back of his arm, where the shirt was ripped. Three deep red lines in a row. "My dog knows his business. He didn't bite you. These are scratches. Come." He pulled Ivan's arm to the sink and began to wash it with soap.

The whole back wall of the room was a sliding glass door. It was half open and outside you could hear the sea on the rocks below. Nothing was visible, but it filled the room with bright white light that made Kevin's eyes blink. Kate walked towards it and stood next to a table looking down while the man was fishing through a drawer in the counter, pulling out ointment and scissors and gauze one by one, still holding Ivan's arm with his other hand. Even though Ivan hadn't put up any fight. He just stood there, his white face blackened with tears. When the man finally let go of Ivan's arm, Kevin looked cautiously for thumbmarks where the fingers had been. But there were none.

Toast crumbs and sections of newspaper lay scattered around a small plate that Kate was standing over. When Kevin walked over to look he saw a weird kind of fruit on it he'd never seen before. It was cut in two and blood red inside with four black spots. Kate's face looked as blank as a sleepwalker's. Even the man noticed and left off cutting tape for Ivan's arm at the sink.

"Are you hungry?" Her face didn't change. It was like she didn't even hear. Ivan looked up from watching the drain in the sink. "It's called a pomegranate," the man said and walked up right behind her, staring with her over her shoulder. "Beautiful isn't it?" But she still didn't move or say anything. So he reached into the pocket of his bathrobe and pulled out a little pen knife with a bright swirling white pearl handle. Kevin had never seen a knife so beautiful.

"Here." He offered her the closed knife, "Try it." His voice sounded funny.  Kevin wouldn't have wanted to try the fruit either when he said it like that.  But when she still didn't say anything he just put the knife on the table in front of her.

"I don't want to," she said.

"You should be open to new things."

She shook her head, "I don't want to."

"Suit yourself." He turned away abruptly. "Now. All of you follow me." And they did, through a series of turns and rooms and corridors until Kevin didn't know which way he was facing  or how to get back out.

They stood on the edge of a wood paneled room, their hands in front of them like they all had invisible handcuffs on. The man walked differently the moment he crossed into the room, like this was his in a way the other rooms weren't. He settled down into a cushioned green armchair at the far end from where he left them in the doorway, like he couldn't get any farther away from them than that and still keep an eye on them. His two thin crossed white legs hung down from the bathrobe, hairy with black. A book spread itself face down on a little claw-footed table next to him, with half glasses on top and a coffee cup. They lay together in a pool of light from a green shaded lamp left on beside the black telephone. Leaves of scribbled yellow paper stacked and littered on the worn oriental rug shone on the floor. The rest of the room was still dim from the fog.

"This is my room." He spoke shyly, so Kevin thought.  Like another kid instead of an adult.  Adults didn't have rooms in that same way. "There's the Gate House too, of course. Where I keep my offices now." Only now he was just talking to hear the sound of his own voice, like it was a room full of other adults instead of them.  "I sleep there quite often because it's closer to town and I prefer not to drive when I...when I go out," he said noticing them again. "Then I'll walk home sometimes on the following day, or take a cab.  But the other rooms here, they belong to the family really, not me. Of course, I'm all that's left of the family, but still it's not the same." He looked in a funny way at Johnny. "Well," he said. "Now, what are you doing here? John, please explain." His tone had changed once more.  He was an adult and they were kids in trouble again.

Johnny cleared his throat, "We didn't mean nothing, Nick."

"Anything, John.  Go on."

"We were just climbing on the rocks and it got foggy.  We just meant to cut back through the Fort Estate and go home.  We didn't try to come here or no-anything."

Nick Ford laughed softly, "Is that what you call it? The Ford

Estate, you mean, John. This is the Ford Estate, what's left of it. The gate house where my offices are used to be its entrance. In fact, you live in the carriage house of the Ford Estate, John. Never mind. The point is that the four of you have been trespassing." He held each of them in his gaze for a while, waiting for some effect to his words. Stony silence.

"Can we go now?" said Kate coolly.

He said nothing and picked up the phone. Dialed looking at her, "Yes. Mrs. Harrigan please. She's one of the weekend guests. Nick Ford. Certainly..." He hung the phone on his shoulder, "Come here," he said to Kate. She squirmed again where she was. "All right," he said, picking up the phone from behind with one hand from the table, standing up so he was above all their heads. Slowly he unthreaded the black chord from the wall with the other. He walked to her, bent slightly and held out the receiver. "Talk to your mother."

Kate held the receiver like a bowl, but he still had the body of the phone.

"Nick?!" it said from her hands, so everybody heard.

Kate put the phone to her ear, "Mom. This is Kate...

"I'm standing here...

"I'm at. I'm at Nick Ford's house. Um, it's like some mansion on the Point...

"Yes, Mr. Ford is here..." Kevin watched the man's face. The man's face was a dark hallway with his eyes getting farther away. She held the phone to him, but turned her head to one side looking closely at the white bandage on Ivan's arm next to hers. "She wants to know if she can talk to you."

"Tell her why you're here."

She looked up from Ivan's bandage, blank.

Ivan whispered in her ear, "We got lost in the fog."

"We got lost in the fog," she repeated. "And Nick Ford's mean dog bit Ivan," she blurted out. "Ivan? Huh?...He's um, just another kid..."

"Johnny?..." Nick Ford stood suddenly close to her, shaking his head and lowering his eyes. She looked at Johnny. He was worried about something and didn't look back, like his eyes were avoiding the phone. Then he shook his head too. "No, not Johnny. Me and some other kids...I don't know where he is. I think he was out maybe riding his bike this morning...Okay...

"She says Put Nick Ford on the phone immediately."

But Nick Ford's eyes remained fixed on the rug, "Tell her That's not necessary.  Only See that your children don't come to my house unannounced in the future."

Kate began to repeat the words when,

"I heard!" burst tinny through the receiver.  A silence while she listened again, then she pulled the phone suddenly away from her ear, like there was a loud noise.  She handed the phone back to Nick Ford who laid the receiver back in its cradle.

"She said Tell Nick he handled the situation very respectably."

"Yes.  Well." He looked at no one and clapped his hands.  "All right, kids.  I'll show you the way out now.  Follow me."

He led them all the way to the road. Kevin, Ivan and Kate were walking ahead, but Nick had his arm on Johnny's shoulder and they were talking together. Johnny was smiling but they were too far behind for Kevin to hear what they were talking about. He stopped where his gate in the wall met the road, close enough for Kevin to hear now, "Goodbye Johnny and remember you're welcome any time," and stayed there on the edge of the road to watch their progress.

He had called ahead, so the guard let them through.  The guard was a thin sallow man with one eye that squinted, who spent all day watching a tiny tv in his little heated guardhouse.  He looked them all over as they passed, burning their faces into his mind.  It made Kevin feel creepy in his back.  He couldn't see beneath the half windows, and wondered if the man had a gun.

After that, they took their time going back, not finding much to say.  Kate in particular was quiet and dragging her feet until Ivan dropped back. They started talking quietly while Kevin walked ahead with Johnny, who was still sort of puffed up from the excitement. Before they parted ways at the path, Kate suddenly grabbed Ivan's good arm and pulled him a little ways up the Garden St. sidewalk, whispered to him in an excited way until Johnny frowned and said,

"C'mon Kate we better get home, and you better think up a story on the way."

"So you will?" she said to Ivan.  "You promise?"

"Okay," said Ivan.

It was already starting to get dark in the path when Kevin and Ivan started to cross.

There used to be a  rowdy bar on one side of this path.  But the Cove Bar got shut down just after he got to this neighborhood, so now it was an empty lot that lurked behind the tangled wall of scrub trees and greenery on that side. The bar got closed after the shoot out between the FBI and some guys. The next day's newspaper said,

SHOOT OUT in the biggest letters it had.

"Right here is where I first met Kate and Johnny," Kevin told Ivan, stopping in the middle of the path where the shadows were almost like night. "I just moved here then and was over at the neighbors' because Didi was gone for work. Like I said, I have to stay over there sometimes. Their place is a real wreck, and they have a million other kids besides, so no one ever even notices when I'm there. Anyway, Bobby and me were playing with the new litter of kittens when the shooting started. Bobby's mom turned white and made us lie on the kitchen floor for an hour.

"I met Johnny and Kate the next day, right here. They had the same idea as me, to sneak through the secret place in the hedge, into the crime scene which was like still roped off on Killdeer so no one could get in. We snuck in there together and picked up blood-stained rocks for souvenirs. I've still got mine. I'll show it to you when we get back."

The path was a funny place, scary funny when you had to cross it sometimes. Not in the daytime, mostly, but at times like this. Like the two falling down pillars on his side and two good ones on theirs. All four were made of the same stuff as the stone walls that kept things separate all over town. Though people in his neighborhood hardly knew about it. Bushes covered it up so much that Vale Place still looked like just another dead end when you looked down it from Hill Street; there was even a beat up little yellow metal Dead End sign to tell you so, nailed crooked to a telephone pole. But some people knew. The pillars had a little graffiti on them, from the big kids who came here some nights to smoke cigarettes. Nothing fancy like the graffiti where he used to live, when he lived next door to Ivan on the other side of town. Just a few words in black spraypaint: 'Fuck,' and 'Peace,' things like that. Also, if you wound up on the wrong side and had to cross it late in the day, like this, you had to remember how it got dark kind of earlier inside. Big black hedges ten feet high all seemed full of hidden things. No one trimmed them and they grew in the nighttime, because grown-ups were afraid to have a common way and wanted their hedges to be walls to keep their backyards safe.

from Kate's diary,
June Twenty-fourth, 1976:


*I'm going to tell someone. I've only
known Ivan a couple days but I am going to
tell him anyways. Kevin used to tell me about
him sometimes though before that because he
missed him and worried because of how he got
into trouble.*

*First thing I gave him a hint about the
path to see how smart he was. When his eyes
looked back at me they said he knew what it
was like to be lied on by a grownup.*

*Then we got caught by the wall in the
fog and Nick's dog had bit Ivan bad and I
knew right then I was going to tell him sometime.*

*I put back the knife so now I can tell
anyone I want.*

*I can't tell Johnny though because if I do
Nick will take him prisoner to make me do
what he wants. He won't take Ivan prisoner*

*though because he is scared of him too like he is scared of me.*

*I'm scared of him too though because he trapped me into his house. I'd never been there before but I knew. But how could I know? That is what scares me most. Before anybody saw his face and his voice all muffly in the fog. But I knew because that's who he really is when no one is looking. When he's alone and nobody's looking he's a black shape waiting. And I knew right away. I saw him when he was waiting for me on the path. And then he turned into Nick Ford just like before and I knew.*

*Sometimes I think it's not Nick Ford at all. But the black shape took over his body. So it was huge and wormy with black hairs of shadow poking everywhere through the skin. But then I can see the black hairs pushing out of my father's nose and I don't know who to trust anymore.*

*I can tell Ivan though because I gave*

*back the penny knife.*

*Tonight my mom and dad are back for dinner. My mom knows Nick Ford made me talk to her on the phone but she doesn't say anything anyways. Nick made me promise not to say about Johnny or he would take him from me. I can't tell Johnny anyways because he likes Nick Ford too much and won't see the shadow inside him.*

*We had to eat porkchops which I hate and Johnny said How come you don't like our neighbor Nick. Then my mother said You should call him Mr. Ford John dear till he tells you otherwise. But she doesn't look at me, she knows she spanked me when it wasn't my fault. Johnny said He said already for me to call him Nick. And my father said Mr. Ford is a very important person in Port Bedford Kitty. I hate when he calls me that. My Dad put his hand on my head after dinner and turned me into a pimply icicle and I couldn't look up at his nose over my head to see if the shadow worms were moving in him too and I ran to my room and shut the door and moved my toy chest to block it because my parents don't allow any locks on the doors except their own two bedrooms and the bathroom in the middle. Johnny and me don't get locks not even in the bathroom because they think we would fight maybe.*

*We don't but I can't tell him anyways.*

*It's starting to get dark. I pulled down my pants and looked at my downthere in the mirror and it was all dim and gray like steel. Then I felt it some too soft. Only I stopped when I heard my mother knock on my door and find out it's blocked. I pulled up my pants and put up my notebook quick to pretend I was doing my homework. Only I remember just in time there's no more school.*

*I say I am writing a story.*

*She doesn't know what to say to that.*

# CHAPTER FOUR

Both Kevin and Ivan felt a little too squirrely to go back to the house right away, so they spent several hours chucking stones; not saying anything as the shadows of the curb started lengthening into the street. They wound up a little late for dinner, snuck in the house without Kevin's sister noticing, because she was on the phone, and into Kevin's room quick to get a long sleeve shirt for Ivan to cover up the bandage with. Not because Kevin thought she'd be mad, he just didn't want to bother her. She worked hard to keep them okay with food and things, and she was mostly always tired.

She was standing in the center of their small kitchen, which had no furniture except a piece of plywood on saw horses by the window for a table, slouched up on one hip, twisting the long, dirty white phone cord with her red painted toe, so she had to pull the receiver up to her ear like it was work to listen. Water bubbled oily in the spaghetti pot.

"Look, Mrs. Caroll, I'm sure it's no big thing. You know how kids get. They have fights all the time; it's just a kid thing. I wouldn't worry about it.

"Yeah, well I do. I'm sure Ivan didn't mean anything. Why don't you just tell him to come on over at six like he was going to.

"What?" she waved at Ivan and Kevin. "They just came in. Look, whatever. I'm making mac and cheese and there's plenty if Bobby decides he wants to. Listen, I'm gonna be late for work if I don't get going." She rolled her eyes at Kevin. "Yes Mrs. Caroll. Okay right, whatever. Gotta go."

It maybe wasn't the best time to talk about getting caught all day at Nick Ford's mansion.

"Bobby said he won't come over because of Ivan," Deirdre said sliding macaroni noisily into the bubbling water so it stopped boiling and made the room silent and steamy. "Mrs. Caroll said Ivan threatened him or something."

"Right," said Ivan. "I didn't even know who he was."

"I don't care," said Kevin. She knew she couldn't get anything out of him when he was like that and he knew she knew it, so she asked Ivan,

"So what's with Bobby and you?" But Ivan just shrugged and

looked sad.

"Beats me."

"Whatever," she said.

Bobby didn't come. It was almost six-thirty. Deirdre was in her bartending clothes and already late, dumping out mac and cheese on two plates so they could eat it in front of the tv.

She rolled Mrs. Carroll's old dishwasher out into the middle of the kitchen before she left, like always, so Kevin could load it up when he was done and start it thumping there. He thought it was a lonely sound.

He remembered how Bobby said he liked it, but that's because there're a thousand kids in his house, so he wasn't always alone when he did it.

After dinner, they got out the sleeping bag for Ivan from the top of the closet by the water heater, and the other one for Kevin even though he already had sheets on his bed, so they could both be the same. Kevin got the bolsters off the couch, to make a mattress for Ivan and he just slept up on his regular bed with his head near the screen window. The moon was shining through, so the room was bright even without the lights on. When they used to play in the salt-marsh, they'd run and hide from the moon and called it Shiner, like it was a big black eye, and mean.

"Remember that?"

Ivan did and said those were good times. Then he said he thought these were going to be good times, too. And so did Kevin.

A car made the turn from Hill St. cascading the bar patterns of the window frame onto the ceiling in its wake. A woman's cigarette voice shouted, "Shut up, just shut the fuck up!" from a living room somewhere nearby. The distant pulse of someone's radio.

"It's better here." Ivan lay on his back, with his arms behind his head, watching the ceiling go by. And Kevin propped on one elbow so he could look down towards him while they talked.

"Today was pretty weird, huh? That guy's house and everything."

"Totally," Ivan agreed. A car starting up, going out for the evening. More bars across the ceiling. "Kate's cool," Ivan added as an afterthought.

"Yeah?" Kevin was already mostly asleep. "That's good."

That night Kevin dreamed he was a rabbit, huddled up small against a big storm until,

"You up?" Ivan's voice floated in. Daylight. Kevin was still a rabbit, curled up tight. He didn't have to get up if he didn't want to.

That's what was so great about summer.

"No."

"Wanna ride bikes today?"

"Yeah." All of the sudden he sprung straight up out of bed and landed so hard the furniture rattled. Then Ivan did the same. Not so loud because he did it from the floor. They were giggling like they had every morning, but today it felt a little forced.

"Kev," Deirdre's voice complained all gravelly and half dead from the other room. "Shut the fuck up and go out and ride bikes or something why don't you?"

"Sorry Didi," and he put a finger to his lips for Ivan. "How's the bandage?" he whispered.

"Seems okay for another day, then maybe we should make a new one."

"Okay. Remind me." They had cereal and snuck outside without another word.

First they finished fixing Ivan's bike up with smaller, fatter wheels; then Kevin took him to the ramp at the old beach parking lot, over by Tock's. As always, Kevin rode the Red Baron, his crazy indestructible bike with the big fat back tire. It was the best jumping bike in the world.

It took Ivan a few tentative tries, jumping too soon, before he got the hang of it.

Then Kate showed up, on her flower banana-seated sissy-bar bicycle. After she did a couple jumps they all three sat on the black top island in the middle of the parkinglot, with the old Red Baron and the other two bikes on their sides.

"So what are you doing right now?" she said to Ivan. Ivan had a long face and his dirty long hair as always was pushed back behind his ears. That was how come you could always tell when his ears got red. It happened almost every time he had to say something.

"Nothin' much." She looked hard at him and he looked hard back, until their eyes softened and Kevin felt he didn't know what they were talking about, even though they didn't say anything.

"Johnny was looking for you, Kev," she said to Kevin with a kind of urgency, then smiling at him. "He said he was going to stop by your house soon."

"Okay, cool."

"You wanta stay here, Ivan?" Her eyes opened wide, like she just thought of it.

"Yeah, Kev, I think I'll stay here. So, I'll see you later back at the house, okay?"

The pavement was drooping, like he had to hold it up with his fingers, until finally he just pushed it down and stood up.    He schlepped up his bicycle. "Okay." His brain felt like it still had squirrels in it, so maybe it wasn't a bad idea to go home.

By the time he got home it was cloudy, so Kevin was just hanging around inside when Johnny showed up.

There was something new and strange about seeing Johnny in his house. Kevin felt unaccountably awkward with him alone there in his living room. He heard the tick and trickle from the old refrigerator turning on in the kitchen behind him. And, in front of him, an enormous space was yawning open that needed to be filled immediately by some distracting activity.

"Wanna play Monopoly?" said Kevin.

"Sure." Johnny also seemed to be feeling the weight of formality between them. Maybe it was just because Kevin was in a bad mood. Johnny just stood there in the center of Kevin's livingroom with his hands crossed in front of him, waiting, not sitting in any of the many ratty chairs or able it seemed to make himself at home in any way. Why was that? Kevin thought. He'd been here many times before with Kate and she always seemed comfortable and he did too. And Kate came often on her own too and that was totally normal too. Only Johnny, he realized, had never been here by himself before, that was it.

The silence was getting heavier. He could hear Johnny breathing. Kevin scratched behind his ear uncomfortably.

"Monopoly isn't very good with two, is it?" said Kevin.

Johnny scratched his head back. "Not really," he admitted. "I thought Kate would come too, but she didn't feel like it and said Why don't you just go over? And I was really bored at home so I figured Why not?"

"Want something to drink?" Kevin suggested.

"Sure." Johnny followed Kevin to the refrigerator in the kitchen, but then Kevin felt embarrassed to open it. He knew there was nothing good inside, just some milk that he remembered tasting a little funny on his cereal this morning. Didi was going shopping tomorrow, so it made sense they'd be getting down to their last stuff, but...he just felt like not opening the fridge right now.

"I feel like just some water," said Kevin, "how 'bout you?"

"Yeah, that's what I feel like too," said Johnny looking sideways like he was looking at someone else in the room to tell him something, only there wasn't anyone of course so he looked back at Kevin.

"Cool," said Kevin and got some jelly jars out of the cabinet, because their couple of glasses were dirty at the moment, and filled them up from the tap. The water had a little orange color Kevin noticed, just from rust, it would taste perfectly fine. Kevin tried it first just to make sure. He handed the other one to Johnny, but he still felt funny about it. Kevin didn't know what was bothering him all of a sudden. Then there seemed to be this funny smell too coming up from behind the couch, like maybe he'd left an old blueberry yogurt cup there or something.

But a sort of light grew up on Johnny's face just at that moment, and he gave Kevin a look he'd given Kevin many times in the past when they and Kate were tooling around the neighborhood together. A wink without winking face that always gave Kevin a good feeling because it said you and me have a secret understanding and Say no more. Kevin raised his eyebrows back and it was even better, because it was just the two of them in Kevin's own house. Johnny tilted up his jar of water then and drained it without stopping once.

"Ahhh," he said and laughed. He and Johnny didn't have a word sort of friendship that was all. So they didn't really know what to say when Kate wasn't around.

"How'd you do that?" said Kevin.

"You just kind of learn how to keep your gullet open," he explained. "It's a lot harder with soda though." He looked at his empty glass jar and laughed again, triumphant for both of them.

It was still the old Johnny Kevin knew and liked and he felt relieved. It was just because Johnny had been acting so weird in the past few days that Kevin hadn't been sure. Weird with Ivan first of all, and that had disappointed Kevin more than he cared to admit, but even weird with Kate like he was angry with what she said all the time which was really strange since normally she just did the talking for both of them and that was perfectly fine with Johnny.

Johnny frowned and suddenly plopped himself down on the rug and leaned in closer to Kevin. "Where's Ivan?" he said.

Kevin's mood fell again. "He went bike riding or something with Kate, but I didn't feel like it."

"Me neither," said Johnny. "I was gonna, but then I just didn't." Johnny stopped and took a breath, like he had something very important he wanted to say.

"What?" said Kevin.

"Kate's been acting weird," he said. "That's really why I wanted to come over today, Kevin. I mean, you're her best friend except me. Don't you think so?"

Kevin didn't know what to say. He hadn't noticed anything different about Kate. It was Johnny who he thought had been acting weird, not Kate. "Not really," Kevin had to admit.

"Well that's because she's been pretending to be normal around you guys, especially Ivan." He stopped again and took another breath to tell Kevin he was about to tell him something secret, "It's different when she's at home though."

"Like how?" said Kevin.

"I don't know, like weird. Like night before last she pulled her whole rug apart." He stretched his shoulders and twined his fingers, turned his arms inside out and over his head, then twisted his neck so it popped. Johnny was so big that when he got confused it took up the whole room. "I mean I know she didn't want to go into Nick's house. Maybe she knew he'd call our mom, but. It wasn't like Nick would hurt us, but that's how she was acting, you know?"

Johnny put his hand under his shirt and rubbed his fat belly again. "Then she told me that about a week ago or something, Nick left the door open to his office and she looked inside even though she knew she wasn't supposed to. But then Nick told Mom his pen knife was missing and mom spanked her for stealing it. 'Member I told you about that knife? Now Kate says he had it all along, because 'member he had it in his pocket yesterday at his house to cut the thinga-majiggy with. I don't know," Johnny groaned. "First, both me and mom know that Kate wouldn't steal. So I asked my mom about it and she said she'd spanked Kate for disobeying, not for stealing. She said Kate was going through a difficult time emotionally and that I should be patient. But it's just weird, because Kate would never lie to me, I know that much. She's being really weird though. Maybe it's one of those things that happens to girls?"

Johnny just sat there on the rug waiting for Kevin to say something. But what was Kevin supposed to say? He didn't know what happened to girls. And Kate had never told him about any of this. "Maybe she just doesn't like this Nick Ford guy," Kevin said finally. "I mean, it's a free country."

"But she does," said Johnny, "That's what's the weirdest. At least she used to. We used to play this game. It's kind of stupid and don't tell anybody but, we used to play this game when we were lit-tle, you know, dress up in dirty clothes from the hamper, and I'd be Nick Ford and she'd be our Mom and we were very important people doing good things all the time. That's how the game went." Johnny paused. "We were really little, we don't play games like that anymore."

"Huh," said Kevin. He didn't know what to say. He felt embar-rassed.

"I guess it wouldn't be that good with two," said Johnny suddenly.

"What?"

"Monopoly. There's always your neighbor, what's his name? Bobby?" Kevin could feel Johnny checking his eyes to see if Kevin was going to say anything to make fun of the dress-up game.

"I guess so," said Kevin cautiously.

"I mean, even if he is a weenie." Johnny laughed. "I don't know, what'you think Nick Ford would do?"

"Maybe he'd say we need him for Monopoly?" said Kevin trying to put Johnny back at ease somehow.

"That's what I think," said Johnny.

It turned out good. Bobby seemed relieved when they got to Kevin's house and Ivan wasn't around. "You really need me, don't you?" He had been eating Twinkies in front of the Saturday morning cartoons with a younger sister and brother. Kevin and Johnny had said that they guessed that they did. They made Bobby be the banker though and, while he was dealing out all the money and they'd already chosen their pieces and had nothing left to do until Bobby was finished, Kevin kept thinking about the strange way Johnny kept talking about this guy, Nick; he had some more questions he wanted to ask.

"Hey Johnny," said Kevin, more relaxed now with Bobby here, sitting down in the big plaid chair as Johnny, more relaxed too, whoomfed down on the couch raising a big cloud of dust, "I've been meaning to ask you," Kevin tried to sound casual about it, "What's the story with this guy Nick. I mean, you and Kate seem to have known him a long time I guess."

"Who's Nick?" said Bobby.

"Just some guy who has an office next to Johnny's house."

"Nick? Just some guy with an office, Kevin? C'mon," said Johnny putting up his big feet on the couch arm, "You know who he is though, right? Isn't he the coolest, don't you think? He's got a really cool sailboat, you should see it. It's made out of solid mahogany." Johnny looked over at Kevin, waiting for him to agree, so Kevin decided he better not say what he really thought: That the guy made him feel really creepy and not just like a normal adult he disliked, the kind that ignored him or talked down to him, but like a guy who looked at him like he knew exactly what he was thinking all the time, but not in a good way.

"I was just wondering who he was," said Kevin cautiously.

"He is the guy who rents our Gate House as an office," Johnny explained for Bobby's benefit, "but that's not all he is by a long shot. He's totally cool. He's like an old old friend of our family, even though he doesn't come to the house much. He's a judge, not just for Port Bedford I don't think, but like for the whole state. That'd be a pretty cool job, don't you think?"

"I guess so," said Kevin.

"Those wigs are pretty stupid though," said Bobby.

Johnny snorted. "Real judges don't wear wigs, Bobby. That's just in the movies."

"Oh," said Bobby."

"Pretty nice guy though?"

"Yeah he is," said Johnny sitting up now. He started to speak rapidly and low, so Kevin had to sit forward in his chair to listen, "I used to pretend sometimes that he was my dad instead of my dad, because you know how dads don't have time for you a lot, like all they say is Not now Johnny and No you can't do that. Well that's how my dad is a lot, but not Nick even though I know Nick is a more important man than my dad. My dad ran his campaign for Judge, you know, but Nick is the judge so that makes him more important."

"You think he's a millionaire?" said Bobby. He was passing out the $500s just then.

"Totally," said Johnny. "You should see his mansion, like we did. Right Kev? Tell him."

"It's pretty big," said Kevin reluctantly.

"Pretty big?" shouted Johnny. "I'm pretty big. You know my house, Bobby? The Carriage House? That's pretty big, right?"

"My house is almost that big too," said Bobby.

"Yeah but that doesn't count: It's totally falling apart," Johnny looked impatiently at Bobby's mad face, "Whatever, okay your house is pretty big too. This is all beside the point because Nick's house, whew, it's a million times bigger than mine is, right Kev?"

"Maybe a thousand times," said Kevin.

"Well anyway, to answer your question, Bobby. He's a millionaire all right. Probably a ten-hundred millionaire, I bet you."

"Are we gonna play or what?" said Bobby.

"Nick invites me into his office all the time and we sit in his big green chairs and talk. And we talk about me, not about him or anything. You know he asks me about my wrestling and everything." Johnny snorted, "I don't even think my dad knows I'm a wrestler."

Kevin was amazed. He couldn't remember ever hearing Johnny say so many words at once.

"And even my dad says he a good man," Johnny went on, "and

my dad hardly likes anybody. He called him a something, philan-thromorph. And I said, What's that? and he said Someone who does good things for no reason at all. So that's why I wasn't worried at all when I found out whose house it was yesterday and I told you it was all right."

"C'mon. Who cares?" said Bobby. "Are we gonna play or what?"

"Nevermind. Yeah," said Kevin. "Let's play. Roll."

It took Kevin about half an hour to finally trade his railroad and utilities for the purple and light blue monopolies, which were his favorite. They reminded him of the streets where he lived. And Bobby had the violets and the orange. Johnny had all the rest plus a big pile of money with $500s hidden everywhere. He put a hotel on Boardwalk and said, "This is Nick Ford's mansion." So Bobby and Kevin got to gang up on him together, and call him rich boy and stuff. Johnny didn't seem to like that much, but he stayed in a pretty good mood anyway, because he won everything in the end and knew he was the biggest.

Deirdre got back from somewhere towards the end of the game and had to start getting ready for work.

Then they were all just sitting in the livingroom relaxing from the game when Deirdre came out of the shower in her bathrobe, rub-bing her hair and Bobby whistled at her. She rolled her eyes and told him to shut up.

"What?" she said, "The, what is it, third day of summer and you kids are bored already?"

"Why? What are you doing, Deirdre?" Bobby said. He was always wise to her, maybe because he knew she wasn't a real parent like his. So he could get away with it.

She made a big face at him, mimicking Bobby's mannerisms when he got cocky. When he tried to get cocky, he always messed it up and spittle wound up coming out of his mouth. "I'm making some cof-fee Bob-bee," she mocked.

"Yeah," said Kevin, "so buzz off." Kevin didn't like it when his friends bugged Deirdre. Ivan never did.

"You tell 'em Kev," she said.

The front door opened and Kate and Ivan came in. They must have seen everybody's bikes and knew Johnny and Kevin were here. Bobby looked uncomfortable when he saw Ivan and said he had to go. Ivan looked at him and shrugged as he left.

"How's it going Kate?" said Deirdre. "Haven't seen you around in a while."

"Good." She was flushed and Deirdre turned away from the

percolator to look at her, crossing her white towel-cloth arms with a different look on her face than she ever gave Kevin.

"Well you look  good, Kate."

"Thanks." Kate looked kind of confused to Kevin.

"You're looking pretty lively there, too, Ivan. Liking it here pretty good so far? You stick around Kate here, Ivan. The two of you are good for each other. I can already tell." Both of them still looked confused even though they were smiling. He figured neither of them got talked to friendly by adults much, and he looked at Deirdre proudly. She always talked like you were as good as she was.

"C'mon Kate," Johnny blustered suddenly, "We oughta be getting home." All of what Johnny said came back to Kevin now. He honestly didn't know what to think. It seemed this time just like it had all week, that Johnny was acting weird and Kate was just being Kate.

"See ya," Kate said.

"See ya," said Ivan.

Deirdre went to work early and Ivan said he was tired. He wanted to read more of his book, *Treasure Island*. So Kevin went over to Bobby's house and watched tv and played with the cats. Ivan was already asleep with the light on, on the couch in the living room, when Kevin got back at nine. Ivan looked happy being asleep, instead of the worried look and red ears he usually wore. Kevin brought out a sleeping bag, unzipped it and put it over him where he was on the sofa, then turned out the light.

"I do too," Ivan said. He must have been dreaming about something, because he was still asleep.

from Kate's diary,
June Twenty-fifth, 1976:


*Johnny is mad at me because he knows
I'm not telling him something and he knows we
promised to tell each other everything so we
will be happy when we are married. But I
don't know if I want to marry Johnny anymore
and maybe I might marry Ivan and just have
Johnny stay my brother.*

*Johnny started getting mad a few days
ago because him and me were playing GI Joes
in the yard and Nick Ford was sitting on the
porch of the Gatehouse pretending to read a
book but he was watching me. But maybe I'm
lying because I was scared to look. And because
I was watching him too even though I wasn't. I
think he is my father in disguise. Because
Nick only shows up when my father is away at
work or on a business trip or gone away with
my mother for a party. Because the hair on his
knuckles is the same is how I know even*

*though he makes sure to change his ring every time.*

*Johnny stopped playing GI Joes and went over to talk to Nick and they talked a long time. Only I kept playing GI Joe climbing a tree and dropping him off to see how he would land. But it wasn't any fun anymore and I was only pretending it was. Then Johnny came running back and all his freckles were smiling and he said that Nick said he would take us sailing some day soon if we both wanted on his big mahogany boat that's the biggest in town harbor so everybody knows it. I said No and went inside and hid in my room and put the chest against the door and didn't answer when Johnny banged on it. Maybe Johnny is mad at me but now I can't help it. I make sure the window is locked too every night.*

*My mom and dad fight all the time now too. They never whisper unless they're fighting and that's how I know.*

*Ivan says adults are basically unpre-*

dictable and the sooner you figure it out the better off you are. Especially when they have the booze. Men are always worst because they hit harder and don't say what's wrong first. Ivan said his dad did things to him. I asked him if he was scared and he said No not anymore because his dad is in jail till Ivan grows up. Nick Ford is the one that puts people in jail so he will never go.

My mom and dad have cocktails every night. Like tonight my dad says Can I fix you a drinkypoo and they laugh so hard they can't talk. They're not fighting anymore. But if I tell my dad tomorrow morning You said Drinkypoo he'll say he never would say a word like that.

Ivan says the only adult I should ever trust is Didi. He says I should never tell my mom what I saw. I wish Johnny hated Nick Ford too.

This isn't my house anymore. The dark carpet on the floor in my room feels rough and prickling now and keeps me awake because I still feel it there, underneath the bed. I can't roll it up without ripping it because it's nailed to the floor. I tried. My father says that carpet cost 900 dollars. He says now I have to live with it like it is. When I pulled at it I found out it's made of just one dark string. Then I couldn't stop.

They didn't punish me like I thought they would. They just stood in the doorway and had worried looks on their faces.

# CHAPTER FIVE

Today Kevin woke up angry about what had happened at Nick Ford's mansion, though he wasn't aware at first that's what he was angry about, that this strange contact with an adult had spoiled the budding prospects of a summer adventure with his friends. It had been developing splendidly until then, but now he felt it transformed, into a very wrong-feeling story.

Two little birds had been brawling in the tin gutters above his window; that's what had disturbed him from his dream, which was all muddled up now in his waking mind. He thought he'd been playing mumbly peg with a beautiful pearl-handled jack knife in a lushly grassed berm by the side of a black summer street. A bright-eyed US postman had strolled by with his big, heavy bag and asked to see the knife. He said he was going to show Kevin the real way to play mumbly peg and spun the knife from his fingers into the thick, green grass. But when Kevin searched the grass to retrieve his knife, he couldn't find it. 'It got lost,' the postman had said; 'look for it;' then he laughed at some private adult joke in himself and slung back his bag and walked off whistling down the street. Kevin, on his hands and knees searched the thick individual blades for his pearl-handled knife, getting more and more upset, when out of the corner of his eye he noticed the receding postman slip a hand into his pocket.

Now one of the birds scooped into view, alighting on the cedar tree at the top of its arc and turning to chitter and glower at the other, which was still in the gutter above. A cat watched from the trunk of the tree, forgetting its hunting poise for the moment to assume a stupefied squat in the middle of the sidewalk.

"Shut up, birds!" Kevin snapped and stung the screen with his fingers so it gave off a rusty tang. Both birds flew away but soon returned to brawl even more noisily with each other in the tin gutter above his window. He ignored them and looked under his bed, more and more upset, for his shoes. He imagined Ivan still rolled in his sleeping bag: "That's a man and a girl bird," he would say.

"Shut up!" Kevin said through his teeth, then pretended to himself he'd said it to the birds. But Ivan would have said something just like that. He was tired of Ivan always knowing everything. The fact that Ivan wasn't even there now to say it made him madder.

There was an extra blanket beside the sleeping bag bunched up on the couch in the livingroom. Didi must've put it on Ivan when she got home from work last night. There was an empty cereal bowl in the sink. Ivan was gone. Kevin's spoon clanged against the side of his own bowl more than was necessary. The ingredients on the box bored him. He knew them all by heart. Putting down his spoon he looked out of the small kitchen window beside the plywood table where he sat, so small it was like a railway window and the other faded little flat-roofed houses scattered around Vale were like boxcars, only none of them connected. And the old tires and pieces of metal in the yards, and rusted broken swing sets, and scavenged pieces of fences made it all into an old junk railroad yard where none of the trains were ever going anywhere again. His mother promised to take him on a train once to see his father, but then she forgot about it. They would have had to get a ride to another town because the railroad in Port Bedford didn't run anymore. The oil tankers didn't come into the port the way they used to because of the energy crisis, and they didn't get put on box cars in the old roundabout. They finished construction of the Interstate highway in 1966, the same year Kevin was born. Stuff got loaded onto trucks now from the piers. This many bananas, that many barrels of oil. These were known as General Facts and they were what you used to start a report in school. He'd learned all this in the unit called Civics during the Social Studies portion of the day. But this was summer and he didn't have to think that way. The way that made his head hurt, like something was too short in there, like something was not right about General Facts but only he seemed to feel it and everyone else just huffed and puffed and stuck their tongues out of the corners of their mouths and scritched away with their pencils while he just sat there staring at the green dotted line for lower case letters, thinking that General Facts maybe weren't true that way, or didn't connect to anything, like junked boxcars and the houses out his kitchen window.

He wondered where was Ivan anyway? Water running in the bathroom. His sister was up now, earlier than usual.

"Hey, Didi."

"Where's Ivan?" she said walking into the kitchen, fully dressed.

"I dunno. He was gone when I got up."

"Well, I was up an hour ago. He must've gone out early. See ya pal. I'm meeting a friend for breakfast downtown. Be back by dinner anyway. What you want anyway?" He gave her a dream list of cupcakes and things and she laughed. "Any plans?"

"Go find Johnny maybe."

"There you go," said Didi grabbing for her bag from the floor. He was going to ask her if she knew anything about Nick Ford, but she was gone too quick. She probably did. She knew everything from working at the bar. He went back to looking at the cereal box, though he hated to. He'd have to remember to ask her next time. It wasn't Kevin's fault that both Kate and Ivan were feeling bad now; the more he thought about it, the madder he got.

He heard the sound of the milkman rattling bottles outside now. No, Kevin decided, he didn't agree with Johnny at all at all. Plus his cereal now was moosh and that made him even madder.

He mined the house for silver and copper—under the bolsters of the couch, behind Didi's dresser, in the yellow junk bowl by the door and finally in the tobacco dust and melted candy and empty lipsticks of Didi's old purse, which she didn't use anymore but still hung battered from the back of her door where the full-length mirror was. That was the motherlode: three blackened quarters, a dime and two green pennies. All together, he found $1.27; stuffed it in his pocket, lit the end of a broken stale cigarette, looked at his face in the mirror then put the butt out and headed for Tock's.

The broken street to the sea wall lay abandoned in the sunshine, but Tock was still there like another stone. Kevin bought a sampling of everything.

"Hey Tock," he said after he paid and Tock was suspiciously inspecting the unrecognizable coins. "Know anything about a guy named Nick Ford. He's not a kid, he's an old guy like you. Lives in a big mansion out there," he said pointing out the Point behind the construction site fence.

Tock looked up from the coins in his hand and his face looked so tired and old for an instant, spreading out with a million dark and pale lines from the outside corners of his eyes all the way to his ears. Kevin had never noticed so many wrinkles on him before. He remembered how he first noticed wrinkles on his father the day after Ivan's dad turned his back on their roofing business and became a fireman instead. The wrinkles were the first sign of how Kevin's dad was going to leave them soon.

"Nick Ford," Tock repeated. It sounded like a curse word in his mouth and in his eyes too; he laughed, sharp, "Sure I do. He's the man. Everybody in this town knows about Nick Ford; knew about his father before that. He's even worse than his father because he's smarter."

"I don't like him," Kevin said. It felt good to say it. Tock stared

at him with a funny look. And then Tock did a funny thing: He took
Kevin's jaw in his tremendous quick rough hand, pulling it over the
counter towards his own. Then he kissed Kevin once on the forehead
and pushed him back so fast Kevin almost lost his balance.

"Don't cross Nick Ford, kid. Take it from me. You're too short."

"Did you?" said Kevin, a little breathless, the odd soft feeling of
lips on his forehead and the scraped sensation on his jaw, like it
would feel to have a beard, he thought.

"Put it this way, my father's father was a fisherman with his
own boat. My father was a fisherman with an even bigger boat. Me,
I started out with a boat, but now I sell candy to kids like you out of
a plywood box."

"I don't get it."

"Neither do I, kid. Don't cross Nick Ford, that's all I'm telling
you." Tock didn't seem in a very good mood after that, so Kevin did-
n't ask him anymore questions.

He brought the candy across the path to the Carriage House,
hoping to find Johnny there at least. As Kevin emerged from the path
he saw Mr. Harrigan in his bright sports car pulling out of Johnny
and Kate's black driveway, red flare of brake lights, an impatient turn
of the body behind the steering wheel, the grey shoulders of a suit
and a flash of blow-dried hair, as if he were considering whether it
was worth his while to run Kevin over in order to save some time.
Apparently not, Mr. Harrigan put it in forward and zipped off down
Garden St. with a stony disgusted look fixed on his face.

Kevin waited for him to round the corner then padded softly
over the purple, blue and red stoned walk, passing the silent Gate
House. Between the colored upside down bells of tulips, with the little black thingamajigs inside them. Kevin approached the Carriage
House, struck by how much it looked like a doll house version of Nick
Ford's real mansion. Dark brown shingle faces edged in black and
high narrow windows, the cones of its gables shimmering lightless
slate like pencil tips; the smaller way it felt, just like Nick Ford's mansion and his face, like it wanted to crawl away from itself if something
would only let it.

Kevin had only been inside here that once, last week when he
first brought Ivan over; never when any parents were around. But
this time the big white station wagon, with the wood sides that were
really metal, was still in the driveway. The mother. He could still hear
the tin echo of her voice from Nick Ford's receiver.

The mother and the father drove separate cars everywhere,
even with the gas rationing and stuff. Kate once told him, like it trou-

bled her, how her parents never had to wait on line like other people's. Her father had told her when she asked that he didn't have the time and, besides, both their license plates were even numbered so they couldn't have filled them up on the same day anyhow if they had to.

No rain today, another sunny blue one, but Kevin was going inside that house to see Johnny today, that was for sure. He felt a kind of stubbornness he knew couldn't be denied. So, taking a deep breath, he stuffed all the candy into the back pockets of his shorts and pulled his big t-shirt over them so no one could tell. Then he knocked resolutely against the frame of the screen door.

After a moment he heard the rustle of someone's newspaper then the sharp click of heels across a tile floor.

"Yes?" The steel shape of Mrs. Harrigan peered through the screen, shimmering because of the climbing morning sun. She couldn't tell who he was. Kevin wished he was a little taller so she might think him an adult. Boy it was sure going to be a hot one today, Kevin told her, wiping off the slick on the back of his neck. "Can I help you?" she said, but it didn't sound very sincere to Kevin.

"Good morning, Mrs. Harrigan," mumbled Kevin in his politest tone, "Is Johnny and Kate around?"

"And you are?" He didn't understand what she meant right away, so he froze for a moment, dumbfounded by the question, really stopping to think what he was, but it was hopeless:

"I'm okay," he said at last, "...I mean, I'm a pretty nice kid once you get to know me." She laughed at that, so it was apparently the right thing to say; broke the ice somehow and she opened the door.

He was looking up into a woman's face floating across the light fabric of her white dress-suit, above a heavy gold chain wound tight around her neck. "I'm sure you are, dear," she said warmly enough, though her smile looked tired already, "but what is your name? From the Town Beach neighborhood, aren't you?" Kevin wasn't sure he liked the sound of that word, 'neighborhood,' in her mouth. It wasn't like someone's door you could knock on if you were in trouble.

"I'm just Kevin. You know, yeah, a kid from the neighborhood." For himself, he tried to put a lot of warmth in the word.

"Yes, John's new friend. He just told me a little about you last night. Live with your sister over on, one of those streets over there?" she waved her hand a little vaguely then fanned her shining make up with it because she was starting to get hot standing out here in the sun on the threshold. Kevin humphed secretly inside himself: New, indeed, as if he'd met Johnny only yesterday.

"Because we played Monopoly at my house yesterday," he said. The heat was too much for her all made up like she was and finally she relinquished the doorway and allowed him to enter. Kevin sort of felt secretly like a knight storming the castle.

He followed her at a slight distance, back into the kitchen where she'd been reading the newspaper before he knocked. It really was cooler in here; Kevin's own house never stayed cool like this. It looked like Nick Ford's a little on the inside too he realized now, dark and gloaming and fabricky. An assortment of gold rings and earrings lay in a neat pile beside her coffee mug on the dark polished table. When she sat down there she looked just like one of those women in perfume ads in the magazines that Deirdre was always reading. Plus Kevin could smell that faint something-like-lilacs that came from the slick pages. She started glancing at the paper again while Kevin just stood there not knowing exactly where to put his hands. He used his back pockets for that normally because the front ones were too tight, but that was out of the question now since they were stuffed to the gills with candy from Tock's.

"John's cleaning up his room," she said at last. "He'll be down in a minute I'm sure." At her own mention of time, she looked nervously at her gold bracelet watch, which had twinkled out magically from under her sleeve when she shook her wrist. "You didn't, by chance, happen to see Kate anywhere in the neighborhood this morning, did you, uh...(she'd already forgotten his name)... I'm late for an appointment as it is..."

"...Kevin," he provided.

"Kevin," she allowed. Only then did Kevin allow himself to shrug in the negative. He was pushing it, he knew. But he was in a stubborn mood and that's just the way it was.

"John!" she called out suddenly, in a stunning voice, making Kevin remember again the piercing voice he'd heard only for a moment through that receiver in Kate's hand. Johnny's voice answered something unintelligible from way upstairs. "Are you finished?" she continued, conversationally, yet with unabated volume.

"Almost," came Johnny's shout in reply, hoarse with frustration.

"Your new friend Kevin is here."

"Hey Kev!" shouted Johnny in a much cheerier voice, "Come on up!"

Mrs. Harrigan now coolly indicated the broad banistered front stairway with her eyes.

"Nice to meet you," mumbled Kevin with not very much pluck.

The stairs were dark red and endless and so thick with carpet that he felt as he climbed them that he was sinking instead of going up. Plus he felt ridiculous, climbing like he had a stick up his butt so the candy wrappers wouldn't crinkle or worse fall out of his pockets. Like Mrs. Harrigan's cool eyes were still on him at the bottom of the stairs though he was afraid to turn around and look. Like she'd been able to see through Nick Ford's telephone that day like on The Jetson's and knew how he'd been there and everything about it. His feet made muffled thuds that vibrated as he climbed so he could feel them all over his body and so could anyone else it felt like. It felt like he was naked.

But when his eyes got safely to the level of the second floor he heard Johnny's strong, comforting voice emerge authoritatively from an open doorway halfway down the carpeted hall: "In here," it said.

Johnny's large, wood-paneled room was filled with the same thick, burgundy carpet as the stairs; it only had one narrow window so the overhead light was on even though Kevin knew outside it was bright morning. Battalions of army toys lay scattered everywhere; so, if he was really cleaning up his room, he hadn't made much progress.

"My mom says I have to finish before I can go out. They're having some big important party tonight and this is where they put the coats."

Kevin looked at the bottoms of his sneakers to make sure they weren't dirty: "So, where do you sleep if the party goes late?"

"Back in Kate's room, on the floor."

"This is a pretty big room," Kevin said.

"I wish it was a little smaller right at the moment," he said, looking around despairingly, "I'm feeling kind of low on energy."

Kevin grinned as, baroquely from his back pockets, he produced package after package of candy, sending them both into the outer reaches of euphoria so they had to start shoving each other around just to calm down.

After about half and hour the room was messier, if anything, and both Johnny and Kevin were sweaty from head to toe. Kevin had big raspberry carpet burns on both his elbows and one on his knee, all throbbing in different rhythms. He'd done pretty well considering Johnny was twice his size. Though just now his ear was pinned to the thick floor, the full weight of Johnny pinning Kevin's head like a vice with his knee. It was hard even to giggle.

"Had enough?" Kevin said through his mooshed up mouth.

"What?" said Johnny and leaned down a little harder.

"I (don't) give up," said Kevin.

"What?" Johnny repeated.

"Ow. Okay, okay." Johnny took his knee off and Kevin sprang up quick as a cricket: "Okay, I'll let you give up this time," Kevin said, smiling and trying to catch his breath. So Johnny started going for him again and Kevin quickly raised his hands, "Only kidding." They both flopped back onto the floor on their backs and stared at the plaster molded ceiling.

"You're a pretty tough kid, Kevin. I know kids a lot bigger who couldn't give me half as good a wrestle."

"You, you and Ivan I bet are the only two kids who could beat me."

"Not wrestling, Ivan couldn't beat me."

"No, you're the strongest," Kevin admitted. "But I remember one time I saw Ivan get in a real fight, I mean with a man and everything, and he did pretty good for a while because he was so mad."

Johnny, suddenly up on his elbows: "Like an adult? Like a teacher or something? That's why he had to switch schools like that isn't it?"

"No, not a teacher, but sort of...It was his Dad," Kevin whispered.

Johnny sat full up, but didn't say anything. He had a look on his face like he was thinking of things he'd never thought of before..."Wow," he said at last, then quickly, "I mean Ivan must be really messed up, right?"

"No he isn't," said Kevin, the mad feeling creeping back.

"That's messed though, isn't it? I mean...I don't like my Dad a lot," he whispered, "but I couldn't ever beat him up, I mean even if I could, know what I mean?"

"That's not how it was."

"I guess that kid, Bobby is right about Ivan, huh? I mean Ivan must be bad news."

"You don't know anything and neither does Bobby Carrol." Kevin's temper had suddenly flashed, "What could you know about it, you and your big stupid house."

A dark look crossed Johnny's face. Realizing he'd just made a tremendous mistake, Kevin stood up and stepped backwards for the door.

"Don't," said Kevin. "Ivan was keeping his Dad off his Mom," he explained.

It took the wind out of Johnny's sails: A thoughtful face grew up on him, which made him look funny somehow. Kevin suddenly saw how Johnny really didn't know anything about anything. Johnny started to pick his nose a little with his thumb, "Ivan's not very lucky," he said at last. He shoveled what was left of the Red Hots into his mouth and munched it over for a while more.

Kevin had never seen Johnny so thoughtful before; he was right, there was something unlucky about Ivan and that's why Kevin had been attracted to him ever since they were kids—like he wanted to protect him somehow from all the things he never deserved. That's why Kevin had brought him to come stay with Deirdre in the first place. "Ivan's Dad broke his arm once and he came to my house and I hid him in the basement until his Dad was gone. Ivan's arm is still crooked; if you don't believe me, Didi knows. She took him to the hospital and she was only eighteen then."

"I guess Kate and me are pretty lucky to have a good family, huh? ...We'll stick together always from now on!" Johnny decided. "You, me, Ivan and Kate okay?"

"Okay!" said Kevin and they slapped two sticky hands together.

Lying quietly on the floor again,  they could hear Mrs. Harrigan's voice rising up from downstairs, but it wasn't talking to them and seemed unaware of its volume:

"...If you ever do something like that to bring shame on me, I swear I'll make that one look like a love pat and Nick Ford won't be there to stop me, you can be sure."

Johnny whispered to Kevin: "Guess Kate's back. Mom's mad as fuck about that thing I told you about with her taking Nick Ford's jack knife, and then when she found out Kate went over there..." Johnny spoke defensively, like he was trying to forget that he'd been there too and Kate was covering for him. "...Mom's got some kind of business meeting with Nick Ford today downtown and then that big party tonight and she's worried because of all that..."

Mrs. Harrigan's strident voice again: "I don't really care if you took it or not. You're going to march your little high-toned fanny over to him tonight, young lady, and I'll be watching you, and you're going to apologize for anything—anything you've done to disturb him in any way. Do I make myself clear? For the jack knife, for going onto his property, for disobeying your mother who's told you time and time again to leave that man in peace. Do you understand me young lady? When I make a rule like that it's for your own good and not to be questioned. Do you understand?"

The house was quiet.

Mrs. Harrigan yelling. "What did you say? I asked you if you understand. Answer me."

"YESSS!" Kate's voice louder then Kevin had ever heard. A few seconds later the front door slammed.

Kevin and Johnny were paralyzed until a few minutes later when they heard Mrs. Harrigan's quick clicking steps on the hard floor of the foyer; the faint tinkling of chains. "John, dear." she called, "I'm going to my meeting now. Make sure that room is clean for coats this evening.

"Okay," Johnny shouted, his voice harsh and frustrated again. Kevin watched his sullen face as they waited silently for the station wagon to pull away. Inside Kevin felt vaguely how this family wasn't so great either, even though he couldn't put his finger on it the way you could at Ivan's. He felt glad to live with Deirdre.

"C'mon," said Johnny once his mother's car was out of hearing. "What're we waiting for? Forget this stupid room, we better go find Kate. She's by herself somewhere now I bet. She's been acting real weird lately, you know. Staring at the walls and ceilings and things." They ran downstairs and out into the street.

But it was like she had disappeared. They looked everywhere for her, for hours it felt like. At the library, over the sea wall even— but still couldn't find her. And then they realized they didn't see Ivan either and they checked and he hadn't been back to Kevin's at all. They saw the neighbor, Bobby, out in his driveway working on his bike, but he hadn't seen them.

There was only one place left and that was the empty lot, where the old Cove Bar had been before the shoot out. They didn't know why Kate might be there, it was a scary place, but there was nowhere else they could think of.

The smooth sea pebbles of the lot were littered with beer cans and broken liquor pints. Leaf shadows, from the bone-like sumacs growing up through a wall of thorns in the back, groped over them in the soft winds, half alive, still searching for the unturned blood-stained stones that Port Bedford's children might have overlooked.

The pink stucco wall of the boarded up bar building caught the full sun, still smattered with white powdering dimples where the bullets had hit it that day. The sky overhead was green, fat with leaves and with the loud disappearing squaw of blue jays. And the white tree trunks at the back of the lot stood like bones in the impenetrable wall of prickers. Kevin heard small groaning noises behind them, like a little wounded animal. Now Johnny heard it too and looked back at Kevin with watery eyes and put a finger to his lips. An image took shape inside of Kevin: Of Kate, crying by herself on the hard-packed dirt behind the hedge.

"We don't know what it is," whispered Johnny. "It might be

dangerous, so I'll go first." It didn't sound dangerous to Kevin, but it did sound weird, not jumpy now like just someone crying, but with long spaces in between. Kevin shrugged uncertainly and followed Johnny soft-footed to the far back corner of the lot where the secret tunnel was through the prickers to the path.

Kevin crawled on his elbows and belly the way Johnny did, like a commando soldier. Scratches burned softly on one cheek and on his leg. He emerged still on his belly next to Johnny on the cool foot-step-smoothed earth, strategically hidden from the place further down where the noise had originated. Only now it was quiet. Then, to their surprise, they heard whispering—two voices. Johnny nodded upwards to the big broad-branched cedar tree above them, like the commanding sergeant he'd become. They climbed sneaky-style into its upper branches. Kevin felt sweaty and his cuts stung with cinnamony dirt from the bark.

He settled onto a smaller branch just above Johnny, who was staring down the vaulted corridor of tree limbs and chewing hard with his mouth so it made his cheek muscles bulge in and out. Kevin had a full view to the pillars now and could see Kate and Ivan in the middle, facing each other. It looked at first like they were holding hands.

Then, when he looked closer, he couldn't believe his eyes. They weren't holding hands at all. Kate and Ivan had their hands in each others pants and were looking at each other. Kevin felt dizzy. He didn't know what else to do, so he started to giggle. Then there was nothing left to do but watch as Kate and Ivan sunk down together and started rolling around on the ground and making those noises again.

Johnny looked back at him with an uncertain smile. So Kevin shoved his arm, giggling again and trying to get Johnny to giggle too. They had caught Kate and Ivan and it was kind of like a joke, right?

Johnny tried to giggle too, pretending like he was holding it back, but Kevin could tell he was faking. Giving that up, Johnny shoved Kevin instead, hard, and that wasn't fake: Kevin almost lost his balance.

That made Kevin kind of mad, so he shoved back hard too. Johnny had just been crouching on his limb and not holding on to anything, or straddling it like Kevin was; so, when Kevin pushed him for real, Johnny teetered, a silly confused look on his face.

There wasn't a sound as he fell. Kevin felt rather than heard a sick thud as Johnny's body landed on the mulch beside the path below.

For a second he thought Johnny was dead.

Down the green corridor, Kate and Ivan were still rolling

around and moaning.

Johnny stood up slowly. He stared ahead in the direction where Ivan was with his sister, not that he could see them from down there. He didn't look back up at Kevin in the tree at all. One of Johnny's fists went up towards him, though. But, instead of shaking it at Kevin, Johnny smacked his own head with it.

Kevin could still see Ivan and Kate rolling around. He could still see Johnny hitting his head. In a sudden flash of fear, Kevin saw the world just stuck like this: like it would go on forever like this, paralyzed in a tree.

"Johnny?" he whispered down to the path below. "You okay?" Johnny looked up at him bewildered; started to shake his head faster and faster. Then, suddenly, Johnny turned and ran away full speed. Away from Kate and Ivan, out the other end towards Vale Place.

from Kate's diary,
June Twenty-sixth, 1976:

*The path was warm and still and sunny around Ivan and me but inside me was cold and moving like a fish. You can't help when it moves in you like that. It gives you the same feeling you had.*

*We were sitting cross-legged with some pebbles we had gathered from down on the sea-wall in the morning. We carried them here in our pockets.*

*Ivan said Who is this one? and his long finger pointed and touched the rock and stayed there. I put my finger on his finger on the rock and said This is the queen of the rocks.*

*Then he asked me where she lived and I said underground. Then I took my finger away and he put his finger on another rock and said Who is this? and I put my finger on his finger on the rock.*

*It wasn't really a game.*
*Shadows don't talk the way people do.*

*They move like a fish inside of you and that's
how you know they're there even though you
can't hear what they're saying.*

*Men are filled with glue but boys don't
have it in them yet.*

*Ivan said How'd you know that? but he
knew in his eyes how I knew.*

*I said to Ivan that it happened exactly
right here on this spot. Ivan happened to get
up and come out from under the hedges like he
had and stand there.*

*Then he said Kate.*

*And I said Oh hi Nick.*

*Then Ivan said What happened? and I
put my finger on his belt buckle and he said
You can tell me if you want.*

*And he said Why do you stand and look
at me that way? You're a temptress. That is not
the look of a child. You are killing God in that
look. You are killing me.*

*And I asked Ivan if I could touch him
down there.*

*And the path was warm and sunny and*

still. And there was still a swimming fish and he said *Your finger is cold.* And my finger was like an icicle and inside his underwear was warm and smooth and dry. Not like him. And Ivan and me both looked all around and the air was green and still and Ivan asked me if he could touch me down there at the same time. I unbuttoned so he could and we both were. Everything was warm then. Both our fingers felt like the same finger. Ivan said *We're inside of a secret now aren't we?* and I said *Yes.*

Shadows melt when you find them out. Then the water has no where to go so it only looks like your crying but inside your happy.

I could feel me starting to shake and I told Ivan I was scared. Then he wrapped his arms around me and held so tight for me that I could hardly breath. And I said *Tighter.* And he said to hold him back and I did tighter too until we fell on the ground and stayed like that, like we were a rock and no one could get to our insides because outside was only our backs.

# CHAPTER SIX

When Didi went to high school and his whole family still lived together out behind the firehouse on the other side of town, Kevin had to start sleeping on the living room couch. There were only two bedrooms, one for his parents off the kitchen and one, just the attic really, up a ladder on the livingroom's back wall, for her. It wasn't okay for a girl in highschool to share her room with a boy, even if it was just her little brother. As Kevin got older something about his sister's life grew thrilling to him. Late on a Saturday night, when their parents were fast asleep, Didi would often sneak in the front door quiet as a cat, though no one ever knew she'd gone out. There was no getting by Kevin of course; he always woke up. To be honest, sometimes he only pretended to sleep: waiting for her.

He would sit up so she could see his shape in the dark and she would either wave at him, or smile and give him a beer-smelling kiss on the forehead, or, sometimes when she was in a really good mood, she'd motion for him to come up the ladder with her and, safe behind her shut door, she'd tell him about the night.

Sometimes it was a keg party somewhere in the saltmarsh or the woods, but other times there was no party and she said it was just her and this or that boy. And it was just the boy she'd want to talk about. On and on.

He remembered asking her on one of these occasions what she and the boy were doing all that time out in the salt marsh and she smiled at him with an odd look he remembered as half worry and half happy:

"Making out," she had whispered hitting him lightly on the shoulder with her open hand. "You'll learn about it one day."

He knew what that meant now, of course, but mostly it came up at school as the butt of jokes: something ridiculous.

Didi then, in his memory, seemed so old and far away from his own life. Now he'd seen his two best friends in the world doing it. Kate and Ivan were still just kids like himself, no matter how tough Ivan acted; no matter how know-it-all Kate pretended to be. They were more like Kevin than anyone and to imagine himself doing that with anyone, let alone his best friend, Kate, gave him a gross feeling.

But the thrilling part came back to him too and haunted his

mind as he patrolled around the neighborhood on his bike not knowing what to do. He couldn't help wondering. He'd known Kate a lot
longer and better than Ivan had. If she wanted to do something like
that, why hadn't she just asked him?

Then there was the way Johnny reacted to what they saw. Like
it was something terrible. And that made Kevin feel like it was all his
fault, not just pushing him out of the tree, that was an accident
after all, but for bringing Ivan to the neighborhood in the first place.
These new, sudden, contradictory feelings presented themselves to
Kevin's heart like a maze he had to get through, and the answer was
waiting in its center like a monster to keep him from getting back out.

The large-stoned concrete blocks that made up the pavement
of Killdeer Ave. precessed one after another beneath the smooth, fat
rear wheel of Kevin's bicycle. He wasn't even looking anymore; he was
thinking. Where would Johnny be? Kevin'd been riding around forever. And there hadn't been a sign, when it hit him: The cave, of course.

He spun that fat wheel around and headed for the sea wall
behind Tock's. He thought of going back to see about Kate and Ivan,
about getting them first maybe.

The picture of Johnny's face, as he fell from the cedar, flung
itself up from Kevin's back tire; Kevin's head recoiled up into the air.
Better not, he thought, steadying the ensuing wobble in his coast.
He'd been staring at his back tire again, his feet on the frame tube,
allowing the pedals to spin on their own for a while with the furious
force of his speed.

Tock had closed for the day, an old plank hatch over the window. A light wind rattled the rusty links on the fence that extended
beyond the wall. They sounded just like ringing rigging from the dragboats down at the port and that made him shiver. The dragboats at
Commercial Harbor were the most dangerous place in Port Bedford.
A place where adults' eyes turned down if you even talked about
going there. Tock lived in East Bedford though, which was on the far
side of Commercial Harbor and most people in Port Bedford never
even went there at all. But Tock told Kevin it was a nice place and to
not listen to bigots.

The air smelled like night already. Kevin looked out across the
ocean to see if it might be getting dark. Because the ocean was where
the sunrise came from, but it was where the dark came from too. He
thought again about the dragboats.

Though the high coast cast a long shadow onto the water, still,
Kevin thought trying to cheer himself, out in Infinity the sun is
always shining. He could even still see it glittering near the horizon

with gold. Kevin was going to be a fisherman maybe, like Tock used to be. So far though, to his shame, Kevin had never even been on a real boat. Just his and Ivan's raft was all, and that was a long time ago.

He leaned his bike against the wall and swung himself quickly around the fence. It had become an ordinary crossing. He scrambled down the old wall and into the blue and gray shade of the rocks. Night was down here already, like the insides of a pocket.

"Johnny!" It was hard without sunlight to recognize which was their cave. "Hey Johnny." Kevin poked his head in one triangular black space. That wasn't it, no smell of water inside. Once Kevin's eyes adjusted, he found that it wasn't quite night after all, but that time of day when the forms of things grew confusing. "Joh-ne-e!" The quiet slop of the ocean. The wind was dying because of sunset. The out of reach sky dazzled red and orange and pink. "Infinity," Kevin whispered. He liked the sound of the word. Like something magic to chase away the maze feeling in his stomach. He doggedly turned his eyes to what was real in front of him. Two blocks and a blue square. Three pillars of wan lightness in a row and, next to them, a black space like a huge mouth. That was it! He crawled in and sat down.

"Johnny?" he said.

"What." came Johnny's voice, quiet and sad, not an arm's length from Kevin's ear.

"Hey," said Kevin quietly.

"Hey," said Johnny too. Kevin could smell the salt strong.

"Why're you crying?" said Kevin.

Johnny's breath smelled like a maze too, tangled and musty like the hallways of that mansion. "I never get anything until it's too late. I mean, I knew Kate was acting weird on me all week. But I just let it go. I figured she'd come talk to me after a while like she always does. Then she goes and cuts me like that." Kevin felt himself blushing in the dark.

A growing feeling squinted through Kevin's eyes, even in the dark. It was growing stronger in that dark cave, stronger than anything else, even Johnny. Everybody but Kevin himself was lost. Here in the dark Kevin felt the great weight of a growing responsibility. It was up to him, Kevin Hawkins, single handedly to save the summer.

"Okay, what's so bad really?" said Kevin cautiously.

"She did it to cut me," said Johnny proud in his clear copper voice like moist pennies. "She wanted me to see how, how gross she really is. How she's not. I saw what I saw."

"Well, so did I," said Kevin. "You don't see me hiding in a cave do you?" Suddenly they both laughed.

"If there was any light I could," said Johnny.

Kevin felt a tingling in his skinny ribs. "There's some secret here, Johnny, isn't there?" He could hear the back and forth quiet of Johnny rubbing his belly in the dark. But Kevin was determined to get the secret out of him; he stayed silent until he could see Johnny's shape relaxing and widening in the dark. Then he plunged: "It's a secret about Kate, isn't it?"

"He was right," said Johnny.

"Who was?"

"She wouldn't go sailing with him and me so I couldn't go. He told me she was doing some strange things and then not telling the truth about them after."

"Who?"

"My, you know, our family friend, Nick. He said he wasn't sure what was wrong with her, but not to be mad if Kate told me something that wasn't true. And that maybe she'd get better after a while. He said until then I had to be extra nice to her."

"What does he got to do with anything?" It was starting to feel uncomfortable sitting cross-legged in the dark.

"He's..." Johnny seemed to want to say more, but stopped himself. "He wouldn't lie to me."

Kevin could hardly see and it made him need to do something with his hands to make up for it. He found a long fringe on his cut off shorts which was tickling his knee and started to twist it up into a big knot and press it hard into his thigh with his thumb.

"When Kate and me grew up we were going to get married."

"I don't think brothers can marry sisters, Johnny."

"Trust me," said Johnny. "We could have. We promised each other."

"Okay," said Kevin, skeptically.

"But then Kate just started getting weird about it. Like when Nick was going to take us sailing in his huge cool boat, Kate told me that he was actually a shadow monster in disguise. But I still thought, Okay. But then, after that, every time Nick was nice to me, she'd do something mean. And then all the stuff with the jack knife happened, but even then I couldn't believe it."

"You already told me about that."

Johnny spoke slowly now: "For the first time this morning I started to not believe her some. What happened. Well, Kate and Mom or, Kev? Kate probably told didn't she?"

"What?," said Kevin, "I didn't talk to them at all."

"Forget it. We both saw them."

"Now who you talking about?" said Kevin exasperated by Johnny's willful mysteriousness. He wasn't going to tell Kevin the secret after all.

"You know who: Kate and Ivan. And I know enough about things to know what that was."

Kevin kept silent, he didn't know exactly what, but he thought he had enough of an idea anyway, "You mean they were making out," said Kevin nervously. He untangled his legs and moved away from Johnny a little.

"I remember every single thing that was going on in my head while I watched. And then it all started to make sense. How she didn't like Nick Ford because he always liked me more than her, and how she stole his jack knife to get back at me. And how, when she got caught she got Ivan to help her because he's a tough guy and not from around here. And they planned it all so they could sneak the knife back into the pocket of Nick's bathrobe when he wasn't looking. Because what would Nick have it in his bathrobe for?" As Johnny talked, Kevin was talking to himself inside. His mind kept repeating A maze, over and over, "Only Nick was too nice to say anything about it then, and decided to punish her by calling our Mom and making Kate talk to her."

Kevin was speechless. All of that couldn't be true, it went against everything he felt about Kate, and everything he felt about Ivan. And there was that guy Nick Ford again at the bottom of it. Finally Kevin said, "You aren't mad at me are you? For pushing you out of the tree? It was an accident."

"What? No. I didn't even feel it really."

"Good, then I'll tell you what I think. There's something else going on. There has to be."

"What?"

"So there's got to be some mistake, that's all. Something neither of us get."

Johnny blew a breathy whistle. "I don't know," he said, "I'm not so smart sometimes, but I believe what I see."

"That doesn't include what that guy Nick said. What if he's lying?"

"But it makes sense though, doesn't it?" demanded Johnny.

"Sort of," admitted Kevin. "But not with Kate. And not with Ivan neither. I've known him since I was born."

"Nick isn't lying, not to me. Just trust me on that one, Hawkins, okay?"

"Okay," said Kevin because there was nothing else he could say if he didn't want Johnny to get mad at him. And he did trust Johnny after all. Just not Nick Ford.

"Nick is the one who told me the truth," said Johnny, "when no one else would, not even Kate. He's not lying," whispered Johnny, more to himself.

Kevin looked outside the cave to find no more sun on the water anywhere. "Maybe we should go home now, Johnny."

"I'm not going home."

"You can't stay here, Johnny. The tide, remember?"

"I know where I'm going. Don't try to follow me either."

"You can't tell me?" moaned Kevin.

"If I tell anybody, it'll be you, Kev."

"Yeah?"

"I knew I could count on you. That's why I said Yeah when you came in here." Crossing alone back around the fence in the dark seemed only a small thing to Kevin now. It felt good to be counted on.

"Promise you won't do anything crazy," Kevin said, "without telling me first. Let's meet somewhere, tomorrow, okay?"

"Tomorrow," said Johnny's voice in the dark. Kevin knew suddenly with his ribs that Johnny respected him even if he couldn't tell him the secret just yet. "If," Johnny reiterated, "you promise not to follow me. We'll meet at noon, far away from here, okay, so no one else will know. Maybe I'll tell you the secret then if I can."

"How bout at the port, by the dragboats," said Kevin. It was all he could think of in his present mood. It was the worst place he could think of.

"Okay," Johnny said, accepting his dare. "Tomorrow."

"Tomorrow," said Kevin and felt older suddenly, a man with a secret of his own, even if it was one that he hadn't quite heard yet. "And I'm going to find out what's really going on by then, you'll see. And Kate..."

"I don't want to talk about her anymore, she cut me."

"Whatever."

"Goodbye, Kev. Thanks I guess." Their hands found each other and made a strong handshake in the dark.

"Okay," Kevin said. "Goodbye..."

It really was night in Port Bedford when Kevin got back to the level of its streets. As he was rounding the fence, he thought he saw the shape of Johnny emerging from the cave and making its way further up the coast, below. But Kevin couldn't be sure and held himself to the promise not to follow.

He got on his bike and rode carefully home.

When Kevin finally made it through the front door of his own house he saw no one at first. Then he heard Didi and Ivan laughing and the sound of clapping. So he walked back to the living room where a light was already on.

Ivan was sitting close to Deirdre on the low plaid couch. He had an arm around her so it looked like Deirdre had a hand growing out of her armpit.

As Kevin walked into the living room the two of them fell into a larger picture. They were sitting like an audience watching Kate. She faced them on the carpet. The footlocker coffee table was slid out of the way. She was dancing for them, crazily like a go-go girl.

Didi half glanced at Kevin as he came in, the other half still watching Kate. "Come 'ere, Bubba," said Didi rubbing her thin flared red nose with the back of her hand before it beckoned. Kevin thought again about how she'd call him up the ladder in the old days.

Kate stopped dancing when she saw Kevin. She stood awkwardly on one foot and looked at him and he looked back at her, just as blank faced. Kevin curled up at Deirdre's feet and she put her two hands on the top of his head, "Where you been?"

"Thought you had to go to work," said Kevin, looked up into her eyes.

"What's wrong?" she said.

Now Kevin noticed that his sister's eyes were really red and smeared with mascara. "Look who's talking."

"Don't worry, I just didn't feel like going, that's all."

They made circle eyes at each other and Deirdre started to laugh. Ivan tickled her in the side, then Kate started to dance again with just her head, singing a thumpy tune. Finally Kevin started to tickle Deirdre's feet from underneath until she was in near hysterics.

"You guys!" shrieked Didi and she burst out laughing again pedaling her feet to keep them from Kevin's little fingers and squirming her body back away from Ivan. "What do I need a boyfriend for?" Didi laughed, tense at first, but loosening. "Fuck him. Fuck that arrogant son of a bitch." She laughed and laughed. Kate hugged her then and put her head in Deirdre's lap.

"You're our mom," said Kate.

"You're my little boogers," said Deirdre and burst out laughing again. "Hey, it's almost nine o'clock," she said noticing her little wristwatch and unslumping herself and extricating her curvy hip from between the two bolsters. "Shouldn't you be heading home, Kate?"

Kate frowned.

Kevin felt itchy all of the sudden, and got up and sat down in the chair across.

Deirdre sat up and looked at them all hard for the first time.

Kate was still frowning and said, "You can't make me."

"Now come on," said Deirdre. "You want to see Johnny at least."

"Johnny won't be there," said Kevin angrily.

Kate looked questioningly at Kevin, "He won't?"

"Nope," said Kevin.

Kate took off her blurry glasses, "Why won't he?"

Ivan sat up to look at Kate, "Did he run away or something?"

"Don't ask me where he is," said Kevin, "because I don't know."

"What the hell is going on here?" said Deirdre.

"I don't care why," said Kate. "Why isn't he going back?"

"I'm not sure," said Kevin evasively.

"You should stay here with us then, if your parents are having a party," said Ivan.

Now Deirdre just blinked until finally she said, "Excuse me. I'm missing something here." Deirdre, Kevin had guessed by now, must have called in sick tonight, even though she wasn't, because of 'boy trouble' as she called it. "I'm sorry, this is just a little too weird for me. This was supposed to be my stay-home-and-feel-sorry-for-myself-night tonight," she said, talking to herself now. She got up and opened a drawer in the bureau. She poured some liquor into her coffee cup, "You know, the more I think about it, there's been something weird with you guys all along tonight. Hasn't there?"

Ivan and Kate looked at the same spot on the rug.

"There's something going on here," Didi said, scanning Kate and Ivan now particularly. "I can smell it."

Kate started to taunt, "You can't make me. Nobody can make me do anything."

"And why's that?" said Deirdre.

"Because," said Kate.

"Listen, Kate. I'm going to call your folks."

When Deirdre started for the phone, Kate started to dance again, even more crazily and shook her head.

"This is a new dance I made up called the Godkiller," said Kate. Kate and Didi were looking at each other in that way again that didn't have anything to do with Kevin and Ivan. "My mom hates for me to dance. And she plugs up her ears whenever I come near her."

"What is it, Honey?" Deirdre said to Kate with a whole new voice, her eyes opening, holding her and petting her back. But that made Kate dance harder and backwards from Deirdre. "Okay you guys," said Deirdre suddenly to the two boys, "it's past your bedtime. Go to bed, okay? Kate and me are going to have some girl talk. She's going to lie down on my bed. Okay Kate?"

"No," said Kate still dancing, stretching her head like an upside down grandfatherclock.

"For a little while and then I'll take you home myself, I promise, and make sure everything's okay. Okay?"

The dancing slowed, tock tick tock tick, "Promise?"

"What did I say?"

Kate hesitated. "Nothing," she said. But not with very much conviction.

Kevin and Ivan just stood there. Inside of a maze, thought Kevin again.

"Go and get to your room Kev, I mean it." Didi put a hand on Kate's small shoulder and ushered her into Didi's bedroom. Then Didi poked her head back out into the living room. "Good night," she pronounced. Then she gently shut the door, so Ivan and Kevin were standing in the living room all by themselves.

"Good night," came Didi's stern voice again through the door.

from Kate's diary,
June Twenty-seventh, 1976:


*Didi was watching me. She took me to her room.*

*She was looking at me with smeary black crazy woman eyes and I wasn't scared of looking back at them. I could stare at them for a long time just the way I do in the bathroom mirror at night when I can't sleep. Because Didi is me.*

*I was watching me be a grownup in the mirror.*

*So what's going on with you Kate?*

*Her voice was scared too. Like mine when it talks to itself.*

*I said It wasn't me.*

*She said What?*

*I said What?*

*She said Look I know that look.*

*I said Why?*

*She said Why are you acting like that?*

*I said Why are you acting like that? But
she doesn't get mad like I wanted her to.*

*She held me so I could smell how safe
her breasts are. They felt good on my face but
different. I'll have them too one day but now
they're just the tiniest little bumps that no one
knows but me yet..*

*If there was another girl to tell though I
would.*

*I think my mother used to be a girl
when I see old pictures from then and they are
me instead of her. And she's holding hands
with a boy who looks like Johnny. But she's not
my friend if she yells at me like she did this
morning first thing. I tried to be friends
because I told the truth. I said I never took
Nick Ford's penny knife he lent it to me and I
gave it back later. She said I was betraying
her. She said How could you do this to me?
After she felt sorry for herself and put her hand
on my head and called me her little girl but
it's too late I don't want to be friends anymore.*

*I'm Me all by myself. Her little girl is a flat faced old picture with yellow bumpy edges.*

*She wants me to be in her picture with Johnny but I won't. I want Johnny to be my twin brother like always but he isn't anymore and now Kevin says he's gone.*

*He's got Johnny I know he does. He's making Johnny wrestle with shadows inside on purpose so he can't listen to me. I couldn't tell Didi because she isn't me. I knew she had a patch of black wormy moss on her downthere too even though I couldn't see it. I wanted to tell Didi like I told Ivan, but I couldn't because I knew it wasn't safe even though it felt safe.*

*I wish I had a friend who is a girl.*

*My girlfriend would be just my age and she'd be named for a flower. Daisy or Rose or Dandelion. And we would take bubble baths together and Didi would come in and talk to us while she peed and then she'd hand us bath oils and things to make us smell like flowers.*

*She'd tell us all what to do too when a shadow comes out of someone.*

*Dandelion would runaway first thing as soon as she saw it and bring back a big flash-light from her garage and shine it right on Nick Ford so he was blind and his shadow would have to hide. So it would be just Nick and he would be nice to me again like he was before in the Gatehouse when I showed him some of my diaries one day. He said I was special and not like other people.*

*While he was being nice and before the shadow could get back inside him Didi would sneak up behind him though with a big kitchen knife bigger than the penny knife to cut the shadow right off his heels. Then I'd forget about Nick Ford and Dandelion and me would chase the shadow back past Tock's with the flashlight and over the sea wall till it was safe where it belongs all the way up inside the sea wall cave with me and Kevin and Ivan and Johnny and then I'd let them meet*

Dandelion and she would like my twin brother and marry him one day instead of me. And I would marry Ivan maybe or maybe no one. Nick Ford would just be standing all by himself on the path with Didi smiling just for himself because he was all better now. And my mom and dad would be all better too.

But there is no Dandelion

I said to Didi I can't because my mouth is full of glue.

Didi hugged me good and said Okay Kate Okay Kate Okay.

# CHAPTER SEVEN

Finally, when they
still half way up
"I ain't g
path gives m
take walks
since I c
toward
arou

About half an hour later, Didi
room. "Change of plans," said Deird:
room, where Kevin and Ivan were si
really having anything to say to one

Didi smiled at both of them the same.
Kevin: That Ivan and he were still best friends and understo
other like always, even after what Kevin saw on the path.

No other adult could make him feel that way. In Kevin's expe-
rience, adults were not to be trusted with only one exception; that
exception was Deirdre who used to be a kid herself, before she found
her own place. And still would be probably if she didn't have to work
all the time. She was twenty-two years old. Kevin's parents had her
when they were highschool sweethearts and not even married, just
before his dad had to go away to the Korean war to drive a jeep. His
mom was only fifteen then. They never had another baby until Kevin,
twelve years later, and Kevin was pretty sure that he was just a big
mistake for them, because Kevin's dad was already sort of messed up
in the head from that war and then, when Kevin was tiny, it was even
more messed up from Vietnam where his dad met Ivan's dad who was
a lot younger. Ivan's dad was messed up too. And both their moms
were messed up too, mostly because his and Ivan's dads were messed
up he guessed. So, growing up, Deirdre had been the only one either
of them could count on.

Looking at her face, Kevin knew he could count on her now,
when he was feeling secretly all weird inside with Ivan because of
Kate, and Kate because of Ivan too.

"I'm taking Kate home," said Didi. "You two punks come with
me, so we don't get into trouble on the way, okay?" Kevin grinned
thankfully: Now he could just think about how Ivan and he were
there now together, to protect Didi from anything bad happening, and
Kate too.

The night was still hot and muggy. Cicada swelled in and out
of hearing as the four of them strolled, Deirdre barefoot, over the just
now cooling pavement of the street. The pavement on Vale was crumbling pretty good, so Deirdre, whose feet were still tender because it
was early in the summer, teetered and they needed to wait up for her.

had reached the pillars of the path and Didi was
the street, she called for them to come back.

oing that way," she said. "It's full of glass. Besides that
e the creeps; let's go the long way. I hardly ever get to
with you guys anyway. I haven't had a night off to spend
n't remember when." So they turned around and started out
s Hill Street, to hook up with Beach Avenue and the long way
nd to Garden Street.

A car cruised them by on the corner of Vale and Hill, thumping
disco beat through closed windows. The guys inside were checking
Deirdre out. It was a Saturday night. Ivan gave Kevin a look and they
both stooped down to pick up handfuls of rocks from the driveway
they were passing, but the car moved on, accelerating down the street
and leaving a squeal of rubber as it rounded the corner on to Beach.
Didi laughed,

"Those kids probably can't get into the Beachcomber tonight
because I'm not working."

"Did you ever, you know get into trouble coming home from the
bar late at night?" Kate asked.

"A couple of tight spots," Didi admitted. "But don't you worry,
we got Kev and Ivan with us tonight." Kevin knew she was just joking, but he tried to look a little tough anyway.

When they finally got to Garden Street, cars clung to both
curbs—from the corner of Beach Avenue to three quarters of the way
to Estate Road. Large cars shining primary colors, and black, and
their hard waxes caught the mercury vapor incandescence of the
streetlights.

There were so many cars that Kevin and Ivan started to count
them, strutting cockily down the still night street, while Kate hung
behind close, almost touching Deirdre's side.

"Thirty-five...I bet there are forty-two cars," said Kevin.

"Forty-seven I got," said Ivan.

"Can't I just stay over at your house, Didi?" said Kate. Didi
looked down into her face, and stooped to wipe some dirt or something off of Kate's face which she must've seen in the streetlight they
were under,

"We'll see, we'll ask your parents and, if they say it's okay, well
it's okay by me."

"Did you hear that?!" Kate ran to catch up with the boys, "Didi
says it's okay for me to stay over." Yes, Kevin had heard. Blood rushed
to his ears; Ivan looked nervously happy... "Maybe I can sleep in
Deirdre's room with her, if it's okay." Kate bit her lip, "Is that okay,

Didi?"

"Sure, why not. But we'll have to find out what your parents think first."

"They won't care. They don't care about me at all when a party's going on; they're too busy smiling always."

Didi laughed even though she tried not to. "That's not very nice," she said.

All the lights were lit in the narrow windows of the Carriage House, and an ethereal thread of piano notes hovered out above the summer lawn, suspended by the huzzah of many voices and the mood-lifting tinkle of icecubes...Kevin liked the sound of parties. Not birthday parties, those tended to make him sad and grumpy, especially his own. Adult parties. He even liked the sound of the Beachcomber, the bar where his sister worked, when it was full on a Saturday night, but adult parties particularly. Like a feeling of promise that wasn't any less because it never panned out. Adults seemed like a lot more than they really were at parties and, even though that made things even worse later on, Kevin almost felt it was worth it. Even though he hated the dog-ends of parties worse than anything on this earth, because there was no help for a kid then. But at first, like now when the ice cubes still tinkled and the sound of adults laughing was full of warmth and play and more like children, like children looking after themselves—it was like a wish, that the world could be more than what it would most certainly end up as before long. It was too hard sometimes for Kevin to think about later.

As the four of them approached the door, Kevin found himself wondering what sort of a party people like Mr. and Mrs. Harrigan might have...or Nick Ford, would he really be here? He had overheard, in the midst of Mrs. Harrigan's tirade to Kate, that Kate was to apologize to Nick Ford for everything at the party. This party. So much had happened to Kevin today. A thousand pieces of information, any one of which might be important to figuring out what was going on, were mixed up like a washing machine inside of him.

"It'd be better to go around back," said Kate, appraising the situation, "where the trellace and the patio is, by the pool. No one will know we're here if we come in the front probably."

So they crossed the narrow side strip of lawn that lay thick and green-black between the dark wall of the house and the black hedge. The voices grew louder and the grass grew bright green just around the corner, lit from above by floodlights beneath a green and white striped awning. Kevin loved to watch parties and this one was brighter than anything he'd ever imagined. And, glowing aquamarine from its depths, bordered in tile, a huge rectangle of pool water stood glassy. Around it stood bright, summery formal adults clustered in threes and fours and sixes. In all his time of knowing Johnny and Kate, Kevin never knew they had a pool. He felt a little crestfallen they'd never told him about it.

"Nice digs, Kate," said Deirdre.

Mrs. Harrigan, standing in a crowd of several by an aluminum awning pole, suddenly spotted them lurking there hesitantly in the penumbra of the side lawn. She disengaged herself from her company with a single wave of her hand; approached now rapidly as if to prevent them coming further across the eaves of light into this forbidden world. The floral figure of her dress grew and darkened. The dazzling light of her hair continued to shine and grow while the rest of her slipped towards them into the darkness.

"Where the hell have you been?" she whispered furiously at Kate, ignoring Kevin and Ivan and even Deirdre completely.

Suddenly Kevin thought of his own mother: How different she was from this terrible, spectacular figure. His mom was a pretty woman too, pretty like Deirdre. About how soft and talky his mom was and how much she'd needed him all the time before, but now hardly saw him at all. How not like Mrs. Harrigan who wouldn't need anyone ever it felt like. It always seemed like Mrs. Harrigan was doing you some kind of big favor by even ignoring you like she was doing to Kevin now. But Mrs. Harrigan wasn't ignoring Kate; maybe she thought she was doing Kate a favor by yelling at her in a whisper to one side instead of out loud in front of everybody.

Kevin looked over and noticed his sister's expression and the way she held her body: Forward-like, like invisible hands were holding it back from behind by the waist. Her shoulders were forward too, like she was protecting something inside her ribcage. Didi didn't like to be ignored—she knew how to do it though. You have to, she had said to Kevin, when you work in a bar. You have to know how to protect yourself when you're too busy to take a table's drink order, or if a drunk guy is making the moves on you or something. But she also had said she didn't get off on it like a lot of people. Didi never put up with it when someone ignored her for no good reason. And Kevin could tell Didi didn't think Mrs. Harrigan had any good reason for ignoring her now. You don't see me acting better than anyone, Didi would always say, so you better not act better than me. Even at a fancy party like this one when she was only barefoot. Didi was kind of oversensitive that way, Kevin thought. Except so was he. Kevin never stopped to think either, he just did—like he did this morning when Mrs. Harrigan came to the door.

Didi had a big smile on her face that showed her back teeth, which were kind of green inside for some reason. That smile was the sign; when she smiled super-polite like that, Kevin knew she was about to lose it. Usually when it happened to involve him, Kevin tried to clear out of the room as fast as he could, but now with Mrs. Harrigan in her sights, he was eager to wait and to watch.

"Now you go and get changed," said Mrs. Harrigan out loud to Kate after she had finished her secret lecture, "right upstairs through the side door. Then come back to me and we'll speak to Mr. Ford together." Mrs. Harrigan spoke like the matter was already decided.

"Didi said I could stay over at her house tonight if I wanted." Kate's voice was timid and firm all at once.

Her mother looked surprised, "Didi?"

"This is my sister, Deirdre," Kevin jumped in suddenly. He cast a quick look back to Ivan to reassure himself that his friend was behind him; he could tell he was. Then Kevin took Didi's clenched hand in both of his and stepped forward.

But, though her arm traveled with him, Deirdre's feet stayed firmly planted. Kevin's arm lifted hers into an unintended barricade which cut off Mrs. Harrigan's direct exit back to the party. All three stood a moment, embarrassed, quite close together.

"Kate was over at our house," said Didi, pulling Kevin back close to her side, "and it got late before I realized. She was a little upset about something, so I decided we'd better walk her back home."

"Upset about what?" said Mrs. Harrigan coldly, not acknowledging the introduction.

"And this is my friend Ivan who's staying with us," Kevin continued doggedly. "And this is Mrs. Harrigan, Kate's mom."

"Pleased to meet you," said Ivan, picking up the ball from Kevin perfectly, standing close to Kate, raising his hand half way in the air like he did when he greeted someone he didn't know.

"I don't know about what," Deirdre answered. "But I told her she could stay over with us, if it's all right with you. Seeing how there's a big party..."

At that moment a man's voice by the pool rose for all to hear: "...So he said, 'I know, Juan, but if my wife doesn't have another baby so we can qualify, then where in the hell will I get the money to put gas in my car?'" This was followed by a general roar of laughter and boisterous applause. "I swear to God," the man cried out, pleased with himself. Kevin saw him now, he had a red face and white slacks, and one of those Hawaiian shirts on. "It was that little dark guy,

pumping gas at the Shell station on Harbor Rd. I overheard him talking to one of his buddies while he was filling me up. Believe me I
heard. I was waiting on that damn line for an hour and a half."

"...and the party doesn't show signs of letting up much," Didi
went on. "And it's no trouble putting Kate up for the night if you'd
like."

"I'm sure, it's a very kind gesture Miss...?"

"Deirdre Hawkins."

"Miss Hawkins, but I believe we'll manage..."

"Where's Johnny?" Kate blurted out.

"We'll discuss that later," said Mrs. Harrigan, her face growing
redder and redder—she put a hand to her face like a headache was
coming on; looked anxiously back over her shoulder. "Listen," she
said to Deirdre, "I really don't have time to deal with this right now."
Several members of the party were already glancing over to the shaded corner of the house between phrases of conversation to watch the
strange visitors confronting their hostess.

"I won't stay here alone, if Johnny's not here," said Kate, her
voice growing shrieky.

"You'll do what I tell you to do, Katharine," snapped Mrs.
Harrigan. "I said we'd discuss it later. And right now you'll march
upstairs and change into a dress, and come straight back down to
me, understood?"

Kate just glared at her mother.

"My God," said Mrs. Harrigan to Deirdre. "She's only ten years
old. I can't wait for adolescence."

"It's okay," said Deirdre soothingly to Kate, "we'll wait for you."

"Can I sleep over then?" Kate asked cautiously. Mrs. Harrigan
raised her hand in frustration then checked it, realizing where she
was. Kevin suddenly wondered if she ever hit Kate when they were by
themselves; again he remembered the argument he'd overheard
downstairs from Johnny's room that morning. Probably she never did
much, Kevin decided. Just threats mostly was his guess. Because he
thought of Ivan's dad and mom. When they had hit Ivan, growing up,
there was never a threat beforehand. It always just came from
nowhere; then afterwards they'd try to explain how he'd deserved it.

"We'll discuss that later," said Mrs. Harrigan, using her raised
hand now to adjust her hair. It was done up some fancy way on the
top of her head that made it look like a sculpture. "You know what I
said," Mrs. Harrigan resumed, "I'm not going to stand here and make
deals with you. Now, go on." These last words she spoke sort of gently and patted Kate off with them. Kate ran to the side door and they

all could hear her quick steps up the wooden stairs. "...You can...wait here if you'd like," said Mrs. Harrigan to Deirdre. "If you'll excuse me." A smile bloomed out of nowhere on her face as she pivoted to return to the light of the party.

But she hadn't gotten half way back across the lawn when a deep tranquil melodious voice rose over her from the crowd and across to the penumbra where Deirdre, Ivan and Kevin still stood.

"Is that Deirdre?"

"Yeah?" answered Deirdre back, in the loud husky voice she got from being a bartender; it struck Kevin odd that she'd be using her bartender's voice here.

He couldn't tell where the deep voice had come from right away, when a large man emerged from the people at the poolside and began to plow like a crossing ship through the wake of where Mrs. Harrigan had just been. He nodded cursorily to Mrs. Harrigan as he passed. Mrs. Harrigan stopped in her tracks and turned to look at his back. The features of her face had softened, every one. It was like a total transformation, but just for a second. But Kevin saw it because she was standing directly beneath the biggest flood light.

He was a large handsome, dark-haired man with black eyes in a pale face; well dressed in a coarse white suit, a short heavy glass in his hand. His hair, though, was a little longer than seemed typical to Kevin for well-dressed people, but neatly groomed like a movie star's.

"It is Deirdre. You're the last person I'd expect to see in a place like this. Thank God, these people are really boring the hell out of me. I was half thinking of walking over to the Beachcomber, but really I'm obliged to stay...but, this is perfect....Now I won't be bored."

Something about the fanciness in his language struck Kevin as familiar.

It was Nick Ford. Kevin hadn't recognized him without the bathrobe and hat.

Nick, unlike Mrs. Harrigan, seemed unbothered that Deirdre was barefooted and in jeans, though everyone else here was nicely dressed, or that they were standing alone in the shadows by the corner of the house and he seemed only just then to notice Ivan and Kevin beside her.

"You must be older than you look, Deirdre. Didn't know you had kids."

Didi laughed, "Nick, this is my little brother Kevin and his friend Ivan. This is Nick Ford," she said turning to them with a smile that said to Kevin I like him, "who comes into the bar where I work." Kevin glowered and Ivan stood puffed up, tucking his hair back behind his ears.

"Yeah, we know already," Ivan said. Nick Ford paled suddenly like he was going to get angry; then, just as suddenly, burst out laughing and clapped a tremendous hand on both of their shoulders so strong that Kevin could feel it in his knees.

"Now I know where I know you two from, the little trespassers. Don't worry, no harm done. You all just caught me a little by surprise. I'm not used to entertaining in my bathrobe, you know. Hope I wasn't too gruff. I can be sometimes I know. How's the arm, by the way?" he said to Ivan.

"Fine," Ivan said, low and short.

"Tough kid," Nick said to Deirdre, with nothing but praise and pleasantness in his tone.

"What arm?" said Deirdre.

"Nothing," said Ivan, "...I just got bit by his dog is all."

"Very tough kid," Nick observed, laughing, more complimentary still. "Don't worry, Deirdre, I disinfected it before they left." His tone was so convincing that Kevin was almost ready to doubt his judgment of the man. Almost.

"Uh, you kids might fill me in every once in a while," muttered Deirdre.

"Well I was going to," said Kevin, "but you've been real busy working a lot and..."

"Kev," she put her arm around him, "You're gonna break my heart. I know I have. You gotta let me know about this stuff though. I'll always have the time, kid, if you let me know. At least I'll try to." She put a hand on her forehead, sort of Like Mrs. Harrigan had just done, "What the hell am I doing trying to raise a kid, Nick? I mean, Jesus, I should be going to fraternity parties or something."

Nick's face was still in the light and, to Kevin's amazement, his black eyes had filled up with tears. Flushing, Nick turned his face away while putting an arm around Deirdre's shoulder at the same time. It was an awkward shy sort of gesture, Kevin thought.

"It's an odd world," Nick said. "C'mon. I'll introduce you to all these stuffed-shirts. It'll be fun."

Deirdre laughed, "Why not. You guys wait here," she said to Kevin and Ivan. "I'll be right back." Kevin stared at the black grass between him and his sister, sinking like a pit and growing as she walked away towards the light with Nick Ford.

They passed Mrs. Harrigan, still in the floodlight. She looked as furiously towards Deirdre as Kevin looked towards Nick.

"Well, how do you like that?" Kevin muttered.

"I don't," said Ivan. "I'm telling you Kev, that guy is a bad man. I mean, we've got to do something." There was a special urgency in Ivan's voice that Kevin knew well from their times before. "Listen...I have to tell you something...that guy hurt Kate...she told me about it—he, listen, he's a fucked up man and we have to keep him away from her. And we have to keep him away from Deirdre too, I'm telling you. And ourselves too." He was talking so fast it was hard for Kevin to follow. "I'm telling you, Kev, we've got to have a plan and quick!"

"Whoa, what're you talking about? You mean the stuff at the mansion or not? I mean I don't like him either I guess, but..."

"No, No nolisten it's way more than that. I promised not to tell but Kate and me. But..." Ivan was getting muddled like he didn't know exactly how to begin.

Kevin maybe knew part of what he was talking about then so he said, "I saw you guys on the path today. I mean I was in the tree and I saw what you guys were doing to each other..."

Ivan's face fell open like a steamed clam,

"It's not..."

"I better tell you that Johnny saw too. He was in the tree with me, and then he ran away. And I don't know where in fuck he is," said Kevin sternly. Now Ivan looked like he just got hit by a truck.

After a second, the face of Kevin's oldest friend started to pull itself back together like a strong muscle, but it was still terribly pale,

"Nick Ford is a molester, Kevin. He was hiding in the bushes on the path and he got Kate." It was a vague and sinister word to Kevin's ears—something waiting for children, something teachers warned against with pale bothered faces. "And if he finds out you and me know too, after the mansion and stuff...I think he'd come after us too."

"So, you're telling me he did like you and Kate were doing," Kevin shoved Ivan angrily in the chest. Kevin was sort of scared by how angry he was. The whole thing had mostly seemed like a kind of joke until this moment. Something funny like farting, or throwing up. But now Kevin sort of felt like throwing up himself. He could feel all the candy he'd eaten today and the end of Deirdre's stale cigarette all gyrating and shimmying inside him.

"Yeah," said Ivan scornfully, "like you're even listening. I thought you said Kate was your friend. Do you know anything about it, what it's like, Kev? Huh?! If Nick Ford comes after you, you'll find out." He pushed Kevin back so it felt like a blackjack in Kevin's chest and then this weird picture came into Kevin's mind—a memory sort of, of his mother, in her bedroom, drunk and petting him and telling him everything was all right, while a strange man outside beat on the door over and over and shouted, Come out here, bitch. "...You don't know, do you?" Ivan went on. "Well, I do. I know what it's like. It hurts you real bad inside and makes you feel crazy."

"If that guy touches my sister, or Kate ever again," Kevin burst out, "Or me. Or you. I'll kill him." Kevin didn't want to feel angry anymore as soon as he said it. He wondered for a second if he might not be getting a fever or something from smoking that cigarette.

It seemed to scare Ivan as well, "Okay, C'mon," he said hesitantly, "I know how it feels, but right now we need to think about what to do."

"What happened to Kate? Tell me that first," Kevin said. But it so happened that Kate was standing just behind him as he now could read from Ivan's eyes. She had appeared from the side door as they were talking. Kevin turned around and she stood there like a statue, pale in a light blue lacy dress, white stockings and shiny black strap over shoes.

*The girl lives in a beautiful house
and there's a path across the street that goes to
a hole
and the hole is terrible and empty.*

*But it used to be a beautiful secret cave
lined with black moss softer than velvet.
That's where the path was supposed to go.*

*It's for the girl to go visit her friends in.*

*The hole happens one day when there is
a neighbor man.*

*The neighbor man happens one day
when the girl has a mother and the neighbor
man and the mother are friends from before
when the girl's mother was also a girl and
when the path was for her to go see him
instead of for this girl to go see her friends on.
When the man comes to be their neighbor it's
only in the day time.*

*The reason for this is magic stones.*

No one knows how magic stones work
but they're made out of all the light that fireflies leave on the trees and bushes in the path.
Working guys rake it up at night and bring it
in secret to the candy man and he pushes it
into stones for them to build everything with.

The neighbor man doesn't like the light.
That's why he hates the candyman and spends
all the daytimes in his dark office. And the little girl hardly ever sees him even then.

The hole starts one day when the man
wants to be alone with the girl . He says that
the girl looks like her mother did when she was
his friend.

The girl is scared even though she knows
the man is her mother's friend from before.
The mother and the man never talk to each
other now. The mother only says the neighbor
man's name sometimes when she wants the
father to change his mind.

When the neighbor man sees how the girl
is scared of the dark, he reaches into the black

moss cave and pulls out a patch of black moss into the daylight so she can see it. Maybe the man thinks she's scared of the cave. But its not the cave she's scared of. She is scared of him now for pulling the moss out when he shouldn't have.

He pulls down his pants and puts the moss on top of his thing which makes it stick straight out.

Then the neighbor man asks the girl if she thinks it is pretty.

She doesn't think so because the black spot makes a shadow on the path.

And that's how the hole starts only it's small at first.

# CHAPTER EIGHT

"I feel stupid," Kate said to Kevin. "And I'm not going to apologize to him anyway. I'll die first."

"Ivan told me," Kevin blurted out. Kate's eyes got burning bright on Ivan when Kevin said that, and he thought for a second she was going to start go-go dancing again. But maybe she couldn't with that funny looking dress on.

"I know I promised," said Ivan, dim-eyed, "but I had to, Look!" And Ivan's eyes flashed up suddenly across the lawn. Nick had his arm around Deirdre. She had a drink in her hand and was already arguing with someone about something.

"I was going to tell you anyway," Kate said and put a hand on Kevin's shoulder. "I'm glad you know. But," Kevin felt a little weird from her hand, "it's not something that just happened," she whispered, "It's still there. It's here. So if you feel like cold all of a sudden," she said like she was straining for the words, "and you can't remember why, it'll feel like a shadow crossing, just be careful then, okay? It's hard to explain."

"Okay," he said. He didn't say anything about seeing her and Ivan on the path, maybe he would later—how that made him feel cold. And Ivan didn't say anything about it now either, but you could tell he was thinking about it, the way he stared down at the ground and kept tucking his hair back behind his ears.

But for right now Kevin looked back into the eyes of his friend Kate and felt all right. "Nothing's going to happen to you or to Didi, or us either. Ivan and me'll call the police if we have to, won't we Ivan?" Kevin saw that night again in his mind, that night he'd hardly remembered about that much until today. The guy was pounding on the door again, yelling for his mom, like the scene was just picking up where it left off after a commercial in his mind. Now he saw himself again, barefoot and small in only his underwears, standing in the cold dark of the kitchen dialing 911 on the phone and wincing each time the dial wound back off his finger. The noise it made.

"Solid," said Ivan.

"We can all count on each other," said Kevin, trying to sound a little too important and in charge. "That's the important thing."

They all three put their left arms together, hand-to-wrist, in a triangle.

Just then Mrs. Harrigan spotted Kate and crossed back over the lawn.

"C'mon now," she said to Kate. "You look sweet," and took her daughter by the arm. Kevin couldn't help feeling that the little look she shot at him was particularly venomous now.

But that didn't stop Kevin and Ivan, uninvited, from following them into the midst of the throng by the pool.

Didi and Nick stood at the center of a circle of three or four couples.

A fat man with a bald, shining head and strings of sweaty hair was speaking heatedly to Nick,

"You're laughing at me, but it's your own idea."

"It may have been," laughed Nick, "but it's just that: an idea, among others. For you, Bill, it seems to have become a virtue of Messianic proportions." Kevin stood with Ivan at the very edge of the circle. He couldn't make heads or tails of what they were talking about. He felt his forehead constricting as he listened desperately for some clue in the words to orient him. There was no clue in Nick's face either, which smiled back blandly at the fat man.

"Your idea will save this country," said the fat man angrily. "By removing the feeling of shame that keeps us down. Look at us, backing down again, from a ragtag group of Arab tribes. It must  stop." Kevin felt a sudden flush of danger; maybe rag tag Arab tribes meant Didi and Ivan and himself. "Our shame blurs the line, that's the brilliance of your idea, Nick.  Could they stand on their own against the interests of the most powerful nation on earth without it? Damn Nixon, the Democrats have made him a symbol for it.  But it's beyond Nixon, it's our own guilt we can't defeat. Remove that and the whole world will benefit—rich and poor alike." Kevin's whole body relaxed. Nixon, that was the clue. They were talking about politics, that was all, not anything real.

"Maybe," said Nick indifferently. "In any case you're too large a figure, and it's much too hot a night. Really. There's still four months till election day."

Politics were weird. Kevin noticed how careful adults always were around them; the careful way Nick Ford held his body right now, the grumpy flushed face of the bald man. For himself, Kevin didn't understand the passion, but he could recognize it as one. And in the faces of Ivan and of Kate now, he found confirmation of his own vague malaise. Politics was something they, as children, were excused from, but still it often left them in a precarious position. Strange actions could be inspired suddenly in this sort of conversation, by unknown forces that couldn't be predicted. Two adults could be talking about how many people made this much at their jobs and how many didn't work—or something of the kind that seemed pretty ordinary on the surface and not personal at all, when out of the blue a bottle might get smashed against the wall. Kevin remembered that at the fourth of July barbecue one year that his dad and mom had behind the garage; it was a long time ago but Didi would remember too, he bet; might even be thinking of it now, because she thought she was old enough to get involved in the argument and the bottle his dad threw only just missed her eye.

Whatever was being talked about here was dangerous too. Dangerous enough that Mrs. Harrigan dared not interrupt, even though it was plain she was hell-bent on getting Kate to make her apology to Nick while she had her in her hands.

Kevin looked at Didi and felt his throat tightening. She was wearing the same expression as at that barbecue four years ago when Kevin's dad finally left them for good. Only now she was an adult too. The frown: Kevin knew she was about to say something even though she knew it was better not to. It wasn't long in coming either.

"Maybe I don't exactly understand what you're talking about," Deirdre said, to the bald man. "But if you're saying what I think you're saying, which is that regular people are somehow going to be better off if you make it so rich people can do whatever they want to get richer, I'd say—nothing personal—that you're full of shit and, I'm sorry, I don't exactly see too many Working Joes in this crowd to agree or disagree."

A damp silence, heavy and thick: So all the other adults had to hold it up with their eyebrows to keep it from hitting the ground. The writing was on the wall; Kevin and Ivan and Didi were going to get kicked out now—finally. To tell the truth, Kevin had been expecting it to happen a lot sooner.

Nick smiled faintly, but his eyes seemed very amused, "That, of course, is true," he said.

"You, I assume," said the bald man, a mean sort of glint in his small eyes, "are what we might identify as a 'wage earner?'"

"I work at a bar," said Didi angrily. "Yeah."

"Noble pursuit," said the man, and a general chuckle lightened the mood, so even Deirdre smiled a little, and several people took sips from their glasses. "She makes an honest objection," he said to his audience. "So, with her permission, let's take this young woman's case as an example, shall we?" But he didn't ask her permission and was about to go on with his point when Nick said,

"This 'young woman' is here at my invitation, not as an 'example,' Bill," he looked sidelong at Mrs. Harrigan standing there with Kate and seemed about to say something. But after he said, 'here at my invitation,' Mrs. Harrigan kept silent and had the sort of expression you have when you've just lost at checkers. She was holding so tightly to Kate's arm that Kate was wincing. But Mrs. Harrigan seemed totally unaware of her.

"Do you mind?" said the bald man.

"Why should I mind?" said Deirdre hotly.

"How old are you?" said the man.

"Why? How old are you?" said Didi and everyone laughed, so Kevin saw she'd scored a point somehow.

And the bald man smiled too, "If I were trying to win your company for the evening, I might say I'm forty-seven. As it is, sadly, I'm fifty-three." Everyone seemed to like what he said too: Not laughing this time, but all looking more like they were smiling to themselves. But Didi turned bright red, so Kevin would have liked to hit somebody for it if he could only figure out quick enough who or why.

Kevin was about to shout something like, 'She's smarter than you are, so shut up,' but he wasn't totally sure that was what it was about and, before he could decide, Deirdre said, "Dream on," and that shut the guy up for a minute somehow, and pulled the color back out of her face and back into his. Kevin was relieved, understanding only that she'd somehow defended herself.

"All right," said the man. "Twenty-eight and adequate guess?"

"Sure, if it's adequate to be wrong." The crowd didn't seem to approve of her saying that and many of them started to fidget and look uncomfortable. "I'm twenty-two, if you want to know."

Everyone, the bald man included, looked like they'd just lost their socks.

"Very young to be a mother, if you'll forgive me," he said. "Are you on any kind of, assistance?"

Didi gave him her laser-beam look, "That's my younger brother Kevin and his friend Ivan," she said.

"We're friends with Kate," Kevin blurted out. "And Didi's our adult; that's the only reason she's here anyway. No one invited us." He shot a dirty look at Nick Ford..."My sister doesn't care about your dumb party." Kevin knew he might have gone a little far; now it was Mrs. Harrigan who turned bright red. Kevin was actually finding it sort of fun to watch the way it traveled around—like there was someone in the shadows shining a colored flashlight first on this person, then on that one.

"I invited Deirdre to join us, as I said," said Nick, an odd faint smile on his face. Kevin couldn't imagine what words could make him blush. Maybe the words didn't even exist and certainly, if they did, they were sure to be words that Kevin wouldn't know. The thought of this man as his opponent scared Kevin down deep now for the first time. What to do? What to do? He was going to lose. He was going to lose Deirdre and there was nothing he could do about it.

"Actually," said Mrs. Harrigan interrupting sweetly and addressing Deirdre, "I've been looking forward to meeting you. I just met Kevin for the first time this morning. A new summer friend of my son, John, I believe." She put all the stress on the word, 'summer.'

"Actually," Deirdre said, in the mimicking way that she had, "Johnny and Kate have been coming to my place for nearly two years now." The red in Mrs. Harrigan's face now drained white, but Kevin didn't know where it had gone this time, like they were all through with the little man in the bushes with the red flashlight now, and things were starting to get serious. Now Mrs. Harrigan flashed her cold look at Kate,

"My children are quite secretive at times," she pronounced generally. "Especially this one. I had no idea," she said to Didi and in a proud and dignified tone, "forgive me."

"Hey, kids are kids," said Deirdre with real warmth. "They've got their own world, know what I mean? Maybe I'm just closer to it, that's all. Really, I didn't mean it like that; and really, it was just an accident I crashed you party. Nick comes into the Beachcomber sometimes, so he recognized me. Me and Kevin didn't mean to spoil anything. Listen, I better get going."

"On the contrary," said the bald man, "I thank Nick for bringing you. You give us the occasion to speak concretely about something that troubles us all, secretly."

Kevin felt something tickling his foot.

"Look at us, the so-called powerful, the so-called leaders of Port Bedford. So reluctant, so fearful to put a name on it."

Kevin felt the something crawl towards his ankle and, realizing it was some kind of bug, jerked his leg back totally repulsed.

"I, for one, am not in the least ashamed of my position in Society. No Nick," said the man holding up his hand to prevent Nick from interrupting him, Nick who was standing way too close to Kevin's sister. "I won't pretend your talent for thought, Nick, nor even your fearlessness. Only it seems, though, you'd prefer to leave it to my likes to recognize, defend and believe in what you conceive of."

Kevin noticed the bug now, fat and black, humming under his chin. He started with a tiny cry and swatted the air in front of him and, to his surprise, the bug glowed out a bright lemon spot.

"Perhaps you are right, in that respect, to become a judge and leave the politicking to the likes of me, ha, ha," he clapped Nick on the shoulder, coming dangerously close to touching Kevin's sister as he did so. Consciousness was creeping into Kevin too now that the bald man was a little drunk. An uneasy smile circulated between Ivan, Kate and himself. Deirdre somehow had another drink in her hand too. Nick looked at the man coolly. But the man didn't seem to notice and went on talking,

"...My point is only this, Let's be honest," he said to the general circle, which had grown quite a bit larger—the most magnetic conversation in the yard—"With the exception of our—why not say it—exceptional Mr. Ford, who is equally at home among any company: women, men, poor, rich...even children," he observed with a cursory glance at them, "we were every one of us put a little out of ease by this young lady's appearance in our conversation..."

"Bill, please," said Mrs. Harrigan, "really you've been a little heavy on the gin and tonics tonight."

"No, I mean it," said Bill "This is my whole point...it's true, she's dressed differently, carries herself differently and, well, makes us all feel guilty, in a word. I mean, my God, a girl of her age raising two children, not even her own, on limited means. In our secret heart of hearts, doesn't she stand here, forgive me," he said, turning to Deirdre, "but I'm speaking openly here, God forgive me. Stands here as an accusation to our more comfortable lifestyles. Guilt in short."

The firefly wandered off, oblivious to the conversation.

"Therefore, I would ask this of the elite of Port Bedford, assembled here tonight," he said, wobbling a little as he raised one finger in the air, "Is it this woman (or these people if you prefer) that inhibits us, or ourselves. Ourselves, I'm saying, from acting. Acting from ideas that are naturally, naturally, mind you, our own?"

Kevin all the while had been doggedly trying to follow the thread of this man's talk, but there didn't seem to be one. So far as Kevin could tell this guy wasn't at all being kept from doing anything he felt like, if that's what he was talking about.

"And not only ourselves, don't we inhibit her as well in this? Does self-effacement do, not only us any good, but her as well?" The circle of people was dead silent. Kevin felt more lost than ever. He just wished he had a pin though, so he could pop that red fat guy like a balloon.

"No!" he shouted. "And it winds up hurting everyone rich and poor. It's our responsibility to change this hypocritical state of affairs. It's time, so to speak, for us to come out of the closet." The bald man looked wryly at Nick, "Perhaps not your choice of words, but have I stated the idea fairly, Nick?"

"The honorable Judge Ford," said Nick smiling faintly still, "Why ask me?"

"Why ask you? Why ask you?!" said the fat man in a spray of sweat and spit. "You are our Jefferson and I am but a Jeffersonian..." The way the man gesticulated reminded Kevin more, actually, of George Washington, crossing the Delaware so he could get to the President's Day sale before it was over.

"The practical man was Hamilton," said Nick laughing.

"Quite right, quite right. The foot is on the other shoe!" said the bald man, happily prodding Nick in the ribs," the crowd laughed again as he raised his glass, "To a new Hamiltonianism—power to the States; unshackle us, we who have the means, and we will lead the way to a new Golden Age for America."

"You do have ambitions, don't you, Bill?" said Nick. A general cheer now; then Mr. Harrigan, who had joined the crowd, spoke for the first time Kevin had ever heard,

"Indeed," he pronounced in a thin controlled voice. "William Gunn for President in 1980; we could do far, far worse."

"Hm," said Nick thoughtfully. "The name at least is problematic."

"Ah, my name," said the bald man with a mock dramatic gesture, "And what is in a name?"

"Only what you put there," said Nick. He wasn't as drunk as Bill Gunn, Kevin didn't think.

"Seriously," Bill Gunn said, still glowing from the applause and returning to his questioning of Deirdre, "I'm interested. Do you get assistance, you know, through B.C.W., Medicaid? AFDC maybe? Now there's a program near and dear to all of our hearts. Well, how 'bout it?" The crowd again was quiet. Everywhere around him, Kevin could feel the apprehension; the anger beneath it. Then he noticed how Mrs. Harrigan's eye went like a magnet to Deirdre, as Nick put his arm protectively back around her waist. Kevin was so confused now that he didn't know who was trying to hurt his sister or who was trying to help her. He saw the firefly light up again, but it was far away by the hedge now.

Kevin didn't want Nick Ford's arm to be around his sister any more than Mrs. Harrigan did. But he also knew what those letters were. Gunn was taking about welfare checks. Kevin's mother got them every month in the mailbox and was always waiting for them. Kevin knew what Bill Gunn meant. He meant that people like Deirdre and him were worse than ragtag Arabs even.

"What's it to you?" Deirdre said carefully.

"Oh nothing, nothing at all," he said smiling. Kevin didn't believe him for as far as he could throw him. "Let us assume," he said spreading his arms out like a balloon again. If Kevin had a pin in his pocket he probably would have really stuck him this time, just to see what happened. "That you support yourself completely."

"You're right about that Mr. President," she snapped. "I'd give you about twenty minutes in my shoes before you keeled over with heat stroke." Kevin couldn't keep from laughing and to his horror, the only other face that thought it was funny was Nick Ford's. Their eyes met for half a second. Kevin felt like someone just soaked him in gasoline and Nick's eyes were a match.

"Look," said Bill Gunn angrily. "If I go and buy that bar where Nick tells me you work, and don't think I don't have the money; and if you in fact are as good a worker as you say, and I have the sense to capitalize, don't you see that your life will improve as well? It's called a raise. You will share in my success just as you have invested your worth, by fulfilling your job with, with your character."

Although he was still totally bewildered by the conversation, Kevin saw in that instant, by the change on his sister's face, that Bill Gunn had crossed the fatal line. Deirdre's hands shot from her sides like rockets,

"Hey, Fuck you, Bub." In that same motion, to Kevin's delight, she had pulled her side completely away from Nick's. Now she turned back towards him and pointed both fingers like two little pistols at his brain. "Don't expect me to vote for your friend, here, Nick." Nobody moved. Everybody's eyes were on Deirdre. She looked back at all of them and laughed. Then she turned and walked towards Kevin and Ivan, "C'mon," she said to them, "Oh, Kate." Kate was still at Mrs. Harrigan's arm—the mother still clutching the daughter. "Come if you want to."

Kate looked uncertainly at her mother, "All right," she said, slowly trying to extricate herself as gently as possible from her mother's vacillating hand.

Mrs. Harrigan smiled and rolled her eyes for the audience, "We had a deal, young lady."

Kate looked at Nick Ford and then she looked at Deirdre,

"Okay, Mom," Kate said and smiled sweetly too. The crowd murmured in approval as Kate kissed her mother on the cheek. "I'll get my toothbrush and..."

"Yes, later dear. I'll take a moment with you now, if you don't mind."

Kate withdrew with Kevin and Ivan; hurried to Didi's side and whispered something quickly to her.

"Sure, Kate," Deirdre said in a perfectly loud voice, "No problem."

"Nick?" Mrs. Harrigan said, turning to Nick Ford appealingly, the softness of her tone surprised Kevin again, he'd never heard one like that from her mouth yet. It was like a girl asking a boy out for a date or something, "Since my husband seems rather unavailable at the moment." Mr. Harrigan, Kevin observed, had indeed withdrawn to one side, right on the edge of the pool in fact, and was heatedly speaking to Bill Gunn in whispers; Bill Gunn didn't seem to be saying anything; he just listened with his head down and to one side, like he was opening up his ear to let Mr. Harrigan pour words in easier. "Would you mind, terribly," Mrs. Harrigan went on, "my borrowing you for a male presence, for a moment?"

Nick Ford nodded his head. His face was unreadable to Kevin.

"You'll excuse us," Mrs. Harrigan said to the party. She put her arm in Nick's and together they shepherded Kate, together with Deirdre, Ivan and Kevin, away from the party and back into the dark. "Kate," she said pulling her along with her now, "We'll go around to the living room; your friends can wait outside if they'd like."

Deirdre stopped, so they all had to stop. "No, that's okay," she looked straight at Nick, "We'll come in."

Nick smiled. "Most Certainly you'll come in," he said.

"Please," said Mrs. Harrigan weakly.

Suddenly Kevin had the uncomfortable feeling they were all trapped in Nick Ford's mansion again. But they weren't. This was Kate's house. But if anyone there was acting like it was his house it wasn't Kate, who stood looking down at the living room carpet. Not even Mrs. Harrigan looked at home.

"Can I fix you a drink?" Nick said to Deirdre, walking immediately toward the liquor cabinet.

"Sure," said Didi. "Got any Southern Comfort?"

"I don't think," he said bending his knees to peer inside, holding the doors open in his hands like wings, "that they do." The cabinet was made out of that same dark wood and the room had old smelling velvet wingback chairs and a couch. There were books, mostly spy novels and things like the kind Kevin's dad used to read— fat, shiny lettered spines, mixed in with a lot of things bound like schoolbooks, but whole bunches of the same color and size grouped together. "So that's your drink is it?"

"Whatever," Didi said.

"Carol, a martini?"

"That would be wonderful, Nick."

"Been a while since I've been inside here, hasn't it Carol? Since before the kids were born, no?" Mrs. Harrigan seemed to shrink away from him a little.

"Nick, you know yourself we invite you all the time."

"I know, I know," he answered rudely. "Wouldn't mind some Southern Comfort myself," he muttered to Deirdre. Kevin, Ivan and Kate had all grouped themselves together on the couch, "Bourbon?" he asked Deirdre.

"Yeah, whatever. Like I said. Listen, these guys are up way past their bedtime."

Kevin actually was feeling a little sleepy, only there was too much going on to be sleepy so he felt grumpy instead.

"Nice place you've got here," said Ivan. I never saw the living room last time I was here."

"You were here?" said Mrs. Harrigan, her eyes widening.

"We were just picking up Kate and Johnny one time," he said, "We, uh, didn't go inside or anything," he lied.

Nick studied Ivan curiously, like he was stopping to consider him for the first time.

"Anyway," said Mrs. Harrigan, "I'd like for Kate to say something to Mr. Ford and I'm not sure it wouldn't be easier for her without her friends."

"Why?" said Kate looking oddly at her mother, as if she mightn't have heard right. "It's like you said: They're my friends."

Mrs. Harrigan flushed, "Of course they are, dear. Well?" she said after a pause.

"And afterwards I'll get my tooth brush and stuff and stay over with Didi..." Kate waited.

"It's really no problem," Didi interjected, "I've got a fold-out she can sleep on in the living room; I'll fix them breakfast in the morning and send her back."

"That's very generous..."

"I'll just jot down my phone number here..." she scribbled on a pen and pad set by the phone, next to Kevin's arm, so Kevin couldn't help noticing her sidelong glance up at Nick. Kevin kicked the base of the couch where he was sitting, loud with his sneaker. Since there was no response, he did it again. Mrs. Harrigan was just about to say something, but the noise had interrupted her.

Then out of the blue, Kate bolted up from the couch, put both hands behind her back and blurted out as fast as she could: "I'm really sorry, about taking your losing your pen knife,"

"My pen knife...?" His eyes were full of surprise, for half a second, then he roared out laughing, "Is that what this is all about?" He looked for just a fraction of a second at Kevin and Ivan before bowing to Kate, "Apology accepted, though." Kevin saw or imagined a mischievous twinkle in his eyes. "The funny thing is, I found it again under the desk. Only minutes after I mentioned it to you Carol. I'd just misplaced it, I suppose." To his amazement, Kevin saw Mrs. Harrigan's eyes filling up with tears.

"Oh Nick," she said, "How can you..."

He looked back at her, frowning, "I forgot to mention that I suppose. I'm sure I should have kept my suspicions to myself at the time, but I hardly thought..."

Kate looked mad, her head bowed down. Mrs. Harrigan was bright red, even her arms.

"You're a good girl, Katharine," said Nick. "I just couldn't imagine where I left it was all. As I said, when you were admiring it that day, it was given to me when I was a boy, by another boy my age and... Well, I'm sentimental about it I guess."

"Well?" said Mrs. Harrigan to Kate with a strangled voice. "It's not as if that's the only thing you've done lately to harass Mr. Ford, is it?"

Kate's mouth fell open as she stared at her mother, her face went completely pale. Kevin couldn't even tell if she was angry or scared or what. Her eyes fell mechanically back down to the carpet and she labored on like each word weighed a million pounds, "And it was just a big mistake about cutting across your yard..."

"Not to worry," said Nick grandly. "Just call in the future if you'd like to visit; you're welcome anytime. Sorry I can't extend the invitation to you two," he said appraising Kevin and Ivan again with a menacing look, like if they said one word he might just snap their necks, "but I'm a rather busy man, you see. Kate is almost family, *Is* family actually. Carol and I are cousins, did you know? Carol and I have always underplayed that fact. We've only just recently told Katharine and John, in fact." Nick seemed to be talking to Deirdre. "Carol and I grew up together." In a flash Kevin remembered what

Johnny had said about the dress-up game he and Kate used to play. Kevin couldn't help a knowing look at Mrs. Harrigan. Mrs. Harrigan eyed the two boys without comment.

"But..." Kate said

"Mr. Ford...Your cousin, is being very generous with you, Katharine. Thank him."

"Thank you," said Kate. Her voice was strangled though, just as strangled as Mrs. Harrigan's had been a moment before.

"All right," said Mrs. Harrigan, "That's that." She looked like she was ready to run for her life. When she looked at Nick there were tears in her eyes again. She didn't even bother to apologize to Kate for accusing her of stealing the knife when it wasn't true. "I'm going back to my company now. It's very kind of you to offer to look after Kate," but instead of looking at Deirdre, Mrs. Harrigan was looking at the notepad where Deirdre had written down her name, as if that were the real Deirdre, not the person in front of her. "And, if, if you, Nick, feel it's most appropriate, under the circumstances." Nick nodded, half-smiling. "All right then, I defer. Your visit certainly turned out to be lively..." she said scanning the notepad like it was Deirdre again, "Miss Hawkins, or is it Ms.?" Finally she stared up at Didi with a scary face.

"Whatever," said Deirdre.

"Run up and get your things," said Mrs. Harrigan to her daughter. Kate hurried up the stairs, not waiting for her mother to change her mind.

Kevin began to suspect that all of this might somehow have to do with Johnny's disappearance too. He looked at Ivan, still sitting next to him on the gold velvet couch, his arms crossed so it made his muscles seem bigger. In his mind, Kevin was still seeing Ivan from this afternoon, touching Kate; being touched by her. Kevin felt all mixed up with envy and disgust; he wondered what Johnny was thinking about it all. And had Kate taken that knife or not, he couldn't even say. He'd seen it that day at the mansion, they all had and Nick knew it. He still looked at Ivan. There was something adult in his friend too, something not understood that made Kevin uneasy.

As soon as Kate had reached the top of the stairs, Mrs. Harrigan hurried to the bathroom. She returned a moment later, fully composed like nothing had happened and returned to her party without a glance at any of them.

Now just Nick and Didi were the only adults in the room. Kevin felt ignored. He was used to feeling invisible around adults, but not around his sister. Seeing her, not three feet away, looking into Nick's eyes and completely unaware that Kevin was on the planet made him lonelier than he'd felt in years. Plus Kevin felt secretly awkward too, just to be sitting alone next to his friend after what he and Johnny saw. He longed to tell Ivan, so Ivan could explain, "Don't be dumb, Kevin: it's just this way," but that would have to wait till they got home and into Kevin's room. And right now Kevin couldn't see at all what way it was. He tried again to giggle to himself, but it still felt fake. Ivan seemed to notice the strangeness of Kevin's expression and the not-funny laugh from his lips,

"What's up, Kev?" he said. So Kevin turned his attention to Nick and his sister instead of answering, as if that were the cause. They were standing close together in the corner by the open cabinet. Ivan nodded silently.

"...I'll bet you do," Deirdre was saying to Nick about something. A tough open smile.

"Jerk," Kevin whispered to Ivan, but for some reason he didn't feel like getting close to his friends ear so it came out louder than he wanted; Nick and Deirdre both heard something and stopped their conversation,

"What?" said Didi, sort of fake-motherly to Kevin, but really she was embarrassed.

"Nothing," Kevin said. He couldn't help sounding surly and accusing too.

"You guys are drunk, aren't you?" Ivan said. He wasn't very afraid of adults after all he'd been through with his dad. Not even a guy like Nick Ford.

Nick laughed, "Not by a long shot," he said.

Deirdre smiled at Nick, "Oh, I've seen old St. Nicholas drunk, Ivan; believe me, he's not drunk."

Nick frowned, "That's what you get for trying to get friendly with your bartender."

She said, "I got a file on you. So watch your step here—because your playing with fire. I'm over-worked. I got two kids to think of who aren't even mine, and a third tonight," she added, but she wasn't mad, it was something different—like rough play—"I'm lonely as hell, so watch your step, Judge, because if you cross me, you'll find out the meaning of the word Bitch."

Kevin was confused though. He approved of what she was saying—like she was standing up to him like no one else, not even the adults at the party seemed to do, but the voice didn't match up to the words somehow: Like her voice was saying I like you; I think you're nice, instead of what it really said.

And that seemed to be the way Nick took it, even though he still looked pretty impressed.

"You're very unique, Deirdre Hawkins," he said.

"Yeah," Deirdre laughed air through her nose, "Unique with kids."

"Where's Kate?" said Kevin, "C'mon let's get out of here." Nick and Deirdre looked at each other significantly and that made him furious. "C'mon," he said. "Kate!" he shouted up the stairs. "C'mon let's go."

Kate came down the stairs then, with a little backpack and her regular clothes from before.

"Where's Johnny?" she said.

"I don't know, hon," said Deirdre. "Maybe he's sleeping over somewhere too, because of the party. Your momma didn't seem too worried about it, I'm sure she knows where he is."

Kevin, though, wasn't so sure. He thought, when he saw him as it was getting dark, that Johnny didn't know where he was going, and might be sleeping in the rocks of the sea wall somewhere for all Kevin knew. At least it wasn't cold outside, and Kevin had promised— not to look for him, not to follow him, not to tell—until their meeting tomorrow by the dragboats. There was that at least. Why had Kevin chosen the dragboats? Now, late at night when things always seem less sure than before, he regretted the bold suggestion. He had wanted to show Johnny how tough he was too—but it was a dangerous place for a kid or for anyone sometimes, and he could just as well have chosen his schooyard or anywhere. Well, anyway, at least he knew he could find him tomorrow. He knew too that Johnny would keep his promise unless he were really in trouble.

Nick took a few steps away from Deirdre when Kate came the rest of the way down the stairs.

"In fact," Nick said to Kate, "Johnny's at my house."

Everyone's jaw dropped at once, and Didi's too.

"So you see," he said, smiling at Deirdre, "I have a kid now too."

*I want to sleep in Deirdre's bed but don't ask when we get back to their house. It's real late and Didi is tired. She brings out sheets for the couch and Ivan and Kevin go to sleep in Kevin's room.*

*I am all alone in the dark in their living room except the moon is shining on dirty white boards from the next door house. And there aren't any curtains to pull in Didi's living room because there's nothing to hide here like at my house.*

*I'm glad the moon isn't coming in here though just lighting up the dirty boards outside and a little piece of the street and a rusty bicycle.*

*Every time a car goes by all the walls get scary. I can't sleep even though I try. The couch is scratchy all over me and makes the sheets twisty.*

*I can hear snores from the boys' room. It's Ivan because I remember his stuffy nose from today.*

*Before the first black spot boys don't have black hair all over them. After they get it it spreads and that's what a man is.*

*Boys have hair on their heads of course but that kind smells like toast and butter and not like eels in low tide mud.*

*Boys don't need any black moss to keep their things warm. Boys are different, with them it's always the best time of day on the path and never night.*

*In the best time of day all the buildings and everything are made out of magic stones. The girl wears her sunglasses by the pool because it's so bright. And a boy's thing never gets cold and stays soft and wiggly.*

*And it's okay for anyone to play with them. Even the girl used to sometimes on her brother. It never gets cold or makes anybody a different person. It's just for fun and maybe* only a little stupid. And the girl and her brother don't do that anymore anyway, and they only did it when they were in a stupid mood and both of them had the giggles. There's only a shadow when the neighborman reaches down and pulls off the black moss from where it's supposed to stay.

I'm still not sleeping and then Kevin is standing in the living room doorway in his not so white boys underwears. I can tell he's Kevin because his shape is the same size as me. He sees I'm awake and says he got up to take a pee.

He says I saw you, you and Ivan. Me and Johnny did from a tree.

I say So? but stand up because the couch is burning me. I stand near the window where the moon is coming in now. Kevin does too and looks at the dirty white boards with me and the rusty bicycle and the piece of street. His bottom lip is full of moon like a cup.

He says I think my sister likes Nick Ford.

*I say Nick Ford pulled black moss from a secret place. So he's not Nick Ford really, but something else.*

*Kevin doesn't understand so I say A shadow. It's everywhere now, but it comes from Nick Ford's eyeballs. All men can get it from him though. Once its started, it goes from one to the other so you never know where it is. I've seen it in my dad and Bill Gunn too, sneaking half way out when you're not looking. Ivan knows his dad's got it too.*

*Kevin says I don't have it. Not in me it isn't.*

*I say No it's not in boys yet. It comes from the black moss*

*I say its supposed to be hidden, but it's not anymore.*

*He says there's no black moss anywhere he's ever seen. He says I don't think there's such a thing.*

*But I know where it is, so now I have to find it and show him. It's on the path and I'll* show him where.

I say we have to find it now right away
because we talked about it and I run out the
front door of their house and into the moon
even though I'm only wearing my nightgown
and Kevin runs after me even though all he
has on is his boys underwears.

I'm in the moon in the place on the path and I
say Here. I get on my knees and dig around the
dirt of the bushes to find it. Kevin just stands
there so I say Help me.

Kevin is on his hands and knees too,
looking.

He says What's this? and holds it up for
everyone to see in the moon.

It's black and stiff.

I snatch it from him to hide it fast
under my nightgown. It feels ugly there.

# CHAPTER NINE

Kevin'd seen Ivan sleepwalk before. It happened pretty often and he'd also do strange things. He'd even talk to you sometimes, or even go outside. But he wouldn't answer your questions like Kate was doing. And Ivan's eyes would have this funny, empty look; Kate's were looking straight at him. Kevin knew you're not supposed to wake up somebody who's sleepwalking, but he decided to try an experiment.

"What were you doing with Ivan here yesterday?" he said. Kevin didn't say it in a bad way or to surprise her. He said it because he wanted to know, and somehow he just couldn't bring himself to ask Ivan about it. And maybe she was asleep anyway.

Then Kevin could tell that Kate could tell; that she was thinking about it even though she didn't look mad or defensive. He didn't think sleep walkers thought about things much. They started slowly back to Vale Place.

"A kind of magic, I guess," she answered slowly and thoughtfully, as they approached Kevin's house again. "To make the shadow thing go away. Because if you catch them in daylight they turn to stones…. It's not just Nick that does that, you know. Ivan's dad too. He told me all about that too; that's how it started. They all do a little."

"Who?" said Kevin.

"Men. So you never know where it is. But it comes from Nick's eyeballs. That's where it comes from first. Even Ivan's dad got it from him.

"Did you know Ivan sleepwalks sometimes?" said Kevin.

"No, he never told me. I never have," said Kate. "Have you?"

"No. We're still friends, right?" said Kevin.

"We're best friends," said Kate.

"So okay good," said Kevin, nodding to the little lump in the belly of Kate's nightgown where she was still holding it in her hands away from her skin. "That's a piece of a shadow that used to be moss or something?

Kate nodded.

"It's not girl's underwears maybe?"

"Well that's what it really is, of course," said Kate with a don't-be-stupid look; blushing a little, he thought, but it was hard for Kevin to tell in the streetlight.

"Are they yours?"

"Not anymore."

"I'm going somewhere after breakfast." They were walking back into the house so they were talking in whispers now.

"So?"

"I'm gonna meet Johnny." She waited. "Johnny ran away somewhere because of you and Ivan I think." They walked into the front hallway next to his bedroom door.

"I know where he went," said Kate. Ivan's snores from the bedroom stopped suddenly and he said something in his sleep Kevin couldn't understand and rolled back over.

"Why would he go to Nick Ford's do you think?" said Kevin.

"Because," said Kate, "I knew he would."

"Well I'm not going to meet him there."

"That's smart," said Kate.

"Anything you want me to tell him from you?"

Kevin felt like kissing her on the cheek for some reason, but he didn't. He just raised his eyebrows. She raised hers back. "No," she said. He crossed the dark threshold into his room.

The last thing Kevin heard before falling back to sleep was the voice of Kate asking Didi if she could get into her bed. Then the sleepy grunt of Didi saying yes. Then everything was quiet: The even breaths of Ivan beside him.

Suddenly sunbeams were so thick across the floor of Kevin's room you could spread them on toast, which he could already smell wafting from the kitchen, even before the toaster's first springy pop. Ivan was sitting upright, cross-legged, deep eyes sparkling, on the bolster bed below Kevin's own. Kevin lay with his eyes open, looking at Ivan but not really awake yet.

"I love this summer," Ivan said. Metal clatter and sizzling margarine. The hoarse morning voice of Deirdre and the higher voice of Kate murmured as they cooked.

A feeling of family flooded through Kevin as he lay there still, still with his eyes open, watching Ivan's happy face but also not yet looking at anything at all.

"...You toast it first and then you soak it in the eggs. See..." Kate was chattering, "...It's good."

"Don't think we got syrup," mumbled Deirdre.

"Look," Kate said, "we can use jam," and then their conversation dropped back down to a murmur.

"We're the men comin' in for breakfast," Kevin drawled. Ivan looked a little shy at first, but played along.

"Well, sit on down, cowboys," said Didi, leaning the old melted Teflon spatula on the hip of her white towel robe like a six shooter.

Kate wore the same blue cotton night gown down to her toes. And there was a broad line of black dirt across her knees. So, it hadn't been a dream, Kevin thought. Straight white-gold hair in every direction—the crease from the pillow still on her cheek. She wouldn't look at him.

"What does that make me?" she asked.

No one said anything for a minute.

"A cowgirl, I guess," said Didi.

After breakfast, they took Kate home like Deirdre promised. Kevin felt like Kate was avoiding him a little. There was no one up on the whole of Garden St. it seemed. Kate thanked everybody, without looking at anybody, waved, walked resolutely up her porch steps and opened the front door with a key from her pocket.

"You call me, hon, if you need anything. Or come over," said Deirdre. "Meanwhile, I'm gonna find out more about this on my own from Nick."

Kate frowned, waved her hand again and disappeared.

Didi had to go into town, she said, so Kevin and Ivan walked her to the busstop and then were on their own. They went back to the house.

At eleven, Kevin sprang up from the couch where he was starting to nod off. He walked outside, Ivan behind him and picked up his bike. He told Ivan he was riding to Commercial Harbor to meet with Johnny.

Ivan lent him his pocket knife, because Kevin was going to the dragboats and that was a dangerous place. "I used to go down there sometimes," was all Ivan said.

It was a Sunday morning, hazy and a little windy even on Market, the inland avenue Kevin rode through the center of town. Most of the downtown shops were closed, except for one or two of the breakfast and newspaper joints. So Kevin sailed through the five lights of town, red or green, since there was hardly any traffic anyway; only the syncopated bump of his tires as he crossed raised tar joints in the blocks of concrete pavement. Black uneven lines, bubbled and jagged with tire tracks from the heatwave of recent days. The tar was solid again, the wind was much cooler this morning than it had been. In fact Kevin had his sweatshirt zipped up all the way to his neck and still felt a chill.

It wasn't even July until tomorrow, but the air made him think of the fall; of how all the people close to him were changing shape. He remembered the things Kate had said and thought of the manhood waiting inside of himself like the egg of a shadow, waiting and growing behind some bad thought until the black hairs would come out of his skin and take him over. It was too soon to be this cold; he just wanted more than anything for summer to come back.

At the far end of down town, the wooden bones of the big roller coaster humped up above the thick carpet of treetops and back down again, and beyond that the blue steel of the ferry docks poked up, and beyond that all the riggings of the fishing boats, like a thousand crazily tuned tv antennae. That was where he was heading, and to the worst place in it too, the dragboats.

More than the other fishing boats—the small lobster boats that went around dropping and picking up their pots, or the long-liners who fished with strings of hooks—the draggers were big and dirty. They were as industrial looking as the big tankers almost, even though hardly any of them were more than fifty feet long. They dragged a big sock net behind them from thick rusty cables, along the bottom of the ocean, dragging up whatever they could find, then the men would separate fish from the old tires and other slimy junk with shovels. And the men, like the boats were bigger and dirtier too than the other fishermen and more dangerous, drunk and armed and stooping to anything because they couldn't go lower, because they never had money and had nothing to lose. Kevin knew most of this from Deirdre, who knew a few of them, and also from Ivan, because his dad used to hang out down there a lot, even though he was never a fisherman himself. Most of them lived either in East Bedford or else on the boats themselves.

Kevin stopped his bike at the familiar—safer—public ferry dock from where he could see the whole harbor at once and build up his courage. The sheltered water stretched out gray-black and ruffled silky like snakeskin from the even off-shore breeze, which carried the salty smell of oil from some big tanker discharging from deeper down the harbor behind him. A single seagull on the ferrydocks highest piling stuck up his neck and laughed at Kevin, ha ha ha-ha ha.

The actual shape of Port Bedford Harbor, as Kevin learned it in General Facts, was this:

Port Bedford Harbor was shaped like two unequal lobes of a brain, or like a misdrawn heart—with a long jetty in the center made of dynamited rock to divide the two parts: Commercial Harbor on the left; Town on the right. Kevin got back on his bike and rode now past the small launching beach by the ferry dock to the turn for the jetty road that ran along the jetty's back out into the water a quarter of a mile or so, where all the fishbuying houses had piers, and where the fishingboats first came in to unload from the ocean. The jetty itself extended long past the fishbuyer road, a mile or more, to protect both harbors from storms: Town from Nor'easters, which were never big enough to pose a serious threat to the big tankers or even fishingboats on Commercialside. Town harbor was naturally protected from sou'westers—the hurricane storms—by an inward sweep in the land. It was the jetty's job to protect the bigger boats on Commercialside from sou'westers.

Looking back into Town Harbor from the start of Jetty Rd., Kevin could see the full array tricked out before him. All the beautiful yachts and sailboats were nestled into that inward curve of land: Moored off private piers; ending finally where Town Harbor deeped at the ferry dock, which was nearest to the center of town.

The fishbuying houses were nearest to town in Commercial Harbor; they shot off on piers to the left at the end of the jetty road. That could be a tricky place for a kid too. The older kids who worked the winches would stare at you while they worked and would even try to sell you things sometimes and ran mysterious errands for the big guys hidden in the back. From here, Kevin could just see the rigging of the fishingboats from over the fishbuyers' bowing shingled roofs—where old names were written in lighter shingles: General Fish, Fishcorp, were two that he could read from this angle now. In reality, the slips of the fishing boats weren't really behind the fishbuyers; that's why they looked so small. They were all the way on the opposite side coast of Commercial Harbor and their entrance was a mile further down Harbor Rd. Commercial Harbor was by far the larger lobe—Town was hardly anything in comparison. Kevin saw it stretching endlessly inland from where he stood into a wire and steel girdered marshy wasteland. He could just barely see the dirty white top of the big tanker's pilot house and the tips of red letters which he knew spelled ESSO, the gas station company that owned that particular tanker. He knew where the tanker was, too, docked far in from where he could see from here, where the oil holding tanks and the railroads were and the tankers came in to discharge. It was naturally the deepest part of the harbor but had to be dredged all the time anyway because it dwindled at last, behind the tracks and warehouses into a mirey garbage strewn salt marsh that itself narrowed finally into the slow flowing tidal stream know as Blind Brook. Not many people knew that Blind Brook came from there, but Kevin did, because his mom's house was way out right near there.

Standing here on Jetty Rd. comparing the two, it suddenly seemed weird to Kevin that people from Port Bedford only went to Town Harbor and never to Commercial at all. It was clear from here that Commercial was about ninety percent of the harbor. And yet, for people in Port Bedford it was like it didn't even really exist. Their boats were here and not there, and they strolled on Sundays here and would never go there to save their lives—because Town Harbor was all painted and nice he guessed, with taffy and ice cream and the amusement park nearby. But everything real, Kevin guessed, was probably going on over there. That's why he told Johnny to meet him by the draggers where no one ever went. Because in a place like that maybe there was a way to find out what was really happening, underneath all the crazy stuff that didn't make sense on the surface in Kevin's life right now.

A guy named Herbert Ford had first conceived of the jetty some date a long time ago—Kevin got back on his bike and started pedaling fast down the part of Harbor Rd. he didn't know well which led to Commercialside and each pedal seemed to carry him into bigger dirtier uglier landscape, cinderblock buildings and chainlink fences and barbed wire— And from the simple idea of this pragmatic division (neither lobe of the harbor was sufficiently protected naturally) the small fishing and farming village of Bed Ford had grown into the sizable city Port Bedford was today. Kevin had written a report on the harbor for an extra credit in the geography unit. He liked boats more than most things in school. Although, to be honest, Kevin remembers copying a good deal of it straight out of some book he found in Killdeer Branch Library.

His head filled with this odd memory of words, Kevin spun up to the fishing dock's chainlinked gate and found Johnny already there waiting.

Johnny looked like a total mess: his eyes were rimmed red and pieces of his hair stuck out like corkscrews. He was wearing different clothes though. Ones Kevin had never seen before, sort of old fashioned looking and rough white cloth. So maybe Nick Ford wasn't lying. Maybe Johnny was really staying with him after all. They were just the sorts of clothes Kevin could imagine hanging around in the closets of that big creepy mansion.

Johnny was sitting on one of the creosote posts at the entrance, his head slumped down into his hands and a bleary look as he greeted Kevin.

"Hi," said Kevin.

"Hi," said Johnny. "Thought you might've forgot."

In the silence, you could hear the riggings and creaks from the metal hulls of the dragboats; then harsh laughter from the cabin of a black rusty one nearest the gate where they stood.

"So," said Johnny, "Nick told me he saw you guys at my parents' party last night; he told me all about what happened." Johnny laughed sort of defensively, "I bet you're surprised I went to Nick's, aren't you?"

Kevin decided not to say anything, waiting just for Johnny to say what he wanted in his own time.

"I was going to ask you if you brought any candy," said Johnny trying to change the subject, "but I didn't, because I'm not so sure now, if I should even eat candy anymore, because everything's sort of different for me now."

"I don't have any anyway," said Kevin.

"Oh, okay," Johnny said. "Never mind then. " He looked disappointed.

"Okay," said Kevin hesitantly. Johnny looked different, more than just the clothes. He was sitting up straighter than he usually did now, maybe.

"Did she ask about me?" said Johnny. He winced like he wished he hadn't asked.

"Sure she did," said Kevin. "I told her I was going to see you today."

John frowned and didn't say anything for a long time.

"She's not really my sister, Kevin. Did she tell you that?" Johnny looked up at him hard. Kevin started running the sole of his sneaker back and forth over the spikes of his bike sprocket, looking down.

"Jeez."

"We figured it out last year on our birthday, but we kept it secret from everybody. Everything started to get worse after that." Johnny blew out a big sigh. "Now it's finally over. I'm glad." He didn't look glad though. Kevin had known there was something mysterious about Kate and Johnny being twins for a long time. He kept rubbing his sneaker back and forth, tearing at the rubber.

"I'm not like Kate, Kevin. I don't like secrets, especially secrets against me. And I don't like to have to keep them either. It's just too complicated. When I used to think we were twins I thought I should be like Kate. But now I know I'm different. I always felt different and didn't know why. I've just never known where I fit in really. Even with you Kevin, so now I, I just want to tell the whole story I guess."

"Okay," said Kevin, but he could hardly hear his own voice. He was still thinking about Kate and the black underwear he saw.

"Our parents were going to be away that weekend when our birthday was supposed to be last year, August fifth, remember?"

"Yeah, I remember," said Kevin. He was very good about remembering people's birthdays, Ivan's, Didi's, his mom, his dad: It was like a role call in his mind.

"They said we were going to have our birthdays on August first instead. Then we heard our mom and dad arguing about it late at night when we were supposed to be asleep, but me and Kate were up and listening at the top of the stairs. Dad was saying how the party they were going to was too important to cancel; mom said they couldn't just not be there for their children's birthday even though she knew it was too important, too.

"Then he said, Well Johnny's real birthday is August first after all and it would only be fair to celebrate on his birthday for once.

"Kate and me had our birthday with our parents last year; then, remember on the fifth we met you, Kev, and got candy and took you with us to the movies. Remember: That's when Kate told you how our birthdays were really five days apart even though we were still twins?"

Kevin remembered. They took their bikes to Town Theater and, even though it was rated R, they saw this movie called "Ben" where this rat named Ben becomes king of the rats and gets them to kill all the people and take over a city, because the rat is sad about something. Because they killed his owner. The people in real life were wearing rubber suits covered with peanut butter, but it was scary anyway and Kevin hadn't been able to sleep for nights.

"That was a cool movie," said Kevin.

"Yeah it was," said Johnny.

"Hey," said Kevin. "I don't have any candy, but I got a cigarette out of Didi's purse if you want to try a little.

Johnny lifted his head from its slump and looked around nervously. "A cigarette? Have you done that before?"

"Just a little bit yesterday. It sort of made me dizzy, but it was kind of cool."

"Not right here though," said Johnny appraising, "what if a car comes? Let's climb down the rocks and sit under the dock ramp. Then I'll tell you the rest."

It was almost dead low tide—the whole place reeked black mud, so the ramp down to the floating finger docks of the dragboats was steep and the barnacled rocks underneath were all exposed. They had to move carefully so as not to cut themselves.

The cigarette that Kevin pulled from his shirt pocket said KOOL in green letters and it tasted cool at first; he lit it and puffed, and Johnny puffed and waved it with his hand, and continued in a chattering voice, like it was no big deal: "Then in the winter Kate and me found out I was adopted." Kevin took another puff, his eyes felt wide. Like he was just watching himself listening to Johnny from up above the ramp somehow.

"Are you dizzy yet?" said Johnny.

"Adopted," said Kevin; "Fuck." Johnny took the cigarette from him and sucked it with tremendous lungs so it glowed like a bright orange splotch in Kevin's brain.

"Now I'm dizzy too," said Johnny. Kevin took back the cigarette and tamped it out on his rock, then put it absently back into his shirt pocket. It stunk almost as bad as the mud. All the smells were getting stronger. "I almost told you yesterday," said Johnny, "because I thought you probably knew; because I figured Kate would give it away even though she promised not to..."

"She didn't," said Kevin. "She doesn't tell other people's secrets, only hers when she want to."

"Kate thinks if we tell anybody, someone will come and take me away, but I don't care anymore, because I'm at Nick's now." Johnny frowned. "We found out by listening on the phone last Christmas day. Mom was talking to our aunt Harriet, which is her little sister; only they didn't know we were upstairs listening on the other phone. They were talking about who my real mother was. Aunt Harriet said she was probably a prostitute now and on her back in some room high on heroin." Johnny looked flabby and sad. "I remember how Kate pushed down the button and she was really mad at our parents for not telling us. And she was scared too if they found out we knew, they'd send me away to an orphanage or something. I just didn't feel that good; I said I was going to run away I think. But Kate said not to. She said how we would always just keep it as our special secret and, and we'd get married one day. Like Nick and our mom was gonna when they were our age."

"They were?" said Kevin.

"They should've," said Johnny angrily.

"Do you think Nick loves your mom better than your dad does?" Kevin thought of how Nick was making the moves on Deirdre and thought that Nick had been mean to Mrs. Harrigan if anything at the party. But he hoped it was true because they deserved each other and anyway that would get him away from Deirdre.

"That's what I think," said Johnny as if Kevin had finally

guessed. "I'm going to help them." Kevin started to pick at the hole in the bottom of his sneaker, tearing at the rubber. "I always thought Kate was going to help too. It was both our plan. And then she just changed. She's been acting so weird for like two weeks. Then, with yesterday and the tree and everything. That's how come I decided I'm through with her stupid secrets. So that's why I decided to run away again," he said sort of wearily, "Kate's just like her dad after all I guess." Johnny had a mean look on his face. "Gimme that cigarette again," he said. "And you better not tell Otrusky any of this, Hawkins, I swear."

"I won't, okay?" said Kevin, but he looked hard back, and shoved the rest of the cigarette into Johnny's hand. Kevin wanted to say too that maybe Johnny didn't understand about Kate, and he was just thinking how when Johnny said softly, "I know you won't because you're my friend, and I don't want him to know."

Kevin struck him a match; how could he say about Nick Ford now?

Heavy wooden footsteps from the ramp above, so the whole ramp shook over their heads. Johnny quickly stumped out the cigarette.

"...Shit yeah," came a man's voice. "Don't tell me about it. Thirty cents a pound, that's bullshit for sole."

"Fuck him is what I say."

"Fuck him is damn right, fuck him..." the receding tramp on the finger dock, until two large stooped backs suddenly came into view, out the low edge of the ramp that Kevin and Johnny were facing, one with a bottle in his hand, booted fisherman, they stopped at the rusty black boat where the laughter had come from, boarded and disappeared. Several voices inside rose up to greet them.

"Who's walking on my bridge?" whispered Johnny in such a hoarse low voice that he sounded like the devil. They both started to giggle.

"Anyway," said Johnny, "Everything's okay now. Nick said he was going to call my mom. He promised I can stay with him at least for the summer if I want. Then he said it might be too busy with his work and things and me going to school, but we'd see. We're going for a trip together on his boat," Johnny said. "He said we could pick up stuff for me tonight. So it looks like I'll be staying in Nick Ford's mansion, I guess," said Johnny dreamily.

The oily water Kevin watched between the toes of his sneakers swished in and out and made the fleshy tangles of seaweed seem to blow and breathe all on their own. Kevin always felt a little repulsed by this kind of seaweed, black strings of pale blisters that you could pop between your fingers. Kevin was popping them in fact, having picked one end up out of the water between the two toes of his sneakers, breaking the blisters one by one with gross squirts while the rest of the string wallowed in the slow slop. How could he tell Johnny now what he'd come to tell him, about what Nick Ford did to Kate? And what did Nick do exactly? Molested the word was still shifting into uncertain shapes that wouldn't fit to any picture Kevin tried to put in its place.

Kevin was about to try again, and it was like Johnny sensed something in Kevin's face he didn't want to hear and looked away down into the water. Then Kevin remembered the way Nick Ford had turned away from Didi with tears in his eyes when she told him how hard it was for her sometimes. Kevin saw Nick Ford's face: His cheekbones, his black eyes, the coarse black hair the way it was under the business man's hat when they caught him by surprise. Kevin rubbed his eyes, like they were going crazy. "I just want to know one thing, Johnny," Kevin blurted out, "Why him? I don't like him, Johnny. None of us do."

Johnny's eyes were two huge circles, like bullet holes made by Kevin's own words. He suddenly picked up a huge black rock and pushed it off his shoulder into the water: A huge crack when it hit the surface, then the swoosh of water coming over when it sank; then an ear popping thud as water shot high into the sky with all the air it'd caught.

"Yo!" shouted someone from the black boat, "What the hell was that?" An unshaven burnt face poking out the galley door of the black dragger.

"Relax, Concho, another voice shouted from within. You're just being paranoid, take another hit," then the sound of prolonged coughing and laughter until all was quiet again.

"What'd you do that for?" scolded Kevin in a whisper. Inside he was worried, not just for his safety if some crazy draggerman caught them, but because it was becoming more and more difficult for Kevin to guess what Johnny would do next. Johnny's eyes were wide and exhausted at the same time and Kevin noticed Johnny had a new habit he'd never had much before. Every time there was a silence, Johnny would rub his nose: Almost hit it over and over with the bottom of his thumb, like there was a booger there, only there wasn't. It was just red on that one nostril from his doing that so much.

"Because I just told you," Johnny hissed. "I just told you, Kevin, and you still don't get it."

from Kate's diary,
June Thirtieth, 1976:

*I came home but it's not home without
my brother. There's no noise at all here now.
Every room has its mouth open and Johnny's
most of all when I look in at his red carpet
and no Johnny reminds me of a bloody hole
where the tooth is gone. It hurts too like it
wasn't supposed to come out. I think about
how much it must hurt too for Johnny to be a
tooth all by himself under Nick's pillow waiting to get turned into a nickel. I wish it wasn't
true that Nick was his dad because then it
wouldn't be so hard for him to know what the
right thing was. It's because Nick is his dad
that he thinks it's the right thing to be there
and not listen to me anymore because I'm not
really his sister. I know it hurts him bad and
that's why he pretends it doesn't. But I don't
care if I'm not his sister anymore because he's
still my brother because only I can decide if he*

*is or isn't so tough luck.*

*My mom was in her bedroom in front of the mirror getting ready. She saw me in her door in the mirror and didn't turn around. She said What is it Kate?*

*Her table is shaped like a white kidney bean. It's full of different shaped bottles and jars and velvet boxes tangled full of bracelets and necklaces.*

*I was just wearing my dirty tennis shorts and my knees are skinned and I forgot to comb my hair before I left Didi's.*

*I said I'm home.*

*She said I see that but she doesn't turn around so she was really seeing me backwards. She was still so mad at me I could tell by her back and the quick way she fiddled with her earring.*

*I said I have to tell you something mom. It made my insides swimmy like a fish.*

*She said I'm late for an appointment Kate. I stayed there in her mirror anyways* until she let out a long angry breath like she does when I hear sometimes late at night alone in the living room way after my dad has gone to bed.

She said What is it Kate? and spun around on her stool with eyes looking everywhere but at me. I think most moms are easier to talk to than my mom. I felt small. Dad's hifi was coming up through the floor and kept pushing my tongue up to the roof of my mouth.

I said I saw you and Nick Ford doing it once in the window of the Gatehouse.

She said Doing what? What on earth are you talking about now? Eyes everywhere but looking at me.

I said It was a accident. I wasn't spying. Then my mom looked at me. She looked a long time not saying anything. She was white under her makeup and she looked like she was going to be sick.

She said Kate and Don't be upset and You should have come to me sooner.

*I said I would've mom but he got me first and jumped out and made me be quiet he*

*She said Katharine don't lie as well please*

*I said He hurt me mom he*

*But she wouldn't let me finish because her eyes looked straight at me and didn't try to believe me anymore.*

*She said Please no more. I know when you're inventing something. I know Kate because I used to do it too Kate when I was upset. And now I know what you're upset about. You must try Kate Listen to me you must fight to separate what you saw and what you've invented. You must try very hard to be an adult and not be angry with Mr. Ford.*

*I tried to tell her but she wasn't listening and then all I could say was Mom then I started to cry. It felt horrible but it just kept coming up and up every time I tried to say. She put her hand on my shoulder and it almost didn't weigh anything.*

*Her voice was soft and musicky now. She said Mr. Ford was never trying to hurt me Kate even if that's what it looked like to you. I. Its hard for a little girl to face this so young. I wanted to be there with Mr. Ford Kate. I asked him to invite me in. I didn't think you were home.*

*I said Why*

*She took me over to her bed and sat me down on the edge. And then she pulled the stool from her table and sat down too with her hand on my knee. She said I don't want to marry Mr. Ford Kate he's like a very good friend.*

*I said Is that why you let him take Johnny. I was talking loud and she put a finger on her lips Quiet Listen to me.*

*I said No I won't. I wasn't going to listen because she wasn't listening. I covered my ears but I could hear her anyways.*

*She said Nick is my cousin. We grew up together like you and Johnny. We still have feelings for each other like, like you and Johnny might when you grow up. Your father knows this. He's always known and he understands that. You mustn't mention it to him though. You must promise to keep it to yourself.*

*I said Why.*

*She said because it would upset him if you knew.*

*I said When's my brother coming home*

*She said We'll see. He's visiting Mr. Ford for a while and then we'll see, Kate.*

*Then I stood up and was yelling He's tricking you. No mom he's doing it purpose. He's taking Johnny to get at me Mom. He wants to make me do things I don't want to. He's a shadow monster.*

*My mom slapped me. Not hard but I was so surprised I stopped.*

*She whispered Stop that right now Kate.*

*My dad's voice yelled up the stairs Carol?*

*She yelled back It's fine Jason I'm dealing with it. She whispered Nick Ford is not trying to do anything to you Kate. You're upset and confused. There are reasons why he and Johnny should try to be together. We have to see. Johnny is growing up now and so are you. Now sit back down.*

*I sat back down.*

*She said Johnny is not really your brother Kate. Your father and I decided to keep that from you both until you were old enough.*

*I felt sick*

*Johnny knows that and that's why he wants to stay with Mr. Ford right now.*

*I said You lied on me. I knew for a long time you were lying on me and Johnny.*

*She said No Kate we were trying to protect you until you were old enough. Maybe we made a mistake but we thought it was best for you both. Now you must try to understand. John is your cousin. Like Mr. Ford is my cousin.*

*Her eyes were shiny.*

*I said I thought  you weren't going to*

*marry Nick Ford.*

*She sighed angry Of course not because I married your father first but that doesn't mean you can't marry Johnny one day if you want. She said That's why it's best you're apart from him for now.*

*I said Nick Ford is a shadow monster and he wants to eat my brother. I said He did bad things to me I didn't want to and you won't believe me.*

*My mom didn't get mad this time but put her hand on my forehead. Her voice was musicky. She said When I was your age I got very upset too. I got very upset and it took a long time to get better. Mr. Ford's father Mr. Ford senior helped me to get better. You must try to understand that Mr. Ford is trying to help you now too like his father did for me. He wants what's best for you just like Mr. Ford senior did for me.*

*And then I saw it. The dark hole was right there in the room between me and my* mom and it was growing so big I couldn't hardly jump over it. And I ran away into my room and pulled the chest in front of the door.

Then she was knocking soft on the door Kate. But I wouldn't answer.

She said Kate please.

I said Go away because I'm writing a story.

Then my dad was there too on the other side of the door.

They said Kate come out. We know you're upset. Please come out.

But I didn't and they went away.

# CHAPTER TEN

"Hey. You two!" A raspy woman's voice. Kevin, surprised to hear a woman's voice here, raspy or not, took his eyes reluctantly from Johnny's angry face and scanned the finger docks where the voice had come from. A dark, longhaired figure stood on the stern deck of the big black rusty dragger, in yellow oilskin overalls, arms crossed tightly, smoke rising against the sky behind one shoulder. "Whatcha doing down there?" she asked.

"Talking," said Kevin, responding to the fact that her voice didn't sound particularly mean, just kind of curious. Johnny looked up at her listlessly.

"Two talking little boys," she said, leaning her hands over the stern now to get a closer view and taking a long pull from her cigarette. "Were you listening too, or just talking?"

"Yeah we were." said Johnny, "I mean you have to listen when you talk don't you? Otherwise your not talking." Johnny just said it just to say something, but she seemed to think about that one for a second.

"The whole world should be kids. Hey, listen, how 'bout coming on over here. I won't bite you."

The man's voice again from inside the open cabin door: "Yo. Arlene. Who are you talking to?"

"Just a couple of kids. Let's take a break for a minute how 'bout though? We're all talking and nobody's listening anyway." She laughed a hoarse, friendly laugh. "You have to listen to talk. So let's just take a break. I want to talk to these kids a minute, all right?"

Kevin thought that was nice, how she took Johnny's words so serious; he sort of warmed right up to her in spite of himself.

"Kids!?" said a different man's voice also hidden inside the cabin, but which sounded sort of familiar to Kevin for a second, "What the fuck are kids doing down here?" but then Kevin couldn't place the voice again. He didn't know any draggermen anyway, though maybe Ivan did. Didi said they tended to be bad news. So he was already preparing for the worst. "All right," said the still sort of familiar voice, "You and kids, Arlene, I swear. Let's take that break boys," the voice said to others inside, "then we'll talk about my plan."

"C'mon," said Arlene to Kevin and Johnny with a big rough

friendly beckoning from her cigarette hand. "I won't bite you." The way she beckoned was like she expected them to dive straight into the water and swim over.

"What do you think?" said Johnny; you could tell he was curious for an adventure. But Johnny's last words 'You still don't get it.' were still echoing through Kevin's head. He wasn't sure of Johnny anymore, for that reason also he sort of welcomed the idea of not being alone with him. Plus the truth was he'd never been invited onto a dragboat before, or any boat for that matter, except for once a ferry to one of the big islands that surrounded Port Bedford.

"Okay," said Kevin, to Johnny and the woman, Arlene, both. Johnny picked up the end of the cigarette and put it into the pocket of his shirt, and they climbed up the rocks to the steep ramp, even steeper now since the tide had gone down more.

Kevin felt like he weighed a million pounds when he went down the ramp, it was so steep; each forceful step shuddered the ramp against the rhythm of the even larger shudders from Johnny's steps. The first several of the floating finger docks were grounded askew on their barnacled Styrofoam undersides. The field of black silky mud around them smelled even more powerfully its fertile decay, freckled white with razor slivers of clam shell and able, Kevin knew, to trap a little boy and suck him down without a thought, if he were foolish enough to try to walk on it.

The boat was called the *Sierra Madre* and there was a salt-pocked aluminum railed gang plank leading up to its low stern. "C'mon over," said Arlene, invitingly standing to one side of the plank, "Ever been on a dragboat before?" Both Johnny and he shook their heads shyly. The two big cable spools and the smelly net hanging from a big steel boom overhead were a little overwhelming.

"God," she said, putting a caressing hand onto Kevin's head as soon as he touched the deck. Kevin shied away, like her fingers were full of electricity, "Did I scare you? My little boy Steven looked just like you." Kevin froze. He allowed his head to be petted for some reason but it made his skin go all prickly. "Sorry," she said; then her face darkened, "The bitch who married Stevie's father won't let me see him anymore." She smiled at Kevin again, "What's this crazy lady talking about, right?" She tapped his cheek, "Don't worry, I said I wouldn't bite. Want to see inside?"

"Sure," said Johnny. A strange moist sawdusty smoky smell was coming from in there and, when they entered behind Arlene, the three men inside all started shouting, "Arlene don't bring them in," "Hey wait." "Yo." and "Great, now they'll run back home and tell their at all of a sudden.

"We all have to have a special knife, you know," Tock went on, enigmatically, the way he said things so often. And suddenly it was like they were all back at the candystand by the sea wall and it was just an ordinary day. "So, why don't you two sit down and tell us how you got yours, and then we'll each tell you how we got ours? That's what fisherman do in the galleys of their dragboats, you might as well know. It's like a friendship thing. That's just what we were doing before you got here. Sit on down," Tock said. "Want anything to drink?"

"What do you got?" said Johnny looking at his ease again. There was something different about Tock still though, like Kevin's dad when he'd had too much to drink. Kevin didn't feel quite safe again yet.

"Hell, I don't know. Water? Some soda, I think. Hell, we got a bottle of gin if you want it."

"Fuck," said Johnny to Kevin, "want to share one of those beers? I had one before and it was good."

"Now you're talking," said Tock.

"I'll have a soda," said Kevin. "And maybe a sip of beer," he added, seeing Johnny's disappointment

"Arlene?" said Tock.

"Fuck you, get it yourself, if you want to corrupt kids," she said. "I work for a living. All I see you doing is sitting on your ass talking about revolutions and shit. Feeding beer to kids, Tock, that's a great way to start the new world."

"Listen, Arlene," said Tock, "kids can make choices just as good as adults; don't think they can't." Meanwhile everyone put their jack knives on the table, so so did Kevin and then, more reluctantly, Johnny.

"So where'd you get that knife, Kevin?" It was always surprising when Tock used your name.

"I got it from the Mad Russian," Kevin said, because he wanted to be friendly because the truth was he was feeling a little scared even though he knew it was just Tock. That was the joke that Tock himself made about Ivan and Kevin hoped he'd remember it and let them go. But Tock didn't laugh, or even seem to notice anything unusual in the phrase.

"Yeah, I know," Tock said, "But the Mad Russian just got sent to prison last week, for robbing a liquor store, so how'd you get his knife?"

"What'd you mean?" said Kevin, sipping from the beer can Tock handed him. It tasted bitter and salty like surf water, but kind of okay. Then he decided Tock had got the joke and was making one of his own, "I guess you knew he was going to prison," said Kevin ,"and that's why you gave him a free atomic fireball, huh?"

"Who you talking about?" said Tock.

"Ivan."

"The Mad Russian? Shit," said Tock, like he'd just figured something out. "That kid, your new friend, is named Ivan too, isn't he? I never forget a name. Not even a kid's. That's why I called him the Mad Russian, I wasn't even thinking about, but. Man, I could feel it even then, there was something familiar looking about him. I don't suppose, Kevin, that your friend Ivan happens to be an Ivan Jr.?"

"Ivan does have a kid named Ivan, I think," said Arlene.

"I borrowed it from him, that's all," said Kevin cautiously.

"Yeah?" interrupted the big, bearded draggermen. "But that sure in hell don't explain the other one;" he pointed at Johnny's knife. "How'd you get that one, kid? These kids are fucking spies, Tock, I swear." But he laughed and shook his head like he didn't care all that much if they were spies or not. He was just having a good time.

"Quit being paranoid, Concho," Tock said. "You smoke too much of that shit, I swear to the Lord."

The big man mock-saluted him, crossed his arms over his belly which was so big his t-shirt didn't cover it, and started to smile to himself again.

"I got it from my dad," said Johnny defensively.

"Yeah? And how'd your dad get it?" Concho said, lumbering up clumsily and swaying over Johnny now like some kind of interrogator, stroking his beard and after a while just stroking the air like he forgot exactly where his face was for a second.

"It's his," said Johnny.

"His is it, hm? Listen, don't dick around with us, kid." The big fisherman seemed to enjoy playing the tough guy, even though his voice was very soft and far away. "because we know who's knife that is. We gave him the fucking thing uh," Concho stared off into space a while "... a, way long time ago."

"Yeah?" said Johnny, being just as tough, standing up himself. "Well who's is it then?" He reached over and took the beer can from Kevin's hand; took a big armed big swig.

"Nuh uh, Nuh uh," said Concho trying to keep a straight face. "I asked you first. Who's your father? Tell me that first." Concho was huge, but Johnny was huge for a kid.

"Children, children," said Tock laughing at them both. "See,

Arlene, I've corrupted Concho too."

But Concho still stood over Johnny waiting for his answer, and even though he was still smiling, Kevin started to feel a little scared. Kevin was busy trying to picture the thin, feather-haired, gray suited Mr. Harrigan with any kind of knife at all, even one as small as that, when Johnny said, looking significantly at Kevin first, quietly but proudly, "Nick Ford is my father." Silence. Like a big huge black hole in the boat, growing between Johnny and himself like a mouth.

"Bullshit," said the other draggerman. "And, bullshit or not, that's a pretty stupid thing to say outloud on these piers."

"Well? How did I get this knife then, you tell me?" Johnny countered.

Kevin was staring at Tock though, not at them. His face was old again, those dark and light lines coming out from his eyes again like a shattered windshield. Tock's big hand was digging itself into his curly black hair which was so thick his hand was almost hidden. Then he bent over like he had a stomach ache. Now everyone was looking at him, even Concho and Johnny. But when he came up again, instead of the groan of pain Kevin was expecting to hear, there was a roaring laugh and the lines around his eyes were rays from an angry bright sun.

"Serendipity," he roared so loud the cabinets shook. So Kevin thought the word some magic incantation. Tock noticed Kevin's look of confusion and, ever the instructor, said "Sort of means Speak of the Devil, which was what just exactly what we were doing when you two boys walked in."

Concho chuckled, "Devil, exactamundo."

"And you're his spawn. Spawn," said Tock to Johnny suddenly, like it was Johnny's name. His voice was so forceful Johnny had to look at him. Whatever language Tock was talking in, Kevin felt sure it wasn't Spanish or Portuguese with words like spawn and serendipity and must've been Mongolian or wherever it was that Tock was from. Tock took Johnny's face and pinched it in his tremendous hand and drew it towards him so Kevin thought he was going to kiss Johnny on the forehead maybe like he had done to Kevin the other day. But he didn't. He just stared at it. Johnny's face had a big smooshed up grin like he thought this was all a big joke.

"You know what?" said Tock. "He actually looks like him. I know what old Nickey used to look like as a kid. In the eyes he does."

He released Johnny's face which was bright red now with a left over smile and Johnny said, "Jeez, Tock," rubbing his jaw and clearly impressed by the strength of Tock's hand, "I thought my head was going to pop." Johnny laughed again, more uncertainly, hoping maybe to get a laugh back. But Tock's face still wasn't friendly. His hand was shaking as a matter of fact, so he must've been squeezing Johnny pretty hard. Tock looked at it like it'd just touched a spider or something.

"That was a mistake," he said, to Arlene and the draggermen it sounded like. "I won't touch you," he said to Johnny, but the smile was gone from Johnny's face now. Kevin was relieved though. It seemed like Johnny's smile was what'd been making Tock angry somehow. "I won't touch you ever again, as a matter of fact, kid. Unless you cross me your own damn self." Tock eyed Concho like he expected him to say something and wanted to shut him up."

Concho didn't catch the look though, "But wait Tock," he said, "Don't you see this is perfect? It's an opportunity made in heaven, man. Maybe you forgot what Nick did to you, but I don't. I'm your friend man and I remember. That was the beginning. He did it to all of us." Kevin didn't understand exactly what it was they were talking about, but it wasn't good for Johnny he could see that. And, judging by his paling face, Johnny was beginning to see that too.

"Unlike my jolly friend." said Tock to Johnny, "You're lucky I don't buy this sins of the father bullshit."

"That's right," said Arlene.

"Right it's right," said Tock. "Why do you think I let Nick in with us in the first place, Concho? To give him a chance you know. He was his father's son now wasn't he?"

"And it got you the pinta," said Concho sulkily.

"That's right," said Tock icily back, "And is it this kid's fault?"

Concho wasn't enjoying himself anymore, you could tell he didn't like to fight with Tock. "It's a good idea though anyway," he said sulkily, "I mean he did walk right into our laps. You know, man, use the tools at hand."

"I know whose fault it is all right," said Tock in a whisper, the lines back in his face. "Don't you worry about that."

Kevin thought back to the party on Garden Street when he didn't understand what was going on either. Was this just politics too, he wondered? It still felt dangerous whatever it was. Kevin began to sincerely regret he'd ever suggested the dragboats as a place to meet.

"But you know, Johnny, this is very  interesting," said Tock, leaning way back as if to keep as far away from him as possible, to not be tempted to touch him again, "Concho's right about that. That's probably the most interesting thing I've heard in a long while. Have you told anyone?"

Johnny looked uncertain, and he looked up at Tock appealingly, his voice was shy. "I don't understand all this, Tock. Why is everybody being like this. I, I mean he is my dad. I could tell people if I wanted, couldn't I?"

Kevin turned his head away. He couldn't help it.

"C'mon Kevin," Johnny said, nudging him with his elbow. "He's really a nice guy. He's important. People look up to him. Maybe you just got off on a bad foot or something?" Kevin didn't know what to say, so he just stared at the kerosene flame in the lamp.

"Trust me on this, Little Mr. Ford," said Tock quietly, "keep this to yourself for now. Remember something. I never forget a name. Though I hardly ever use them unless you're my friend, or were once." Then he stared hard at both of them, "Knives either," Tock added, that secret look in his eye.

Again something had changed in Tock's tone and his eyes felt unbearably bright on Kevin's skin in the dark smoky room.

"Here. Look at this:" He opened his own knife; held the big blade over the chimney of the kerosene lamp. "I can't explain it, but let me show you something you should never forget:" Tock continued to pass the blade of the knife hypnotically back and forth over the glass chimney of the lamp. This is why you need to keep quiet about everything you've seen here." He laughed softly in time to the knife, following the blade with his eyes. "There's no way to explain it," he said again. "It can never make sense, only this is the way it is."

The big man, Concho, was leaning over the lamp with a faraway look into Tock's eyes, then he let out a laugh of disbelief. "You said my idea was crazy?"

Kevin cast a quick look over his shoulder, the cabin door was still open at least. Meanwhile, Tock's voice flashed out angrily at Concho, there was no warning to tell he was about to be mad at anyone,

"You still don't get it, Concho; you never will. Just do what I tell you is all. I could never show you if I had a lifetime. Your skin's a hundred feet thick my friend. And that's too thick for me to get through." But Tock's eyes still followed the knife, back and forth. "How 'bout you and Manny go out and take a walk around the docks for a while? This is between me and these, fellahs."

"Aw, Tock. What about Arlene, then?" Tock glanced up at her. She was still leaning on the stove sipping her beer. "Arlene knows, already. She can stay." Manny, the smaller man spoke up then, a little indignant. "All right Tock. All he means, Concho," he said to his partner, "is that Arlene is just as crazy as he is. C'mon." The two of them hulked out of the cabin leaving Kevin and Johnny alone with Tock and Arlene.

Now Tock looked at Johnny, it wasn't at all a friendly look Kevin thought, and passed the knife near him.

The knife passed so near Johnny that Kevin, without thinking shot a quick hand to his own knife, Ivan's knife, on the table.

What happened next, Kevin was never really able to sort out. It felt like time had shifted to a slower speed even though it all happened in just an instant. Everything was just hanging in the air—the thick smell of kerosene and the charring knife blade and the lingering sawdust smell of the marijuana and the stale tinny hints of breath and beer, and the fishy smell underneath it all—Several things happened all at once: Johnny opened his mouth to say something, but what it would have been, or if he said it, Kevin never knew. Also Arlene got up from the stove and moved towards Tock as if to stop him from doing something. But Tock's eyes never left off looking straight into Johnny's and it seemed as if he hadn't moved at all.

But Tock had moved, or at least the hand with the knife had, quick as lightning. But the hand with the knife hadn't moved where Kevin was anticipating, into Johnny; instead it moved to the side, to Kevin, even though Tock's eyes were still fixed straight on Johnny's. And before Kevin, his own arm extended to Ivan's knife on the table, could react, Tock's hand and knife were gone, completely disappeared under the table, his eyes still on Johnny's. Tock's knife hadn't stabbed Kevin, that wasn't it. The movement was too quiet and quick and soft. Tock had simply touched Kevin's arm with the flat side of the knife's tip.

Kevin winced, not understanding, the flat part of a knife shouldn't hurt, but Kevin felt, not a cut, but a thin, swelling throb. Then he saw a red, triangular mark rise up in the middle of his forearm. For some reason though, Kevin refused to let go of the knife or even move his hand from the table.

"Hot, isn't it?" said Tock, turning his eyes, kindly and sad now, to Kevin's.

"What'd you do that for? said Kevin, holding back tears. Tock looked at him hard, but not unfriendly somehow. It almost looked like Tock was about to cry too. He looked very, very old.

Johnny's mouth and eyes gaped open. "Hey," he said to Tock, his voice quavering, "You were going to stab me with that thing, weren't you?"

"Because I care about you," said Tock to Kevin, ignoring Johnny. "Because I could. Look, let me show you something." He held up his own forearm. There was a faded little brown triangular scar there. "My uncle did it to me when I was about your age and a lot worse than that one, that sucker was glowing when he did it. And I just remembered that all of a sudden. 'Member I said I'd tell you what happened to me my fifth grade summer? Well now I'm showing you. This was the beginning. It's a good lesson to learn, Kevin. Think about it." Kevin actually tried a little to think about it, but it just wouldn't make any sense; he only felt a pressing urge to run away and cry. He didn't even understand why he didn't. The hot knife had just come from nowhere. From someone he thought of as his friend, because Tock had always sort of reminded him of his Dad.

"Okay," said Kevin, "I will." Unfortunately it came out kind of choky, so everybody could tell now that Kevin wanted to cry. And that was making it even harder not to. He turned his face helplessly to Johnny; Johnny looked like he was about to cry too, and Tock hadn't even touched him. That helped somehow.

"I bet you will," said Tock. "That's why I showed you. You particularly, Kevin." Arlene moved towards Kevin, to put her arms around him and protect him maybe, but Tock put up a hand to make her stop. So suddenly that she did, like she was frozen halfway reaching Kevin. Then she relaxed, and laughed and moved back to the stove.

"You think about it too, John Ford," said Tock, his eyes back on him like they'd never left. "You better think about it hard. Nick was there too that day."

Ivan's face came into Kevin's mind. Kevin suddenly understood that this must have been how Ivan felt, when Nick Ford's dog bit him. It was just like that. Out of nowhere, something that didn't make sense, but there it was. Kevin wondered with an odd calm whether he should put a bandage on his now too. Or if Tock, like Nick, would offer one.

"Here," said Tock, offering him the marijuana cigarette from the ashtray, "That was the first time I smoked too, my uncle gave it to me. It's to help the pain; all of it, Kevin, not just that little burn, that won't hurt soon enough. Only if you want to, of course," he said, still holding it out—a peace offering somehow.

"Sure," said Kevin, his voice a little sob, "I'll try it."

Tock laughed, "Okay, my curious little man, but first, think. Hell, I started smoking when I was younger than you. I never got you that soda you asked for, remember?"

"I'm not thirsty anymore," said Kevin.

"You will be," laughed Tock. "Oh, by the way," he said to

Johnny, "This ain't like the knife. It's for anybody. Don't mind giving you some too. Nick smoked with me too that day. Might open your mind up before it's too late. Didn't help your father in the end, I guess, but there's no harm in trying. Unfortunately, he always preferred the white stuff." Arlene laughed hoarsely. Kevin didn't know what the white stuff was. Johnny was looking down at the table like he was trying hard not to listen.

Was Nick Ford really Johnny's father? It still seemed so impossible to Kevin that he suspected that was at the root of why nothing at all here was making sense. Kate was right. You couldn't keep track of anyone, it seemed. So why should that wet, sawdusty smelling thing in his fingers be any different.

"Whatever," Kevin said. That's what Deirdre always said in situations like this.

Then he went ahead and drew in the smoke to his lungs. The orange flower on the end of the hand-rolled cigarette still blossoming, he gave it to Johnny who was big-grinning and soon it was blossoming for him too.

It was curious. No big deal that much, Kevin thought as he began to feel funny. The pain and confusion with Tock did start to break though, just sort of melted into tingles all over.

"Well, thanks, Tock," he said. They all began to look like clowns, too, as he began to feel one himself, all of their faces growing larger and rosy with the kerosene light and laughing as Arlene took the cigarette too.

"To the revolution," said Arlene as she smoked.

Kevin took Johnny's hand and stood up. "I think we better go now."

"Okay," said Tock. "No hard feelings now, eh?" Kevin stood a moment trying to examine exactly how it was he felt. There were no hard feelings certainly; no particular feelings at all really, just the one: a rising wave of tingles. He watched Johnny's grin getting only larger and larger.

"Nope," answered Kevin. "No hard feelings."

"Be careful now," said Arlene.

"And remember the Narcs," said Tock laughing. "Don't tell anyone about any of this."

"We won't," said Kevin, uncertainly. Johnny pulled at his hand and they started out of the cabin

"Wait," said Tock.

"What?" said Kevin.

"Your knives."

Kevin took them both and put them into his pocket. Johnny was laughing, saying over and over, This is cool. Their backs were covered by laughter from the cabin; wavering, it seemed somehow to Kevin, between warm and friendly, to sinister and then back again.

Johnny and Kevin laughed and laughed too as they worked their way back up the ramp from the docks. But Kevin didn't even know why.

Back on Harbor Rd. their laughter stopped like a lead brick. It was obviously way too much to think of riding their bikes back to the neighborhood, so they decided to leave them where they were—locked up to the crossbar of a guard rail on Harbor Rd, by the pier entrance—and walk across the road to this big grassy field sloping down to a tangle of blooming rose bushes, full of dandelions and buttercups. The bushes, they discovered, were hollow underneath.

Feeling safer for the moment, Kevin lay on his back on the slope under the bushes and closed his eyes, or opened them again to watch the sunlight through the green and red. And, maybe it was the slight slope, but Kevin found his whole prone body floating head over heels. Then, like sinking into deep warm water, he fell asleep.

*My mother thinks she is punishing me. But I'd rather be here than anywhere else. A library in the summertime is the best hiding place.*

*They open up the big round windows to let the wind in. Wind is made out of wishes.*

*The librarians here are all ladies who are my friends. They're like what I think nuns should be like or witches each one is different but they're all together too and secret. Maybe they think I'll be one of them one day because even though they're always busy they're never in a rush and all five of them smile at me at least twice a day each because I am so quiet and that's their favorite thing.*

*The way I choose books here is when the sun falls on them. That's my rule. The sun makes spots that cross all over the library from morning till afternoon. I read all kinds of dif-*

ferent things that way. But when I don't like
something I write here in my book instead.
There's always a big pile of books I've chosen in
front of me at my table at the end of the day.
Then I help the librarians put them away and
we talk about them.

Then my mother comes to get me at five
thirty sharp. Then I go home and go to my
room until dinner and then I have to go to bed
but I read then too with my flashlight or write
some more. I think I'll be pale as the librarians soon. In the morning my mother drops me
off in her car again at the library. My mother
says that this is because I'm grounded.

Just now at the desk I told Roberta that.
I hadn't told her yet because I didn't want her
to think I was bad. She's the palest and my
favorite. Roberta is the Circulation Librarian
and wears a different colored blouse for every
day but the same colored Kleenex in her sleeve
because I never remember her not having a
cold. In real life she has a squeaky voice but

*when she whispers its like a music box.*
*Roberta can laugh and whisper at the same*
*time. I told Roberta that the reason I was here*
*was because I was grounded and she told me*
*back You most certainly are.*

*My mother thinks I should spend my day*
*thinking about what I've done and why it was*
*wrong. I look out the window and think about*
*the hole out there and how the magic stones*
*are broken. I tried twice to tell her how bad he*
*was really and how it was all his fault not*
*mine but both times she started right away*
*talking fast how good he was how he did this*
*and that and how all the good things our fam-*
*ily has are because of him and she can't listen*
*to me. I say I don't think we have such good*
*things. I say how I don't even have Johnny*
*anymore because he took him away. My mother*
*says I am ungrateful. That's why I broke the*
*windows maybe. But now it's even worse. She*
*won't listen to me at all now. She only feels my*
*forehead and covers my mouth with her hand*

*all smelling from dishwater after dinner. She*
*says Why would a little girl break windows?*
*And I start to say about him and she says*
*Katharine please your imagination.*

   *I wish it could be my imagination*
*because then my brother wouldn't feel bad*
*inside because he loves me. If it was my imagi-*
*nation he would never have a real dad that*
*was a shadow monster.*

   *Here in the library where it's safe I make*
*believe it's my imagination and that I never*
*ever had to go home where the little girl was*
*left alone in the yard where the neighbor man*
*was more hot and bothered every day.*

   *He told the girl's mom once that he*
*would never go into the swimming pool even*
*though he had it built for her mom who loved*
*it and wore her bikini and big glasses on the*
*weekends there while he was working. He said*
*it hurt his eyes so he couldn't read and it made*
*his breathing shallow and If it got any shal-*
*lower he was afraid it might put him into an*

early grave because of all the young women he was with every night. The girl's mother rolled her eyes as she always did when the man talked about his young women. But he always did end up talking about that until sometimes the girl's mother cried and told him to go to hell. The girl's dad was never around at those times.

The girl didn't care so much why they got the pool built though. She just loved the pool more than anything because she loved to swim in it. And then the man would almost always come out of the Gatehouse where he was working to watch her because no one should swim unsupervised. And he would stand there in his long sleeves and pants all sweating and bothered when it was just the two of them and watch her. He said he had piles of thinking and reading to do and he told the girl one day she spent so much time in the water that she was like a fish. He said the pool is a bad place for a fish and that the place for a fish was the ocean.

The girl started to visit him then sometimes in the Gatehouse where he worked right next to her house instead of just swimming all the time so she wouldn't turn into a fish.

The man said he didn't like how bright it was. He said he was always so stuffy and he never got out anymore like when he was young like the girl and used to like to walk on the path. He liked to complain all the time how he never had time anymore with all of his important work. He said What he needed was to get out in the ocean on his boat and then he invited the girl. She asked if her brother could come too but he said No just the two of them. Then he said they'd have to go way far for her to really swim because the harbor was getting more like a swimming pool every day. It was even starting to smell like one.

He said no one in his right mind would go swimming in there unless he was planning to drown himself.

# CHAPTER ELEVEN

When Johnny and Kevin woke up, almost simultaneously, it was nearly night.

The long-haired, t-shirted silhouette of Ivan stooped over them, his voice high with panic, "C'mon you guys, wake up. Quit fooling around."

They got up, rubbing their eyes as they emerged from under the bush.

"What's up?" said Kevin.

"What's up?!" Ivan burst out in a relief of exasperation. "You've been gone more than seven hours. I just thought you were dead that's what's up. You guys look like a mess," he added more softly, his face strung funny with worry. "What happened?"

Johnny laughed, "We took a nap I guess," and Kevin shrugged, not sure what else to say. For starters, he was uneasy and uncertain about what had happened in the dragboat—about the Narcs; about the rest of it he didn't even want to remember yet.

"There's trouble," said Ivan. "Big trouble." Kevin and Johnny just stared at him stupidly. "I mean, the cops could be there already." Still, Kevin and Johnny just stared at him. "Are you guys listening? I went back over to your house, Johnny, to find Kate. And she was just walking around the yard there, picking up rocks and she wouldn't even talk to me for a long time.

Johnny was frowning from the first mention of Kate.

"I tried to stop her," Ivan explained. "But I wasn't going to make her stop, know what I mean?" he said to Kevin.

"Stop what?" said Kevin, panic rising through the fog in his brain.

"Throwing rocks. She just kept at it until she'd put one through every window of Nick Ford's office. That's when I told her we'd better clear out before the police came, but she still wouldn't go. She just sat down where she was and said I'm waiting for Johnny to come back. C'mon Johnny. Maybe we can still get there before your folks get back, or the cops."

The three boys had been slowly making their way back up the hill, across the road; to their bikes. Johnny was unlocking his, still frowning, but finally once it was unlocked he straightened up and opened his mouth.

"I better go," Johnny said. "I've gotta get home."

"All right! Let's go," said Ivan. "She might be getting arrested right now."

"I mean home," said Johnny looking at Ivan then Kevin half shamefully. "Nick said he was cooking me dinner."

Without a word more of even goodbye, Big Johnny got up on his bike and rode away into the murky twilight of Harbor Rd.

Ivan stood speechless. Kevin shrugged helplessly.

Finally, they got on their bikes and started back to the neighborhood, there was nothing else to do. It wasn't like they could just follow Johnny to Nick Ford's mansion. And probably, by now, Kate was already in big trouble for a long time. Maybe she was getting arrested even. How quickly it had happened, Kevin thought as he rode. The pedals were heavy. He had invited Ivan to come and it was just the two of them again and his other friends were out of reach. It wasn't really Ivan's fault, even though he was probably the reason why Johnny wouldn't help his sister, but why did it always seem to happen this way, that whenever Ivan showed up everything started to get bad again and then it was just the two of them left one more time to make the best of it?

As they passed Town Harbor, the ferryboat parkinglot was filled up with cars, which seemed strange because there weren't any ferries to any of the islands after five and it must've been nine o'clock by now.

"Look," said Ivan, "look at those."

The masts from three anchored pirate ships rose up above everything else in the harbor, like six giant trees full of horizontal leafless branches black against the last high orange glow of the eastern sky. The yachts of Port Bedford, even Nick Ford's tremendous mahogany one, bobbed around those big painted wood ships like toys. Their three decks were lit up by hanging lanterns swinging gently between red white and blue ribbons.

Still on their bikes, the boys stood at the end of the ferry dock watching a white wood rowboat full of people shuttle from one ship to another. And the decks of all three ships were full of people too and laughter, and the tinkle of icecubes drifted back across the slick still water. Kevin remembered then, the headlines of the newspaper from yesterday, about the tall ships that might be stopping in Port Bedford on their way down to Operation Sail, the big bicentennial thing down south. That didn't make their appearance now any less portentous.

"Wish we had one of those," Ivan said, "and a crew full of

pirates. I'd tell them to break windows all over town." Kevin looked sharply at his friend.

"Why didn't you try to stop her or something?" said Kevin, "You didn't put her up to it did you?"

"Why would I do something like that?" said Ivan, hackling.

"I don't know," said Kevin. He felt guilty for the suggestion. "It's just not like Kate to do something like that ."

"But it's like me, I suppose."

"I didn't mean that."

"Oh yes you did. And why isn't it like her? If somebody hit you, you don't think you'd hit him back any way you could?"

"Sure she would," said Kevin, though he was less sure that he himself would and maybe that was it. "But...why doesn't she just tell her mom or something. That's what I'd do, or Didi I mean."

"I told her to stop; she told me to mind my own business."

"That sounds like Kate, I guess."

"What? You don't believe me now? We're not friends anymore like we used to be?"

"Sure we are. Why do you have to be so tough all the time though?"

Kevin picked up a pebble and chucked it into the water.

Ivan chucked one too.

"Did you know Johnny is adopted?" said Kevin

"Kate told me," said Ivan, looking at the ground.

Kevin felt a little jealous again that Kate had decided to tell Ivan something and yet keep it from himself, "Do you know who his real father is?"

"No," said Ivan looking back up, "Kate wouldn't tell me."

Kevin plopped another stone into the water, half trying to skip it, but it wouldn't go, "Nick Ford, that's who."

Ivan's face fell and he was silent for a long time, "Boy. And we think we got problems."

"We need a pirate ship."

"With cannons." After they laughed a little, it seemed even more silent.

Still each on their own bikes, Kevin leaned over and put his hand on Ivan's shoulder; he could feel the roughness of the t-shirt; the warm, stringy boniness of Ivan like something really solid. "We'll tell Didi. That'll be helping."

"Maybe," said Ivan, "or maybe it'll just ruin things for her too. That's probably what will happen."

Kevin reached into his pocket, "here's your knife," he said, then felt at the same time Nick Ford's pearl handled one still in his pocket.

As they rode home, close, in the dark, Kevin told Ivan the story of what happened to him on the dragboats, over the noise of rushing wind. But for some reason he left out the part about Tock burning him with the knife, not because he wanted to keep anything secret from his friend now. He just didn't know exactly what had happened, or what to say about it. Ivan didn't seem to notice he'd left anything out though. What struck Ivan most seemed to be how much Tock seemed to hate Nick Ford. You were right after all, Kevin." he said. "Your Tock is an important person to know."

As they passed Garden St. they saw a parked police car in front of the Gatehouse which was dark: The jagged edges of its broken glass catching the streetlights like teeth. And a big black Mercedes. Kevin had to believe it was real now. The Carriage House living room was all lit up. He could see the policeman on the couch laughing and drinking coffee and unmistakably over him like a commanding officer, the large silhouette of Nick Ford moving his hands, telling the story to make the policeman laugh. Mr. and Mrs. Harrigan were sitting in chairs, listening. Kevin could see the light on in Kate's room too. Had she been able to tell them what Nick Ford had done to deserve getting his windows broken and much more? Why did she do it? Kevin suddenly saw himself earlier today in the dragboat galley, thoughtlessly pulling Ivan's knife out in front of all those fisherman. Wasn't that pointless and crazy? No wonder Tock did that to him maybe. The rocks were like that maybe. Kate and him were still alike in ways that she and Ivan never could be. In spite of everything, the thought comforted him. Maybe she would say. And the policeman would go and put Nick Ford in jail and Johnny would come back to the Carriage House and everything would be normal again. But Kevin couldn't forget how soft Mrs. Harrigan was when Nick Ford was around and guessed that Mrs. Harrigan would believe anything Nick Ford said over Kate no matter what. Kate probably knew that too. And the way the policeman was laughing at Nick Ford's joke whatever it was. Suddenly Kevin understood the rocks. His heart went up into her window and felt her, alone in her room and scared, listening to the laughter downstairs.

"Let's get out of here," said Ivan through his teeth, "Or else I'm gonna throw rocks through those windows too."

That night, the boys were left to themselves. It seemed recently that Didi was gone all the time. She must've been working extra hours or something.

Kevin heard her come in finally. The sound of the turning knob woke him. It was already starting to get light out. He wondered groggily where she'd been all this time because the Beachcomber closed at two. By the time Kevin got up for the morning though, she was fast asleep so he couldn't ask her.

It was a really dumb idea to try and find Johnny at Nick Ford's mansion, even though he was the only one who could tell the truth so Kate's parents would believe it; Kevin and Ivan confirmed the idea's stupidity to each other every so often over their cereal: Nick, they reminded each other, had more or less particularly forbidden them from coming anywhere near his house ever again, that night at the party. Maybe Didi was too busy to notice, but Kevin could still feel the threat in Nick's eyes as he said it to them. And too, Kevin remembered the yellow eyes of the gatekeeper. Plus, what could they do there anyway? Johnny had turned his back on them after all, as much as on Kate. Kevin couldn't blame him though: Nick was his father, how could you ask someone to not like his father?

So it was against their better judgment they found themselves making their way around the fence at Tock's candy stand and up the coast. To see what they could see was what they told themselves; to spy is what they intended. But they didn't get far. When they got to the end of the Fort Estate, the fence, instead of just ending like it had last time they were here, now took a sharp left and, brand new, marched straight down the rocks and into the water, the whole thing topped with lethal coils of razor wire. Nick Ford, they knew without question, had done this because of them and suddenly Kevin felt very naked and visible standing there on the coast. Without even speaking, they hurried back to the sea wall. It was still early morning.

They crossed the path to the Carriage house several times after that, more for something to occupy themselves; there was no one at home. Finally they'd even gone around back and tossed pebbles at Kate's window. But they hadn't tried for long. It made them nervous, looking around for watching neighbors. After what Kate had done, after what had happened to Kevin on the dragboat, after finding the new fence, the feeling was growing stronger and stronger that somehow Kevin's private doings with his friends would no longer be overlooked by the adult population; like they might know somehow what he was thinking even. Like everywhere was enemy territory all of the sudden. The only place he could feel safe today was Didi's house.

But, home again, Didi was no longer asleep, she was gone; so they went back to check Kate's house one more time. Kevin felt like he was going in circles

This time there was a glass truck parked out front and a guy on a step ladder outside the Gate house putting in new panes of glass with a razor blade and a can of putty. Finally, they extracted an important piece of information: The hippyish looking workman, finally, in answer to their incessant chatter, blurted out, "Look, I'm going to be here half the night as it is. All these windows have to be replaced by tomorrow, because the guy's got an important client or something he's got to meet here at eleven. I got my own life too, you know. I don't want to be here any longer than I have to, even if I am getting paid triple time, know what I mean?"

Kevin and Ivan knew exactly what he meant, even though he didn't know it himself. He meant Nick Ford would be here tomorrow at the Gate House and that meant he wouldn't be in his mansion and Johnny would probably be there alone. If they were ever going to get Johnny back to their side, tomorrow was the time. That was all they wanted to know, but once started the glass man kept on talking, like he was talking to himself, "I don't know why he don't replace the whole windows, " he complained. "This is a real pain in the ass; it's not like he don't got the money. But no, he says, I like these windows. Fuck it, he's got the money to pay me triple time, even if the sills are rotten..." The man went on muttering as he angrily chipped away old putty with a knife, but Kevin and Ivan didn't wait to hear any more; they went back to the path to sit on its hard dirt  to think.

Kevin though only pretended to think. He looked up at the glowing green leaves overhead and remembered instead when his dad and Ivan's dad had a roofing company together with an old green pickup truck with Hawkins & Otrusky Roofing painted in yellow on the side. He summoned a special memory of his dad, sunburned and unshaven and smiling, eating a sandwich straddled up on the peak of someone's roof as Kevin was walking home from school. He was beckoning to Kevin, "Come on up here, kiddo," he said to Kevin. "Don't be afraid, I ain't gonna let you fall."

The business had lasted less than a year though all together, because their two dads argued all the time; then they had to sell the truck. That time on the roof was the last clear memory Kevin had of his dad in a good mood with him. His dad left Kevin and Didi and their mom not long after the business fell apart. Ivan's dad got a lot worse after that too. Kevin cried and cried. His mom just stared at the refrigerator door like his dad might just pop out of it with a fresh beer in his hand. Didi was the one. She invited Kevin up to her private room in the attic and held him tight. "You'll always have me, Kev."

"Remember last night, we said we need a boat?" said Ivan suddenly. "We do have a boat, remember. At least I think so. I actually checked last summer and it was still there."

Of course Kevin remembered. Ivan was talking about their raft from when they used to be neighbors out by the salt marsh. They started to build it just after their dads got back from the war. They'd hid it way back in the marsh in a cave made from a solid mat of bent over reeds. "That old raft would last about half a minute on the ocean though even if we could drag it there. It weighs about a million pounds."

But Ivan was all smiles now, "I've been thinking. Remember that branch we found off of Blind Brook, way up the salt marshes, that one where there's that old stone bridge, remember, that you can only get under a low tide so we never went up? And remember how the water was flowing in from there and not out when the tide was coming in?"

"Yeah?" said Kevin eagerly.

"That's called an estuary." said Ivan like the brain he was, "Well I think low tide tomorrow is around  eleven."

"It's getting later, and it was getting low this morning, remember? Maybe before eleven even."

"Okay before eleven. That's even better timing, because where could that estuary go to the ocean if you think about it?" continued Ivan like he was a professor of brooks or something. "Well I bet it's somewhere out on the point; where else could it go from over there?"

Kevin giggled suddenly. That would give that stupid dog a surprise if they could somehow sneak in from the other direction. Something to try, an adventure and what was more, just him and Ivan, like the old days, on the raft. Even if it went wrong it was better than just moping around. And it'd be a chance, he thought to get back to the kind of friends they were before Kevin moved away. Ivan's eyes said he was thinking the same thing.

"We'd have to get up super early," said Ivan, the raft might need more Styrofoam, I'll have to sneak a hammer and nails out of my mom's garage too."

"And it's a long bike ride," Kevin agreed, "we'll need to get up at the crack of dawn."

The mood, like a hand on the back of his neck which had been there without his being aware since he left Tock on the dragboat, lifted now. The afternoon flew by swiftly and pleasantly and Kevin enjoyed Ivan's company more than he had yet since he came to stay.

Tomorrow they would surprise Johnny; Kevin felt certain that he and Ivan together could bring him around. Then Johnny could get Kate out of trouble by telling the real story.

It began to get late though, and still no sign of Deirdre, and with twilight, Kevin felt the hand creeping back to the back of his neck. She should be here, he thought. Tonight of all nights. He wanted to tell her everything. He called the bar, but Janine answered instead of Didi. She was pissed because Didi took the night off and she had to fill in at the last minute. Then it had him, the old feeling: Kevin was worried. Ivan was watching tv, laughing at some stupid show. Kevin wished he could see Kate. She was his best friend for when he was worried this way. She didn't care at all how tough he was.

As the room darkened, bluing with the changing light from the television screen, Kevin felt a growing dread that he would never see Kate again; that Didi had left him, like their dad.

Ivan never really could understand when Kevin felt bad for no good reason. It always had to be for something. For Ivan it always had to be simple, like someone did something to you so his advice could be to do something back and then you'd feel better. But Kate wasn't like that before now. That's why Kevin thought Ivan was behind the rocks. She always knew just the right thing to say to make Kevin feel better about something confusing. She'd say Some things are for no reason and they're just as important or even more because they're mysterious.

So, even though he knew it was probably a bad idea, Kevin tried Kate's house just once on the telephone. It was an unlisted number, but Kate had told it to him one day when just she and Johnny were home. It was in the winter and Deirdre had a boyfriend and was gone a lot. He had played with Kate that day after school and for no reason at all he had started to cry. Kate didn't laugh at him or ask him why. She just said to call her up if he felt like it and gave him the secret number.

Mrs. Harrigan answered the phone this time, "Who is this?"

Resisting the impulse to hang up, Kevin stammered who he was.

"How did you get this number, young man?"

He ignored the question and asked was Kate home? Mrs. Harrigan said yes she was, but she was grounded for a month and not allowed to see her friends or speak with them. Kevin wanted to say something, but broken windows and Mrs. Harrigan's tone were hard to argue against, so he just said, "Oh." He could hear voices in the background.

By then it was nine o'clock and still no Deirdre; he made mac and cheese for them while Ivan packed some supplies for the dawn's journey, squares of chicken meat and cheese and apples and crackers and then they went to bed even though it was still a little bit light out.

"You never even told Johnny anything about what Nick did to Kate, did you?" said Ivan from his sleeping place on the floor.

Kevin quickened with anger, wishing Ivan had just gone to sleep and left him alone, "Well first of all she told you everything about it not me. I was with Johnny in the tree, remember?"

"That was because I told her first, about something my dad did to me once."

"What was that?" said Kevin sharply.

"I don't really feel like talking about it now, Kev," said Ivan lamely.

"See!" said Kevin sitting straight up now in his bed. "No one wants to tell me anything. Alls everybody keeps telling me is You still don't get it. So how am I supposed to tell Johnny? Maybe I'm stupid or something so you think I can't understand, right?"

Ivan was sitting up now too. "It's not that," he said quietly. "It just never happened to you is all. The thing."

"What do you mean?" said Kevin more quietly and felt suddenly very uncomfortable next to his friend.

"Okay, if you want to know," Ivan began sullenly, Kevin regretted his insistence now and wished more than anything for Ivan to shut up, but he didn't: "There was some times I don't remember very well. But I know mom was never there. He made me touch him, maybe. That's all. No big deal. After he got out of the shower or something. I can't really remember, all right? It was a long time ago. It was around when we were adding pontoons to the raft, maybe, I don't know. I just didn't feel like talking about it." Those days flooded vividly back to Kevin now, how furious Ivan was in his work. Their raft was going to be an escape pod for them to run away on, like Tom Sawyer and Huckleberry Finn.

"Oh," said Kevin.

That seemed to make Ivan angry now. "He's in jail now so it doesn't matter. I hope he stays there forever. But that guy Nick's still doing it, to Kate. When we talked about it I remembered all kinds of bad feelings I forgot about. It makes me crazy, Kevin. I feel like it's happening to me all over again." Ivan groaned and twisted on the bolsters.

"Johnny would've just said I was making it up, you know," said Kevin. "Nick's his dad, Ivan."

"So?"

"You think Johnny will see it like that? Nick never did anything to him I guess."

"That's stupid, Kevin. How could Nick do all that to Kate without Johnny feeling something at least?"

"I dunno."

"So?" Ivan rolled away from Kevin with a quick, violent motion, so he was facing towards the door. Kevin felt horrible.

"Sorry," said Kevin, even though he knew it wasn't exactly the right thing.

"It's not your fault," said Ivan.

"It's Nick Ford's fault," said Kevin. "He's behind everything, even your dad. Kate said so."

Ivan rolled back around towards Kevin again, a smile on his face. "We'll get him. You watch!"

"No, you watch," Kevin laughed. A good warm laugh like he hadn't felt in a while. Ivan and him were back together again, that's what he was laughing about really. And he fell asleep still smiling.

Kevin's electric alarm went off before they knew it, and Deirdre was safe and snoring softly in her bed. It was the fourth of July. The darkness outside grayed in places by the time they were out on their bikes, reaching the outskirts of their old neighborhood on the far side of the port.

Harry's Sweetshop, on the edge of the old neighborhood, was the earliest thing open in all of Port Bedford and the only place sure to be open on the Fourth. Because the truckers stopped there before heading back out onto the Interstate and they never stopped for anything, not even the two hundredth birthday of America. Its yellow lights blurred out into the heavy fog of first light. Kevin and Ivan spent the night before gathering change for this purpose, with not much success until Kevin had found one of those new two dollar bills in Didi's red Things Box on top of her dresser. She'd find out of course, such a unique thing; he'd have to tell her something eventually he knew. But later was like the fog, and maybe she would have given it to him anyway or not care or something. Still, in the cold shaky morning, his taking it bothered him; let some of the fog's blurry uncomfortableness slip through his body and into his mood, making it feel fragile and achy. Something about how weird it felt that the person who is the best to you is the one you wind up taking stuff from without asking.

But he and Ivan were both chilled now from the bike ride, and Kevin had to think of his friend too. Hot chocolate and bear claws was an important ritual for starting on such a risky adventure; their first real adventure where they might get into real trouble; they both sensed this new seriousness. But also one where Ivan and him together, invincible, could really do something important.

Even with a name like Sweet Shop, Harry's was a very adult and early morning serious place; that's why they'd chosen it. As Ivan in front of him pushed open the thick, green painted door so the bell tinkled, Kevin discovered that there had been no fog at all outside, only his inner mood: The blurriness was all from the steam beaded up on the insides of the plate glass, from all the good-smelling baking going on in the back.

They climbed onto two free swivel stools at the low Formica counter which was mostly mint green, but worn white in some places from too many elbows. Everybody in there, in fact, seemed to be resting their heads on heavy elbows. There were three or four fishermen or truckers at the counter staring in a line into their coffee cups and one guy on the stool next to Kevin with his head in one hand, cigarette smoking and looking sideways up at the big rust spot in the white tin squares of the ceiling.

Even the old crushed little white-haired guy behind the register was propped up on his elbows. Kevin had always assumed that was Harry, but he'd never asked him to be sure. He took their order wordlessly, not bothering to move. Kevin felt out of place and the immediate need to seem more depressed than was his nature in order to fit in. He tried his best to make his voice glum and not too squeaky: "Two hot chocolates and a couple of bear claws."

"You kids got a paper route or something?" grunted Harry.

"Yeah," Ivan grunted back. He was pretty good at this stuff, because Harry seemed impressed enough and left them alone after that. Plus Kevin felt like they fit in more after that. Except that the News was playing loud on the radio, and the News, especially the super droning early morning news never failed to make Kevin feel more alone and inadequate to understand the true nature of what was going on around him; not adult enough to appreciate it.

Ivan was quiet and everyone else seemed to be listening, so Kevin started to let phrases here and there into his ears in spite of himself; in spite of the muddled feeling it inspired. Meanwhile, he occupied himself by looking into the men's faces and trying to guess what they were feeling as they stared into their cups so he might have a better idea himself. But their faces too were impenetrable. He looked at the farthest man whose face was bristly and sagging, like that guy Bill Gunn looked at the party when Mr. Harrigan seemed to be pouring stuff into his ear. In fact, all of their faces looked exactly like what Kevin thought the News itself would look like if it took over someone's body—marshy and never quite taking shape as any expression in particular. Kevin heard something about global inflation and then about a plane full of hijackers

"You think the raft is rotted?" said Kevin, more to break the silence.

Ivan said back, through a mouth full of bear claw, "Nah." and nothing else, like it was very important here to just say single words if you were going to say anything at all.

So Kevin just said, "Hmmph." and went back to his hot chocolate.

But the News just chattered on and on:

"In a landmark decision," said the radio, "the Supreme Court has upheld the death penalty as constitutional, maintaining that it does not constitute 'cruel and unusual punishment.'"

Kevin fell at last to busting up blobs of chocolate powder in his cup with his spoon, feeling some small satisfaction from the activity—as if each dry blob were a General Fact and it was Kevin's job to let the water in so it could go away— when 'Nicholas Ford' caught his ear from the fresh voice of the local Port Bedford announcer who'd just come back on the air: "Port Bedford's own, who has recently been appointed to the Eighth District Circuit Court of Appeals, says he supports Steven's opinion in principal and has long been an advocate of the reinstitution of the death penalty in this country."

"There are several cases pending in our own state," said a familiar voice. Ivan and Kevin both sat transfixed with sudden panic while Nick Ford's actual voice came through the radio itself. It was Nick for sure, except it sounded more tinny, like he was talking through the telephone or something. "...that the law of the people," said Nick's voice, "must be equal to punishing the greatest crime of an individual is as essential to today's society as the system of checks and balances among the branches of government was two hundred years ago. It's our only defense, I think, against the potential despotism of aberrant individual appetites."

Kevin looked to Ivan who, like Kate, knew a lot of big words, "What do you think he's talking about?"

"I don't know," Ivan admitted. "Aberrant means weird I think."

"I'm scared of him, Ivan."

"Maybe he's scared of us too." said Ivan. "Think about that. Why else would he put up that fence?"

Nick Ford was powerful all right, that's one thing Kevin was certain of now, if he could even talk to them straight through the radio like that. Feeling very vulnerable all of the sudden in this early morning shop full of men, Kevin slid off his stool and walked up to the cash register to pay. Then, when he pulled out Deirdre's two dollar bill along with the change they had found—eight-five cents—spreading it all out on the counter, he felt a sudden wave of shame again about taking it from Deirdre. Harry stood behind the register eyeing him. The tab was two dollars and ten cents.

"Um, this is all we have," said Kevin, "but I was wondering Can I keep this two dollar bill somehow? It's my only one and I want to save it."

Harry picked it up and examined it. "I heard about these," he said, "First one I seen." He had a serious look that said he sort of wanted it; "Look, he said, showing it to the nearest trucker, the one who'd been smoking his cigarette up at the ceiling. "Jefferson on the front and all those guys signing the Declaration of Independence on the back. Real pretty, I think. Sorry though," said Harry turning back to Kevin, "If you didn't want to use it you shouldn't of ate the bear claws."

The trucker laughed at Harry and reached into his pocket. He pulled out a tremendous bank roll and peeled off two singles and put them by the register, "Keep it," he said to Kevin. "That'll be worth money some day."

"Thanks," said Kevin, keeping his eyes firmly planted on the tile floor, unable to believe his luck and slipping the bill back into his pocket as inconspicuously as possible. Then he and Ivan slipped together out of the door and into the first thick rays of morning.

from Kate's diary,
July Third, 1976:


*There's nothing to do at night but twist
the carpet string together.*

*I'm making a noose because that's the
one knot you're never supposed to tie ever.*

*Johnny taught me how to tie it once. He
said it was illegal to make one and it had to
have thirteen loops or it wouldn't work.*

*The phone rang downstairs. I think it
was Kevin maybe. I miss him more than Ivan
right now or Johnny even because I just want a
friend more than anything. I want to sneak
out of my room and call him back, but I'm
afraid. I don't want to go to the library again
tomorrow. If I don't see the ocean for another
day I think I'll die.*

*It was a bad time for Kevin to try and
call because Nick was in the living room again
with my parents just like last night too and
that will make him want to go after Kevin*

*now too for poking his nose in and Ivan too because he already hates him because the dog bit him..*

*I snuck out from my room to listen at the top of the stairs*

*Nick Ford's voice said Who's that? and tinkled its ice cubes.*

*My mom said Your new floozy's little brother.*

*Nick's voice said You see Jason this is a non issue. He said We're all adults here aren't we? He said Trust me your career is about to take a big turn for the better. He said Let me go up and talk to her and then I got scared but I couldn't move because they'd hear. He said She's upset about John that's all. It's a hard change for a little girl to lose her brother all of a sudden. He said I'll talk to her. She's a good girl and after all she wants what's best for him too.*

*I shouted in my head No don't dad.*

*My dad's voice said All right Nick if you*

*think you can get through to her go ahead and try. It's you she thinks she's angry at after all.*

*How could they have? I ran to my room and pushed the chest in front of the door.*

*His heavy steps went one by one up the stairs like drums in my head and I looked out the window. All I could see is the stupid pool outside my window. If I jumped from here I'd probably crack my skull on the bottom before I drowned. I wish I could live with Didi and Kevin now and never have a pool again.*

*So I jumped in my bed under the covers in the farthest corner away.*

*Kate*

*I'm not home.*

*The knob turned and the heavy chest slid on the carpet so there's not even a noise for them to hear downstairs.*

*There's a whoosh and the covers are gone from the bed and I'm bunched up in the light.*

*He said Lie on your back Kate and don't make a sound.*

*I do.*

*Lift your night gown.*

*I do.*

*Higher.*

*I do.*

*Lie absolutely still and listen. His thick
ring finger makes circles from my to hip to my
belly button to my leg to my other leg to my
hip again.*

*He said Relax and you'll see I'm not
going to hurt you. The finger stops in the middle then starts to make very little soft circles.
He said You see?*

*My middle felt tingles like it was falling
asleep.*

*Look. And I lifted my head. And his fin-
ger ring was a gold watch going back and forth
to hypnotize my middle.*

*He said Johnny. It went inside to the
first knuckle and I watched it and it hurt. He
put his other finger to his lip and I bit my lip.
He said Is fine. Johnny is fine. He'll inherit my*

*house one day and the harbor too. So don't you worry. Look.*

*I watched the bigger knuckle disappear and the ring was cold and close to me and I couldn't stop from making a noise even though my mouth was shut.*

*He said Shh do you like that? You've been bad about keeping our secret haven't you?*

*I shake my head No*

*Haven't you?*

*I nod my head Yes*

*He said Listen careful Kate. Not another word or I'll have to send you away to a place where only I can visit.*

*His finger was the chest moving backwards.*

*He put back my night gown.*

*He put back my covers and tucked me in and patted my head.*

*He said What do you promise?*

*I nodded my head.*

*He said There's a good girl and kissed me*

goodnight on the cheek so every hair of his beard was a knife sticking into me.

He turned off the light and closed the door.

I get up in the dark and look out the window. I'm cold and my belly hurts.

That other girl had a pool too because that's how the story goes. But it wasn't fun to swim with the man watching her. She could feel how mad he was because she wouldn't go sailing with him. He was so mad that little by little he dug up all the black moss by the roots and stuck it over all the stones and made them dark.

Once he started he had to keep on adding more and more because what the magic stones are really is firefly hives where the fireflies make light the same way bees make honey.

The neighborman made all the fireflies fly away to make the stars and it was night.

# CHAPTER TWELVE

Ivan's house had a strange car parked out front. The thing Kevin most remembered about Ivan's house was how it always smelled wet and like cat pee, especially in the garage underneath which was carpeted for some reason, but also in the apartment part above.

The garage had an overhead door that they managed to raise a foot or so without making much racket then slide under. Ivan turned on the light so they could rummage through his dad's old dust-covered workbench for two hammers, a coffee can of miscellaneous nails and a ball of twine. They didn't worry too much about noise, now that Ivan Sr. was permanently out of the picture. Ivan's mom never got up before noon in her life. So it surprised Kevin when Ivan suddenly put a finger to his lips.

"The car out front," he whispered. "Who knows who that guy is?"

Still, it turned out to be no problem to get the stuff out. But, as Kevin slipped back out beneath the door after Ivan, he knew his friend's mood had changed. The way you can tell it's about to rain. Changed to something harder. Kevin knew it wouldn't do any good, but he tried to say something to soften it.

"Hey, it's going to be another perfect day, I bet," he said as he got back on his bike.

"Put a hammer in your belt," said Ivan dismissively, "if you still want to do this." As if it were all just another one of Kevin's harebrained ideas.

Now on the way to the marsh they would have to pass Kevin's old house too, many blocks further back, but also on the same street.

He closed his eyes as he passed, afraid to be spotted. But, unable to resist the urge, Kevin threw a quick glance behind him to his mom's house, in spite of himself. It looked both the same and different too: Smaller and older, like his leaving it behind had made the white painted shingles more yellow. The empty flower pot on the porch was kicked over with some dirt and cigarette butts spilled out. The little beige beat up car out front meant that his mom had a boyfriend over too, just like Ivan's. His name was Carl and Kevin didn't like him. He'd hoped and expected that Carl would be out of the picture by now. Thinking of his mom made Kevin sad. The guy was half her age and making her cook him breakfast and probably still didn't have a job, living instead off his mom's welfare checks and, if Kevin were there, he'd probably be walking around without a shirt trying to boss Kevin around too. All of her boyfriends since his dad left were like that.

Kevin's and Ivan's moms' street didn't have a name so far as they knew; it was paved sort of, but mostly gravel and pot holes and everyone just called it The houses behind the fire house, and there were tons of them, mostly half falling apart like the street itself. But the great thing was that it was right on the edge of the saltmarsh behind the tanker discharge station across the Interstate that made the mouth to Blind Brook: Even though the house yards were full of brackish oily water half of the time and nothing would grow there, not even dandelions, and the ground floors of every house flooded a lot, which was why the carpet in Ivan's garage was wet all of the time. But, just like the Port dwindled down to Blind Brook, the street behind the firehouse dwindled down to a little single track after a while, which Kevin and Ivan rode now into the high tassels of reeds. They rubbed together in low rattling whispers.

Their raft, as it turned out, was in remarkably good shape considering it'd been several seasons since they'd sailed it. Pulling the old thing out from it's bent-over reed cave left Kevin and Ivan laughing crazily. They were in the old times again.

The raft had been Kevin and Ivan's comfort and salvation in the springs summers and falls of 1973 and '74, something for them to float on over all the oily sedimented muck in their lives. Those had been the years after their fathers got home from Viet Nam and were weird. Everything was so uncertain at home all of the sudden. At home, Didi was their only chance in those days. In the springs and summers and falls they had ridden out every chance they could get down the dirt track strewn with beer bottles and junkfood wrappers just like it still was and into to quiet of the reeds: To the raft cave to take off their shoes and drag their creation, though it weighed more than both of them put together, the ten yards to the standing pool they called Launching Cove. In the winter, however, with the plants and trees, all their hope went to sleep. But through the springs and summers and falls each day, they floated and explored, and made up stories together to carry them through. Like Shiner, the big, black-eyed moon out to get them. Or the Monster Mice who lived in the reeds and were ten feet tall, or how Kevin and Ivan were whale hunters, only the whales were horseshoe crabs instead, older and stranger and as mysterious as whales if not as tremendous; more dangerous and warlike for their size, spines and lances rising to meet Kevin's and Ivan's own, which doubled as poles to push their raft about, made from green sumac saplings hatcheted out at the roots and whittled to points; which tripled as paddles when the water was deeper, old cedar shingles lashed to the other end.

During those two years, the raft (and Didi at home) were everything to them. It was like riding back in time when Kevin sat again by the cave of crushed down reeds still there and still growing. Growing smaller, it struck him, like his mom's house, from the last time he'd seen it, but growing still, and still there. And still still, everything was absolutely still as it always had been in this clear blue July morning. With a whoop, he leaped into the reeds and Ivan behind him. They found a good spot and, simultaneously, holding hands and tensing their bodies as one body, they let themselves fall backwards. The thick stand of reeds softened their fall as it always had done in the past. All around him again, the high thick protecting wall of reeds towered, waving gently against the deep unlimited blue of the sky.

"Shall we check out the raft?" said Ivan after a while.

"Let's." It only needed minor repairs and a short search for flotsam Styrofoam on the water's edge to supplement what had crumbled away. Then they ditched their shoes, with the hammers and nails and twine, with their bikes in the cave and dragged the raft down to Launching Cove. It was far lighter than it ever had been before, and seemed smaller too, so, without even breaking a sweat they were launched and on their way.

The bow of their raft was a pointed fence post with a shorter board on either side in the shape of an upside down 'v' to separate the reeds and leave a path of open water in their wake. Built up from these three keels were whatever scraps of plank and plywood they had foraged from the ocean flotsam that washed back from the port, nailed one on top of the other so they made a sort of crazy step shape climbing higher towards the aft until, crowning it all was a thick, tremendous piece of thick peeling plywood higher than the rest, which served as a quarter deck for Kevin and Ivan to sit on, Indian style, and pole along one on each side, or paddle when the water was deeper. So the bow rode high in the air. Underneath, between the fencepost and two long boards, crammed and lashed and nailed was every shape and size of barnacled Styrofoam washed up onto the shores of Port Bedford, from docks and beer coolers and even the packing for a big color tv someone had left out on the curb for the garbage collectors—all so mish mash that sometimes they left a small trail of floating scraps in their wake. After all was said and done, the thing was unsinkable, at least within the calm tidal waters of the marsh. The ocean itself, Kevin suspected, could very easily smash it back to the bits that it came from.

"The tide's almost ebb already," said Ivan, "we better go." Ivan knew a lot about the tides.

Neither Kevin nor Ivan felt the need to speak as they poled into the narrowing reed-filled mouth of Blind Brook. Even though Kevin's own mouth was full of questions about the people in their lives, his eyes and ears and nose were empty and hungry for the marshland banks lurching past with the staggered pushes of their poles: The little white egret fluting up to a tassel, the big muddy fish peeking out from the ring of a sunken truck tire, the swirl of mud underwater where his pole touched the bottom in the dead still water, and the black smelling vapors that rose to the surface. And Ivan, older than in Kevin's memory as it was now awakened, and harder, and more muscular beside him; his skin, like Kevin's own already bronzed.

With the sun burning high in the sky, they reached the old stone bridge where, under it's main arch, the brook was already starting to flow again up into the inland, past suburban back yards of Bedford and finally, Kevin imagined, though he'd never been that far, to fresh water flowing back again from farmlands smelling of sheep and chickens and tractors. These smells were a little theoretical though, extrapolated from Old MacDonald's farm, maybe, and books.

From the smaller arch to the left, and turning back, was a smaller branch that fed into the main one, where water was already sleepily beginning to flow in around the bridge's foot and into the main current of the brook. Up above, Kevin knew that the inland end of the Interstate drove over it's back. The muffled roaring of traffic troubled the damp dark dripping from the pipes underneath.

"Duck down," said Ivan. It was difficult to lie flat on the raft, which they had to do in order to clear the big sewer pipe above them. Kevin felt the sudden drop in temperature as they left the sun. They crossed into a damp darkness, a high swelling murmur like a thousand far off babies, only it turned out to be pigeons roosting and the pipe glowed streams of white from their shit. They also had to keep paddling against the current and, even though it was slight, the motion was difficult lying on their bellies. Kevin's backbone scraped the rusty pipe before they were through.

"Fuck," still under the bridge, and it echoed, 'uck," all around him, so some of the pigeons spilled out to the light in front of them.

"Echo!" shouted Ivan, "echo."

"How we gonna get back, back?" shouted Kevin more to hear his voice resound again so powerfully.

"Who knows?" called Ivan.

"Who's walking on my bridge!" yelled Kevin, imagining the paling faces of anyone who happened to be driving over, the eerie sound of his voice creeping up through their seat cushions. He started to laugh and Ivan did too until their laughter was a landslide of pigeon wings flying in every direction and their raft emerged sideways into the still sunny tidal stream of the other side.

The stream bent through a tunnel of willow trees and soon the banks of reeds gave way to stone walls on one side, a large green lawn opened out on the other with the roof of an unfamiliar estate house visible on the lip of a rolling hill. Then another, then an estate on each side. The sound of a groundskeeper's lawn mower as they slipped thankfully back into fresh reed banks returning. The stream broadened again and hid them from view.

After an hour or so of early afternoon empty estates, a salty light wind told them they were nearing the ocean again. Soon it opened out before them in a small marshy bay. They pulled to the shelter of the reeds and their raft up onto the bank and ate some of the food they had brought.

Since they had never crossed this bay on the coast that day when they first snuck onto Nick Ford's land with Kate and Johnny, Kevin and Ivan now felt more sure in their guess that, by following the coast back down towards the Fort Estate, they'd come to it eventually from the other side. A stone footbridge spanned the marsh and a hardpacked footpath started up into the woods from the water's edge past the two pillars that marked the end of the bridge. To Kevin's chilled surprise, these pillars were identical to those on either side of his own path, between Garden and Vale. He suddenly remembered too, that it was the same stone as the wall they had come against running from Nick Ford's dog. Kevin felt cold. The bridge, the woods, the rolling well-cut hills, the pristine marsh so different from the garbage strewn one by the tanker discharge station where he had grown up, and the ocean. It all seemed unreal—too beautiful, like in a dream. They were at the very tip of the Point, and this, Kevin now felt certain, was the far side of Nick Ford's estate.

They didn't have to go far along the hard packed earth till they came to a fork in the path. The main way continued on into the woods, but on the right a space opened up in the trees to ocean and open sky. There, on a stone bench, between two more pillar's just like their own, sat the back of a large figure, crowned with a gray business man's hat. The whir of a fishing pole casting. He was sitting up on the high back of the stone bench, unaware of them. This was terrible. Nick was supposed to be at his office.

Kevin scanned around quickly for the dog: No sign of that monster at least.

"Maybe we could sneak around to the house," whispered Ivan doubtfully, "talk to Johnny and sneak back out without him seeing us." But he must have said it too loud, because the clicking of the reel slowed and stopped. The figure on the back of the stone bench twisted slowly around.

The face, though, was round and fat and freckled, open-mouthed. Then Kevin felt his own mouth become a muddle of worry and relief as it cried, "Johnny!" Was it really, or was this really Young mister Ford, as Tock had called him?

Johnny leaned the fishing rod, a much nicer one than he had had before, across the bench, and lifted his feet over so he was facing them. The laces of his sneakers were untied and they dangled below him in a patch of sunlight coming through the trees, but he didn't get down. His eyes were wide and surprised.

"You," he said. His face was sad and lonely looking.

"Catch anything?" said Kevin coming closer.

Johnny turned his head away, then back, then down to his untied sneakers.

"That's a pretty nice fishing rod you got," said Ivan coming closer too.

Johnny still didn't say anything. He looked from side to side and seemed to realize he was cornered.

"Sure must be great to have all this place to play in," said Kevin.

"It's okay," said Johnny. His voice was low and hoarse like he hadn't said anything for a long time. He started to smile, but it looked more like he wanted to cry.

"How's it living with your real dad now?" said Kevin.

Johnny looked up defensively, "It's okay." He waited for them to say something but they didn't "I couldn't've helped her anyway if that's what you're thinking. It's not my problem anymore so don't bother to ask me about it okay? So it's okay. I'm okay. Everything's okay, okay?"

"We were just wondering," said Kevin. "You know, if everything's okay."

"You could always stay with us at Didi's, " said Ivan. "You

know, if you didn't like it here or something."

Johnny's face clouded over, then lit up for a second like he'd like to, then cloudy again,

"How'd you get in here?" the voice was Johnny's all right, but he was angry. He jumped down from the back of the bench. Then his eyes narrowed as he approached them.

Kevin had been secretly hoping that Johnny would be happy to see them; that he, as a former trespasser himself, would share in their pride of having overcome the obstacles, the dog, the guard, the new fence that Nick had placed in their path. He had been hoping that this pride he would feel for them in their success would sweep him back to them; make him remember himself, the Johnny that Kevin knew and forget this new young Mister Ford.

In the freckled face before him there was pride, definitely, but not pride in his friends. Something had changed. Kevin's hope vanished.

"You can't be here," said Johnny icily. "You just think you can go anywhere without asking, don't you?"

"We wanted to see you," said Kevin. "To make sure you were okay. It's not like we could just call Nick Ford's house, even if the number was listed."

"Bull," said Johnny. "I saw your face when I said he was my dad. I'm not stupid. A great man like my dad has a lot of enemies because they're all jealous. You saw how those fishermen were when I said his name. And you," said Johnny to Ivan. "Kate put you up to it. You all knew he was my dad all along didn't you? Only no one ever told me."

""That's not true, Johnny," said Kevin, "and you know it. Not even Kate knew he was your dad. He did a bad thing to her, that's why she..."

"None of you can trick me again," Johnny shouted. "You tricked me worse than anybody Kevin, because you pretended you were on my side, but you never told me."

"That's stupid." said Kevin, "How could I know. And why would I care anyway?"

"Because your sister's been here the last two nights that's why," said Johnny.

Johnny's eyes grew intolerably hateful to Kevin. The air was burning between them.

"You lie, Johnny Harrigan," said Kevin.

"It's John Ford!" shrieked Johnny. "Everybody wants to keep me away from my dad because you're all jealous, every single one of you."

But Kevin could hardly listen to Johnny anymore. Not Didi.

"Give me back my knife," said Johnny. "My dad gave it to me."

As a matter of fact, it was still in Kevin's pocket, but he didn't say a word.

"Actually, he gave it to Kate, first, Johnny," said Ivan. "That's the kind of guy he is, gives it to Kate, steals it back then gives it to you. You have to tell them what he did, Johnny. You have to tell them. They won't believe her. It doesn't matter if he's your dad."

Johnny's voice unsteady: "He told me it wasn't true. He promised it wasn't." And Johnny started to toe the dirt, with an intricate step which Kevin couldn't fathom at first until he saw that it was to block the path of an ant so it had to keep on switching directions; then Johnny's toe would catch up and block its way again.

But Kevin couldn't listen now. Not Didi.

"Who're you going to believe Johnny," Ivan was saying, "Kate or, or him?"

"You're not going to keep me from living with my dad and that's all I have to say about it." Johnny crossed his arms, his ears bright red like he was putting all of his strength into making them not listen to anything.

"You know already, don't you Johnny?" said Ivan. "You had to know. You know."

"I'm not listening to you." said Johnny. He covered his ears and started to go, "La la lala la."

"You wanna know what we're doing here?" shouted Ivan. "That's easy, we snuck here What are you doing here, and with that stupid hat on? When you know."

"Jealous," Johnny shot back.

"Actually," said Ivan, scratching his head like an intellectual and looking around him, "I was just trying to figure out the best spot where I can puke."

Slowly an awareness crept over Kevin: The two of them wanted to fight, and they were going to. Johnny crouching low now, into a practiced wrestling pose; Ivan, still without his shirt on, leaning back casually with his arms crossed on his ribs, like the tough guy he was. Ivan spoke before Johnny had a chance to charge:

"Nick hid on the path," said Ivan, "And you know it, because she told you. He was waiting for her and he grabbed her into the bushes and he made her take off his pants, and do things to him, and he wouldn't let her go until she did."

Johnny turned his head away just like he'd got hit in the face;

then he started to shake it again, like he had that other time; then he hit it with his fist. He fixed Kevin suddenly with a watery, wide-eyed, drowning gaze,

"Won't you guys please just leave me alone?" he whispered. "It's not fair. You don't understand how it is, how I'm. How much I'm trying to be good. You're not helping me. You're not helping Kate either, you're not helping anybody. You think you are, but you aren't."

"Listen, Johnny," said Kevin, "Kate said."

Johnny's eyes shut like traps. Snap.

"Didi was here. Both nights. I saw her. He doesn't love her though, he loves my mom. And she loves him not my old dad."

"You better stop lying," said Kevin.

"You're trespassing," said Johnny. Then his tone changed to something lower, meaner: "Ask your sister if you don't believe me."

"What's that supposed to mean," said Kevin under his breath, feeling all the dangerousness in his own voice and Johnny felt it too.

"It's not my fault if she likes my dad," Johnny said quickly. "Or his either. She came here first late at night after I was in bed and then left super early so they thought I wouldn't know, but I got up and saw her leave and it was her. My dad didn't ask her. She just comes."

"You're lying," shouted Kevin.

"Ivan's lying," Johnny shouted back. Johnny turned to Ivan who was staring at him straight through his eyebrows.

"You know it's true, Johnny."

"La la lala la. Idiots," said Johnny.

Kevin's world was spinning. Deirdre hadn't come home night before last and he knew it. "You're lying," he said again.

"Then get out of here. Run home to your sister if you don't believe me; ask her and see what she does, she can't deny it. I saw her. Get out of here!" he bellowed, "or I'll go let the dog loose."

"You would do that?" said Kevin probing deep into his eyes without finding anything to show Johnny wouldn't.

"Yeah I would," said Johnny, hard as ice. "You're just here because you want to mess up the only good thing that's ever happened to me."

Kevin couldn't help it; he suddenly started to cry, "You're not my friend anymore, John Ford."

"I guess I'm not," said Johnny with disgust.

"C'mon, Ivan. Let's get out of here."

"I feel sorry for you, Johnny," said Ivan.

"Guess we know where your dad lives," said Johnny. "So maybe you can go live with him, huh Ivan?"

Ivan went for Johnny, but Kevin got to Ivan first and grabbed him back. Ivan could have broken free if he'd wanted, but he probably was feeling as sick about the whole thing as Kevin was.

"We'll see who's right," said Kevin. "All I know though, is Kate would never ever set a dog on me no matter what. And oh," Kevin tapped his pocket, "I guess I lost your knife, Mr. Ford."

"Just get off my land," said Johnny and went back to the bench as if Kevin and Ivan didn't even exist, between the pillars that were the path pillars, and he didn't even bother to turn around again to see if they were leaving. His shoulders were jiggling up and down. Kevin had no idea what could be going on inside of Johnny, how it was he was trying so hard to be good. He believed him though, Johnny didn't lie, but it was beyond Kevin to understand him. A sharp wind swept up from the sea and blew Johnny's fishing rod over with a light clatter. Johnny's shoulders kept on jiggling and he made no move to pick it up. The air was dead still then. The whole forest was still except for Johnny's shoulders.

from Kate's diary,
July Fourth, 1976:

*Now that it's finally summer my mom
says I'm getting sick and have to stay home. I
can't even go to the library anymore. They
make me stay in my room and say it doesn't
matter if I don't have a fever. Tomorrow I have
to see a special kind of doctor where it doesn't
matter if you have a fever or not.*

*It's because I tried to tell my mom.*

*It was the most beautiful knife in the
world though, and he gave it to the little girl.
He did. She didn't make it up. She didn't even
want to take it though even though he could
tell how much she wanted to. But he made her.
He said it was because she was so special.*

*The shadows didn't know where to go
but the girl found out they all jumped into the
man through the black holes in his eyes
straight through the center of his eyeballs and
into his brain.*

*But she didn't know. She just thought he looked a little weird that day when he asked her in, she felt like it sounded oozy though and didn't really want to. She had dried off and changed from the pool and was on her way to the library like every day while her brother was at wrestling to write in her book and talk with her favorite the circulation librarian to find a new good book to bring home because she was way ahead on all her homework like always.*

*The man said that he was writing a book and would she like to come inside to see? He'd never shown it to anyone. Only once to someone way back when she was a very very small girl and used to run around like a little pink thing in the yard without any clothes on.*

*He put a stack of typewriter pages on his desk and then when the girl tried to read them he leaned against her from behind to show her over her shoulder. But he was leaning funny All the way from her legs to up past where they stopped.*

*The girl felt a hard part there in the middle only she didn't even know what that part was yet. She thought then that it was his knee maybe. She thought it would be rude for her to turn around to see because she was supposed to be looking at the book instead.*

*But she couldn't make sense of it. The letters didn't make any sense and she didn't know what they were saying. He felt weird and shadowy against her like that but she was scared to move. She didn't know the shadow was creeping out for the first time and suffocating her skin so it felt hot and itchy. She didn't know what to say so she just said that it looked hard.*

*He laughed oozy and leaned over her more.*

*She said she had to go to the library then because she did every day and thank you for showing her the book. He stood up quick and said to remember not to stay too late because things were more dangerous after dark.*

*I never took the penny knife even if I wanted it. I put it back and ran away.*

*My mother says it's natural for me to feel upset that Johnny is back with his real father now. But I mustn't lie too. I must try to understand. She says the doctor will help me to understand these things.*

*The fire flies are far away and all together looking for a new home. There are no more stars. The moon is all of them going away.*

# CHAPTER THIRTEEN

But the way back was blocked. What had been a bridge this morning was now a wall of stones, its arches submerged by the rising, swift flowing brook. The way out beneath it had shrunk to a damp black slot, big enough for a pigeon to fly through maybe but no longer for themselves. Overhead, the Interstate roared louder and closer, tearing the air around them. The sudden thunder of a truck made Kevin duck, then his eyes crept slowly up to a small green sign, bolted to the stone at eye level, full of meaningless numbers, and up, through a high grimy chainlink fence to the gray steel top of the truck shooting by at death speed.

Ivan started to backpaddle, cursing. The sleepy current was strengthening, drawing them in.

"Help, why don't you Kevin." And Kevin, trying to overcome a weariness, or a daze, finally joined the effort to get back to the bank; then Kevin stabbed his pole into its muddy slope and the raft was still. How could Johnny have left them like this?

The problem—even though they might find an okay place to stash the raft further back on the branch; leave it for some time when they could time the tide better—the problem was where they were in Port Bedford and how what was meant to keep them out was now keeping them in. By Kevin's reckoning, and Ivan agreed with him, they were not off of the point until they crossed the Interstate. Therefore, once back up on the land, the only way out was past the sallow guard; if they were stopped there, Johnny would certainly be no help in his present mood. And they'd still have to sneak in all over again some other day to get the raft, or abandon it. And, once Nick found out how Ivan and Kevin got on his land this time—as he surely would since Johnny was so brainwashed by his charm that he'd be sure to give him a full account—Who knows? maybe a steel gate would be on this arch before long.

More trucks thundered by, percussing the continuous zoom of cars like kettle drums. It was getting near rush hour and that amplified his urgency. He needed to get home right away no matter what the cost. Didi would be leaving for work again before long, less than two hours from now probably and, if what Johnny said was true, she was in danger. Look what Nick Ford's charms had done to Johnny;

how they made Kate's mom not listen to a word she said. Look what Nick Ford had done to Kate. Kevin had to tell Didi everything, to warn her before it was too late.

Ivan agreed, but there was only one way to get back they could think of and neither of them liked it much. They back paddled the raft to the first substantial reed bank and hid it, though Ivan had some misgivings over the spot: The roof of the Point's first estate loomed ominously visible across the long field. But Kevin felt too tired and too pressed for time to look for something better, it wasn't a regular sort of tiredness from doing too much. He felt tired because of Johnny; the enormity of it washed over him, how much and how quickly Johnny had changed with the discovery Nick was his real dad. Kevin had lost a friend.

Ivan put on Kevin's backpack with what was left of the food and, on foot, they followed the brook bank pathless through a low tangly brush back to the foot of the bridge and scaled the bank.

They had agreed if there were any other way to get off the Point they would take it, but after following the bridge fence for a while, it just dropped off finally into a simple guard rail and a shoulder opened up on the highway, thin crumbling and garbage strewn. There was no other way.

Fighting the sinking feeling of fear, Kevin hopped the guard rail onto the Interstate itself. He was inside the noise now. The sleepy brook was gone, replaced by a glaring  deafening river of danger, rattling panels only inches from Kevin's ears. This place did not belong in Port Bedford at all, Kevin thought. This was nowhere. The gravely glass strewn shoulder they walked on, single file, wasn't meant for people or for anything.

It was too loud and scary for them to even talk. Ivan was behind him but separate, Kevin was alone, trapped in his own nightmare. To calm himself, he watched how the drivers' faces repeated the same exact expression as they noticed the two boys on the shoulder: First a look of surprise and then, just before the face in the driver's seat blurred by it seemed to change to a sort of tisk tisk face expanding in size and volume until the car was past and the blank backs of their heads disappeared to specks, continuing their speeding unslowable way.

He walked on like that for miles and hours it felt like, threading a path between traffic and guard rail, checking now and again to make sure Ivan was still behind him, hoping no police car would see them before they reached the first off-ramp. It was the one for the amusement park, he'd known that for about half an hour because the signs were for cars and so started miles before the exit.

At last they returned to Port Bedford past the slower speed signs of the ramp and the ones, facing the other direction, saying Wrong Way Go Back, and the ones across the median forbidding entrance to pedestrians and horses and scooters, and kids, Kevin almost expected to see. When he finally found his feet firmly again on Harbor Rd., the end nearer to Didi's house, exhausted, overwhelmed and, Kevin never felt so thankful, but he knew inside by that stinging feeling in the top of his throat he was very near the threshold of tears.

"I can't believe we just did that," said Ivan sounding not nearly as upset as Kevin felt, but maybe he was. Ivan was better than Kevin at keeping stuff like that way inside. Kevin couldn't manage to say anything at all for fear of choking up on the words. When he finally brought out, "How are we ever going to get our raft back?" it still came out as a whine. The loss cut him deep, it was surprising how much since, before yesterday, he'd hardly even thought about the raft or those days. But now that it was gone, the loss felt heavy and significant and his feelings for it were all mixed up with his feelings for Didi too. And Nick Ford loomed large in his mind as the source and the danger. Who was he? Where had he come from and why had he come into Kevin's life just now, when everything seemed to be going so good. If the Interstate was a nightmare, he was waking up to something real. That man was here in Kevin's world, just outside of his awareness, choosing the people Kevin loved one by one and drawing them out of his reach.

They decided not to pick up their bikes either and headed straight back to Vale Place. A blockbuster firecracker went off from somewhere near Beach Ave., a deep soft thump in Kevin's chest; then a wide slow echo off of the pavement everywhere. That's how you could tell it was a blockbuster and not a gunfire, like the one's he heard that day from the Cove Bar whose echoes cracked then trailed off like wind.

Both sides of this part of Harbor Rd. had the biggest oldest maple trees in town. They buckled up the blocks of sidewalk with their roots. Their wide green leaves hung still overhead in a lofty solid roof that spanned the whole street. No cars were passing, which was a tremendous relief after the Interstate. But the cyclical thrum from the cicada overhead still echoed the panicking passage of trucks to Kevin's ears and all the exhaust still seemed to tingle on his damp sooty skin.

Ivan's shoulders sagged and one of his sneakers caught the

edge of a pushed up block of cement. He lurched forward, but Kevin caught him before he fell. After that it felt like the last mile home just seemed to grow and grow.

"Shit," Ivan said when they got to Beach Ave. So Kevin started singing a breathy rhythm to keep their spirits up and their feet from dragging. After a block or two he added some words, little by little: "Nick Ford," then "Death Lord," then "Stick a needle in his gourd." The rhythm and their walk got faster and Ivan joined in, until they were walking so fast that they were almost running. That way, and because they were grinning so much now, they got to the doorstep of 3 Vale almost before they knew it, completely out of breath collapsing on the stoop.

Kevin almost never looked at his house from the outside, since he was always on his way out or in: It looked less sturdy than he remembered, walls tipping maybe or the flat roof was squashed up a tiny bit. Ivan also seemed reluctant to go in.

"Maybe we shouldn't even tell her," said Ivan.

"Maybe not," Kevin said. "Nick Ford..." he began again automatically his song, but there was nowhere left to walk.

Didi, it turned out was in the bathroom taking a bath. They could hear the water swishing around in the tub as they came in.

"Kev? Is that you? Hold on. I need to talk to you guys before I go to work."

Kevin walked up to the bathroom, leaving Ivan standing in the hallway with the bag of left over food. Kevin put his whole body and the side of his face against the moist unpainted wood of the door, one hand on the fingerprinted gold chromed knob. Then, without knocking he walked blind into the steam already talking,

"Is Nick Ford your boyfriend?" he said. He was looking down at her full length as the steam rushed out of the room, from the side of the tub. Didi's body lay submerged beneath the translucent water, except for the oval of her face which broke the surface. A swirl of pink curves in the soapiness as she pulled up her head and a streaming wake of dark hair behind; then an elbow up over the curved white edge of the tub, then her soft reddened breasts like two children's faces in there with her, glistening and fresh now above the surface as she leaned out her body, "Jesus Kevin, you scared me. Couldn't you even knock or say something or?"

It wasn't that he was exactly troubled. Kevin saw parts of Deirdre's body naked all the time, while she was dressing for example, or just at home in her underwear and a t-shirt, or when the front of her robe fell open and showed her breast where the butterfly tattoo was. But never her whole shape like this. The flow of water from her hair quieted to a drip and the bathwater stilled.

She leaned her other elbow back on the far edge by the wall so the bottom curves of her breasts made circles in the water and, at the center of her body underneath was a broad, dark place. Kevin thought back to the night when Kate ran out to the path looking for black moss. How it grows over the down there of grown ups.

"No, Kevin. He's not my boyfriend," she said, relaxed again, "he's...he's strange," she laughed oddly and swished up her knee so that a drop of water touched Kevin on the face.

As if the single drop bowled him over, Kevin sat down on the closed toilet lid, his legs shedding their last strength from kneeling on the raft, the Interstate and all that walking. He just collapsed, what was left of his strength streamed out down his spine like the water had from his sisters hair. It was true.

"I knew you weren't," he said full of relief he didn't fully feel. "But that's where you were the other night, wasn't it?"

"You little spy!" she said sitting straight up in the tub, but only halfway indignant.

"We got it out of Johnny," he said, no longer able to conceal his countless worries from her. Didi seemed to be studying his face

"Nick was so sure he was asleep," Deirdre laughed. " A lot he knows about kids. Let me get dressed Kevin. Is Ivan here? I want to ask both of you about something."

"Yeah. We want to talk to you about something too. Okay. Sorry about busting in on you, Deed."

"I've got nothing to hide from you, Kevin," she said, smiling, looking at him curiously, wondering maybe what it was they had to tell her. Kevin himself wasn't sure exactly himself, he just needed to unburden himself from all the stuff he'd been keeping secret so long. And to warn her.

"Me neither," he said.

"So?" said Didi.

"So," said Kevin looking straight at her, feeling her warmth.

"So get the fuck out of here and let me get dressed."

"I borrowed your two dollar bill," he began, "but I..."

"Out!" and a splash of water chased him from the room.

Kevin looked at Ivan uncertainly, standing in the hallway still, "She said it wasn't true."

The friendly sound of water draining from the tub and after a few moments Deirdre emerged from the bathroom in her white soft tericloth robe, still combing her hair, holding its ends close to her breast and running the dirty pink comb through it lovingly, again and again even though the tangles were long gone.

She walked through the livingroom where Kevin and Ivan had sprawled themselves: Ivan on the couch and Kevin in Didi's big frayed plaid chair because it felt like being in her lap. She smiled at them, continuing to comb and went to the kitchen; put the comb down on the counter and opened the cabinet with a magnetic pop, pulled out the coffee tin. So Kevin got up from the chair, motioning for Ivan to follow him into the kitchen. They sat down at the plywood kitchen table watching Deirdre pour coffee into the basket of the electric percolator, fill it with water and plug it in. Soon the warm sound of bubbling water began, the liquid bubbles darkening in the top, and the good, burnt smell filling the room. Didi leaned her hips against the counter so she was facing them.

"I wanted to ask you guys about Kate. How's she doing?"

"She's grounded," Kevin said.

"What for?"

"For breaking all of Nick Ford's windows."

A high sharp giggle burst from Didi's lips, though her face seemed to say it wasn't so funny, "When?"

"A couple of days ago."

"He somehow forgot to mention that," muttered Deirdre. "It started really because I worried about Kate." Her tone shifted nervously. "She said some things to me that other night when she stayed here. Kevin, I think maybe she's in trouble inside. It's not like her to break windows is it?"

"I guess not," said Kevin.

"The thing is, I've been worried for her since that party. She's crying out I think. You guys know her better than me. So that's why I'm asking. I think you're old enough to know what I'm talking about. It's just that, well, I see a lot of myself in Kate. Bad things can happen to a girl her age and, well to be honest, I don't think Mrs. Harrigan is worth a rat's ass, so I feel sort of responsible for her."

It was Kevin and Ivan's turn to giggle.

"I guess, if you saw Johnny," said Deirdre, "he told you the reason he's living with Nick now."

"Nick's his real dad, he told me," said Kevin glumly.

"You don't like Nick much, do you, Kev?" said Didi, serious like Kevin was an adult. Kevin was silent. "It must be hard for Kate, I know, but the truth is, you guys, Nick did the right thing. Johnny is probably better off with his real dad." Kevin felt Ivan's obstinate silence beside him, and he felt his own obstinate silence too. "I'm not saying everybody is better off with their real dads," she added quickly. "I'm just saying that for Johnny I think it's the right thing. Damn," she said, but now she was talking to herself. "I can't believe I've gotten myself all messed up in all this."

"How messed up?" said Kevin almost angry—the doubt creeping in once again that it was Nick Ford she was messed up with.

"I care about you, hon," said Deirdre simply. "And you have great friends Kevin. And I care about them too. You're lucky though. Not everyone can choose good friends like you have—like Ivan here, and Kate. Lord knows I haven't." Kevin felt himself blushing with pleasure and he looked over to see Ivan looking proud. He found himself wishing he could freeze this moment forever and keep it safe in a jar.

"And you," Kevin added, so Didi blushed too. Everything was perfect until he saw tears in her eyes and that made Kevin sad. It didn't exactly spoil it, but it made him remember that, really, it was no good saving anything because it always changed.

"I'm glad you think so," said Didi, "but like I said, I think one of your friends at least is in trouble. Not just in trouble for breaking windows or whatever—but, real trouble in herself. I'd have her come live here if I thought I could get away with it. I swear I would."

Kevin looked at her hopefully until she lowered her eyes.

"I can't Kevin. There are laws if nothing else. I guess what I'm saying is, I think she needs you guys right now."

"We tried to go see her," said Ivan, but Mrs. Harrigan won't let us anymore."

"Listen," she said pouring coffee then sipping it with the mug in both hands. "This may seem like a weird question, but I want to know if, well, did anything ever happen to Kate that you know of? I asked Nick, I thought he might know. That's why I first went over there with him, night before last after work. He was at the bar at closing and I walked home with him. He knows the family and I wanted to know if...He's worried about her too. He cares a great deal about Kate I think. But he's a strange one, I," Didi fumbled.

Kevin looked at Ivan to see what he was thinking. Now was the time to tell her of course since she was asking. Ivan's face looked unsure, he was leaving it up to Kevin; Kevin found himself suddenly wishing he could leave it up to Ivan, after all, Ivan knew more about it but.

"Maybe you guys don't really know what I'm talking about do you?" she seemed to be studying Kevin's face again. "The thing is, this is the biggest night of the year at the bar tonight and I know Nick is going to show up there and Well the truth is, I said he wasn't my boyfriend, and he isn't—I think he wants to be though, Kevin. But he's a strange one. He told me plenty; we talked about ourselves last night until it got light out, but there's something. I don't know. I just don't have a firm fix—something makes me, I don't know, and. I guess I just wanted to find out what you guys knew about him before I saw him again tonight." She drank down about half her cup of coffee then and filled it up right away from the pot.

"You do like him don't you?" said Kevin, not angry anymore, but worried. Worried for Didi, worried for himself.

"No Kev. Not in a permanent way I don't think...I think he's very attractive, I guess. I mean there's something very interesting about him, but, no, I'm not at all sure I like him if that's...I guess sometimes. Well, I'm not so sure sometimes, Kev, that I'm as good at picking friends as you are." She laughed and put up her hands. "I guess I'm asking for advice from my little brother."

"We think he's a jerk," said Kevin carefully.

"Why?" said Deirdre.

"Because he is," said Ivan.

Deirdre laughed, "Okay," she said. "Whatever." Kevin felt the moment slipping away. It was like there was nothing he could do about it and soon he'd never be able to tell Didi and if he couldn't tell her that, then it would be like he'd lose her little by little and then there'd be no adult at all and he'd be alone. He just needed to say...What? He couldn't think of the words or what they should mean even and all the while Didi leaning her hips on the counter was receding farther and farther like the car drivers on the Interstate with no way for him to stop them for help. Panic was creeping up his legs now, like ants from the floor. Like he was sinking into an ocean of ants until it was all the way up to his neck tickling it horribly, until he couldn't bear it anymore and Kevin shrieked,

"It was him!" and everything froze even the ants around his neck. But he'd stopped sinking at least. Deirdre's face was pale:

"What was him?" she said slowly. But Kevin's mouth was frozen now with everything else. He wanted to say but couldn't. Then it was Ivan's voice, quiet and even:

"What happened to Kate," it said.

Deirdre was staring out the kitchen window like she just realized she'd forgotten something very important in the yard. She glanced back at them, a quick wrinkled red glance, then went back to staring out the window.

"Shit." she said. "Shit, shit, shit. I knew `it. Oh god I should never have let him touch me. Oh god," she said, touching her face, "Shit."

from Kate's diary,
July Fourth, 1976:


*Nick was all sweaty and red when he was himself again.*

*The shadow was back inside of him so he couldn't look at me.*

*I was myself then.*

*But I didn't know where I was and it felt like just a second ago I was looking at his super secret typewriter pages.*

*But all of the sudden I was sitting on the ground in the dark instead.*

*He said that it wasn't him.*

*He said that it wasn't me.*

*I tried to think if it was me and it wasn't. But I couldn't say anything because I forgot how to talk. All I could remember was when I forgot how to read when he showed me the typewriter pages that were his book.*

*I didn't remember I was at the library until later. But I asked Roberta and I was. She*

*says she helped me pick out a book which was*
*The Secret Garden because it was the first*
*book her mother ever read to her.*

*I have The Secret Garden against my lap*
*with my hands on the outside.*

*I can't let hands be in there.*

*He waves them in front of my eyes to see*
*if I am awake.*

*He asks if I'm okay.*

*I say no but I don't. I can't remember*
*how to talk.*

*He gets redder and redder.*

*He says that I've been acting very strange*
*and that he just came to the path to breathe a*
*little.*

*He says I must've been taken sick sud-*
*denly.*

*He says Don't you see? You wouldn't have*
*acted that way if you'd known it was me.*

*He says it's lucky it was him. Or else*
*something might have happened. It could have*
*been a terrible person I met on the path.*

*He tells me to hurry back home now and jump in the pool first Because you feel very hot and then jump straight into bed.*

*He says I am very very hot and there must be something wrong with me.*

*He says I should be in bed.*

*I still can't talk. I can run though. He says I can.*

*I run away as fast as I can and I do exactly what he says so he doesn't come back to get me.*

*I go to bed still soaking wet from the pool. I am scared to look for a towel.*

*When I wake up this morning I feel sick and fuzzy. It's hard to remember what order things go or if I maybe dreamt some.*

*I woke up in the middle of the night and the whole sky was orangey red like dawn only it wasn't dawn.*

# CHAPTER FOURTEEN

A bottle rocket screamed by the window, probably launched by some of the older kids from the vicinity of the pillars at the end of Vale. Pop. Warming up for tonight. Starting after noon, all around town, some distant, some close, ash cans and bricks of firecrackers and blockbusters had begun going off. Didi had a face like they were all aimed at her. Ivan and Kevin hung around her in the kitchen, blabbering about  each large explosion—whether it was an ash can, which was a tenth of a stick of dynamite, or a blockbuster, which was an eighth, or vice versa. But that only made Kevin's sister quieter. She looked like a painting.

She had changed into her tight bar clothes already, pouring herself yet another cup of coffee, but not moving otherwise.

"Are you mad at us, Didi?" Kevin finally said.

She walked away into the livingroom, like she didn't hear and flicked on the tv so she could watch some of Operation Sail. Kevin followed her to the doorway.

All the old tall ships in the world were swarming around the screen, down to New York Harbor around the Statue of Liberty to celebrate America's 200th birthday.  Little sailors stood, like migrating birds, all over the masts.

"Kevin, Ivan. Come look," she said from the doorway of the living room, even though she wasn't looking at the screen herself. She was staring absently out the window like she'd been doing all day.

Now she was looking at him, or rather not looking because every time Kevin tried to catch her eye, she turned it away. "Ain't they fine? Better than fireworks. I'd just stay home and watch this on tv if I could. Port Bedford a hundred years ago or something used to be filled with boats like that. Now it's just ugly and polluted from the tankers."

The harbor just now was a sore subject for Kevin, "We want  to go down to the harbor to watch the fireworks." Deirdre had already said no, without explanation.

"You can see them here from the roof," Didi said. "People are crazy on a night like this and I really don't want you wandering around the harbor."

"Why?" said Kevin.

"Because I've got a bad feeling, that's why." She looked annoyed.

"So? Just because you're in a bad mood doesn't mean everybody has to be."

"Look," snapped Deirdre, "I hear things, okay? The fishermen come into the bar every day talking shit. And tonight they'll be drunk."

"Do you have to go to work?" said Ivan.

"I have to, hon. It's going to be the busiest night of the year; maybe ever. Beachcomber is probably the best place in town to see the fireworks. This is a big deal you know. There won't be another Fourth like this for a hundred years.

"We'll be a hundred and ten then," Kevin said after taking a second for the calculation, "it's not fair."

"Life isn't fair, little brother."

"But..."

"Don't argue with me Kev, not now. It's not like I'm going to have a whole lot of fun tonight myself. It's not like I've had any fun since..." she didn't finish, but Kevin felt his face swelling bright red and he concentrated on the tips of his sneakers. Since what? Did she mean since she found out the truth about Nick—or did she mean since Kevin'd moved in with her, that was what. To tie her down and keep her from doing all the things she wanted to do.

It was like Didi could read the thoughts right off of Kevin's face and she hugged him. "C'mon, Kev," she said, "it's just one night. If there was someone..." The problem was that the Carroll's, who took him with them last year to the harbor, were away for this Fourth, camping in their trailer. Kevin and Ivan both just kept looking at their shoes.

"It's okay," said Kevin. "I understand."

Deirdre suddenly laughed, "You little manipulative shit." Kevin peaked up his eyes to see if her face was as nice feeling as the laugh. She was smiling and shaking her head. "Come on then, but hurry up. Get some jackets. It gets cold at night on the Beachcomber porch."

"All right!" said Kevin and Ivan in chorus, slapping their hands together in a high five.

"I'll call Janine," said Didi, talking more to herself, "and swing it so I can take you home on my break, okay? Fair enough for you?" she fired out, mocking. She pretended she was still angry, but Kevin saw from her eyes that she was as pleased with her decision as he was.

Accompanying Deirdre to the Beachcomber always meant

excitement to Kevin. More than anything else almost: It was a pretty rare event. And never with anyone else his age before. He always considered it his own secret knowledge, something that other kids didn't possess: that glimpse into the bizarre adult world of a bar. As he put on his jacket, though, Kevin suddenly wasn't sure how he felt about sharing this information, even with Ivan.

He disliked this reaction, recognizing it as selfish and told himself so silently. Ivan and he had never been closer than Kevin felt toward him at this moment, and it seemed stupid to resent his coming along. But there was also something half embarrassing about his memory there of his interactions with the drunken adults: half experiences he wasn't at all sure he wanted to have Ivan corroborate. Things that women and men had said to him in their drunkenness, which Didi had been too busy to be aware of, but which she sensed enough of to not want to expose him again unless there was no other choice.

Now, walking behind her, with Ivan along Killdeer, Kevin felt he needed somehow to impress on his friend that his allowing him to accompany him into this taboo world was a dangerous gift. He just hoped Ivan would understand and not make light of it. As Kevin mulled all this anxiously through his mind he was silent and must have pulled a stern face, because Ivan turned to him and asked,

"Don't you like going to the Beachcomber?" Kevin didn't always, actually. He'd probably been there six times all told in all the time he'd been living with Deirdre, and two of those times at least had some unpleasant sensations attached to remembering them even now. So what was it he liked about the bar? Not sitting in the bar itself which was often pretty boring actually, at best, and sometimes awkward or even threatening. He just liked the fact itself, being and occupying space in a place where he was forbidden to be; also the secret relishing and anticipation of that fact, a feeling he was trying very hard to summon now, but not successfully.

The reason was Ivan, walking easily next to him who, by his simple presence, his worldliness, continued to interrupt the chemical connections that would have let Kevin's good feeling flow.

"It's illegal for us to be inside a bar," said Kevin, "that's why Didi has to be so careful."

She had been careful. The last time he went in was in March when the Carrolls were away at a funeral and the heat wasn't working right at 3 Vale, and there was no one at all to watch him. Not even Kevin's mom whom Didi actually called.

So, whenever Kevin did get to go, it was a lot like a snow day at school—something extraordinary.

But Ivan continued to defy all this by his walk, carrying himself along with his most refined No big deal walk. Kevin looked up to Deirdre's back slightly ahead of them—the certain, no-nonsense way of her stride as she prepared herself inside for the chaotic shift to come. It was Deirdre, Kevin suddenly realized, he wanted to himself— the way she kept him protectively by her in the bar and made him feel so important and special among the men who sat there. How they joked with him and were warm and Didi treated them better for it; mixed them better and bigger drinks; said the warmer things that they all seemed to crave. In a funny way, they were just like Kevin: They sat there waiting to be treated special, as someone welcome in the place, as someone whose first name Didi knew and said without thinking.

"The fireworks are going to be extra big this year, I bet," said Ivan as if he were trying to cheer up his friend. "We'll have the best seats in the whole town."

Kevin's mood though was   impenetrable. They walked on in silence.

On the end of the little side street, one street down from Tock's chained off end of Killdeer, Deirdre took out her keys and opened the lock of the bar's entrance: a windowless little blue door in an old brick wall hard against the street. The bar was so well established in Port Bedford that it didn't need any advertisement; Deirdre once told him why it was like that, it had started out as what was known as an Easyspeak, which was an illegal place a long time ago when drinking was against the law. Liquor, Deirdre said, was smuggled through the harbor from other countries in those days, and that's how most rich families in Port Bedford got their money. Deirdre was pretty much of a history buff. If she had been able to go to college, she often said, that would have been her major. Kevin was going to put what she told him about the bar into his General Facts paper on the harbor for school. But the teacher had said he had to say all the books where the facts were from and he guessed he couldn't just say his sister told him, so he just copied other stuff from the library instead.

Even though Deirdre said it was the best bar in town, there was nothing but a peeling white oar handle hanging out front, like a bone above the door with minuscule red painted script saying Beachcomber like that was the boat it came from or something. But when Deirdre finally got all the locks undone and the door opened, the little crumbling street suddenly flooded gold all over Kevin's body and his friend's. And his sister's back became a sunbeamed silhouette before them.

"This is the most beautiful time of day here, Ivan," said Didi. "And no one ever sees it but me and Janine. C'mon inside before somebody sees you." She grabbed them both by the shoulders and pulled them into the light, shutting out the dark, narrow street, and she threw the big black metal bolt again behind her.

The source of all the sunlight in the room was the south wall, which was entirely composed of squares of plate glass, on the shelves of which were different colored seaglass bottles glowing milky blues and greens and ambers. Another little blue door like the front one led out to a high wooden deck overlooking the amusement park and the whole harbor. The deck also wrapped around to the east side of the brick building and looked out to the ocean on a hill between the gaudy new roofs of Ocean Spray apartments and the remains of the Fort Estate. It was the deck and the big window that made the Beachcomber special. Inside, nothing: just a long watersoaked wooden bar with stools and a black iron footrail along the bottom at about the height of Kevin's knees, plus a mirror, behind all the liquor bottles, for customers to look at themselves and also at all the scenery outside the window wall without having to bother to turn around from their drinks; there was a warped watersoaked plank floor with an ancient jukebox and that was it.

"I'm supposed to open up in half an hour," said Deirdre looking at the clock, which she said was always wrong on purpose but only she knew by how much. "I gotta get stuff ready." She flicked Operation Sail back on the barroom tv which hung from the corner ceiling. "You can watch that if you want, or go out on the porch or whatever."

"Hey look," said Ivan, "that's one of the pirate ships that was in town a couple of days ago, I'm sure of it. Remember?"

"Cool," said Kevin, but it made him think of all the weirdness of that day, in the fishingboat with Tock and what Tock did to Kevin with his knife. It came back to him how Tock had told him to come visit. And Kevin wondered if he would and what it would mean if he did. He hadn't had time yet, so it hadn't come up, but Kevin realized in his mind he'd been sort of avoiding the candy stand. Now he unlocked the porch door and stood outside in the low slanting sunshine, looking out at the cranes and down on the roofs of Ocean Spray behind which Tock was probably sitting in his plywood box, maybe wondering why Kevin hadn't come by for some candy. He thought about the old times before he met Kate and Johnny, when it was just him at the candy stand with Tock leaning on his counter telling Kevin stories about the neighborhood in the old days.

Ivan came out on the porch behind him, but Kevin didn't feel like talking about Tock, or any of it, kept his back to Ivan, leaned out over the rail and spaced out on the ocean thinking about how much everything sucked.

Soon Didi unlocked the front door and several young men who'd been waiting outside wandered in and perched themselves on the barstools and put quarters in the jukebox and started making small talk with Deirdre.

"Is that one your little brother?" one in a cut off flannel shirt was saying of Ivan as he walked in from the porch.

"No, the other one," said Deirdre, so Kevin heard it from the porch. "That's Ivan, I've known him since he was born though too. 'Nother?"

"Sure. Why not."

"Hey," Deirdre said to Kevin and Ivan, "You know you guys are going home right after the fireworks, that's the deal right?"

"Deal," said Kevin. The fireworks wouldn't start for another two hours at least when it started to get dark. And they'd probably last half an hour.

"I called Janine because she just lives around the corner. So it's all set. She'll cover while I take you guys back home. Okay?"

"It's not a problem," said Ivan, "we'll be okay you know, we walk that way all the time."

"I know you'd be fine, Ivan. It's just the Fourth. Weird night, you know? So humor me."

Ivan shrugged and asked for a deck of cards, which Didi gave him from under the bar.

Before they knew it, the place was filled with adults. All sorts: a man in a tie and a woman with dangley earrings, and two men in leisure suits and a woman with a short skirt and golden hoops in her ears and some men in t-shirts and boots and one in white tennis shorts and a windbreaker and a woman in green and pink with rope soled elevator shoes. Most of them were taking their drinks out to the tables on the porch—where Didi, with Kevin and Ivan's help, had already put extra benches—for the fireworks.

The sun was red now, and to the west, draining the room altogether of color and flaming only the porch full of people like they were drinking and laughing in a fire. Kevin and Ivan had long ago withdrawn inside, where it was only slightly less crowded with tremen-

dous sweaty smoky bodies, and onto two stools in safety behind the
barrier of the bar, by the glass washing sink. Their two sets of hands
plunged into the suds, washing glasses for Didi who had a string of
hair dropped out of its braid and stuck fast across her forehead as
she tried grimly to keep up with the men who stood leaning between
occupied stools waiting for their orders, for them and their partners
out on the porch. She hadn't had time yet to turn the lights on inside,
so the main light in the room came from the tv's blue and gray flash-
ings over Ivan's shoulder. It filled the bar with cold light while the
porch outside continued to burn red against a yellow sky. The seven
o'clock news was on, Walter Cronkite's familiar white moustache
flashing between pictures of the tall ships in New York Harbor and
the face of the President of the United States and foreign news and
crowds of people with protest signs. There was no sound from the tv
and Kevin was a little overwhelmed at the moment by the actual
crowd here at the Beachcomber. He went back to concentrating on
getting every speck off the glass he was washing for Didi, and handed it to her as she looked around for one, and she smiled at him
wearily so the room didn't feel so cold for a second. An Elton John
song he knew was blaring from the jukebox and Kevin yelled into her
ear:

"You want me to turn the lights on for you?" and she nodded
and pointed to the wall on the customer side of the bar. Kevin looked
at the tv again: It was the local newscaster man and then the big hotel
lobby in the center of Port Bedford and a close-up of the sweating
smiling face of Bill Gunn and, as the camera panned backwards, Nick
Ford was at the table next to him, looking handsome and bored.
Kevin mistrusted the tv even more now and hit Ivan on the shoulder
and pointed to it, but by the time Ivan looked up from the sink it was
gone and there were shots of Commercial Harbor where the fireworks
were getting set up instead.

"It'll be a better view from here, I bet," shouted Ivan. Kevin
shrugged off the confusion of communicating what was no longer
there and ducked under the space in the bar and wormed his way
through the waists of people for the light switch. The tv had left him
feeling afraid again and then, half way across the room it happened:
A black suited, white cuffed arm came down to stop him. Kevin
looked up and his terror was complete. It was Nick Ford himself, in
the very same suit he'd just seen a second before on the tv, sweaty
and man smelling, a cold sweating drink glass in his hand, a drop of
which hit the back of Kevin's hand and seemed to freeze all his blood.
Nick looked down at him with a strange, red-faced smile. Kevin

looked around; he was blocked in, nowhere to go, the edges of his vision starting to go black. Nick Ford's tremendous face lurching down—cologne and an alcoholic wind from his mouth and a deafening bellow piercing Kevin's ear: "Tell your sister I want to talk with her. When she gets the chance," he smiled. Kevin nodded helplessly then, released, ran for the light switch, flicked it on and stopped to breathe against the wall. With yellow light suddenly everywhere, the whole crowd looked sharply at Kevin, as if he'd caught them all in terrible crimes. But the light adjusting in his eyes made them all seem smaller too, like startled rabbits and not so terrifying. Instead of crossing the crowd and risking another encounter with Nick Ford, he followed the wall around the entire perimeter of the room. But Nick was at its center now; Kevin could feel his eyes boring into him everywhere. The uncertainty was unbearable, so Kevin stopped and turned to face him. Nick wasn't looking at him. Kevin saw him laughing down to a shiny-eyed woman in a white dress; then Kevin slipped back under the bar and hid, motioning for Ivan to get down off the stool.

Ivan seemed to think it was a joke, smiled and got down among the extra bottles with him.

"Knock it off you guys," Didi yelled down to them. "You've got to be cool okay, and try to stay out of my way."

"It's him," Kevin mouthed to her, pointing through the bar towards the crowd. Didi must have seen him then, because she blanched and dropped down to a squat beside them.

"Did he say anything to you?"

"He grabbed me and said he wanted to talk to you when you had the chance."

"Great," said Deirdre. She glanced into the crowd, "He seems to be working up a back up plan already anyway. I'm too fucking busy to deal with that asshole now," she said; she looked worried. "What should I do, Kev?"

Kevin looked down on the ground and shook his head violently.

"I'll go tell him you're too busy," said Ivan. "I ain't scared of him."

"No, thanks though," said Didi, "Just ignore him." She went back to pouring beers, violent and fast, like the long white porcelain taps were people's necks she was choking one after the other.

Even though the rush was slowing; people were already starting to empty out onto the porch as it grew dark enough, repelled also, Kevin felt, by the revealing light inside. Nick seemed to be practically the only one inside suddenly and there were no more customers. He was staring at her, eyes shining soft and kindly.

"Go enjoy the fireworks," Deirdre said to Nick, cool as cucumber. "Because you won't be getting none from me."

"You couldn't be mad," he said, smiling innocently, "about that little girl I was just talking to, Deirdre really..."

But Deirdre cut him off sharp, "Which little girl is that?"

Kevin watched, in awe, as Nick Ford's face began to swell, first from his neck above the tight white collar then up through his cheeks and into his eyes, bloating purple red, like the way Kevin imagined a drowned man would look after floating in the ocean for a week. Kevin was terrified; he grabbed for Ivan's arm.

"Well go on," she said. He shook his head like he was choking and then, like some evil sorcerer bringing himself back from the dead, he brought back his normal features and all the awfulness in his face concentrated itself into a single, thin unnatural smile. He walked out onto the porch.

"Asshole," said Didi to his back. He paused in his step but didn't turn around.

Now that the room was empty, Didi came out from behind the bar; her legs were shaking. To hide it, Didi walked to the porch doorway and leaned her back against the jamb, half turned, as if to keep an eye on the front entrance. Kevin and Ivan, looking at one another knowingly took there stations in front of her, like two small knights at her knees, leaning back against the fronts of her legs, steadying them. The crowd outside was too tall for Kevin to see where exactly Nick was anymore.

The first dimly glowing salvo shot its way up into the air. A moment. Then it bloomed green with people's collective ooh, like the light itself was coming from their desire filled mouths—expanding and dissipating and falling down among them in separating sprouts of light that went out with tinkles in their glasses so it made the icecubes sparkle. Kevin fixed his eyes on one couple at a table between two torsos. They leaned together and hugged each other like the light had been love that filled them and now they were afraid that it was gone.

"I love fireworks," Deirdre said. "Ivan! look at that one."

"It's like grapes," said Ivan. Several bright compact flashes then a wait then thumps in Kevin's chest.

"Boom," said Kevin.

"Deirdre," said a voice. The thump in Kevin's chest was deeper than any firework could make. Nick had appeared from nowhere, black in the doorway.

"You're blocking the fireworks," Deirdre said coolly.

"Excuse me," Nick said and his large figure drifted to the side next to Deirdre's shoulder. "I want to say something, knowing you'd be working tonight, I," he whispered. "It's been. From our conversation, I. I don't have many real friends. None in fact," he laughed. "You may find that surprising?"

"No, not really," said Deirdre. Nick looked at her like that wasn't at all the answer he expected.

"You see more keenly than the people I'm used to," he said.

"You're the judge," she said. "I guess you should know."

"Yes..." he said, but Deirdre snorted before he was through speaking.

"Will you hear my side?" he said. "Listen without prejudice?"

"Why?"

"May I see you alone sometime tonight?" Kevin tightened his grip on Deirdre's leg.

"No," Kevin blurted. He could feel Nick Ford's eyes burning into the top of his head, but Kevin was too afraid to look up this time.

"A devious mind will always see a plot, young man," muttered Nick Ford angrily, then his voice mellowed, "I'm sincere, Deirdre. Believe me or not."

"Sorry," said Deirdre. Her face lit up gold for a moment. "I'm busy." Then Nick's face was purple; then green.

"I understand," he said looking down at Ivan and Kevin. I understand your little friends here have been doing a little amateur detective work. "The three of you how 'bout?" he said. Black eyes to Kevin and Ivan. "I'd prefer it really. It will help me to be clear. So there's no misunderstanding. I only want to tell you the truth, that's all."

"Clear about what?" said Deirdre; the light was red.

"Apparently there is need for clarity," said Nick frowning. "I don't... People's opinions of me or what they think they know about me is unimportant as a rule."

"Whatever," said Deirdre. "I have to get back to the bar. And, by the way, if you want my professional opinion, you've had quite a few tonight haven't you?"

"Quite a few," he said smiling and the light was orange red, but from much lower down this time.

There was something weird about the light. A different kind of murmur, lowered and uncertain, was coming from the crowd on the porch. A lone man's voice burst out, "Holy Shit!" and suddenly the whole porch erupted into loud, frantic conversation. Now Kevin could see searchlights combing the harbor. Something had gone wrong with the fireworks before the grand finale. The sound of sirens and the sky seemed blacker than ordinary night and people on the porch started shouting, "The harbor's on fire!" at Deirdre, like there was something she could do about it.

"Yeah?" Deirdre fired back at them. "What do you want from me, a pitcher of water? I'll turn on the tv, okay?" Deirdre hurried back to the bar because some of the people were rushing inside shouting for her to turn up the volume; for her to call this place and that on the bar phone.

Nick Ford was still standing frozen in the porch doorway. People had to squeeze around him to get back inside.

"Damnit!" his voice erupted. The whole bar went silent, afraid to look at him.

"Hope you got insurance," said Deirdre coldly. Some of the other local business men looked at her, their eyes full of hostility. Everyone there probably knew that Nick Ford owned practically everything in the harbor.

There was a live newsbreak going on, a reporter standing against the backdrop of a flaming pier saying it was unclear whether this was started by a piece of fireworks or whether, as some seem to be suggesting, it was arson. "None of the private fishing boats is affected; the fires took place on company owned boats off the fish-buyers' piers..." An angry Nick Ford stood alone in the center of the room watching the screen, the others in a wide circle around him.

"I know exactly which boat, that bastard. I have to go," he said to Didi. "I'll try to find you later." He was grabbing his suitcoat from a hook by the bar when he stopped, "Had you heard anything about this?" he whispered to Deirdre.

Deirdre shrugged. "You hear a lot of things around here," she said. "Never thought they'd have the guts."

"Remember, please, that I was here when this happened. It may prove helpful to me later; we'll see." His walk was purposeful but calm as he left the Beachcomber. The crowd seemed to approve. Deirdre crossed her arms tight over her chest and smiled for the first time all day.

from Kate's diary,
July Fifth, 1976:

*I put the dead firefly rocks in a pile and broke all his windows for the ones still stuck in the moss inside. So they could escape to the moon.*

*That's why my mom and dad want to send me to the doctors and because I touched the knife. That's why he told my brother not to be my brother and come live with him instead.*

*His name is Doctor Weir and I kept wanting to say Weird. His office was full of green chairs and he had hairs coming out of his nose so much I didn't think he could breathe. The way he breathed was noisy and full of ooze and I felt sick. He made me sit in a big green chair across from his desk. I couldn't see what his hands were doing under the desk and that made me scared.*

*I said Aren't you the kind of doctor that makes people lie down on the couch.*

*And he said I could if I want.*

*I said No I didn't want to.*

*And he said How do you feel about your cousin Johnny being gone?*

*And I said I don't know how do you feel?*

*And he said My feelings don't matter here.*

*And I said he's not my cousin he's my brother.*

*And he said Are you angry at his father for taking him back?*

*And I said No*

*And he said Why not?*

*And I said Why do you keep asking me dumb questions?*

*And he said What do you want me to ask?*

*And I said What do you want me to ask?*

# CHAPTER FIFTEEN

Everybody was talking about the fire. Janine came in about an hour after Nick left and agreed to cover for the rest of the night because she knew she could make a lot in tips. Everyone was so excited about the fire they wanted to stay and drink and have theories. Least it wasn't the discharge station, some people said. Others laughed and said they would have loved to have seen that. Kevin wondered how big the headlines would be tomorrow, or if anyone got killed, or if he would have the chance to get down to the harbor tomorrow for charred pieces of fishingboats. Searchlights still swept crazily around the harbor which glowed orangy yellow over the tree tops. He could smell the smoke on the air even from here, sharp with hints of tar and salt in it. Sirens were coming from everywhere and the big firehouse horns were still bellowing at each other from both sides of town as Kevin and Ivan walked beside Deirdre back down Killdeer. Fireworks were still going off too, everywhere, on top of everything and then they heard shouting from a sidestreet they were passing and the thump of running feet.

A group of four older kids came flying by, grinning and looking behind themselves wild eyed.

The rapid fire of three blockbusters and the rumble of metal, like maybe they set them off in a garbage can. When the older kids saw Kevin and Ivan and Deirdre standing in the street watching them, they stopped and looked panicked; started hitting each other on the shoulders and then each bolted in a separate direction.

All in all, Kevin decided, this was the most spectacular Fourth of July ever; anything less would have only disappointed his expectations for a bicentennial; he didn't care how many old boats were sailing around. To tell the truth he wouldn't have minded if the whole town went up in flames.

"I'm glad I'm not going back," said Deirdre. "I don't need this kind of scene no matter how much I would've made in tips. When we get back I'm locking all the doors and fixing *myself* a drink!"

And that's exactly what she did, locking both bolts fast and pouring herself a big glass of Southern Comfort with ice. Ivan and Kevin decided on chocolate milk.

Didi had turned up the radio and the three of them were doing the twist on the rug when a loud knock made them freeze, hor-rorstricken, and Didi jumped for the radio and shut it off. The same knock again. They just stood there in their bare feet on the rug look-ing at each other. They didn't know anyone who on any night would come and knock on their door. Mrs. Carroll would shout Halooo! and Kevin's mom would just walk right in. Or if the door was locked, she'd yell something anyway. And Didi never had brought a boyfriend here, though Kevin knew she had them sometimes. But then she always went to the guy's house and was home by first thing in the morning.

So Kevin knew exactly who it was; it alarmed him that he could do to them what they had done to him—find them unexpectedly at their own house.

Deirdre, grim-faced, walked down the hall.

The sound of the knob being tried. "Deirdre, open the damn door please." A tired almost frantic sounding Nick Ford.

"Fuck no," said Deirdre.

"Look. I just lost hundreds of thousands of dollars; can't you spare me a minute and a drink at least? I'd like to save my emotion-al life anyway, if I can." Kevin felt his forehead breaking into a tiny beaded sweat. He knew this scene way too well. He ran to the kitchen, put his hand on the phone, ready to call 911.

"How do you know where I live?" said Deirdre.

"Looked it up in the phone book. Do I have to stand out here talking on the street like a criminal? If you'll just let me in I'll tell you the whole story. I'd no intention of hiding anything, Deirdre." Ivan was rummaging through the kitchen drawer now for a butcher knife or something, but all he could find was the percolator on the counter. He had it in his hand looking down the hall, fierce and uncertain.

"Deirdre. I didn't do what you think I did. Won't you just let me explain the whole story? The lowest criminal has that right in this country, does he not?"

"Put that down," said Deirdre, looking over her shoulder to Ivan in the kitchen doorway with the silver pot in his fist. "I'm going to go ahead and let him in. One condition," she says through the door to Nick, "If I ask you to leave, your promise, you'll leave, no questions."

"My word of honor," said Nick.

Kevin's sister inched back the bolt uncertainly. He was wearing his gray hat even though it didn't match the suit and his shirt front was open and it wasn't white anymore, it was gray and sweaty and there was a streak of soot across his cheek.

"May I come in?" he said, his face a self-mocking smile.

"Are the cops after you or anything?" said Deirdre suspiciously. He stared at her, dumfounded for a second then burst into an almost crying sort of laughter.

"Noo. No," he said when he got the better of his hysterics, "not me. But I sent their asses out to find him and his little band of politicos and to hold them tight if they catch them. I told them they could reach me at this number; hope you don't mind."

"Mind?" said Deirdre, furious. "Why should I mind? Did I ever happen to give you my phone number?"

"Well, no actually I had to look it up. Sorry. I just wanted them to be able to reach me. They don't know whose number it is if you're worried about that for some reason." Kevin didn't like the way Nick looked at Deirdre then, as if he might suspect that she was a criminal."

"Whatever," said Deirdre and walked away from the open door; leaving Nick there to decide on his own whether he should come in or not now. Nick didn't look like he was planning to kill any of them right away anyway.

"Do you two mind if I come in?" Nick said to Kevin and Ivan in the kitchen doorway, mock polite, threat in his eyes the moment Didi's back was turned.

"Whatever," Kevin answered for them both, turning and pretending to be doing something important in the kitchen, to still be close to the phone, and the knives and things. Ivan just glowered. It wasn't okay with him at all.

"It's not my house," said Ivan.

"It'll be all right, guys," said Deirdre. "I've got it under control."

"I'm not a monster, boys. No matter what you've heard. In fact, I'm proud to say, I've never committed an act of violence against another human being in my entire life. Unlike some old acquaintances of mine."

Deirdre snorted. "I suppose those fishermen burned your harbor down because you were such a nice guy." Nick swelled purple red, paled again a second after.

"Legitimate business is not violence."

"Could've fooled me."

"Maybe we could save our political differences for another time."

"Your dog bit me," said Ivan.

"That, as you know, was an accident," said Nick, losing his temper. "Had you not been trespassing on my land..." He took off his hat, midsentence, a still sort of stunned look on his face, threw it on the coffee table and just flopped down in the big plaid chair. Didi's chair.

"Could I trouble you for a drink?"

Didi laughed at him. "Do you know who did it?"

"Do you?"

"Could've been any one."

"Oh no," said Nick distractedly. "Only one. I know who did it. Tom Tock did it and no one else."

"The coffee cart guy?"

"The same. My father had a share in his father's fishingboat. He grew up in one of my father's apartments. We've had, differences."

Kevin grabbed Ivan's arm like his life depended on it (he still wasn't entirely sure it didn't). Ivan looked back at him seriously, showing Kevin he had no intention of revealing their connection to Tock. Nick seemed to be thinking, paid them no attention.

"Southern Comfort," said Nick absently. "That's your drink. However you like to make it."

"I don't like to make it," said Deirdre, losing just a little bit of her cool, but he didn't seem to notice that either. "That's why I buy it. It comes sweet in the bottle." She dropped the bottle into his lap. He was able to catch it just before it hit home.

"I don't suppose I could trouble you for a shower?" he said. He smelled thickly of burnt tar and sweat, looked at her hopefully, angrily.

"You've got a lot of fucking nerve," said Deirdre, showing her back teeth in a dangerous smile. "If you've got something to say about what you've been doing to Kate, then say it or get the fuck out."

"My cousin's daughter..." said Nick, looking at Kevin and Ivan now, a dull gleam in his eye. He stood up over all of them. Deirdre sat down farthest away from him on the couch. She crossed her legs tight because she was wearing a really short skirt still from the bar. "...has a complicated history. Her mother spent some time in an institution starting right about her age, eight years as a matter of fact. I have consulted with the family doctor. Unfortunately, he believes that recent signs indicate the same seems to be happening to Katharine." Didi frowned, but didn't look up at Nick. "Seems to first present with the stress of early puberty: delusions, outbursts of violence, paranoia." She looked at Kevin and Ivan with an I-don't-believe-him look. "The good news is, in Carol's case at least, with the help of proper care, she completely recovered herself at eighteen and has had a completely normal and fulfilling adulthood." He paused, looking back and forth coolly from Didi on the couch to Kevin and Ivan in the kitchen doorway, his tone had been the certain calm of a seasoned official; now his tone turned more confidential. "I don't tell you this lightly,

Deirdre. In fact I had to convince myself it was necessary." Ivan raised his eyebrows at Kevin like How boring. "What I've said is what you might call a dark Ford family secret. It could be very damaging to Carol and especially to her husband if it became public knowledge. I didn't want to tell your boys for obvious reasons." Liar, liar, thought Kevin, "But it seems they have been reasoning on their own. Kevin, Ivan," he said, his dark eyes on them, filled with secret codes of murder, "you must never, never mention this to Kate, first of all, but also not to Johnny. I have never told him any of this."

Kevin wasn't as stupid as he used to be. He knew it was a lie, that Nick Ford was a liar, that Nick had done the things she said, even if she mixed it up with things like black moss sometimes. But he felt more afraid than ever now; he was beginning to figure out that the truth didn't matter all that much sometimes.

"I think I've said enough, more than enough in front of the boys." His eye felt still full of murder when it brushed across Kevin. "When I realized what you were thinking, I knew I had to speak with you. Don't misunderstand me, Deirdre, I have vices, plenty and plenty, but that I'm glad to say is not among them. I'll tell you more of the story, but maybe you should send the boys to bed now?"

"They can do what they want," said Didi. "Why don't you guys watch the tv or something?" Right, as if they wouldn't listen.

Refusing to put more than half their backs to the enemy, they sat sideways on the carpet and turned the tv on, low volume: some weird stupid late night science fiction movie that was totally fake.

Nick leaned out from the plaid chair to talk just into Didi's ear. But Didi stayed away at the far end of the couch, not leaning back at all. So Nick had to speak loud enough for them to hear everything anyway. They weren't even pretending to pay attention to the movie. "I was a young man, just out of college when my father died. Provided for, useless. I spent all my free time hanging out at the dragboats, with Tock and the boys, smoking pot and talking big stupid ideas. We all thought we were very radical. I must have been about your age."

"This sure is a dumb movie," said Kevin.

"Totally," said Ivan.

Kevin had never really thought about an age difference between Nick and his sister, but now he realized it was obviously tremendous. Maybe it was because Nick, however creepy the message, mostly meant something when he spoke to you, like Didi, not like most adults who spoke like they thought you were a moron.

Nick tried to lower his voice and lean closer, but Didi wasn't buying. "A young lady sort of camping out down there with the fishermen wound up pregnant with what would become my son."

Johnny.

"Carol had just gotten released from the institution then. She'd met an ambitious young man in New York. To make a long story short, I invited them out here and gave them the Carriage House. They agreed to raise my child along with theirs. She was pregnant too."

Kate.

"What happened to the mother?" said Didi in a perfectly loud voice, so Kevin and Ivan started to giggle.

"That was a funny part," said Ivan to the tv screen.

"Totally," said Kevin. They could feel the threat of Nick scowling down on them. They both kept their eyes on the screen. This slimy thing like jello was spilling through the vents of a movie theater and everybody was screaming.

Nick's voice was clipped and defensive, "She was a heroin addict, lost, wanted to kill herself, lacked the nerve. Hopeless. Half crazy."

"Well?" said Deirdre.

"She's provided for, for life. She's in California in a treatment center."

"Convenient," said Didi.

Nick raised his voice to a shout, "I'm not telling you all this so you can laugh at me, you know." Then the voice lowered again to its low, hoarse, confidential whisper, "Deirdre. When you walked home with me the other night. The first one, closing the bar, I swear I didn't think we were talking about the Harrigans for any reason but that it was our only common reference. I left myself out of their story. It was too soon."

"You never laid a finger on Kate?"

"Never. I swear. I tried to be a favorite uncle to her and Johnny equally. I won't deny she was my favorite, even though Johnny's my blood. She's got talent. Unruly talent. You should read her journals sometime if she'll let you. I want to say, don't hold this against Carol either. She's had a very difficult life. As petty and superficial as she must appear to you, there's a girl just like her daughter in that woman's heart. I believe she's done her honest best with a very difficult situation. I only hope the girl doesn't have to go through what she's been through."

"Her name is Kate," said Deirdre in a low, dangerous voice. But, to Kevin's surprise it was Nick's, not her voice that exploded. All of a sudden he stood up from the chair to loom huge above all of them.

"Don't you think I know that?" he shouted. "I named her

myself!"

Kevin could feel the heat from Ivan's fury beside him. Ivan just kept staring at Nick, who'd sat back down and was staring at the rug. Ivan was trying to bore a hole through the top of Nick's head with his eyes. Maybe Nick could feel it because he looked up then and stared straight back into Ivan's eyes. And Ivan kept right on staring back, saying with his eyes that he knew exactly what Nick did to Kate from more than words.

Kevin thought again of Ivan and Kate on the path; how strange it was, like they were in a play and not themselves. I know, said Ivan's eyes, So don't try to change it. And Nick's eyes said back, You think you do, but if you cross me there'll be trouble. Kevin felt frightened for Ivan because Ivan didn't seem to be frightened for himself. But the only thing Kevin could do was help his friend stare so there was two against one. Nick had to move his eyes back and forth between them. There was sweat on Nick Ford's forehead. Kevin pretended he was saying through his eyes that him and Ivan and Kate were all one person and they could change from one into the other just like he could. They could be anywhere, too, waiting for him. Kevin felt for a second like he was Kate. At that moment Nick Ford looked afraid of him and looked away.

"I'm not afraid of you," Ivan shouted suddenly so some of his spit even hit Nick right in the face. "My dad used to lie all the time too and say I fell down the stairs or something." Nick's eyes flashed and he stood up full height.

"Leave!" said Deirdre in a low voice. "I'll call the fucking police if you don't." Nick's face turned instantly sad.

"I'm sorry," he said. Sat back down. "I lost my temper. I'm losing my temper with a ten-year-old. You've got to understand it's been a very long night for me. It began with an endorsement of Bill Gunn, a political monster I more or less created. I don't really approve of his ideas, you know," he laughed. "If you want me to go, Deirdre. I'll go."

"Go."

"Do you believe me when I say I never laid a finger on Kate?"

"I don't know," said Deirdre. "Just go, okay?"

"I care what you think, Deirdre."

"Right. Whatever. Just go."

"I apologize to Ivan. Ivan, listen to me. I'm not blaming Kate for what she's invented or for anything else she's told you. And Kate wasn't lying to you; that's not it. It's difficult to understand, but you're a sharp kid. What she told you is true for her. That doesn't always mean it's what actually happened in reality. Do you see?" Ivan was silent. Furious.

"If you want me to go, Deirdre, I'll go. But if I could just have a few minutes alone to tell you more. More about myself, I feel it would help."

Deirdre, her face turning red, "I know enough about little girls to know that something happened to Kate. I may not know what happened exactly but I, of all people, know that something did."

"Maybe so," he said thoughtfully. "If so, it wasn't me." He glanced at the coffee pot Ivan had left on the counter, "Might I..."

Kevin understood that Nick had no intention of leaving even though he was pretending like he did. They were all like that. Kevin looked nervously at the phone, which was all the way on the other-side of the kitchen. He could never make it without Nick pulling out the cord.

"I'm only here because I care what you think, Deirdre. That's the only reason. I won't say that twice. When you showed up at that stupid party of Carol's, I knew." Kevin wanted to gag. "Send the boys to bed and I'll tell you the whole story. Tock, Carol, Johnny's mother, everything..."

"Get out of my house," said Deirdre.

Nick's voice went cold. "You're making a mistake." He gave Ivan and Kevin quick death stares. "You're all making a mistake."

"I've made mistakes before," said Deirdre. "Now get out."

His throat was choked and swelling. Slowly he picked up his hat. "I'll hold you to concealing what I've told you about the family, and to assuring me that they say nothing of it to anyone. Shouldn't be a problem since you don't seem to believe me anyway." He smiled thinly. "Maybe you'll reconsider," he said, eyes furiously on the floor.

Slow heavy steps down the hallway and the door was shut at last.

The windows outside the livingroom lamps were growing gray and sheer. But Kevin and Ivan were both wide awake and staring at Deirdre as she collapsed into the plaid chair where he'd been sitting, with her head in her hands.

She hit her head with the butt of her fist. Kevin thought of Johnny making that same exact gesture.

from Kate's diary,
July Fifth, 1976:


*He won't scare me anymore ever. Because I don't care anymore what happens. He lied on me again. He said Be a good girl or I'll send you away. But I didn't tell anyone anything since then and he's downstairs again anyways talking to my parents about this school where my mom went when she was my age. He's going to send me away anyways to a school in the summertime where he'll be alone with me whenever he wants to.*

*Now I know for sure It doesn't matter if I do what he says because he keeps coming back anyways. So I don't care anymore if he comes up here and puts his whole arm in me so I split in two I won't be scared anymore. I don't care. I hate him. I'm going to get him back.*

*1. Find something he's scared of*
*2. Get him back with it.*

*I'm going to hurt him till he leaves me alone forever. I don't care if it takes my whole life. I'm going to get him back.*

# CHAPTER SIXTEEN

Kevin and Ivan crouched, one behind each Garden Street pillar of the path, and waited for Mr. and Mrs. Harrigan to leave the Carriage House for the morning. Kevin noticed Ivan's eyes drooping shut now and again. It had been hard to get up after going to bed so late. Kevin felt like a big electric fan was vibrating through him and his eyes felt full of vinegar. The morning air wasn't fresh and exhilarating either like it was supposed to be, like it used to be. It smelled rancid still from Nick Ford breathing it first. Even the trees felt sick.

By the time the sun was fully lighting up the drooping tree leaves, Mr. Harrigan left for work, snapping shut the door of his sportscar and running over imaginary children in his hurry.

It was a long time after that, though, before they saw Mrs. Harrigan. She walked hesitantly out a few steps onto the porch and stopped, staring at the large key ring in her hand. For half a second Kevin thought it was the maid or something. She wore dungarees and a baggy blue sweatshirt, blond hair hanging down dead straight.

"Remember what Nick Ford said about her?" whispered Ivan, peering. "I've been thinking she's a real jerk, but if Nick wasn't lying maybe she's just had a tough time is all." Mrs. Harrigan did look a little like Kate at the moment, Kevin's eyes were better than Ivan's though neither of them saw all that well really. Kevin knew it wasn't Kate of course by the way the round breast shapes lifted the front of her sweatshirt and by her size. But still, even though he knew it was Mrs. Harrigan he also had to think twice about his opinion of her when, instead of marching straight up to the station wagon, she sat plop down on the top step and leaned her head into her hand, exactly like something Kate might do if she were sad; then she looked back over her shoulder through the still open front door and up the stairs. Then she crossed her arms over her lap and bent way forward like she had a stomach ache. Then she sprung fast again to her feet even though no one called her or anything. The other Mrs. Harrigan had taken over again, Kevin could see it in the clipped movements as she turned back to the open door and called up the stairs in a shrill voice,

"I'll be back before one to take you to the doctor." She turned away from the house, starting to shut the door behind her, when she stopped again with it still halfway open. "I'm trusting you," she shouted. She stopped, looking quickly around her, realizing the whole neighborhood could hear maybe, but she couldn't find anyone looking, because Kevin and Ivan were hidden, "If you need anything while I'm out," she said, "Call your uncle Nick. The number's by the phone." She shut the front door but still kept facing it for a second more, just holding the handle; then she locked two bolts with two separate keys and hurried down the steps to the stationwagon.

The side door was locked too. And the back door by the pool. But the window next to it was open and Ivan deftly popped out the screen with his pocket knife. He then Kevin hopped inside and he replaced it undamaged.

Kevin found himself in a large wood paneled room where he'd never been before. A skinny, expensive looking stereo was still illuminated and soft orchestra music was coming out of the speakers so he was scared for a second that an adult was still there after all. But then he figured someone had just forgotten to turn it off because it was playing so low. So he relaxed enough to look around: a big leather chair and a television set and a whole wall of framed photographs, mostly of Mr. Harrigan shaking hands with other men in suits and half the time with an American flag behind them.

The largest and most centrally displayed of these was of Mr. Harrigan and an old man with totally black shiny hair in front of a big blue banner which you could only read part of "...in '76 for a new America." It was signed 'Best wishes Jason' and then some sort of crazy signature.

Ivan, though, wasn't at all interested in the photographs; he paced the floor back and forth and kept looking back over his shoulder at Kevin while Kevin was perusing the wall.

"C'mon," said Ivan. "This room gives me the creeps." Kevin thought it was pretty interesting and wanted to look at the bookshelf too, but he shrugged and followed Ivan through a dark, shiny wood-floored dining room that made Kevin's sneakers squeak so Ivan had to turn around and hiss, "Shhh." But by then they were on the carpet of the living room where they had been before, that night of the party when Kevin first realized that Nick liked Deirdre and then they were on the foot of the stairs. Ivan cleared his throat then and called up carefully,

"Kate? Kate, it's us." Ivan could really sound just like a man sometimes; Kevin thought then how deep his voice was for a kid. But maybe he was just still so secretly impressed from the handy way Ivan had popped open the window screen. There was no answer. At least there was no one else in the house.

"Kate?" called Ivan a little more forcefully, moving half way up the stairs this time. Then they heard the unmistakably quiet sound of a doorknob clicking shut. Kevin was right on Ivan's heels going up the stairs so they saw its top corner too, at the far end of the hallway, closing. When they got to the door, though, Kevin felt uncertain what to do next.

"Kate?" Ivan said, starting to open the door.

"I'm sick," pleaded a thin strange voice. "You can't come in."

"But it's us," said Kevin, "Me and Ivan." and Ivan swung open the door.

Kate was just a huge pair of eyes above the silk hem of her gray blanket. She flipped it down like a cloud and beamed.

"Hey," she said. But behind the smile she looked terrible, thin and sick-looking and red lines still from the pillow.

"What's the matter with you?" Kevin asked.

"Nothing. I've just been in bed too long. They make me stay in bed so I don't get anxiety attacks. But having to stay in bed in the summertime makes me more nervous than anything. My mother's coming back after lunch to take me back to the doctor, but it's the kind that makes you sit in a chair and talk. I'm supposed to not get upset. I'm not sick but they want me to be. And I still feel terrible. I feel like I'm suffocating." She sat straight up in the bed and threw back the covers all the way so she was just sitting there cross-legged in her long blue nightgown. "You guys, I've got to get out of here."

"It's pretty beautiful outside today," Kevin suggested. He was lying in a way. As much to himself as to Kate. It looked beautiful enough: Blue sky and everything. But it didn't feel right. Kind of flat or something

"Is it?" said Kate, but she was looking with her eyes at Ivan and Ivan's eyes were looking back into hers. "I thought you were him again," she said. "Then I heard Kevin and knew you weren't."

"Are you still grounded?" said Kevin.

"I think so," she said. "It's hard to tell. They want to make me go to a summer school now when I get better."

"Didi knows everything," Kevin said. "She doesn't believe what Nick Ford says."

"What did he say?" Kate whispered, like she was afraid of her own voice.

"He says you made it all up in your head," said Ivan angrily.

"Oh."

Ivan pushed his hair back behind his ears even though it was already there, "He was lying. I could tell."

"I don't know," said Kate. "I can't remember what happened very good anymore; everything keeps changing." She pulled up the covers again over her head even and bunched herself into a little ball, "maybe I should just stay here," said her voice, muffled through the blanket, "because what if there really is something wrong with me like my mom says?"

"It's beautiful out," said Kevin. "It really is."

"He was lying about it," said Ivan. "I could tell."

"Really?" said Kate, peaking back out a little.

"Didi thinks so," said Kevin. "She wants you to come and stay with us." Of course, Kevin realized, she hadn't said that in so many words, but he felt sure she'd back him up if it came down to it.

"She does?" said Kate, pulling down the cover a little farther.

"She kind of sent us to come get you," said Kevin.

Kate's frown was gone, "I'll get some stuff," she said, "Let's go."

When Kate had dressed, each of the three of them carried a bag down the stairs; they were half way out the door and Kate stopped.

"I can't."

"Can't what?" said Ivan.

"You don't understand. I can't just leave without saying good-bye. My mom will lose it. She'll think I went crazy and died."

"So what?" said Ivan, "They're gonna send you away anyhow."

"I'm not like you," she snapped. "I don't hate my parents. They never tried to hurt me at all."

"Fine," said Ivan. Kevin could tell he was hurt. Kate looked like she was considering again whether to go back up to bed.

Ivan marched noisily into the kitchen where there was a pen and a notepad by the phone, came back and shoved it into her hands. "Write a note. C'mon Kev." He grabbed Kevin's arm.

"But..."

"C'mon!" There was no arguing with Ivan in a mood like this.

"But Kate?" said Kevin.

"Fine," said Kate grabbing the pad, leaving the bags in the hall and storming into the kitchen, throwing herself into a chair and ignoring them. There was no arguing with her either.

"She'll come," said Ivan once they had crossed the street and were back behind the pillars of the path. Kevin thought maybe that Ivan had been trying to make her mad on purpose so she would. Like Kevin upstairs, making up that Deirdre had invited her to come live with them, just to make it feel more sure. Kevin felt sure Deirdre would want her to stay once she understood the situation. Still, he was putting himself in a tricky situation. But it was just a matter of timing. Deirdre would have left for work by the time they got back; then Kate could be already settled in. Maybe he could go over to the bar then, it was a slow night, and explain the situation with Deirdre who'd understand of course.

Kate was standing, sweaty, at the head of the path, all three of her bags balanced.

"So let's go," she said and slung off two, handing one to each of them.

In the full light of the morning outside though, Kate looked even thinner than she did inside, and Kevin started to worry that she might really be sick and need to stay in bed and that maybe he and Ivan were doing something dangerous by talking her into going outside. Then he thought that was ridiculous, because it was summertime and it was warmer outside than inside anyway. And at night Deirdre's would be just as good as the stuffy, dark Carriage House. So he kept his concern to himself as the three of them, each with one of Kate's bags, stepped into the shade of the path.

"It's so beautiful," said Kate looking at the leaves and tree trunks all around her like she hadn't been outside for a thousand years. "I feel like it's the first day of summer all over again."

Kevin added glumly to himself, 'and full of sweaty liars,' but he looked at Kate and faked a smile.

"I've got three dollars," she said taking off her shoes and putting them in the pack, "that's a whole dollar each." Kevin and Ivan took off their sneakers too and put them in the pack with Kate's. "Let's go to Tock's," she shouted and started to run.

It seemed like years since Kevin had seen Kate, her hair galloping behind her with her speed. But really it had been less than a week. She stopped at the other end of the path to re-sling the daypack to the other shoulder and to let them catch up with her. Then she picked up a stick off the ground and ran it along the tree trunks like they were a giant picket fence. If she was sick before maybe, Kevin could tell she was better now; her face was bright red.

"I'm sick and tired of them," she said. "My mom is the worst. She treats me like I'm some kind of lightbulb, or an egg or something now. She keeps looking at me with these eyes." Kate made a circle gesture with her two hands, "and says, 'I understand what you're going through.' Yeah right. And that's not the worst because this morning they both came into my bedroom to tell me about this stupid sleepaway summerschool like they were giving me a birthday present or something. It's on an island somewhere way out past the end of the harbor so you can't leave." Then she suddenly changed the subject, "what've you guys been doing since I've been grounded? And what about Johnny?"

Kevin didn't know where to begin and neither, he noticed, did Ivan. But their faces must have looked pretty sneaky and guilty because all of the sudden Kate burst out laughing.

"It wasn't fair for you guys to be getting in trouble without me. Now you have to tell me all about everything I missed, but first," she said, a huge grin growing, "you've got to catch me," the words trailed away as she took off full speed towards Tock's, all three of them now running as hard as they could. The sound of their slapping bare feet was everywhere.

Ivan was in the lead at first; then Kevin; then Kate; then Kevin again. Kate, Kevin until finally both of them stopped around the middle of Killdeer to let Ivan catch up.

"I had the heaviest bag," Ivan gasped. He was red-faced and sweaty and funny looking.

"Bull," said Kate. "There's nothing in there but clothes. I have all the books."

They walked now or wove rather, roughly along the middle of the street flushed and breathing, so the leaves above them were alive with it. A gusty wind was blowing from the sea. The same street, the same summer, the same Tock's candy stand waiting at the end, but nothing was the same. Kevin knew he lingered behind the others now because he was afraid to find Tock patiently waiting there, even though he thought it unlikely after the events of last night. But why go if the candy stand was empty? And maybe now was the time to let Kate know that it probably would be. And what if it wasn't? Tock waited there in Kevin's mind with a hot knife in his hand. Not that Kevin was afraid of him exactly, sensing that he had no desire to hurt Kevin particularly. Rather it was what Tock was trying to tell Kevin particularly that frightened him: How ugly it all was. He wanted to put the meeting off as long as he could manage. But, "Come and see me," was what Tock had said, and Kevin had agreed he would.

Farther and farther ahead, Ivan and Kate talked quietly between themselves. In the growing distance Kevin thought he saw a blurry gray thing floating, an almost shape that remained whether he closed or opened his eyes. Whenever it tried to approach him, he slowed down even more so it would keep its distance. Until Kevin considered just turning back on his own and returning alone to the safety of Deirdre; he knew she was home on the couch waiting for him too. But he soon forgot about that idea and started to wonder about what Kate and Ivan might be talking about now that he was out of hearing. They seemed to be leaning into one another as they walked and talked. Probably Ivan was just filling Kate in on all the adventures they'd had while she was grounded. But maybe not. Maybe, if he caught up to them now, they might look at him with that look like he was interrupting what he didn't understand again. But his worry vanished instantly when Ivan turned around suddenly and yelled back,

"Hey c'mon Kevin. Hurry up!" And all his worries about Tock vanished too as he trotted up to join them again.

Kate was laughing at it all. "A lots been happening without me," she said half angrily.

"Now it's all three of us again," said Kevin. "I'm the brains of course."

"Bull," Kate said, "I'm the brains, you're the booger."

*Dear Mom*

*As you might have noticed I'm not here anymore. I am not crazy or dead but rather have decided to go to Deirdre's for a while who invited me because I'm not understood here anymore and you think there's something wrong with me and  there isn't and that's wrong for you to think so when it was Nick Ford who did it not me.*

*So long as you believe him and not me I'm not coming back. Tell Dad that I'm sorry too. But what am I supposed to do? Why won't you just listen to me and not make me go away to school just because you did? I'm not going to any crazy school to get better because I'm fine and that's final.*

*Your daughter,*

*Katharine Harrigan*

*P.S. If you try to make me go I'll run away and won't come back.*

# CHAPTER SEVENTEEN

They crossed Estate Road and onto the chained off part of Killdeer. Kevin almost thought he saw Tock's hulking figure in the candy stand but really it was all closed and locked up.

"I guess I knew he wouldn't be open," said Kevin

"Well why didn't you say so before we ran all the way over here," said Kate crossing her arms in mild exasperation.

"We could go down on the sea wall," Kevin suggested.

"All right," said Kate, "but I really wanted some candy, you know."

"I forgot all about the fire," said Ivan.

"What fire?" said Kate.

"Boy you've really been out of it if you didn't hear about that," said Ivan jumping up onto the fence and starting to work his way around, then he froze half way, looking down and then giving Kevin and Kate a quick glance, "There's someone down there." Kevin peered over the wall and saw Tock working his way up the rocks towards them.

"Kevin," shouted Tock, "I thought you guys might show up here after a while. C'mon down. An excellent hideout, by the way. Hope you don't mind if I've borrowed it for a while." Tock was wearing a big green army coat without a shirt underneath and had a cup of coffee in his hand. There was little choice now but to climb down; he was just Tock after all. When they did they saw he'd made a nice little set up in the caves of the rocks a little further down and out of sight. With a fishing line cast out and a sleeping bag under a canvas tarp tied fast with rope to block the wind and a little cook stove, which was still boiling water. Another man was sitting there too, Kevin now noticed, a little further down the shore with another big fishing rod cast into the water. Even from here Kevin could tell the man was fat and bearded: Kevin knew who it was.

"How's it going?" said Kevin just because he couldn't think of anything else to say.

"It's been better and it could be worse," said Tock mysteriously. "Things got a little hot last night down at the harbor where I been staying. Now the whole place is just swarming with police and reporters asking questions. I'm not real fond of questions, so that's

why I'm here for a while," he said, and laughed. "Just keeping out of
sight for a while, you know? The way you guys like to sometimes."
Kate and Ivan were staring at the other man who had put down his
rod and turned towards them. "Oh that's just my old friend Concho,
he'll keep your secret just as good as me. Won't he Kevin?" A light in
his eye.

Kevin had been trying to forget about what had happened in
the drag boat, but the sight of Concho made it all come flooding back.
He felt sick and his arm started to hurt again.

"I know what you mean about having a secret place," said Kate.
"It's okay with us if you want to use our place for a while, don't you
think?" she asked Kevin and Ivan.

"Yeah, sure," said Ivan. Kevin wanted to agree, but he couldn't
get any words out. He didn't want to not look at Tock, which was
what his eyes were telling him to do; so he stared at him instead,
which wasn't exactly what he wanted to do either, but it was the best
he could manage under the circumstances. He felt like it was turning
out to be a hard stare, which wasn't exactly how he felt or anything,
so he decided he'd better try to put a smile on it, even though his eyes
just seemed to have to stay the same way or else they'd just go
straight down to the ground where they wanted to be. The resulting
expression made Kevin feel foolish, like he was standing there naked,
and that got him mad so he blurted out,

"You lit the harbor on fire didn't you?"

Kate's jaw dropped. Tock raised his eyebrows in a funny way.
Concho sauntered up; he was half a head taller than Tock even, and
half a width wider.

"Hey, Kevin."

Kate looked at the big strange Concho, took one look at Kevin's
expression and hunched her shoulders up like a turtle. Ivan looked
uneasy too.

"He's an old friend," said Tock. "Since we were kids. You can
trust him. Just came to bring me a few odds and ends for my camp."
Concho put his hands to his heart and smiled such a goofy smile that
both Kate and Ivan had to laugh.

"You're a smart kid," said Tock to Kevin. "You think and do at
the same time. I like that about you. It's a risky business though.
That's how you wind up in tricky situations."

"Like what?" said Kevin, falling back to a confrontational tone.

"Like I don't know. Like fires on dragboats maybe."

"So it's true then isn't it?" said Ivan. "You did it to get Nick, just
like he said."

"The fire's true all right," said Tock. "Just go down to the harbor: All those burnt out company boats and counting houses on the jetty, it's a damn shame." He pulled out his knife and thumbed it over his knuckles and back into his pocket. Kevin felt dizzy and sick all of the sudden and wished he'd gone straight back to Deirdre's like he'd wanted. "But how it happened now," Tock went on casually as if the knife had never been there at all, "now that's another story. I might tell you one thing, and somebody else might tell you different. They say you're supposed to let the judge decide, but I'm not so sure. The judge has his own story too, now doesn't he? I know he does, because I've known him since I was one and he was born. It's like I was telling you, Kevin. We've all got our own stories, just like we've all got our own knives. That's what a fisherman knows." He half winked at Concho when he said it.

"Was he always evil inside?" said Kate, looking Tock straight in the eyes. "Do you know about that ?"

Tock looked at Concho and Concho looked him back. They both seemed impressed.

"Evil?" said Tock, his eyes growing round. "That's a big word for a little girl."

"I know what it means."

"Not sure I do," Tock said thoughtfully, "He always had a mean streak all right, sometimes. Not mean exactly, more like a nothing, like a blank, if you see what I mean."

"A shadow," said Kate. "I've seen it." Tock didn't say anything for a while, sat down on a big stone and just stared at her.

"Me I can't see what's not there. Maybe I'm not as deep as you are, honey. I don't like what I can't see. It's always sneaking up and biting you in the back, know what I mean?"

"It comes from his eyeballs," said Kate excitedly, sitting down now on the rock right next to him. That made Kevin nervous. He wanted to sit next to Tock like that himself, but he still didn't trust him; he knew he might do anything.

"Now maybe it does," said Tock putting his hands on his knees and staring down between the rocks. "Never show him your back; I learned that mistake. I'll tell you my story with him, though. How 'bout that?" Kate nodded.

"Nicholas Junior, as he was called in those days, wasn't exactly like he is now. And I didn't know a lot of things in those days. I even kind of liked him up until about when we were fifteen. We used to call him Enjay and I took him on the sly to hang out with the other boys and me."

"That's right," said Concho with a heavy nod.

"You know, mostly Portuguese and Puerto Rican boys from East Bedford, like Concho here." Kevin and Ivan sat down too. Whatever else, Tock had a good storytelling voice.

"His father found out about that, though. Maybe it's a little like your hanging out with Kevin and Ivan here, but even more. Get the picture? Got me in big trouble. We'd like started a little gang over there you know. That's when Nick started to change, when his father got to him. He was always out to fuck me up after that; to fuck all of us up, you know, anybody." Kevin thought of Johnny siding with Nick now. He thought of the knife, and Tock's uncle, and suddenly in a flash he could see Tock too as a curly headed fifth grader and how they would have been friends. "I trusted him. Well, so much for his harbor, eh?"

"Whoosh," said Concho, twirling his fingers.

"This is his cousin's daughter, Concho."

Concho looked at Kate, "What're you talking?"

"Listen what she's saying, ballast brain. Listen how she's saying it. She's not even a teenager yet, Concho. Can't you see what's going on here? Makes me sick."

Kate's eyes were riveted to Tock's.

"You know?" whispered Kate.

"I can guess," said Tock.

Ivan had his chin in his hands like he was listening to a story in the library. So Tock turned to him now.

"Your dad, Ivan, I know him too. Got into our group a little later on, just off the boat from Russia there. Met him just after I got out. Could hardly speak a word of English, but Nick was long gone by then and the gang was more a political thing."

"I think that Nick helped my dad start his politics business," said Kate. "My mom says we owe him everything. She doesn't believe he's evil. But I know. I just was wondering how he got that way. I just thought maybe you would know, but maybe you don't. Maybe he's just that way to me."

"Now you have a story of your own maybe?" said Tock to Kate suddenly.

Kate looked back at him oddly, "But there's always one story that's true, isn't there?"

"Is there?" said Tock. "I don't know." Then he laughed to himself and muttered, "maybe the only way to find out for sure is by lighting a fire under it. Like your friend Kevin here just did, by asking me a question like that one. Isn't that right Kevin? Sometimes, before you

know what something is, it's gotta come right up and burn you first."
This inspired and even longer session of Tock laughing to himself.
They were afraid to interrupt him, so they just sat there until it was
done and he reached into his pocket for a cigarette.

"Yeah," said Kevin sullenly, "I know what you mean."

"I didn't mean nothing," said Tock, lighting it and exhaling.
"Just showing you what it's like to be fucked with. Trust me, it's a lesson for your own good."

"Why should we trust you?" said Ivan, not understanding what
Tock was referring to. "Did you do it or not?"

"What do you care? Trust me because I can help you kids,
that's why, if you're stupid enough to fuck with a guy like Nick Ford.
You don't even know who you're up against. But, as to who did what,
that's hard to say sometimes. Maybe your friend Kevin started the
fire. What do you think about that?" Kevin felt his throat tighten up.
He was just starting to warm to him again and Tock was springing
another trap.

"You're an arsonist," Kevin said. He couldn't believe he said it
and he thought suddenly about bolting for it, with the vague notion
how maybe Kate and Ivan would follow. But maybe they would really think that Kevin did it then. Anyway his legs wouldn't move any
more than he could take his eyes off of Tock's, which were stony and
unreadable like a thousand locked rooms. He wished he could have
just kept his mouth shut for once. Now it was too late and Tock did-
n't say anything, but just sat there curiously observing as Kevin
squirmed.

"I'm not saying you lit the match or anything," Tock said finally, after he'd made Kevin as uncomfortable as possible. "Maybe you
just started a few things in motion that day, when you came on the
*Sierra Madre* with Nick's fat bastard little boy. Maybe you just lit a
match in me, ever think about that? Maybe I saw all over again what
happened to me happening to you. You could go to jail yourself one
day, Kevin. All it takes is someone to narc on you. Maybe I turned
around and burned you with it, before it's too late. Maybe you got me
thinking I been letting things slide too long."

"Hey," Kate shouted, "that fat bastard you're talking about's my
twin brother!"

"Is he?"

"You shut up!" she snapped at Tock, unintimidated. "I think we
should leave now," she said to Kevin and Ivan.

"Hold on one minute," said Tock. "You can't just start something and not finish it. Now Kevin here just accused me of being an

arsonist. They could put a guy away for a long time for something like that. Don't get me wrong, I'm not threatening you. I like you guys, always have; you're my favorite kids in the neighborhood. Even your big fat brother, maybe it's still not too late for him," he said smiling at Kate. But she didn't smile and looked like she was trying to turn him into ashes now with her look instead. "So all I want is a promise because I trust you. I leveled with you, right? Was I talking to you just now like you were a bunch of stupid kids? No, I laid it right on the line about me, fisherman to fisherman. All I need back is your word, your fisherman's word not to narc on me. Deal?"

They all looked at him blankly.

"Narc," he said. "It means, 'to tell:' Don't tell on me, okay?"

Kate and Ivan looked at Kevin until he shrugged.

"Okay, we promise," said Kate for all of them.

"Kevin?" said Tock.

'Yeah, I promise. What do I care anyway."

"'At a boy," said Concho.

"My feelings exactly," said Tock and clapped Kevin on the back, "and you won't tell anyone I'm down here, right?" Kevin nodded. "I can't get enough of this guy," Tock confided to Concho. "And just because I like you so much, I'll give you a promise, how's that? If you ever need something done, and you'll know when you do, just let me know." He was winking again. "And, oh, hey," he said laughing and scooping out something from his pocket, "I know I'm closed for a while, so this one's on me." It was a handful of Atomic Fireballs.

"Thanks," they all said, not knowing what else to say and wanting to be polite. Kate stood looking at Tock, she was standing up on a rock so they were eye to eye.

"You'd help me?" she said.

"I would," said Tock, meeting her eyes and smiling.

Kevin felt weird though, because even as he said Thanks, he didn't know if he was saying it for just the fireballs or for something else.

The day was at its hottest by the time they got back up onto Killdeer, even though the sun was already starting to go down. There didn't seem to be any shadows anywhere, it was so hot and bright still. None of them was wearing any sneakers and Kevin was thankful for the white cement because it was cooler but even that was getting hot on the soles of his feet because of the larger darker rocks embedded in it and he had to carefully avoid the bubbling black shiny liquid seams of tar, and the darker hotter asphalt of Hill Street was still ahead.

"I should put on my sneakers," Kate moaned as she hopped and limped. "I've been inside too long so my feet got all soft again."

"We'll go quick on Hill Street," Ivan said.

"Ouch," it was very, very hot and all the houses and trees around them looked flatter and flatter from so much light.

"I bet it's a hundred degrees."

"No way," said Kevin.

I bet I gave Port Bedford my fever," Kate said. They all giggled.

"We'll make it stay in bed now," said Ivan.

"Then send it away to a special school for towns in the summertime," said Kevin, as a joke, but it didn't come out funny. "Deirdre isn't going to let them," he said quickly. "Last night she told Nick 'over my dead body.'"

"She did?" said Kate.

"Then she kicked him right out of our house." Kevin knew that's not exactly how it happened but he thought it might cheer Kate up if he said it.

"Didi's going to be all of our moms now isn't she?" said Kate and started to whistle some tuneless nothing that sounded so silly that they all laughed.

"So what do you think Tock meant about all that?" said Kevin bringing up the subject that was on all of their minds right now.

"He wants to get even with Nick about something," said Ivan, "and he knows we do too."

"Is that what we want?" said Kevin.

"You know what I go to sleep wishing every night?" said Kate. She spoke in her secret voice that Kevin and Ivan both recognized. They stopped walking. "I go to bed every night wishing that he would die. I don't care if it makes me a bad person." Kevin was stunned. But Ivan was shaking his head,

"Just wishing doesn't do any good at all. That's what I think."

None of them seemed to have an answer to that and they were quiet, hopping carefully down Hill Street and onto the broken pavement of Vale and finally to the warm shade of Kevin's porch: The door was wide open. Kevin's feet were throbbing so he sat down on the porch to rub them and it wasn't until then that he noticed two cars he recognized parked out front. The little beat up one belonged to Ivan's mother and the other, an immaculate white station wagon, could only mean Mrs. Harrigan. He was about to warn Kate and Ivan when his own mother's face suddenly appeared in the doorway.

"You guys are in a lot of trouble," she said.

The front hallway seemed longer than it ever had before. Kevin felt all the heat from the street pouring out of his face. Then, standing behind the couch with her arms crossed, tall white dress, the figure of Mrs. Harrigan stood terribly in the frame of his own kitchen doorway, behind Ivan's mom who was lounging on the couch. Mrs. Harrigans' hair was pulled tight like a helmet on her scalp and her face looked like she was really really late for an appointment.

"Hi Mrs. Harrigan," he mumbled. "Actually my sister says there aren't supposed to be people in the house when she's not here."

"I'm here to pick up my daughter, young man," she said, steely, not even bothering to look at him, her eyes going right over his head and straight down the hallway.

"How'd you find me?" said Kate, guiltily.

"It wasn't hard to figure out from the letter you left," said Mrs. Harrigan. "You missed a very expensive doctor's appointment that we still had to pay for."

"What about what I said?"

Mrs. Harrigan's face turned angry, "We'll discuss that later, Katharine." Kevin could tell from her tone that whatever was in Kate's letter hadn't gone over well.

Familiar fingers appeared on his own shoulders, wrinkled knuckles, a familiar set of rings and that particular shade of short frosty pink nails. Kevin turned around. It'd been more than a month since Kevin had looked into his mother's soft, round worried face, her gray and black long hair banded girlishly still in the loose pony tail she always wore.

"Hon, it's time for you to come home now too," she said. "This all has gone way too far. I forget sometimes that your sister is still just a kid herself, but she's really made a mess of things this time."

"Where's Didi?"

"She's at work, hon, where she should be, not taking days off all the time and getting mixed up in other people's problems."

"But..." Kevin said.

"I've talked to Carl," said Kevin's mother coaxingly, "and he says we can work it out this time." Kevin's heart sunk a thousand feet at the very mention of the name. Carl was his mom's latest boyfriend. He'd never liked any of them much, but that guy in particular was surly and a jerk and not much older than Deirdre even. Kevin hated his guts and had been hoping his mother would have ditched him by now. He hated him ever since the first moment he set eyes on him and the feeling was mutual. And what about Ivan then? he suddenly thought. He couldn't believe it: Ivan's mother was here to take him back too, standing now, tall behind his own mother's face was her familiar, lazy, indifferent long hawkish tough face looking down at Ivan behind him.

"Get your stuff, Ivan," was all she said; then to Kevin, "Hi Kev, how's it going?"

"Hi Judy," said Kevin. He felt sick.

"Are we all ready to stop acting like a bunch of little hoodlums now?" said Mrs. Harrigan. "If it's you children's intention to turn all of your mothers gray with worry, you've certainly been doing a fine job so far. I think that Judy and May will agree?"

"Ivan's a punk," said Ivan's mom. "Always has been and always will be I guess. Who the hell knows where I went wrong." Kevin thought she might be drunk, but it was always hard to tell with Judy because she drank all the time. Kevin noticed what looked like a smile of triumph on Mrs. Harrigan's face and remembered how he himself had forced his way into her house that one time to visit Johnny. Kevin was beaten now, though, and he knew it. Reluctantly, he stepped back out of her way as she walked down the hallway with Ivan's mom behind her and then Kevin's own small mother stopped to hug him so he felt like he would start to cry and his body filled up with prickly heat.

"How've you been hon," she said muffled against his ear.

"Good I guess," mumbled Kevin.

"I've missed you," she said.

"I've been okay," he stammered out, hoping she'd finish hugging him before he collapsed. "I've just been real busy lately." Inside of her arms the whole hallway went black and he couldn't even think anymore of Kate and Ivan seeing their own mothers. He couldn't fight anything anymore it felt like, as his mother's smell, which always reminded him of warm tangerines, surrounded him again.

"It'll be better this time, Kev," she whispered, "I swear."

"I missed you too, mom," he said. When he followed his mom back onto the porch everything was blurry so he couldn't think. Ivan's mom had a friendly hand on Ivan's shoulder now.

"C'mon kiddo," she said, "why don't you get your stuff?"

And Kate's mom wouldn't touch Kate at all, like she still thought she was contagious maybe. She stood there cold and white in the heat over Kate who sat alone now on the porch step staring at the sidewalk.

"You seem to have recovered quite miraculously, Katharine," said Mrs. Harrigan.

They put Kate's bags in the stationwagon like three obedient children. Mrs. Harrigan was talking to Kate in a quick whisper: "Well

I'm glad your feeling better. And now you've had a little time with your friends so you ought to be all taken care of and ready to go. We've packed what you need and your uncle Nick will take you, himself, to the island tomorrow and get you registered..." The only sign of disobedience from Kate was when she kicked a rock with her shoe on the sidewalk then wandered a whole circle around the car before she would get in. And before she would get in she stuck her tongue out at Kevin and Ivan to let them know she was still in good spirits . "Meet me at the mailboat to say goodbye," she said. And then, instead of getting into the front seat she walked halfway around the car again and got into the far back seat instead. She did that deliberately it seemed. Then Kate finally got in like her mother was a taxi driver, but before her mother could pull away she popped her head back out the window and over the roof to talk to Ivan who was standing out on the sidewalk, looking about as forlorn as a boy could look, his tall mother hovering over him like he was a suitcase she didn't exactly know what to do with. "You'll come and say goodbye at the mailboat won't you?" she shouted. Her voice sounded surprisingly cheerful.

"Kate!" her mother finally shouted in exasperation from the driver's seat. But Kate slid her torso farther out the car window and as the stationwagon pulled away she stuck her fist out like Tock.

from Kate's diary,
July Sixth, 1976:


*When Kevin and Ivan told me that Tock
the candyman lit fire to all the fishbuyer docks
and all the fishbuyer boats where Nick makes
his money I couldn't believe it but I was glad.
Then we went to see him and I saw the fire in
his eyes and I laughed with him because fire is
way better than rocks to break a shadow with.
He said to come back and see him and we both
knew he meant Nick. He knew all about Nick
and my mom since before I was born even.
And I felt like dancing because there is someone big to help me now. I'm going to tell him
everything and he's going to tell me too. I don't
care what my mom thinks anymore. I don't
care what Nick does to me now because I'm
smarter and I'll get him back worse.
When Kevin first brought me and
Johnny to see Tock he said he was the most
important person in his whole neighborhood. I
thought he was scary sometimes but I liked*

*him too. And now I know I do because he's scary for Nick and not for me because Nick tricked him or something. And I'm scary for Nick too.*

*And Didi and Ivan and even Kevin though he doesn't understand really. And I didn't even care when my mom came to get me and I put my fist up the way Tock taught Kevin.*

*I'm not scared anymore even though I am because Nick is downstairs talking to my parents again and I'm listening at the top of the stairs.*

*Because he says he'll take me himself to the school. Because he says the captain of the mailboat that goes there is a personal friend. I'm not scared.*

*I don't care. I'll runaway.*

*The sky over the pool was on fire. Red sky in the morning sailor take warning. I had my backpack and the black trunk full of clothes and things from my room to pack in my bag. I put my diary in my backpack because I* didn't care if I never saw the stuff in that trunk. I wished I had a bomb to put in the trunk but I didn't so I put the noose of carpet string instead and locked it up with the Masterlock.

My mom called me down for a big good-bye breakfast and said Your uncle will be here soon.

And I said So? and didn't touch all the food.

And my dad said Eat something Kitty. Not too much because the sea might make you sick but something or you'll feel worse.

I said What do you care? and didn't eat anything anyways.

My dad said I'm sure you'll come to enjoy it in time.

And I said I doubt it.

And my dad put down his paper and shouted Eat your food damnit.

So I ate some.

Nick came in his big car and him and my dad put the big black trunk in the car trunk. I watched them from the kitchen window and Nick put his hand on my dad's shoulder. My mom gave me a pile of envelopes with our address and stamps on them. She kissed the top of my head and said We love you Kate.

I didn't say anything.

The big car door was open for me like a mouth and Nick was inside with his hands on the wheel. I couldn't look at him. I was scared I couldn't help it.

But he liked that I could tell. He thought I was scared of him forever now but I wasn't. I wished Tock would be there to light the mailboat on fire.

He said It's all right get in don't worry.

I got in because I don't care.

The insides of the car were gray and quiet so you couldn't hear anything outside and he didn't say anything until we were almost at the harbor. Then he said I think you'll like my island it's beautiful. I'll make sure they treat you special.

I didn't say anything.

# CHAPTER EIGHTEEN

The mailboat to the islands, which was to deliver Kate to the school, left the ferry dock of Port Bedford usually at around nine in the morning, just after the ferry made it's morning run from the big island, to bring those people and their cars to work in the city, and to transfer what mail there was from the big island to all the little ones that were too small to have cars and so too small to have the ferry too.

Ivan and Kevin promised to meet there at nine tomorrow morning before Kevin would agree to crawl out of the cramped back seat of Judy Otrusky's dirty car. The car whizzed off the several remaining blocks to Ivan's house, leaving Kevin alone with his mother on his old doorstep. His mom made him a nice understanding smile and held his shoulder as she unlocked the door,

"We've missed you around here, bud."

Home. His old angle walled room that used to be the attic, with black light posters he no longer cared for; one in particular that had once been his favorite was curling from the wall with its neglect. It was a brightly colored, gridded square of fluorescent orange and blue drawn to represent a window frame; only, instead of opening onto a landscape or something outside, it closed into a solid empty box. The poster spoke to him in a brand new way, even though he used to look at it a lot in the old days. He felt so dizzy, he sat down in the middle of the floor wishing with all his heart it could just be a cool poster again. It was originally Deirdre's as they all were, from when she was a teenager in this house and used to live in the attic room. When she moved out—a painful day for him, he suddenly remembered—she had bequeathed them to Kevin or more accurately she had discarded them there for him to resuscitate if he wanted, since her tastes had already outgrown them. And he had arranged them after long and painstaking consideration to do them the most honor within the room's inconvenient architecture; it was more the memory of her than the posters themselves: Anything at that time that had once belonged to Deirdre had automatic value for Kevin.

But now, coming back to his old room for the first time in so long, this past remembrance of Deirdre that had been so central in those days filled him with prickles. Why hadn't she been there? Had they forced her to give them up or was it just a convenient excuse for her to have him out of her hair once and for all so she could go back to enjoying her own life again? He didn't hold it against her if that's how it was. He understood how hard it must be with her with boys when her little brother was always hanging around. He knew, because it was just as hard for his mother to have boyfriends when he was there. It was almost like Deirdre and his mom were taking turns with him because he was a bother wherever he was. Kevin wished he could just crawl down into the smelly bottoms of his sneakers and disappear. He sat on his old bed and tried and tried, but he couldn't get any good feelings out of that old room. And his eyes, as he sat cross legged on his bed, listening to his mom preparing dinner in the kitchen, kept fixing on a couple of huge, expensive surf fishing rods, complete with aluminum ground spikes and a big canvas tackle bag piled in the corner. He wished that they were a coming home present for him, but he knew they belonged to his mom's new boyfriend who was just keeping them there because the room had been empty and that way they were out of the way in the small house. Kevin had only really known Carl for a week or so, other than seeing him around from time to time with Kevin's mom. It began on the morning of that first night when his mom had brought Carl home drunk from the bar. But that one week was enough for everybody, and Kevin moved in with his sister on the following Sunday. He never dreamed a piece of trash like Carl could last two years with his mom like he had. Was she planning to marry the guy? Is that why she brought Kevin back? Kevin got more and more worried as he sat there and thought, always with an eye on those fishingrods invading his own and only rightful place in the house, his very own room. She probably couldn't anyway without first getting a divorce from his dad, which she probably couldn't do since they didn't know where he was anyway.

The door slammed, like an answer to Kevin's depressed thoughts, and the raspy voice of Carl hooted from the livingroom below amid the soft bumps of heavy objects dropping. "Honey does that smell good," he whooped. "Got something cookin' for me besides food, little May? I'm in the mood."

"No. Shhh. Kevin's back again. Remember I told you?"

"So? C'mon, May." Kevin heard bumping sounds coming up through the floor. "Do you share your bed with me or him. He's getting a little old now isn't he, May, for that sort of thing?"

"Stop it!" said Kevin's mom.

"I'll stop when I feel like," said Carl, but he must've, because Kevin heard his steps returning to the living room and then the sound of the old tv flicking on and warming up its tubes.

Kevin came down the attic ladder when his mom called him for dinner, past Carl who seemed fully absorbed in the tv and in drinking his beer.

"So how's that hot sister of yours?" said Carl without even taking his eyes off the screen to look at Kevin.

"Shut up," Kevin said.

"C'mon now, kid. Can't we be friends?" said Carl.

"What's for dinner?" said Kevin surly to his mom.

"Frozen pot pies, your favorite right? and salad."

Kevin hadn't liked pot pies that much for a long time, "Mostly mac and cheese is my favorite now."

"That's not true," said his mother. "You know how much you love pot pies." She sounded hurt. "Carl? Are you coming?"

"I'm watching tv," said Carl, as if they didn't know that. "Bring it in here for me May honey, would ya?"

"Carl," Kevin's mom was about to complain when,

"I said I'm watching tv." She just gave Kevin an exasperated complicitous look and brought Carl his meal on a tray. Kevin sort of lost his appetite then: It was happening again already that, despite his best efforts, Kevin was somehow winding up involved as the bad guy between the two of them.

After dinner Kevin said to Carl, "Could you get your fishing rods out of my room?"

"Why, kid?" said Carl. He was a big man with a deeply tanned body and red bulbous nose and blonde curly hair bleached white in places from so much surf fishing.

"Because whatever is in my room is mine; that's why," said Kevin. "So unless you're giving them to me you better put them someplace else."

Carl continued to watch tv, "Don't touch those rigs, kid... Fuckin' Tarkington," he muttered at the football game he was watching. So Kevin climbed back up the ladder and brought both rods down with him in one hand, from which they were stripped before he reached the bottom rung.

"You mother's tit!" shouted Carl, looming over him though Kevin was still three rungs up the ladder—putting one like a priceless heirloom against the wall and still holding the other in his hand and shoving Kevin with it so he fell off the ladder and felt one of the hooks from the big bluefish lure catch his cheek against the tremendous grommet where it was fastened as he fell. In the next instant Carl was pulling the rod away so Kevin wouldn't damage it when he hit the ground. Kevin felt the hook tearing from his face; then, after another second, he hit the carpet and felt like the whole side of his face was wet and on fire. He got up on all fours, watching big drops of blood staining the tan carpet one by one.

"Oh you little shit," said Carl seeing now what had happened. "May," he complained, "this wasn't my fault."

"Oh baby," screamed Kevin's mother running to him. "Just shut up Carl," she said and get me some alcohol and gauze out of the medicine chest, quick. The bleeding stopped after a while, though Kevin kept on crying, to his shame. They decided not to go to the hospital, being uncertain of the cost and, as his mother explained to him, they might end up giving him stitches which would just ruin his pretty face later on. Carl went back to watching football and his mother was trying to clean the stains off the carpet with salt when Kevin finally climbed back up the ladder to his bedroom and closed the door. He lay down his face, tear stained and swollen and burning, good side down on the pillow. The only thing of Carl's left in the room now was his tackle bag. The bag made him angry so Kevin finally got up again and started to rummage through it, carefully unzipping it first and not disturbing the position of anything, until in a pocket on top he found a twenty dollar bill along with a couple of ones. Kevin took the ones and then zipped it back up. He stared hard at the bag again for a while. It shouldn't have been in his room anyway.

Kevin got into bed and turned off the tin cone reading lamp above him. Blue light flowed in then from the one narrow window, because it wasn't even totally dark outside yet. The outside light made all the furniture—the wooden chair, the wicker basket full of outgrown toys, the painted dresser with skewed trackless drawers— appear to be covered in ice. But Kevin and especially the side of his face was sweltering and burning. And the extreme heat of the day was still radiating through the sloping walls of the ceiling from the black tar shingle roof that lay above it. Burning hot and covered in ice; that somehow made his old room familiar. Balling himself up in his single sheet to make himself as small as possible, Kevin fell asleep, the side of his face and the pits of his knees and his shoulders and his elbows all of them sticky with heat.

When he woke up, the light was still blue and he didn't know at first exactly where he was. But he sat up like a shot from the electrocuting sound of his old electric alarmclock and shut it off and then just sat there staring. For a second he thought he was late for school. Then he began to remember a bit of his dream where he'd been looking for some sort of test and hadn't known which schoolroom to go to or if he'd even studied for it. It was a General Facts test and he was supposed to know how many kids got put in jail every year and he was just wandering through all the different classrooms knowing that the time was getting late and trying to figure out where he was supposed to be. Until finally two big policemen that looked like Carl and somebody else, his dad maybe, stopped him and said they knew that it was him who burned down the harbor. After that they made him sit down in a chair, and just then was when he heard the electrocuting sound of the alarm clock.

So now he remembered that it was summer and he didn't have to go to school; he'd just set his alarm so he'd know he had plenty of time to get to the ferry dock to see Kate off before nine. But still Kevin just sat up in bed staring at nothing. There was a yellow and brown oozy spot on his pillow where his cheek had been and his whole face ached now like a bruise. He felt his hair sticking out everywhere and his sheet around his ankles was all twisted and hot. Why was he in his mom's house anyway? Then he heard Carl snoring away downstairs in his mom's room and Kevin suddenly remembered it all. He slipped on his shorts and shirt and shoes and stole out of the house without even trying to look around for some breakfast.

His first stop was the reed cave where he'd left his bike the other day along with Ivan's, which was still there. It was a sort of cloudy morning, he began to see as the sun rose up a little, but thin enough clouds that the whole sky was a uniform soft pink that reflected off the reed stems and made them seem on fire all around him.

Kevin wandered around the neighborhood aimlessly for a while on his bike so, by the time he got to the ferry dock, Kate was already there waiting and the ferry was already in and they were sliding stuff from the ferry down a ramp to the mailboat. The mailboat had a ramp going down to it because it was not as high in the water as either the ferry or the ferry dock. It was an old low-decked ocean going diesel boat that was supposed to have been in World War II or something once.

And the big flat ferry must have just arrived because a line of cars was still driving off of it, rolling off one by one with the people on the big island coming in for work. As Kevin got closer he spotted Nick down on the deck of the mailboat already, talking to a blond man with a big moustache who reminded Kevin too much at that moment of Carl even though he didn't really look that much like him. This guy had a worn red shirt rolled up around the elbows. He was leaning against the big rubber gunwale of the boat, named the *Sharon K.,* as it said on a painted board on the pilot house wall behind him. There was one other guy on the boat loading all the stuff off the ramp and onto the cargo space on the front deck. He was a big fat guy with a black devil's beard and a long black pony tail. None of the big boxes or crates or sacks of mail seemed to phase him, which impressed Kevin as he watched him; so Kevin walked over to the place in the dock right above him where he could watch, since Kevin didn't want Kate to notice the swollen mark on his face if he could avoid it, since it wasn't really all that big and she probably wouldn't if he kept it out of view while he said goodbye. And anyway Ivan had just rolled up on his bike then, coming to a stop right next to Kate and they were already talking. So Kevin addressed the boatman,

"Nice day," he said, swinging his legs over a pylon top quite precariously as the boatman must've noticed because he stood up from stooping for a box and looked straight up at Kevin's wounded face.

"Depends on how you look at it," said the man. Kevin's eyes opened wide. It was Concho again. But this time Kevin was really glad to see him.

"I look at it from up here," said Kevin. "Need help?" Kevin leapt suddenly from the pylon and onto pretty near the edge of the dock.

"Yeah, little hombre. Sure," said Concho, a look of recognition in his eyes now. "Thanks. Slide those two banana boxes down the ramp for me would ya?" which Kevin did, glad to do something. Then Kevin said,

"I have to go see my friend okay? Because she's leaving."

"Go for it," said Concho and started to pick up the banana boxes from the bottom of the ramp.

"Are the Narcs after Tock now?" said Kevin.

"Probably, mijo, probably," Concho laughed.

"You don't think I'm a spy anymore, do you?" asked Kevin nervously.

Concho smiled up at him. "Naw, don't you worry. Tock told me all about it. I'll watch out for your girlfriend for you, don't you worry." He gave a sidelong look at Nick still talking to the blond man up on the foredeck.

Nick Ford stayed where he was and continued talking in a friendly joking way with the blond man who Kevin guessed now was the Captain, since he wasn't lifting anything and Concho was. Though Nick must've seen them both, him and Ivan, by now, he seemed to be willing to let them say whatever they wanted to Kate before she left. There was no Mr. or Mrs. Harrigan anywhere to be seen. And of course there was no Johnny.

"We're leaving in about ten minutes," was all Nick said, like he was the captain himself.

Kate just seemed to be pretending he wasn't there.

"Kevin, c'mere," she said. "What happened to your face anyway?" Ivan looked at him then too.

"Fishing hook," said Kevin.

"Didn't know you had a rod," she said.

"It's Carl's," said Kevin.

"Oh," said Kate. "What say we take it out for a spin tomorrow if it's sunny?"

Kevin laughed, "Yeah, sure. So when's the first vacation?"

"How can I tell?" said Kate. "I thought this was supposed to be vacation." She frowned. "Some vacation."

"Who knows, maybe it'll be like one of those summer camps," he suggested hopefully.

"Yeah," she said, more from politeness.

Kevin paused for a minute to change the subject then said, "You afraid of him?" indicating Nick Ford with the slightest nod of his head.

"I think nothing will happen," said Kate, also with the slightest nod. "He's only going over to get me registered and then he's coming back he said."

"Here. Take this," Kevin blurted out, producing the pearl handled knife from his back pocket under his stretched out shirt. Kevin kept Kate on purpose between him and Nick's line of vision from down on the deck. Nick didn't look like he was looking at them but you could never tell. At least Nick was probably thinking about them, Kevin told himself, and that was something maybe.

"Are you crazy?" said Kate shoving it back towards him. "This all started because of last time I had that knife."

"Take mine," said Ivan who was sitting down nearby. He stood up and slipped it to her real cool from the side. Kate looked both ways nervously before she took it; then like lightning she stuck it down the front of her shorts.

"Thanks," she said and held the back of Ivan's head and whispered so Kevin could still hear, "If it isn't safe there, that's how I'll know I need it."

The men on the boat were waiting for her now.

"The fat guy's okay," Kevin said suddenly though he still wasn't entirely sure about that. "I'd hang around him if I were going on that boat. Look. He's that friend of Tock's you met."

Kate's eyes lit up, "He is?"

Kevin surveyed the big seaworthy boat half enviously. "Tell me what all the islands are like when you get back," he said.

"Me too," said Ivan. "We've never gotten to go out there ever."

"I'll write it in my diary how 'bout?" said Kate; "then I can show you it when I get back."

"Deal," said Ivan.

"Deal," said Kevin. Then she slung on her knapsack and waved goodbye to both of them low and secret, so it was just for the three of them.

Kevin observed with pleasure how, as the ramp was pulled down, Kate stayed right close to the fat boatman, Concho, with the devil's beard, without getting in his way. Even though the man had scared him before, he was at least one of Tock's fishermen. And she stayed away from Nick and the blonde moustached captain in the pilot house.

And Nick finally spoke to Ivan and Kevin from the open window as the boat backed away. Kevin and Ivan were standing together side by side at the end of the ferry dock now with their bikes. The *Sharon K.* was pulling away and Concho ran everywhere around the dock coiling up lines.

"No nonsense now, boys," was what Nick Ford said to them, shaking his finger; then he turned back inside and said something to the captain, which made the captain smile.

Then Kevin and Ivan were alone again watching the boat disappear among pieces of land; they weren't quite sure which was which or where exactly among them Kate would be going.

"She's tough," said Ivan admiringly.

"So," Kevin said like he could still feel the fishhook in his face.

"So, she's tough. It's better than not isn't it? At least you don't get so scared that way."

"Shut up," said Kevin.

Ivan looked at the bruised scab on Kevin's face closely: "No hey," he said, "I wasn't talking anything about you."

Kevin believed him. "I'm not so tough I don't think," said Kevin.

"I pretend sometimes," said Ivan.

Kevin looked in surprise at this confession. He felt this was a rare moment of openness in Ivan and all of a sudden Kevin didn't know what to put in the emptiness he saw suddenly in his friend's face. All Kevin could think of to say was:

"Wanna spend this two dollars I got?"

"Definitely," said Ivan. "That same two dollar bill? Maybe we can use it all over town all day and never spend it."

"It's a different two dollars, I don't care about these at all," he said waving the two dollar bills in the air.

"Sweetshop?" said Ivan.

"Cool. We can check the paper for when the tide's good for getting the raft back."

They pulled up their kickstands and rode off towards town.

from Kate's diary,
July Seventh, 1976:

*Before we left Ivan gave me his knife
and Kevin showed me the deck guy was Tock's
friend Concho so I felt less scared already.*

*The wind was slapping everything which
was all lashed together in the middle of the
deck. A seagull was following us and I watched
it over the side.*

*The mailboat docked at ten different
beautiful islands and some were full of houses
where I wished I could live and little boats
and old smiley men in yellow rubber pants
who I waved at and they sometimes waved
back and smiled like they were my grandfather.
And at every dock the boatman threw down a
big sack of mail and boxes of vegetables for the
grocery store and sometimes someone would
give him another box to take somewheres else.
The captain and Nick just stood talking on the
dock with them while he did all the work. On*

*the third island I asked him if he wanted help
and handed him things if they weren't too
heavy. It took all day.*

*He smiled at me on the deck while Nick
and the captain were at the controls talking
and laughing. He was winding ropes on the
deck. I said Remember me? He glared at me
suspicious, looking over his shoulder until the
captain wasn't watching him anymore. And
then he smiled and shook his head.*

*Nick turned around and saw us talking
and he didn't like it so he came back down to
the deck. And he said Come into the passenger
cabin with me and I will tell you about the
school you're going to.*

*We were all alone in there with the
round lifesavers and the old worn benches and
he said Sit down. And he closed the door.*

*I said What do you want?*

*He said What do I want? I want you to
tell me what it is you want. Why you look at
me always with those eyes.*

*I said What eyes?*

*He said Those eyes and he was leaning over me again.*

*So I shut my eyes.*

*But just then the door bust open and it was the deck guy.*

*Nick stood up super fast turned around and shouted What the hell are you doing in here?*

*And the deck guy said Yo dude I'm the crew. I go wherever.*

*Nick said What do you want?*

*Concho said I want to sit down and he sat on a bench facing me and Nick and crossed his arms and smiled.*

*Nick said Christ and got up and went out back to the control room with the captain.*

*I said Thanks and then I whispered He's trying to kidnap me. Then I told him all about how he and my parents were making me go to the summerschool even though I did good in school.*

*He said Shit. I dropped out when I was sixteen.*

*He went back out and I followed him. Then I saw the island all alone. And he said That's it, last stop. And I knew it was nowhere. There was no where to escape and I started to cry.*

*He said What is it Linda? I don't know why he called me that but I liked it and wished my name was Linda and not Kate.*

*I said I have to talk to Tock he said to, but now I never can because this stupid island is too far away and I might be here forever.*

*And the boatman laughed a weird laugh and said We'll see because Tock wants to talk to you too. He said I'll tell you a secret. Ford and the captain are going sailing. Ford's got his fancy yacht in the harbor here and I'm taking the Sharon K. back on my own. I'll wait a while Linda before I head back to Bedford town. After they leave you come and see me if you want.*

I said I will.

Nick called from the captain's house Kate come up here and look.

I climbed up the ladder and I was happy because I knew I was going back now.

The captain was steering and talking into the radio with a lady on the island. We were coming into the harbor and I could see Nick's big mahogany boat there. There was a clock in the captain room that said it was already four o'clock.

Nick put his arm around my shoulder and it made me shiver but that made him hold me tighter. He said Look. Nomans Island isn't it beautiful?

It was beautiful but it was scary too. Behind the harbor was the biggest house I ever seen and it was just like my house and Nick's mansion only bigger than both of them put together. It sat up a grassy hill speckled with pale flowers and behind it the hill went higher and higher until it was filled with dark woods.

He said This is the heart and home of the Ford
family Kate. It's where we have lived for 350
years. He said My grandfather John Ford
turned it into a school for special girls after the
family moved to Port Bedford and built the
estate where Johnny and I live. And you and
your parents live in the house that was its
entrance at one time.

It felt like he was talking more to the
captain than me though. Then he said my aunt
went to this school and your mother and now
you.

No I wasn't but I kept my mouth shut. I
could see six or seven girls now on the lawn
playing a game of frisbee and I almost wished
for a second I was going to stay because maybe
someone like Dandelion would be there.

A lady who reminded me of Roberta the
circulation librarian met us at the dock and I
could tell by her voice she was the one the captain was talking to on the radio.

Her hair was short and gray and she had

*a blue wool dress and she said her name was
Miss Parks and she was the headmistress of the
Ford school. And she said they were honored to
have me among her girls. And she said she
remembered my mother and a nice room was
waiting for me  and Your uncle will take you
there and make sure you're settled in and that
dinner was at six in the dining hall and I will
introduce you to the other girls then. She said
to Nick You and Captain Percy will be taking
the Sheherazad back to Port Bedford I understand.*

*He said That's right.*

*She said We'll miss her. She adds so
much grace to Nomans Harbor when she's here,
but now we have Katharine to grace us
instead. And she smiled at me and I liked her
smile and smiled back.*

*Concho had tied up the mailboat and
was on the lawn talking with another
Portuguese man who was leaning over a wheel-
barrow full of grass and a rake. They were
laughing and talking in Portuguese talk so*

*nobody could understand what they were say-*
*ing. But he winked at me before I followed*
*Nick and Miss Parks up to the school. There*
*was another Portuguese man with a big cart*
*with my big black trunk in it who followed us.*

*After Nick and Miss Parks filled out*
*some papers in Miss Parks' office Nick said he*
*would show me my room and the Portuguese*
*man followed us down the long clean dark*
*hallways with the big black trunk on his*
*shoulder. We passed by the rooms where the*
*other girls lived and there was a nice girl I met*
*in the hall and she was skinnier than me even*
*and she said You're new here. Hi I'm Karen.*

*I said Hi I'm Kate. I liked her eyes.*

*She said So you're the new prisoner. Nick*
*scowled at her but she just laughed and ran*
*away.*

*Nick unlocked the door. My room had a*
*bed and a fireplace and old green chairs and a*
*desk and the window had diamond shaped*
*window panes and looked out over the whole*
*harbor and out to all the nothing where it was*

*blurry with clouds.*

*The man put down the trunk and Nick handed him some money and said Thank you you can go now.*

*The man said Gracias Mr. Ford and Nick shut the door behind him and locked it.*

*I thought about Ivan's knife in my pants because I knew what was coming next but if I tried that I knew Concho might leave because Nick would be suspicious. So while Nick was unpacking my trunk and had his back turned putting my things into drawers I put Ivan's knife into the open pocket of my purple pack where I could get it if I had to. I didn't care this time and I wasn't scared. Instead I decided to let him do whatever he wanted.*

*The room is beautiful isn't it Kate?*

*I said Yes.*

*Are you happy?*

*I said Yes. He pet my hair with his hand and I could feel his hand shake. I wanted to be sick but I wasn't.*

*The whole time I watched out the win-*

*dow to the nothing and the clouds coming and
thought about the girl Karen's clear eyes.*

*He said You're a good girl Kate before he
left. He looked at me like he was confused I
had let him do what he wanted. He said You're
an unusually bright and passionate girl. He
said The world will be open to you now. I will
teach you. He said Goodbye for now. We need
to set sail before the weather.*

*I could watch from my new window
when the sails went up on the mahogany boat
and it left with the wind out the harbor. The
mailboat was still there and I took just my
backpack and went down to the harbor and
everybody was going inside for dinner and I
ran quick outside where the boatman Concho
was eating with the two other Portuguese men
in front of a small house where they lived by
the harbor. And I started to shiver and I said
Take me back please. And Concho looked at
the other two Portuguese men with a nod and
said Okay Linda come with me.*

# CHAPTER NINETEEN

Rain fell through that gray blue time like wires, blowing and wobbling and threatening in the wind, like they're only pretending to be soft, and taunting in front of your nose, but really they could cut you like a knife  And you knew they could come at you straight like a snake at any second, crack, so your eyes go black and you feel the goo running down over your lip and into your mouth.

It was that time when everything is quiet; Kevin'd just gotten home from getting the raft back with Ivan, but his mom would be home soon and Carl, who acted like it was really his house and everyone else was just staying because he said they could.  And they'd come pull down the shades one by one. And then the smell of fatty meat in the electric fryer, like a boa constrictor while Kevin would stay in his room and pick at dust in the corners.

But the phone rang before they got back and it was Ivan—calling from a phone booth because Kevin could hear the air, and a car going CHHHHHHH on wet pavement. And Ivan said Kevin could never guess who's with him,

"Who?" Kevin said.

"Kate, man. She snuck out of her boarding school and came back on the mailboat, only nobody knows.  She was outside the store when I got back."

"Like she ran away?"

"Right.  You wanna hear?" Then the sound of wind and rain wires in the phone.

And Kate's voice, "Hey, Kev."

"Where in fuck are you guys?" Kevin said.

"What's this place called, Ivan?...The Harbor Deli," she said.

"Okay, I'll be right there."

Then Ivan's voice again, not sure sounding, "Kev?" so Kevin knew he was going to ask for something,

"What?"

"Food. There's none here. You can stay at my place too if you want, but better bring some food, okay, and some sheets or something maybe....My mom's out of town...I don't know where, and the power is off and the phone and everything is shut off.

"Typical Judy. What a jerk," Kevin said, not feeling like keeping the feeling to himself. "You okay?"

"Yeah, it's okay. Some light comes up from the streetlight downstairs.

"I mean where is she?"

"She probably didn't know everything would get shut off because she doesn't keep track of her bills very good. She left a note that said I could stay here or with you, or at Didi's or Aunt Fay's or something, and not to worry about it. She didn't say when she'd be back..." Click... "dimes gone....t us at my house....kay?"

"Okay!" Kevin shouted because they were getting cut off.

"...Food/ TEN CENTS. PLEASE DEPOSIT TEN..."

Kevin slammed down the phone. He was outa there. Got some sleepingbags and a grocery bag with peanut butter and clam chowder and pickles and Kraft mac and cheese and saltines. No way now he was gonna wait for that guy Carl to get here and find out the food is missing.

He knew, before Ivan even called, he couldn't stay. Out.

Until now, he'd been afraid. But now that he knew that Ivan was out there, and Kate was out there too, he had more courage than when it was just him alone. He felt like he could breathe again.

Out. He could feel that heavy wood door slam behind him. And the invisible dark rain kissing his face. Because he had friends and Forget the rest of it.

Things happen in waves. Like everything will be going along, shitty but normal, and then all at once... Didi called them episodes; Kevin figured this was one. She thought they have to do with the moon. But Kevin wasn't sure, he didn't believe in the horoscope on the radio the way she did. With all the lying and twisting and dangerousness now, Kevin wasn't going to believe in anything but his friends. Out.

He felt all electric inside because the rain was really coming down and the paper bag full of food in his hand was turning to brown mush by the time he got past the fire house. A fog horn moaned out there somewhere from the harbor behind, low like a giant clarinet, and it was foggy and warm everywhere even though it was raining. Good thing he didn't bring so much food that he couldn't hold it up with his shirt arms anyway, even though there was no bag left at all. And his pack was pretty waterproof, because he just got it last spring, with money he made selling papers on the corner in the morning.

Kate was standing in the doorway of Ivan's building when Kevin rounded the corner. Kate: Her face looked new like he was seeing her fresh, and comfortable at the same time like, Kate. She had a striped sailor shirt he could tell was bright colored even though he couldn't tell what bright color, because it was all going gray and blue in the twilight. But he saw something else too: She'd changed a lot, even though it'd only been a day. When she turned to go back inside, not seeing him, he could see something new and cold and maybe even a little cruel on her face. Even in the dark. He wondered if you might be able to see the same thing on his face now too. Her blond hair was glowing as furious as her mother's. Kevin followed her up the thin dark stairway to Ivan's mom's apartment. He wanted to say something, but he couldn't move his tongue.

"Hey Kate," and she nearly jumped out of her skin,

"Fuck!" she yelled, and the wet paper bag fell apart in Kevin's arms and all the stuff went clomping down the stairs.

It's not okay to touch her, he thought.

"It's Kevin," he said. She put her arms around him and squeezed so he felt her flat chest hard against his own.

"What is it?" said Ivan running to the door. Seeing Ivan was no big deal, Kevin had just seen him a little more than an hour ago, even though everything was different now. Kevin showed him the torn paper bag, to show what happened. Now it was only a glimmer of brown, like it's the last color they can see before everything washes into black and blue and gray. Then Ivan looked at Kevin and Kate with a blank face and he said, "I better get a flashlight," and they picked up all the food off the stairs and put it inside. Nothing was broken.

The open door to the apartment was like a black box at the top of the stairs.

None of them wanted to go back into the dark place, and Kate said, "Let's go outside where I can see you guys. Let's walk in the rain. It's too dark in there and I don't like it."

Kevin said, "Maybe we can figure out a plan or something."

Ivan said, "I don't like this time of day at all. It makes me feel crummy."

The rain was starting to make puddles and rivers everywhere; the street was shiny black.

They cut through the woods and the empty field over to Ivan's old school building, which was all closed now. None of them said a word. Even though there ought to have been a lot to say. It was like they were all uncomfortable all at once, so they just keep on walking in the rain. Kevin could feel it creeping up his socks and through his belt now. His shoes were wet to the point of squishing. He kept looking at her, the new look never left her face. And Kevin saw it in Ivan now too. Squish, squish through the field. The hollow straws of grass stuck up black like an unshaven man.

They came up over the bare hill to School Street. A spotlight on the other side washed all the red from the bricks of the building and caught them up in the rainlight still falling. And they kept on walking back into the schoolyard to the seesaws and the jungle gym, until Kate stopped at the foot of the hill that went up to the blacktop. It had a chain link fence around it that was lit black with the last dark blue of the sky. And she climbed up to it with long careful steps, like she was thinking about something, and held onto the fence with her fingers so she was lit up black too, like a shadow shape.

Ivan sat down on the low part of a seesaw after he wiped off some water, and Kevin shook out a swing and started twisting around in it with his heels still dug into the ground. And Kate looked down at them both from over her shoulder and started swaying back and forth like she wanted to say something, but she didn't want to say something either. Her hair was swinging down heavy and wet now but still bright and it was getting harder and harder to see anything inside the strange black shape inside her bright hair.

He and Ivan looked at one another; they didn't know what she was doing really.

"He did it to me, Kevin," she said.

It was super quiet in the schoolyard for a second, then they heard a foghorn. Then Kate cracked up, laughing, and started running around the dripping jungle gym hooting, "Home. Home." Kevin started hooting it too for some reason, over and over; then Ivan joined in too.

"Are you staying?" Kevin said, catching his breath after they were all thoroughly mud spattered. "What happened?" he blurted out. He was angry at himself because he had been trying to make himself not ask that question even though he wanted to know, because maybe Kate didn't feel like talking about it.

"Did you have to use Ivan's knife?" said Kevin, still trying to shut himself up.

"It didn't get that far," said Ivan. Kevin's heart sunk a little. Of course she'd already told Ivan all about it and it was just Kevin who didn't know yet.

"I would've," said Kate, narrowing her eyes. "But I knew I couldn't if I wanted to get off the island. I pictured it. Stick!" she shouted, thrusting out a fist, "right in his saggy belly."

"How could your parents though?" said Kevin, "How could?" Kevin stammered.

"Kate's mom is in love with Nick Ford," Ivan said. Kate frowned at him, like he might be trying to put words in her mouth. "It's true," said Ivan, "It's obvious."

"Shut up," Kate said, then she turned to Kevin, "My mom is worried for me because she thinks I'm lying. That's what happened to her I guess when she got sick. It's a school for liars. And she thinks she got better when she went there. Parents send kids there because you can say whatever you want there and no one will believe you or listen to you, until you learn to shut up; then they let you go. Then you know how to shut up and your parents like you again."

"I don't get it," Kevin said. "I thought it was just a boarding school, and you just needed to have parents with a lot of money to go there. Isn't it, Kate?"

"Sort of," said Kate, "Only like, it's really for kids they think have problems, like it's a school for mixed-up kids."

Kevin had to laugh at that one,

"That's stupid," he said. "Like who isn't mixed up?"

"I hate it there, and I'm not going back."

"How'd you get back?"

"I told Tock's friend on the mailboat. I think he knew what was going on."

"So what now?" said Kevin.

"I'm going to stop wishing and do something," said Kate the anger shining like a statue of cold glass.

Kevin and Ivan just stood there dumbly in the pouring rain.

"What about you, though?" Kate went on as if she hadn't said anything at all. "Ivan says your mom's new boyfriend is a real jerk."

"Yeah," Kevin said. "What about you, Ivan?"

"Shut up," Ivan said. "Let's go to back to my house. There's no one there at least."

The rain was coming down real hard and they were pretty much soaked as much as if they'd been swimming when they got back to Ivan's mom's apartment on the top floor. They climbed up and Ivan unlocked the door in the dark, and found Kevin's sleeping bags with the flashlight. Then they wrapped themselves with the them and ate peanutbutter crackers for a while and pretty soon they didn't have much at all to say again. It was too dark to even see each other at all. And it was getting scarier just being there in that place in the dark, and it smelled like old beer and cat pee from old tenants.

"Pretty great summer vacation, huh?" Ivan said.

After about an hour, they were all starting to feel cold, because it was a cool night and their clothes were still wet.

There was a noise at the bottom of the stairs. Kevin could see enough of Kate and Ivan to know they grabbed each other's hands.

Silence, then, "IVAAN? KEVIIN?"

It was Didi!

They all three shout at once, "DEEDEE!"

"Hey guys," she said in a soft, sad voice finding its way slowly to the top of the stairs. Ivan shined the flashlight on her. She had a long raincoat wrapped around her like she went out in a hurry. She was shaking her head with one hand up to block the light. "Are you guys alone?" she said, a little scared sounding.

"Kate's here too," said Kevin. Ivan turned off the flashlight and then everything was like a soft, blank red glow.

"Oh, Kevin." She almost sounded like she wanted to cry. And Kevin felt like crying and Kate and Ivan too probably but he couldn't see them in the dark. "I figured you'd be here. But why are all the lights off? I only came up because I saw the front door was open downstairs. What's going on here?" But she was talking fast and didn't wait for Kevin to think up an answer, "...Mom is flipped. She called me on the phone in hysterics. Said she didn't know what to do; you were gone and Carl was pissed.

His sister took a second looking at the dark, then they could hear her feeling for the wall and flicking the light switch. When nothing happened, she just sort of sighed. She said, "I tried to call here first, but it's disconnected.

"My mom's not here right now," Ivan said.

Kevin knew she was making a face at Ivan in the dark, not a mean one, just a funny one.

"And who's this one?" she said because her eyes were adjusting and she'd spotted Kate in the dark.

"Hi, Deirdre," Kate said.

"Hi Kate," his sister said, quiet and mothery, the way she always sounded with Kate. "Back from school already?"

"No, not really."

"What!?..." Now Kevin could see enough to see his sister put her hand on her forehead like she's got a headache. "Oh forget it. All you waifs, let's go. Sleep-over at Deirdre's."

"We love you, Didi," Kevin said.

"And you damn well oughta," she said.

from Kate's diary,
July Eighth, 1976:

*Concho told me Tock was still camped out on the end of Killdeer. I went there and climbed around the fence. I told him everything. He called me Linda just like Concho.*

*I said Why do you call me that?*

*He said It just means I understand.*

*I said how they gave me a room by myself at the school where he can get to me whenever he wants. I said I want to get him. I said I want to get him and make him stop forever.*

*He said What do you mean by forever Kate?*

*I said I don't care. The wind was blowing and the sun was going down behind the clouds and it was already dark on the rocks. It started to rain and I didn't know where to go because Ivan and Kevin got taken back to their moms.*

*Tock said I'll help you Kate we'll be
partners okay?*

*I said We'll trap him and then we'll kill
him. And I made a sticking move with my fist
and I was crying*

*He lit a cigarette and asked me if I
wanted one and I said No. He looked at me
and smiled and shook his head and said. Well
we'll see.*

*I said Why do you hate Nick Ford so
much? Did he hurt you too once too?*

*He said Yes.*

*I said He turned on me too and he lied
on me.*

*Tock said he lied on him too.*

*He said when Nick and him were boys
they were best friends. They met through their
dads. Nick's dad gave his dad money to buy his
own boat and his dad did lots of stuff for
Nick's dad at the harbor. He said Nick used to
have his ideas, his ideals you know. About jus-
tice. He's a smart man and they were good*

*ideas. They made sense. Tock said Basically I just started to do what he was talking about as I grew up. I mean shit I never went to college but I read plenty and I believe in straightening things out. And he got scared of me and instead of telling me or arguing he just set me up behind my back. He said he wanted me to get some stuff you know some drugs for him. For him and your mama as a matter of fact Kate.*

*I pictured my mom with a needle in her arm and it scared me.*

*He said We were young. Your mom and Nick were in college.*

*I said I can't believe my mom put needles in her arm.*

*Tock laughed. He said Not her. It was coke. Cocaine they were crazy for it. Never liked it much myself but it's money. It's a powder you snort through your nose.*

*Anyway it was a set up. He worked it out with his dad so he wouldn't get in trouble.*

*The only reason I did it was because they kept the fish prices so low I couldn't make a living. No one could. But I did it for him because we were friends when we were kids. And they popped me. They took my fishingboat that I bought with fishing money and they put me in the pinta for four goddamn years. Your uncle Nick doesn't love no one or nothing and he can't believe his own ideas. That's why I hate him and I'll hate him forever.*

*It was raining hard now and both me and Tock were all wet and he said Shit. And I said I hate him too I'll hate him until he's dead.*

*He smiled and his teeth were brown and dry even though it was raining. He said I got an idea.*

*I said What?*

*He said Partners?*

*I said Partners.*

*He said Good.*

*I liked the way he said that.*

*I said what if they send me back to the island?*

*He said I got you out once didn't I?*

*Now I'm alone in the rain in Kevin and Ivan's old neighborhood. And it's scary and getting dark. And I don't know where to go.*

# CHAPTER TWENTY

Deirdre saw Kevin's face first when they got into 3 Vale and she turned on the light. Her lips were skin-colored from pressing together so hard, almost like she was angry at Kevin, "How'd you get that?"

"Carl," he said. "It was an accident, I guess." Deirdre turned quickly so he couldn't see her expression. She started opening one cabinet after another in the kitchen.

She cooked them all mac and cheese, but didn't seem to want to talk to them at all yet about what had happened; Kevin's mouth felt so full of questions that he kept on having to fill it up with food to keep them from coming out. Where had she been when their parents had come for them, and why hadn't she tried to stop it, and what sinister plot from Nick Ford might have been spun to prevent her, or had Nick charmed her into believing his lies? Simultaneous to his questions was Kevin's own need to answer—he had lied—he had promised Kate that Didi wanted her to live with them without ever asking Deirdre and it was with that in mind Kate decided to escape the island and Kevin shoveled mouthful after mouthful of slippery orange macaroni into his face to keep himself quiet. To hang on if only for one more second to all of them safe and together at 3 Vale again. Kevin couldn't help but be worried in this unexpected moment of happiness, an impossible island waiting for the tide of questions to make it disappear.

"You guys are starving," Deirdre said and she produced orange jello from the fridge and they all had fudge twirl ice cream for dessert. All four of them were laughing then and making jokes around the plywood kitchen table because of how good the ice cream tasted and the rain outside sounded nice now and no one had wanted to eat in front of the tv like Carl because they were having too good of a time with every light in the house on all at once, and the radio playing.

"Unh oh gla," said Kate her jaw wide open to keep the cold of a mouthful of ice cream away from her teeth until she could swallow and giggle how no one had understood her that way. "I'm so glad I can live here."

His sister's face filled with thoughtful surprise, elbows on the splintery plywood table, staring at Kate across her coffee cup. Her quick sideways glance at him told Kevin she'd caught him now. It hadn't seemed like a lie at the time, but suddenly—the despair in his sister's eyes—its magnitude started spreading through Kevin's imagination like cracks in the ice you're about to fall through. His fault. The fault everything was falling through. Why Didi must have gotten in trouble for something she never said. Why Mrs. Harrigan had found them. Why Ivan's mom left. Why Kate ran away from the school.

Kevin smiled sheepishly at his sister. He felt sick.

Kate was looking at Deirdre appealingly, uncertain for a second, sensing something was wrong.

"Of course I want you to stay with us," Deirdre said. "I want it more than anything, baby. You're my girl." Deirdre was winging it, understanding already more than anyone had said. Kevin loved his sister more than his body could contain. He stood up, knocking his fork to the floor, wrapped his arm around her neck and, instead of kissing her ear like it looked like, whispered, "I love you."

It was too late for Didi to go to work now or that's what she said. She didn't say anymore, but looked at Kevin and he could tell she was worried about getting fired this time. It was selfish, but he was glad she was staying home anyway. For tonight anyway there would be nothing lonely in the rhythmical drone of the dishwasher. They were all home now: Didi, and Ivan, and Kate. And nothing could happen to them, or to himself, by being alone. He thought first of Carl, sitting drunk in front of his mom's tv. Then he thought of Johnny—where he might be and what he might be doing. Kevin pictured him rambling around the halls of the big mansion, or sitting with Nick in his study. Was he in danger? If Johnny'd wanted to be here with us he could've, Kevin decided. Didi has plenty of room if he wanted it, Kevin thought.

Now Kevin looked back at Didi, her stretched thin big eyes that made the men in the Beachcomber all want to talk with her, and he thought about how there was even someplace for Nick Ford inside her, and Kevin wondered how much room could possibly be left. And then he thought of Nick Ford as Johnny's father, what it could be like to be alone with no one but that cold terrible person day after day. And did anybody at all really have room inside them for Johnny, if Kevin didn't? Certainly not Nick Ford. And he thought of Johnny in the mansion again, this time all alone, friendless. Well there was nothing Kevin could do about it now. If Johnny came to him maybe, but Kevin couldn't go and find Johnny again after what Johnny had said to him: It was impossible.

And Kevin's worry just kept growing and growing as the

evening went on. When Kevin and Ivan and Kate started up a game
of Monopoly on the livingroom floor, just to break up all the heaviness
a little, Didi withdrew from them. She said she didn't feel like playing
herself and stayed instead alone at the kitchen table where they'd all
been before, like she didn't have any strength to move even. She was
just sitting there through the full first hour of the game, drinking coffee and smoking cigarettes one after the other until their whole little
house was thick with smoke.

She seemed to get edgier too as the game went on. Wouldn't
even look at any of them when she finally walked into the living room.
They were all looking at her, though. Watching her seemed to be
important for all of them, even though the game was pretty close and
interesting.

Didi, who was barefooted, stepped on one of the Monopoly
tokens, one none of them had chosen, which got left on the carpet.
Her voice erupted into a huge swear and then she said, "This house
is a FUCK-ing mess!" The house wasn't at all a mess except for the
Monopoly game. That really was a mess now because she had kicked
it and scattered everything everywhere.

Kevin wasn't looking at his sister anymore but at the carpet
where the gameboard had been but wasn't anymore. Then he only
looked halfway up to Kate and to Ivan sitting in the empty circle with
him. They only looked halfway up too, back up at him and each other.
Didi limped over to her plaid chair and sat down on its edge, bending
down to be in the view of all three of them. Her cheeks were blotchy.

"Okay, listen," she said, "Okay?" she asked, but maybe she was
asking herself and not them, because then she said, "Nothing is okay,
okay? This is deep shit you guys are putting me through now, okay?
I have a life, or I used to. I'm not even talking about my job or anything. Like I could give a fuck, right?" She leaned back in the chair
and it seemed to be okay for them to look up now. "I could get a job
at any bar in town in ten seconds and my dick-brain boss knows that
as good as I do. He knows I'd take half his fucking clientele with me
too."

Didi's voice was full of pain, pain that Kevin felt responsible for
somehow, "Didi..."

"Shut up, for a second, Kev." She spoke angrily and he was
hurt, looked straight back down to the carpet again. "Just listen to
me. You." She bent back down into his field of vision with an I'm sorry
in her eyes for snapping. "All three of you," she went on more slowly,
"are not my kids. Do you know what that means?" They all stayed
quiet. "Hell, I don't know what it means really, but you can bet I don't

have any legal rights here, with you. I don't I got no legal right to have any of you here, not even you Kev if it comes down to it." She lit another cigarette, pulling the mooshed pack from the waist of her jeans. The cigarette was crooked. She stared at it furiously for several seconds, like it was responsible somehow for giving her three grown kids all of a sudden and no one to help her.

She lit it finally. It smoked like an old bent stove pipe. "I know you guys are tired of having to act like grown-ups. None of the adults around here are acting like grown-ups for fucking-christ-on-a bloody-spit-sake, Jesus!" Didi could really swear when she got going. She kind of had a reputation for it when she got mad enough at the Beachcomber. "But you're going to have to help me now; we're all in this together." Her eyes started to fill up with tears. Deirdre, who never cried ever, no matter what, even in the days when things had been most terrible at home and Mom was crying and Kevin was crying too. She looked angrily at the cigarette again like it was the smoke. "I need someone too sometimes, you know." She clenched her eyes to stop it, but she couldn't. "I'm sorry," she said. "I'm sorry, you guys."

None of them said anything. Kevin fidgeted on the carpet, felt his friends fidgeting too. How could they help Deirdre after all?

"Your mom came into the bar yesterday," Deirdre said, and she was talking to Kate now, "To the bar. With my own fucking mother. And Judy." She looked at Ivan. Ivan looked back guiltily. Just saying his mother's name was enough for him to feel like he had to apologize. "Your mom, Kate, had scared the fucking both of them right into the Mothers' Temperance Society." Kate winced. "Look you guys, I'm just in way over my head. She comes in screaming bloody murder about how I had lured her child away from her. Took advantage. Was putting Kate's health in danger. I didn't know what to say, because..." Deirdre stamped out the cigarette angrily. Looked at Kevin. "I didn't know what the hell she was talking about." Didi sat way back in the chair like it was all too much. "She said if I had any contact with you, Kate, she'd have me arrested. And my own fucking mother just stood there cow-eyed and said," and here Deirdre did a perfect imitation of their mother's "serious" voice, desperate and mousy. "'Maybe you better not try to see Kevin for a few days either, dear. I think it's best under the circumstances.' What the fuck circumstances? I wanted to know, but mom just said 'It's one thing for Kevin to have a little vacation with his big sister but,' like two years is some kind of fucking vacation, 'I just think you need a little time is all, to think about why you seem to feel the need to put all the children in Port Bedford under your roof?'" Kevin could see the scene now, exactly, in his mind. Blood shot to his cheeks for his mother's sake. Didi was blushing for her too. "And Judy," said Deirdre to change the subject, "just standing there with her saint's face, looped to the gills. I wanted to smack her. Like all the sudden she just couldn't live with out you Ivan." Ivan's forehead got all wrinkled up. "I'm sorry, hon, I love your mother dearly, but she's a total flake when it comes to you. And then there was *your* mother..." Now it was Kate's turn to blush. "I don't know how she tracked them down so fast or what she said to them, but whatever it was it worked. And it's not even about you, is it? Is it Kate?!" Didi demanded. "It's about Nick, isn't it? She's really just jealous of me because of Nick."

"He did something again," said Kate, not looking up.

Didi's mouth was still open because she was about to say something else. Now she looked at Kate like she was going to throw up instead. And Kate looked like a glass of sour milk that Didi had started to drink by mistake.

Didi stood up from the chair and just stared at the big lamp next to it. She grabbed the lamp, ripping the plug out of the wall and threw it, straight down the hallway and into the front door.

There was a little pop from the lightbulb breaking, but the cloth shade was what hit the door first, so it hardly made any noise other than that.

Then the lamp just sat there, pathetically mangled. Deirdre sat back down again, and lit another cigarette.

"How could he be doing this to me?" Deirdre said. "How could I have been so fucking STUPID?"

"You don't, Didi," Kevin said with a quavering voice, all the building horror and anger and hurt of the past few days trying to get out, "do you?"

"That creep?" said Deirdre angrily. "I never should have. I want! Won't, I won't. Shit." She started to play spider with her fingers on her forehead.

Kevin felt the tiniest pop again, inside of him, like an echo: Nick Ford mattered to his sister. No one could have heard it but Kevin; no one knew his sister well enough but him. It was dead quiet, though he could see they were still talking around him; he saw Ivan's and then Deirdre's mouth moving. But now there was nothing left for Kevin to say, no point in arguing about it, no point in fighting. He couldn't help what he did: Grabbing his knees and curling himself up tighter and tighter and starting to whimper. He knew he was being babyish, but he couldn't stop even after Kate and Ivan both rubbed his back to make him stop. Then he started moving his tongue in a funny way like he was trying to get something bad out of his mouth.

"Stop that!" shouted Didi, finally, and he did. Then Didi started to pace up and down the room.

"Stop that!" shouted Kevin. And she did too.

It was another hour before they came for Kate, Mr. and Mrs. Harrigan together this time. No police or anything, just them. Didi opened the door, pushing aside the broken lamp with it. Mrs. Harrigan stood paused in the doorway, looked down at the broken lamp, back up at Deirdre, smiled. Mr. Harrigan looked straight down the hallway, not even at Kate sitting in plain view on the livingroom floor, but over her head...at nothing. Kevin had never actually seen both Mr. and Mrs. Harrigan standing side by side before and it frightened him. It seemed to frighten Kate too. She just froze up like a statue on the living room floor. Deirdre let them in. They were the same height, taller than everybody, even Deirdre by a head. It was like the house belonged to them immediately when they set foot in it and not to him or Didi even. He felt their noses in the air. The shabbiness of the chairs. The smelly yellowness of the wallpaper in his hall. Mr. and Mrs. Harrigan were here, taller than the room itself even.

Ivan stood against the wall, like he just got caught by the cops. Kevin was standing in back of everybody, in the kitchen doorway. Kate was alone in the middle of the floor. Deirdre's voice was so polite and pleading it was scary, "Would you like to sit down?" No answer. "Could you please sit down and try to listen to what I have to say?"

Mrs. Harrigan turned slowly and looked at her like she was a bug. Mrs. Harrigan raised one cold finger:

"If you—I don't even know what name to call you—If you so much as say one word to me...I'll have you arrested. And, by the by, you are no longer employed at the Beachcomber Bar & Grill."

"Please," Didi said, hysterical, begging. Kevin could feel all the blood in his body come rushing to his face.

"Hup!" Mrs. Harrigan's voice jumped back at her, her whole ringed and braceleted hand raised this time with an angry jingle. "Not-a-word. And I don't condescend to threaten you. I state, my young Miss, a hard and cold fact."

Deirdre's mouth clenched.

"Now," said Mrs. Harrigan, "Allow me to tell you something. I am quite in my cousin's confidence." She scanned Deirdre's face vindictively, "You find that surprising do you? How a little...how a, person," her voice wavering from too much control, "...of your character ever managed to worm your way under the skin of such a noble—I say it and mean it—a noble man. A man so far above you that you couldn't begin to entertain the vaguest conception of who he is. *I'm* not his equal," said Mrs. Harrigan, though the confession seemed to cause her pain. "And you've obviously underestimated me, Ms. Hawk. Don't do it again. I'll have the key thrown into the ocean. Do we understand one another?"

Deirdre didn't say anything, but she looked straight at and through Mrs. Harrigan, it felt like to Kevin, and smiled.

But the strangest of everybody in the room to Kevin was Mr. Harrigan, who Kevin didn't know at all, except that he knew Johnny didn't like him. Kevin really looked at him now for the first time. What must he be thinking and why didn't he say anything? Would Mrs. Harrigan throw the key into the ocean on him too? Kevin wondered. He just stood there with his hands clasped in front of him, looking straight ahead with no expression at all. Like he was just Mrs. Harrigan's butler or something. He refused to even acknowledge Kevin staring at him, though he must have been able to feel it.

But now, suddenly, when Mrs. Harrigan turned to look at him, Mr. Harrigan's face sprung into life, like some great leader that she had just plugged in. He spoke only one word, but it was filled with the power of command:

"Kitty," he said.

And, though she never looked up, her head still hung down, Kate's neck jerked like she'd been stung by the word. Mr. and Mrs. Harrigan stood tall as jailers behind her now. They were ready to leave.

Kate pulled herself slowly, inexorably, to her feet and started the endless walk to the front door under her parents' towering supervision.

Kevin had been standing in the same spot this whole time. He was still standing there, unable to move, staring helplessly and hopelessly at his sister. Her bright red face. She wouldn't even look back at him.

"Hey Mrs. Harrigan," Ivan called suddenly, when they were almost to the door. He was still leaning against the wall, but his arms were crossed now. The way he leaned was Trouble; Kevin wanted to shut his eyes. And, most incredibly, Ivan had spoken very casually, like Mrs. Harrigan was a person of absolutely no consequence. Kate stopped walking, maybe from sheer disbelief. So Mr. and Mrs. Harrigan had to stop too, because she was blocking the door. Mrs. Harrigan turned around, impatient and annoyed by having to do so.

"Say Hi to Nickey for me," said Ivan, "next time you're in bed with him." Everyone froze. Except for Mr. Harrigan who, without warning, went totally berserk. He stormed over to Ivan and pinned his shoulder to the wall with a loud, dull thump.

"You're treading on incredibly thin ice, young man. Do you realize you're this close to becoming a ward of the State?" Mr. Harrigan snapped his finger right under Ivan's nose. But he was trembling all over. "Ivan Otrusky," he said. "Think twice before you say that again."

Ivan looked scared, but hard-scared and he managed to laugh even though Kevin could tell he was faking.

"Jason," said Mrs. Harrigan, her voice clipped and severe. "There's no point in this display. He's just a child. Hasn't this all been ugly enough already? Just go start the car." It was an order. There was no doubt about it.

Mr. Harrigan put his head in his hand and simply followed, his face blank again, as Mrs. Harrigan walked back towards Kate and the door.

But Kate had stopped there because the open doorway was already occupied, so filled that hardly any light from the streetlamp got through. It was filled by a man.

"I saw your car, Carol, and stopped," said a deep voice. Nick Ford stepped inside. He was wearing white deck shoes, blue Levi's, a red alligator shirt. His face was unreadable. He turned and called to the Mercedes parked out by the curb. "John, you can stop hiding in there." The passenger door opened. Then Johnny came in, hesitant, in the exact same outfit as Nick's, with the small addition of some big brown ice cream stains.

"Nick!" Mrs. Harrigan said. She fluttered when she said it like a huge shivering bird. "You really didn't have to see her off a second time." Her head cocked back and forth super-fast, like the needle skipping on a 45. "No, it was nice of you, Nick, really. Ha, ha, sometimes I think you act more like her father than Jason does. I could hardly pull you here, could I dear?"

"Nick," said Mr. Harrigan. His face looked haggard.

Nick wasn't looking anywhere near Kate now that other eyes were on him. Only glancing furtively at Deirdre in the living room every once in a while.

"I just wanted to let you know, I've straightened things out at the school. They're willing to give her another chance." Kate's mouth was tight and hard as a toenail. Her eyes weren't looking anywhere. Johnny was looking at her, though, not listening at all to any of the adults. His forehead was full of I'm sorry wrinkles for Kate.

"Don't be too hard on yourself, Jason," said Nick, "It's a difficult age, as I'm beginning to understand now." He glanced calmly at Johnny. "Still, I wouldn't trade fatherhood for the world."

Kevin could see Mr. Harrigan's face better than anyone else's from his position: angry, humiliated.

"The uniforms were John's idea," said Nick. "We were just on our way to an overnight regatta."

Johnny muttered something inaudible.

"You look very handsome, Johnny," said Mr. Harrigan with a tense face.

"My name is John now," said Johnny coldly.

Mrs. Harrigan smiled sadly at Johnny. "John," she said. "Very adult. Very handsome, just like your, Nick."

Johnny completely ignored her. Nick himself couldn't have done it better. Finally, he jerked away when she tried to fix his collar for him. His only friendly look was for Kate. "How's it going?" he asked Kate. Nick frowned over him.

Kate snorted and shrugged.

"Your brother is talking to you," said Mrs. Harrigan.

"I'm not her brother anymore," said Johnny and, still friendly to Kate, "You can still call me Johnny though."

"Johnny," said Kate softly.

The room filled up with uncomfortable silence. Deirdre was smiling so the whole room could see the back of her teeth.

"So Nick," she said. "I understand you took Kate to that island yourself,"

Suddenly Nick's face looked a little crazy, "That's right."

She walked up to them all slowly, arms crossed, eyeing Nick furiously.

"You think you can shut me up by getting me fired? What do you think I'm gonna come to you begging for my job back? Mrs. Harrigan," said Deirdre, turning to her, "This man has been fucking with your daughter behind your back."

Mrs. Harrigan opened her mouth and blinked.

Deirdre had said it: She had said the impossible to them. Kevin clenched his body for the violence to come. Nothing. Had he imagined it? It was as if there was no one who had heard. Only Ivan and Kate and himself were looking at one another. They had heard all right. But they already knew. Both Mr. and Mrs. Harrigan just looked uncomfortable, like they were both thinking about some private thought that had suddenly occurred to them instead of listening to the conversation. Kevin looked at Johnny for some confirmation, but

Johnny was looking uncertainly at Mrs. Harrigan and then, appealingly, at Nick.

"Don't be ridiculous, John. There are easier ways, Deirdre," said Nick nervously eyeing Mrs. Harrigan. "to settle personal matters between you and me." Deirdre ignored him.

"Didn't Kate tell you so, Mrs. Harrigan?"

Mrs. Harrigan's mouth remained open.

"Kate?" said Deirdre. "Speak up. Is it true or isn't it?"

Kate couldn't answer.

"Don't do this, Deirdre," said Nick.

Mrs. Harrigan had a tremendous wide-open smile, growing and growing. Her arms were trembling.

"Carol," said Mr. Harrigan grabbing her. "Carol, please. Don't allow this woman to upset you. Everything will be fine."

"Of course it will of course it will," said Mrs. Harrigan smiling and shaking her head. "It's time to go now, shall we? Katharine." She put out her hand. To Kevin's surprise, Kate took her mother's hand and held it, petted it, her face distorted and confused. It seemed to calm Mrs. Harrigan down a little. "Thank you dear. You understand. Of course you do. Jason, take us home."

"John," said Nick, calmly.

Johnny started to hit himself on the head and sing softly to himself, "La la lala la."

"John!" Nick's voice rapped out. "What did I tell you about that?"

Johnny put his hand down and stopped singing, "You said it annoys you," said Johnny meekly.

"Well," said Nick.

"I'm sorry," muttered Johnny. Nick put a hand on his head, but Johnny suddenly ran out from beneath it to Kate and hugged her awkwardly,

"Gu, Goobye Kate," said Johnny. His face was confused. "I'm sorry I've, I've got to be with my dad right now." And before he could say more, Nick, ignoring Deirdre, ushered him out the door.

"Kate!" Deirdre shouted.

Kate still held her mother's hand uncertainly in the street. "I should go maybe," she said. Mrs. Harrigan still stood, her hand in her daughter's, staring at nothing, a wide grin on her face.

That night Kevin dreamed that Deirdre was laid out in front of him on red velvet, covered everywhere and up to her chin in dandelions and buttercups. Her face was white and still and slowly it dawned on him that she was dead. Then he could hear the bomb ticking slowly inside his mattress. He woke up suddenly to dead night, covered in sweat and another click. And another. They were coming from the glass of his open window at the foot of his bed. Then a boinging sound from the screen.

Imagining it might be Kate—or even Johnny having come to his senses, throwing rocks from the street to his window, to let him know he'd run away from Nick—Kevin sat up and hurried his face toward the screen. Something flew out and hit him heavily on the cheek, startling him so he cried out a little, then filling him with quick disgust. Just a huge clumsy June bug, out of control in its flight, meaningless.

from Kate's diary,
July Ninth, 1976:

*I saw Ivan sitting on a stone wall next
to a scary looking store with shabby looking
drunk men going in and out for quarts of beer
in paper bags. I couldn't believe it was him.
He was sitting with a tough looking older kid
wearing a blue tough guy jacket with blue fur
on the collar even though it was summer and
an old guy in a stained wet gray t shirt who
had no teeth drinking beer from a paper bag.*

*Ivan looked sad.*

*I said Hey Ivan.*

*He said Kate and couldn't believe it.
And he didn't say goodbye to the man and the
older kid so I knew he couldn't be very good
friends with them.*

*I said Who are they?*

*He said Nobody. They just live around
here. How in fuck did you get back?*

*I asked him to hold me and he did. Tight.*

*I said about the room for me at the*

*school and how he had the key. I said if they make me go back there I think I'll die.*

*I said I'm going to kill Nick Ford.*

*He said Good I'll help you.*

*I had to go back because my mom needed me. I don't want to hurt my mom. I love my mom. She's like an egg now curled up in her bed and I'm scared for her to break.*

*My dad looks like a ghost who forgot to shave.*

*He said You better not upset your mother anymore.*

*I said I won't.*

*I went to my mom's bedroom and there were pills on her nightstand.*

*I said Mom.*

*She said Kate? but her voice was all blurry.*

*I said I will marry Johnny one day when we get old.*

*She smiled and petted my hand and kissed it and put it on her wet cheek.*

*I stayed like that until she fell asleep.*

# CHAPTER TWENTY-ONE

Ivan and Kevin left their bikes hidden under the rose bushes and walked up the already dark hill of grass, back to the twilight on Harbor Rd. and the deep violet reflection of sunset in the open sky over the ocean. They carried windbreakers and sweaters in their backpacks. And a half gallon of orange juice and a bundle of peanut-butter sandwiches. And a chocolate bar and two flashlights and black caps from Woolworth's in town (they had to steal the money from Didi's purse, because it would have been too hard to ask her). All because, for the first time,

"We're going to sea," whispered Ivan.

"To sea." Kevin liked the sound of it and swaggered a little this time through the chainlink gate and down the ramp. For the first time in his life, and in Ivan's too, the harbor was the beginning of the road and not the end. The smell of cold, burnt sour ashes was everywhere. For the first time it really felt like he belonged here.

They'd arranged it with Tock this morning: There was nowhere else to turn.

"They're taking Kate back to a summer school on an island somewhere," Kevin had said. "Do you know where it is?"

"I might."

"The mailboat goes there."

"We want to go there."

"What for?" Tock had said frowning. They'd woken him up. They'd had no choice but to tell Tock the whole story.

"It's on an island somewhere out there." Kevin had pointed out vaguely to the water, "If you take us..."

Tock looked at where Kevin was pointing, "There's nothing that way till the Azores. Portugal. Europe." Then Tock had adjusted Kevin's finger to the left, "There. And yeah...if you help me. Yeah, sure yeah," Tock had said. "Kidnapper. Add that to your list of words."

The tide was medium so the floating ramp wasn't that steep. A steady, stiff sea breeze jostled the docks under their feet as they walked the main way. And it still blew the charred tar smell black across the water mixed with sharper chemical smells like burnt plastic and fiberglass from the burned down fishbuyers on Jetty Road. All the lights from there were dark now. Hinges creaking back and forth in conversation. Stays and wires from the big rigging of the dragboats pinged and hummed the air above. Light spilled over from the occasional boat onto the finger docks to either side, but mostly the way was black dark—the gray painted planks of the dock only a slightly lighter shadow than the blackness of the water to either side. The solitary tocks of their feet resonated hollow underneath them as they passed through the big dragboats and then long-liner boats near the main way's end.

Now the smaller boats began, the high-bowed, low sterned lobster boats in their slips. It seemed brighter here, because most of the lobster boats were white, with dark trim only around their windows.

A bottle smashed farther back among the dragboats, followed by a harsh roll of laughter. Then it was quiet again and the creaking of the docks returned and the drawn-out groan of heavy ropes against their cleats.

At the very end of the main way, they came to a final 'T' and, to the left, a small light shone from the small rectangular cabin windows of an old looking lobster boat. It was the only lobster boat anywhere with a light. Kevin could touch the side window from the finger dock; so he knocked on it,

"Tock," he said. Light spilled through the pilot house and onto the stern deck behind them.

"Get on board," said Tock appearing on the deck. He invited them between two vertical pipes, through the dark pilot house— where only the chrome steering wheel gleamed a little, and the many squares of navigational instruments stayed dark against the windshield, hiding their purposes—and down into a cutty cabin, by a door under the navigational stuff only three quarters Kevin's height. The yellow light was coming from there.

"You still want to go through with this?" said Tock, sounding like he didn't expect an answer. "Come in and let's talk about it." He bent almost double to enter the cabin. They followed, Kevin first. Kevin could stand, but the room was only high enough for Tock to sit hunched over up front. Kevin could see the lights of town harbor spread out before him through the little windows at the level of his eyes, a dark scar in the middle where the fishbuyers used to be before Tock burned them down. Behind him, Ivan had to stoop his head a little when he came in, but there were two maroon wooden benches on either side of them tapered together to a point in the front where Tock sat, knees wide, behind a kerosene lamp that swung gently from a nail at Kevin's neck. The sway of the water was a lot more notice-able in here. Its unrhythmical slap was the largest sound.

"Sit down," Tock said. He looked tremendous because he was wearing a big sweater and yellow oilskin overalls and black rubber boots. "The wind is going to be blowing tonight in open water."

"How can you tell?" said Ivan.

Tock smiled. "The weather report."

Ivan looked disappointed.

"But I knew already," Tock said, still with a smile. "Tonight is the blue moon; not too many of the boys are going out.

The blue moon. Kevin liked the sound of that. "What is it?" he whispered, peering through the salt spattered window east where the moon was indeed breaking through a thick rack of clouds and into clear sky, brightening everything. It was thick and full and yellow.

"It isn't really blue," Tock laughed. "Just the second full moon in one month. It hardly ever happens. It makes the tides funny, and the wind strong. Fishermen say that the fish can see the lines and the net on a full moon."

"Well we're not going fishing," said Ivan.

"No, that's true," said Tock. "It's good for us. Less boats out to see us. Just rough is all. Don't want you fellahs getting sick on the boat. It ain't mine." Tock's big forearms hung like a 'v' between big flat yellow knees, weighted in the middle by his fists, square and scarred. "First let me tell you what we're talking about. The island you're look-ing for is called Noman's Island. It's the last piece of land before you get to open ocean and the fishing banks. It's a private island and the school on it is private too. No docking; no trespassing."

"We already know where Kate's room is," said Ivan sharply. "She told us." He seemed to think Tock wanted to back out.

"Okay, okay. I'm not saying I won't take you. My word is as good with kids as with anyone else." Tock seemed a little offended. "I'm just telling you, what your doing here is not a joke. It's a risky business. I'll take you there, but I can't risk docking. He's not gonna catch old Tock that way, for breaking and entering. I know a place, though. I can anchor without anyone seeing; they can't arrest a guy for anchoring in a cove. Then you'll have to take the dingy and row. It'll be a little sheltered from the wind on the back side of the island but it'll still be a pull for a couple of little guys probably."

"We know how," said Ivan. "If we get caught, you can just leave." Kevin didn't like the sound of that, but he kept quiet.

"Let me put it to you this way, Kevin," said Tock. Kevin noticed that Tock was talking to just him now, like Tock and Ivan had already come to an understanding. "You want to get Kate back, but even if you do it won't last. Everything stays the same as long as he's around, you know. He's not your average Port Bedford snob. He looks; he sees, but still he does just what he wants anyway. He's worse than all of them." He paused, looking at Kevin in an almost fatherly way. Kevin felt like he wanted to be his son maybe, but the memory of the burn on his arm kept his eyes on the ground. He could smell the burning everywhere now. But Tock kept on looking at him like he knew what was going on in Kevin's mind. "I'm a long way from perfect, Kevin. But I like you. If I had a kid I'd like him to be like you." Tock leaned towards him, "'Member I said I'd tell you what I learned when I was how old you are now? Well I'm trying to tell you, if a grown man does something to a kid and makes a kid do something to him too, for no good reason, for no reason at all except he gets off on it? Maybe you think that's me a little, don't you? It's not. I was just trying to show you. But Nick Ford, that's what it comes down to: There's a man who just takes for himself and for no good reason. Here's a guy who spends long weeks trying to get a fine pretty girl like your sister to fall in love with him, eh? Am I right? When he doesn't care for her any more than for a sauce pan, am I right Kevin, eh? Just because it makes him excited. And when that's the same man squeezing money from hard working fishermen and their families, Kevin, week by week, month by month, year by year," and each passage of time Tock marked by a louder fist on the hollow bench beside him till, on the last, the hatch cover skipped up askew and Kevin peeked inside, amid the stowed lines he saw a metal rod, which he suspected might be the barrel of a rifle. Tock slipped the bench hatch back into place so it fell with a clunk.

"So, that's why I'm gonna help you, Kevin. And I don't treat you like just a kid, see? You talk to Tock and you talk to Tock or you don't." Kevin wondered if Tock was drunk, but he didn't think so. But then Tock opened up his knife again, stood up in the cabin, filling the whole of it with his looming stoop. Kevin's heart sank. Tock passed the knife tip back and forth, back and forth again over the heat again in the slot at the top of the hurricane lamp. The periphery of Kevin's sight started going black like the walls of a tunnel. No. This couldn't be happening again. "Remember this?" said Tock, a crazy eye bending down to Kevin. "Sure you do, I see." Kevin's voice box started to jam up in his throat like a lump of spaghetti. He couldn't even warn Ivan of their danger. Ivan's face in the back and forth shadow of Tock's arm was hard, as hard as Tock's and full of anger. "That island belongs, has always belonged, to the Ford family; that is to Nick Ford, get it? It's just the same as if you were breaking into Nick Ford's own house."

The rapidly changing light made Kevin's eyes wiggle just trying to keep up. Like the flicker of a movie. Like a crazed hypnotizer swinging a pocket watch. Then, in his confusion, Kevin started to see pictures in his mind: of Kate naked with her hand over her face and tangled in the shadows with the shape of a man. Then the shape of the man tangled with Ivan's angry face. Then Carl's face tangled with the curves of Didi's body as Kevin had stumbled off a ladder; all to the swaying and yawing back and forth of the boat. Then his eyes came back with dread to the tip of Tock's knife blackening again in the flame. The memory of throbbing in his arm mixing with a throb on his face from Carl's fishhook. The shame of wanting to run again and wanting to cry because he felt the swell and the slap of the water all around him. His eyes stung and his stomach was starting to turn. He couldn't get sick or cry now, embarrass himself in front of Ivan and Tock because, he thought wildly, then he could never go out to sea. No one will take you out to sea ever if you get seasick. They just drop you back on the dock like a cry baby. And Kevin was desperate to go out; he wanted to more than anything.

Then the solution came, a drying glow like the glow of the flame. The feeling, once it started, started to grow. Kevin began at last to get very, very mad.

It was as if that's what Tock's bending crazy eye was waiting for. He took the knife out of the flame. It glowed a dull red, "Remember this, Kevin? It's not me. Now you understand. You get it too, Ivan. I knew you did. Am I right? Am I right?!" he shouted, pointing to the tip of the knife. "Who is this Ivan?" The face of Carl came again huge and distorted to Kevin's mind.

"It's Nick Ford," said Ivan.

"You got it," said Tock. "So spit on it. Both of you."

To his surprise, maybe from relief—knowing now that Tock wouldn't burn him again—Kevin felt saliva flowing into his mouth where it had been dry as a bone before. Both his and Ivan's heads were close over the knife now, so close that Tock could have flicked it up and burned either of their lips if he'd wanted too. But the knife was still and steady. "Go ahead," said Tock.

Together, Kevin and Ivan spat. The blade sizzled.

"Again," said Tock. It sizzled quieter. "Again." This time the knife was quiet. Tock laughed. "Good boys," he said. "Congratulations." He folded the knife and slapped them both on the backs. "You boys are fishermen now. Now you're ready to go to sea."

Kevin understood something else now too, beyond doubt, as he watched Tock's back hulking by him to the door, the close deep smell of his sweat: Tock was crazy.

But, crazy or not, Kevin and Ivan put their sweaters and windbreakers and joined him in the pilot house. Kevin could barely see over the bulkhead through the salt-spattered windshield. Tock turned the key; the big engine rumbled like an unmuffled truck beneath them and then softening as water bubbled out from the stern.

"Cast off, boys," shouted Tock. Ivan and Kevin stared at each other blankly.

"Get onto the dock," he said patiently, "untie the lines and bring 'em back on board with you." Which office Kevin and Ivan performed as nimbly and professionally as they could. It took a second for Kevin to figure out how to get the rope off the cleat without pinching his fingers. The boat was shimmying back and forth, tightening and loosening, impatient to get going.

"The moon is good for seeing," shouted Tock. He steered the boat casually out of the slip and into harbor water, "We won't use the running lights tonight. So you two stay forward with a sharp eye for other boats. And we'll use the radar."

Ivan elbowed Kevin happily, "Radar. Cool." Kevin climbed out the side of the pilot house to the narrow strip of deck leading forward. There was sand mixed in with the chipping paint, so his feet felt secure and he grabbed a wooden handrail on top of the cabin to steady himself. The fresh wind, the silver brightness of the moon electrified him as he peered out to the darkening sea ahead. The wind was cold and filled with empty places where Kevin had never been. But, as Tock plowed the boat slowly down the length of the dark jetty and finally reached and left behind the last red buoys of the harbor, Kevin couldn't help thinking of his warm bed at Didi's; how it might not ever be there for him again.

Past the jetty the wind increased and the steely water got choppier and Kevin was starting to get wet. He spider-crawled backwards to the relative shelter of the walled workdeck and the pilot house. Tock pushed down the throttle stick. The boat's high bow rose to the moon then leveled and skipped in jarring thunks. A big white glowing 'v' spread out behind them, Port Bedford a sinking twinkling dome between it.

Ivan and Kevin moved back to the stern deck behind the pilot house. Soon the small glow of the big island fell behind and then the few lights from Lamb's Island appeared, and Bayberry Island, and another island Kevin couldn't name. Ivan shouted into Kevin's ear that he was going forward and walked a crooked line back to Tock. Kevin stayed leaning over the side looking down into the dark waters, thinking of all the mysterious things beneath its surface. The walls of the stern deck were so low Kevin could touch the water without reaching.

Back in the pilot house, Tock turned on the radar: a sweeping green line in a dark square box. A small desk light on the bulkhead was lit now too, and Tock and Ivan were looking at a nautical chart together. It wasn't like driving a car, Kevin thought looking at them. Both their heads were bowed and Tock was showing Ivan how to read the compass; Tock hardly ever even looked up to actually see where they were going at all. But on they went into blackness, along a shimmer path of moon, the motor roaring full open.

"Careful of the pipes," Tock warned Kevin as he balanced and walked his way forward between the exhaust pipes, which went up through the roof to two big mufflers. "They heat up after a while." They were all wrapped with burnt looking cloth, but Kevin could feel them radiating on his face as he slipped between them. Maybe Tock had heated the knife and burned Kevin just to teach him what it took to be a fisherman. Maybe Tock thought he had what it took. Tock had an arm on Ivan's shoulder. He was letting Ivan be at the wheel. "That's right. So the needle stays on eighty seven. Gentle. Like that." Ivan's face looked focused and important. The heat from the pipes filled the pilot house with a faint metallic smoke. As the boat pitched and yawed along it was hard to stand up straight without holding onto something, but not the pipes even though they were right there. But Tock didn't need to hold onto anything. He stood, tilting this way and that like a gyroscope, like his feet were cemented to the deck. It looked like he was moving, but Kevin realized he was staying straight up and down, immovable, while the boat and Kevin and Ivan moved around him. Kevin stood up with his feet spread wide, trying to mimic him. But he soon gave up when his legs got tired of trying to anticipate which way the boat would move next. Ivan gave up the helm and sat beside Kevin.

The full moon lit a tiny spit of land on the horizon. It was the island, Kevin just knew it somehow. It was right in the belt of the moon.

from Kate's diary,
July Tenth, 1976:

*I'm back in the room at the top of the school on the island. No one said anything about how I ran away because all the girls are bad girls here like me.*

*It's not so bad here when Nick isn't here. Maybe he will only come not so much. I ate dinner next to the girl Karen whose eyes I like. She is as skinny as a bone so there are only her eyes.*

*I said Why are you here?*

*She said Because they think I don't eat enough and she laughed. She was just playing with her food. I liked her laugh it sounded like fruit. I was done with my food and she said You want some of mine?*

*I said Why don't you want to eat?*

*She said Just because. She said Why are you here?*

*I said Just because and we laughed.*

*I think we will be friends.*

# CHAPTER TWENTY-TWO

After about half an hour the signal of the fm radio station, a Port Bedford station, began to fade in and out. Tock backed off the throttle so the boat slowed and quieted. He turned off the radio and spoke in a normal tone now, "We're getting close."

Kevin's and Ivan's windbreakers were dark and they wore dark corduroys, one blue and one brown, which were both Kevin's and so too short for Ivan. So Ivan had to wear black socks too, with his black high-top sneakers. Kevin's sneakers had once been white, but they were so dirty it didn't matter. Now they took the new black caps from the backpack and put them on. Tock chuckled, checking them out over his shoulder as he steered by some buoys.

"A regular couple of commandos," he said. Then he turned off the running lights, but kept the radar on so the whole pilot house glowed faintly green. "I'm taking us to a beach on the north side. The landing dock is on the west. That's where the school is, over there," he said pointing to his right. "You'll have to figure it out." Tock pulled into the cove and cut the engine, letting her coast; then, with unexpected agility, Tock left the pilot house and leaped around it so he was standing high on the foredeck peering out into the darkness. The boat slid silently forward. Tock had a rope and anchor in his hand; he pitched forward and heaved it so it fell far away with an invisible splash. He pulled the boat forward a little and tied them fast. "Well, boys, here we are." Then he leapt like a goat onto the roof of the pilot house where a super-tiny gray plywood skiff was lashed upside down infront of the mufflers. "I threw this little baby together one afternoon for my nephew, with old ply and lots of glue. She leaks a little and she's bluff in the wind. Think you can manage her?"

"We have a raft of our own," said Ivan proudly.

"Good boys," he said. "The oars are down below under the benches. Go fetch 'em Kevin." Kevin caught Tock's eye when he said that. "Ivan. Help me lug her off the roof."

Kevin had almost said Yes sir, but he didn't want to sound ridiculous. He just hurried through the pilot house and down to the cabin and lifted the bench cover he had peeked in before. There was the rifle. He felt like Tock had wanted him to see it all by himself—and several boxes of large bullets. He closed the bench quickly because it scared him, and opened the other, where he found a set of gray oars as long as himself.

Ivan and Tock had the skiff teetering on the gunwale of the stern deck when Kevin came back up. The three of them slid it over the side, Tock grabbing the rope that dangled from its front at the last minute. The skiff bobbed there as high in the water as the lobster boat.

"See you fellah's later," said Tock handing the rope to Kevin. "But, I'll tell you first, I'm pulling out if there's any trouble. Just so you know. Old Tock can't afford no trouble these days boys, so okay?"

Kevin didn't like the sound of that, but said, "we understand," anyway.

"Good boys," said Tock again, clapping them both on the back. "Real fishermen. Onward!" he said. "I'll be waiting." He chuckled again to himself as they climbed into the skiff. "Tock's never been a wheelman before," he said. "First time for everything." With that he gave them his fist in the air like he'd done before and Ivan put the oars into the rowlocks. "Go get 'er!" said Tock laughing, his big arms crossed over his chest, shaking his head, "She'll be expecting you."

Even though the cove was sheltered by a hill full of pine trees, the wind still kept blowing the little skiff off course. Soon, as they blew further and further to the left of the beach, Kevin moved up to join Ivan, hip to hip on the little center bench and took an oar. They kept pretty even after that, both looking over their shoulders to stay on course.

One last small wave lifted them, then the feel in their feet and sound of sand scraping the bottom. They jumped out quickly into about a half foot of returning water. It was icier here than in Port Bedford, soaking into Kevin's sneakers and socks as he held on to keep the boat from being drawn back out with the wave. But they managed to scurry it up the rocky sand before the next little wave rolled in. Now they dragged it to the top of the beach and turned it over into the bushes so it was more or less hidden. The wind was cold too and soon both of their sopping feet were caked in sand.

"This is crazy," said Kevin. His eyes felt round.

Ivan giggled, "Yeah," his voice goofy with excitement. They had come to the head of the beach, to a post stuck in the ground with a round gray-looking lifesaver buoy hung from a nail around a sign saying No Unsupervised Student Swimming and behind it a long dark path going up the hill and into the woods. "This is the swim beach I guess," said Ivan, "so the path probably goes to the school."

At the top of the hill, they stopped in their tracks: two pillars, the exact same as on Garden Street made from the same field rocks, the same big cement knobs at the top.

"This is weird," said Kevin.

"This is very weird," said Ivan.

The pine woods were pitch dark. They flicked on their flashlights and the path turned tawny with pine needles in the beams. And the feeling grew in Kevin with every step that this path, the path at home and the path to his mansion all belonged to Nick Ford.

A sudden cracking of branches immediately to Kevin's left. He dropped his flashlight as he turned towards it. Ivan still held his focused to the ground so it cast a half light into the woods. Nothing.

Ivan shrugged and they went on until, at the top of the hill, the pine trees gave way to a big meadow with an empty dark church in the middle and a little fenced graveyard with very old looking stones. Kevin felt creepy and thought about ghosts. There must be lots of them if this was where all Nick Ford's family was. Meanwhile, Ivan was looking down over the hill—just beyond the church were two more pillars marking the end of the path—to a mansion twice the size of Nick's at least. And the same crazy roofs and dark shingles as his and the Carriage House too only more of them.

A sick feeling growing, Kevin looked down into the harbor. A big, lonely sailboat was moored there, dark and still in the moonlight.

"We can't," moaned Kevin. "This is all a trap. He knows everything we think even. What if he's in Kate's room right now, waiting for us?" Kevin thought of Tock's gun. He wished he'd brought it.

"He won't be," said Ivan. "Johnny's with him, remember? The race? And probably another crew guy too. They're all probably asleep on the boat." This plain common sense calmed Kevin down a little as Ivan had no doubt intended. Things didn't seem quite so supernatural anymore. "And if he is in there," said Ivan menacingly, "He'll be sorry. I'll kick him right in the balls. I wish I had my knife with me, but Kate's got it, so he better watch out."

"And I've still got his," said Kevin pulling out the little pen knife so it shimmered with moon. "If he is there I'll stick it right in his ribs, like this." Kevin jabbed the knife to demonstrate, even though the knife was still closed.

They started to sneak down the hill. No windows were lit anywhere. The lawn was lit with dew already in the moonlight so bright it cast long shadows of themselves ahead of them. And Kevin saw the halo of the moon shimmering around the shadow of his own head. Then it seemed like the shimmer was walking along the lawn ahead of them. Kevin stopped and grabbed Ivan's sleeve. But it kept on walking, like a barefoot woman Kevin thought for a second, then disappeared out towards the harbor.

"What?" whispered Ivan.

"I thought I saw someone for a second," whispered Kevin.

"It's a light house. Out there, see?" Kevin looked out into the ocean and caught a point of light on the horizon just before it winked away.

"That's what it was, you're right."

They circled behind the mansion to keep out of sight of Nick's boat in the harbor. The light house beam swept by them again.

The side door was open. Kate had described to them where the room was that first night after she escaped.

There was a big fire door that said GIRLS. Ivan pushed it open and snuck up the first flight of stairs commando style, indicating for Kevin to follow.

At the end of the second floor hall they saw the closed door of the room. With no more noise than the squishing water in their sneakers, they crept down the hall. Kevin took out Nick's knife and opened it, for the first time ever, he realized. The blade was dark like the metal of a gun and not what he expected. He guessed he'd expected something shiny and bewildering, like the pearl handle. He tested it with a careful thumb as he walked: It was sharp all right, like a razor. Maybe because the opened knife made him nervous, but he tripped on the carpet; his knee thumped loudly against the ground in front of Kate's door.

A desperate whisper came from behind it: "You better not come in. I have a knife." He felt his thumb for wetness; it didn't feel like he'd cut himself at least. Not wanting to risk saying anything in the hallway where other girls might hear, Kevin, already on the ground anyway, shoved his flashlight to the gap in the bottom of the door and flashed it three times in succession.

The door swung open to Kate's smiling face. She was fully clothed, her backpack already on and Ivan's knife gleaming in her hand from the red EXIT sign light in the hallway. "I'm ready." She slipped into the hallway, Kevin and Ivan right behind her, down the stairs, out the side door and they were free.

Kevin broke into a run up the hill, Kate and Ivan racing close behind.

They didn't say a word to one another until they had dragged the skiff down the beach and back into the water. Kate got in and pulled out an oar. Ivan got in next to her and pulled out the other. So Kevin was left to sit in the stern like the captain, or cargo.

Kate wasn't smiling. "Did you see?" she said between strokes. "He's here with Johnny. He's coming to my room tonight. I didn't think you'd get here first. Or I kept thinking he'd catch you." She looked at Kevin grimly and stopped her stroke, "I would have stabbed you." Ivan's stroke put the skiff way off course.

"I could've stabbed you too," said Kevin, terrified at the possibility.

"I almost wish Nick was there," said Ivan. Kevin could already see the gray glow of the lobster boat ahead. "Right in the middle." Kate rowed her oar solo until Kevin said they were pointed right again. "Because now he'd be dead." Ivan started his oar again, in time with Kate's.

Tock was on the deck waiting for them, watching them come. He put his hand up to welcome them. "Damn," he said, reaching out and pulling them along side when they got near enough. "There's hope maybe, if there's more like you kids on the way." He helped each one of them on board like they were all Presidents. They told him how Nick Ford's boat was moored on the other side of the harbor. "Lucky thing we came to the far side," Tock laughed suddenly. "I've half a mind to go pay him a visit in his bunk. He must be such a sweet sleeper. No, not while he's sleeping..." he was speaking to himself as he thoughtfully weighed anchor, then coiled the rope. "He's got to be awake at least; I owe him that much...and..." He took one of the oars from the skiff on the deck and started to row the whole lobster boat away from the land. "...not here. Not on his island. It'd have to be someplace. Someplace we meet as equals," he muttered. The three kids stood silently watching him row, listening to every word. "Someplace where I could tell him my mind..." he laughed. Took another stroke. "Utopia," he said and laughed again, "No place."

Kate and Kevin and Ivan huddled together, a little away from him, looking just at each other.

Soon they were far enough into open water for Tock to start the engine. He took them away at a quiet, reluctant crawl as if he were still half thinking of turning back. In a little while he put the running lights back on and pushed down the throttle.

"Now," he shouted to them, "so far so good. But I've been doing some thinking. It's not good he was in that harbor. Things are going to get a whole lot hotter for you guys and for me too. He'll ask questions. He'll find out how it was before long. That's not good. He couldn't get me for the fire. I was too careful. But this, I don't know. Someone must have seen me leave. And someone will see us coming back. He's got spies in that harbor, people who owe him favors."

"Maybe he'll think I drowned myself," said Kate. "I probably might've if you hadn't showed up like you promised."

Tock looked at her, his eyes sharp, "Hush now, girl," he said. "Life is hard and nothing more. Anyway, you'd just be solving his problems for him. He'd just win again. You'd just be one more to do his work for him. It's a waste of time to think like that."

Kate looked down at the deck like she knew what he was talking about, "Where am I supposed to go, Tock?"

"With us to Didi's," said Kevin too quickly and high-voiced. "We're all going to have a great summer now. We got away. We did it!" he said jumping around the deck, but no one else was jumping.

"You can stay with Didi maybe," said Ivan to Kevin, "but not us. Not for long."

"Of course you can," said Kevin, obstinate. "You're my friends." Tock put the boat into neutral. They were just drifting now in the open sea. His eyes were for all of them now.

"I didn't mean it to be this way," said Tock. "Maybe Arlene was right. But this is the way it is: I'm mixed up in your problems now; so you're mixed up in mine. We have to help each other."

They all three looked at Tock. Could he help them, Kevin wondered? The truth was he could do whatever he wanted to them, and might. He had them here, after all, in the middle of the sea.

"We set him up," said Kate.

"That's right," said Tock. "I'm a fisherman. All I need is good bait. And that's gonna be Kate. See the picture? Just get him to me, on neutral ground. Leave the rest to me."

"Me," said Kate.

"Better than drowning yourself, now isn't it?" Tock said smiling at her. "Unless of course you're losing your nerve."

"I'm not afraid," said Kate icily.

"What're you going to do?" Kevin blurted out.

Tock looked at him seriously, like one adult to another. "Talk to him, Kevin. Maybe he'll listen; who's to say? But he won't trick old Tock. Not this time. On even ground this time. I won't let him go, though, that's for sure. Not this time, Kevin. I made that mistake once. Believing words. Everybody believed him; he's like that: a brilliant fucking con man. Your mother did, Kate, poor soul; she still believes him. I feel for her, you know; I really do."

Kate looked surprised and maybe a little grateful. Kevin was surprised too. Maybe there was more to Mrs. Harrigan than he could see.

"So," said Tock, clapping his hands together suddenly, "Are you fellahs with me?"

"I am," said Ivan loudly.

"I hope he dies," said Kate quietly.

"Kevin?" said Tock.

"What?" said Kevin angrily.

"He'll hurt your sister too, in the end. You can bank on it."

"Shut up about my sister. She can take care of herself," said Kevin. "And she can take care of all of us too. Why don't you just let us go?" he said.

"I'm not gonna hurt you Kevin," said Tock immediately starting the engine again. "You have my word as a fisherman. And I'm not gonna keep you out here. Look. I'm taking you home. Okay?"

"Okay," said Kevin sullenly. He felt like he'd just had enough of everything. All he wanted was to get back safe with his friends to Didi and go to bed. All he wanted was for all of this to not be. Why couldn't it just be that way?

"If I hurt you before," said Tock, "it was to teach you what it took a long time for me to learn. You see now, don't you? I won't hurt you anymore. Promise."

"Let's hear the plan at least, Kevin," said Ivan.

Nick would hurt Didi in the end, Kevin could see that. He already had. And Kate and Ivan and even himself, when he stopped to think. His whole life was just getting worse every day. But he just wanted to be back with Didi. Just for now. He couldn't think about more than that. Just safe with his friends with Didi. Why was that so much to ask? There was no one to ask, that was why.

Kevin looked up from the blank water where he'd been staring, because he felt something. Kate's eyes were on him, full of their friendship and everything he'd meant to her.

"You don't have to," she said. "I'll do it by myself."

"I'll do it," he said. He looked at her and at Ivan and knew then they were the most important thing in the world to him along with Didi. "I want to," he said.

"Good," said Tock. "That's settled. Now here's the plan. Listen closely. There's a pen and paper in the port bench. Go get it." Ivan ran into the cabin for it. "Kate you're going to write Nick a note to tempt him for, you know what."

Kate frowned dangerously, but Tock spoke to her sharply,

"Don't start crying on me. It's time to grow up now. It's nothing new, believe me. It's nothing special. That's the way it's been forever. That's the truth, girl. It's just that no one cares to talk about it; that's all."

"I'm not crying," said Kate looking up at him angrily.

"Well," said Tock, "More ways than one of crying. That's a good girl, anyway," he said with an embarrassed face. "It ain't gonna happen again. I know Nick when there's something he wants. It'll get him there, as crazy as it sounds. He'll be suspicious maybe. But what he wants makes him stupid in the end. It doesn't matter what you write, he'll barely read it once he gets what it means. And he'll show alone because he's too afraid of looking ridiculous. And you'll be alone," Tock held up his hand quickly to stop her from speaking, "Only you won't, see? Because me and the boys will be waiting," he said, taking his hands from the wheel to clap Kevin's shoulder and Ivan's, who had just returned with the pen and paper. "And if anything goes wrong, not that it will, but if something does and they ask you a bunch of questions about it, all you got to say is this: Tell them a dark man did it; that always works no matter what. Remember that: a dark man, and you don't know any more about it. But he sure didn't like Nick Ford," he laughed quietly. "Partners, right? Now we just have to figure out where."

Kate's eyes lit up. "On the path," she said.

"What?" said Tock.

"I want to meet him on the path."

"Between Garden and Vale," said Kevin morosely.

Tock seemed to think for a second. "Okay," said Tock. "That'd be fine." They could already see the glow of Port Bedford in the distance. "Now take the paper and listen. Here's what you're gonna say..."

Kate took the paper. "I know what to say."

*July tenth 1976*
*Dear Nick*

 *I know what I want. I see you even in my bed sometimes when I'm asleep. And sometimes I cry because I think you love Deirdre or my mom and you don't love me and I get angry. I'm not staying at the Ford School because you know there's nothing wrong with me but I was very upset with you for putting me there so you would only see me sometimes and leave me there alone. But I liked what we did there even though I know I'm not supposed to. I pretend you're there when you're not. I think about your big arms and the soft places on your belly. It can be our special secret that no one can ever know but us. I want to stay home and have summer and we can meet on the path like the first time after I saw you. I'll wait for you on the path tomorrow night at eight and if you come I know you love me.*

 *I am yours and waiting for You,*

   *Kate*

# CHAPTER TWENTY-THREE

It wasn't just black anymore on the path. Kevin's eyes were getting used to the dark. He could see Kate now, standing alone in the middle like a gray column of light. And slowly some hints of color too, in her face. Pink's and greens and purples but just barely.

Ivan was an almost imperceptible sound beside him by the trunk of the cedar tree, but Kevin could hear the heavy man's breathing from Tock crouching behind them, against the hedge to the empty lot.

It felt like a long time ago already since Tock had spoken, whispering that it was eight o'clock, the time when Nick was supposed to show. But Kevin wasn't sure how long really. Not very long maybe. The leaves in the trees above stood still. The high pierce of a mosquito passing Kevin's ear. He felt an itchy bite rising on his neck, but he didn't slap the spot. A mournful singing woman's voice rose from far away on Vale, "So..." high and round and hopeless, then lower and desperate, "...phie." It was the older single lady on the corner of Hill calling for her cat, which had been missing for a week, "So...phie."

Kevin tensed and now he heard the unmistakably heavy approach of footsteps on hard packed dirt from the direction of Garden St. A darker place grew in the center of the tree trunks' half suggested forms, and darkened into the shape of a man. Kate stood still and gray with light. The shape stopped. There were hints of color in his face too where he stood, blue and red.

"You are a dirty and cunning little girl, Katharine," said the voice of Nick Ford, and not the voice of Nick Ford because it was lower and trembled and wavered like someone speaking underwater. The night was suddenly hotter and more humid. A cricket started to shriek like a knife. It felt like Kevin could hear Kate's heartbeat just a half step ahead of his own. What could she possibly say now? He could hear Nick's breathing, louder than Tock's though he was three times the distance. "I've felt your eyes, full of desire growing on me this whole year long. It's burning me so I can't stand it. I can't sleep, you're so like...How can the body of a child stand such passion? It's no wonder you got sick. Don't just stand there and say nothing. Say something, please. Tell me all my senses are wrong, that you aren't burning inside. Where is the innocence you should have, Katharine?

Say something. Laugh at me even," he said angrily, "just say something before I touch you." The man shape started to approach her, "Is
it you?" his voice was a whimper. He stopped not a foot from her. "I
can smell you now," he said, "talc and wind. That's your fragrance; I
have nightmares about it. Why?" his voice clipped short. "Tell me why
you met me here? What do you want from me? Tell me what you
want, Kate. Anything and I'll give it to you. Anything. Say something,
Kate. Please. You're trembling." His dark hand reached toward her.

Kevin couldn't stand it. He crouched, pushing his hands into
his cheeks as hard as he could, the pearl handle of the knife in his
left hand pushing into the bone. Why didn't Tock do something? The
hand was on her cheek.

"I'll take you out of that school. I'll send Johnny away and have
you come live with me. Would you like that?" Tock's breathing was
deafening in Kevin's ears, but Nick seemed deaf, his shape leaning
unchanged toward the gray still shape of Kate. The sound of his
breathing filled everywhere. The feeling returned that Kevin had had
when Johnny fell from the cedar, and Kate and Ivan on the path did-
n't hear. That the world was stuck; it would never move again, just
stay like this always. He heard a tiny clicking. Ivan was grinding his
teeth. Kate still didn't say anything. Maybe she'd had a heart attack.
Kate had insisted that Tock not come out until she gave him the
word. But she was probably so scared she couldn't talk.

Kate lifted her hands slowly to Nick's on her cheek. She took
his hand and put it to her mouth. Her body jerked. Nick's body jerked
too.

"You little!" Nick cried in a hissing shout, pulling back. "You bit
me, you little cunt. I'll..."

"Tock!" said Kate, stepping back.

"Tock?!" said Nick.

"Hello, Enjay," said Tock standing up and walking into the path
between them. "Always wondered what you did with your evenings.
Where's the innocence you used to have? You used to be such a nice
kid."

The bitten hand went to Nick's forehead now. "Shit," he said.
But Kevin only half heard because he and Ivan were moving now,
according to plan, to block off the path behind him.

"And Kevin," said Kevin.

"And Ivan," said Ivan, "and we both have knives."

"And me too," said Kate, from behind Tock, opening Tock's big
bonehandled knife so the blade caught a gray gleam from the sky.

Suddenly, Nick laughed. "And you, Tom? I suppose you have a gun."

"Nope," said Tock, "just my Mediterranean good looks. We never had a gang as good as this one when we were kids, now did we? I just borrowed them. You're a hard man to get on an equal footing these days, you know."

"You call this equal, Tom?" It was trying to be cool, but Nick Ford's voice filled with panic.

"That's right," said Tock. "How does it feel?"

"Not very pleasant," said Nick.

"No? I'm sorry for you, I really am. You always hated to be embarrassed worse than anything." Tock reached over his shoulder to Kate. "Give me my knife," he said. Nick looked over his shoulder to Ivan and Kevin standing shoulder to shoulder in the path. "Give it to me, Kate," said Tock. Nick turned his head back to Tock and Kate, behind him.

"You are doing this to me, Kate," Nick said, huge and menacing. "It's you, you little witch. It's all you," but now his voice was full of fear. "I hope you understand, if you give him that knife, you'll be murdering me."

"Why?" said Tock. "Don't you trust me, Enjay?"

Nick laughed again, more like a sob, "That's what's sticking in your throat all this time, isn't it Tommy? That I was born with privilege and you weren't. That's it, isn't it? You just can't stand that. So you set my fishingboats on fire, so you use children to humiliate me, all because you're still a child yourself, crying 'It's not fair, it's not fair.'"

"That's it isn't it?" said Tock back, mocking. "I moved on from that when I was ten. I don't cry, Enjay, that's the difference. I do something about it. The knife, Kate."

"Don't do it, Kate!" said Nick, commanding.

She handed Tock's knife back to him then moved quickly away.

Kevin wanted it to stop. He wanted to go to sleep.

"Let's be fair, though," said Tock. "I have my knife now so you ought to have yours, no? Fair's fair. Kevin, toss Mr. Ford his knife back. Don't get too close, though."

Kevin tossed the little penknife out in front of Nick. He felt more defenseless than ever. Tock stood in front of Nick, his big open knife, five times its size, in his right hand.

"Fair?" said Nick.

"Fair," said Tock. "You should've chosen yourself a bigger knife."

"You think I'm just going to pick that up, Tom? You really think it's that easy to turn me into a back alley hood like yourself?"

"Pick it up, Enjay," said Tock in a low voice.

"Why'd you bring the children into it, Tom?" said Nick.

"Oh no," said Tock, looking down for a second to the ground. "You brought them into it. You..." But Tock never had a chance to finish because at that moment, when his eyes were off of Nick, Nick turned towards Kevin and Ivan and started to charge through them back towards Garden. Kevin threw up his arms to protect himself, catching a glimpse of Tock in the air over Nick's shoulder as he did.

When Kevin took his arms away from his eyes, Nick was kneeling in front of him, eye to eye. Tock held Nick's head by the hair with his left hand. Nick was holding Tock's arm. Ivan held his ground next to Kevin, his jackknife point out. His hand was shaking. But Nick wasn't coming any closer.

Then came Tock's knife, a dull flash from behind below Nick's chin. Then Tock and the knife disappeared in the darkness.

Nick sat with his back against the cedar tree, smiling at Kevin. A dark smiling line. Smiling in his throat and darkening underneath like a beard. Smiling at Kevin now forever. The barest hint of red growing in the darkness.

Tock again, reappearing from the darkness, dark-edged knife first, pointing down. Suddenly Ivan and Kate were there huddled up next to Kevin, touching him, and he was touching them. Like they had all lost something in each other's pockets. Nick was trying to get up from the tree trunk, bubbling weak words from his mouth, "Oh God, oh god," he was saying. He scrabbled himself up off the tree and, when Kate came towards him, his eyes were filled with terror, "No, please," he whispered and feebly raised an arm to ward off the blow.

Kate had nothing but her small fist. She shook it at his face.

"Let him go," said Tock.

Kevin and Ivan stepped back, watched Nick stagger towards Garden St.

"Make it if you can, you fuck," Tock hissed. "Fuck with those kids, touch that girl again, and I'll come back and finish it. That's a promise."

"Oh God, oh god," spluttered Nick, stumbling down the path.

"Remember, fellahs," whispered Tock when Nick was out of earshot, "You never seen my boat. Tock's going fishing down South and I don't plan on being bothered. No one knows I got my boat back. Banker'll figure it burned with the rest. Nothing more I can do; the fire finished me off for this town anyhow, so I'll be moving on."

Kevin couldn't hold it back anymore and he started to cry. "What about us?" he sobbed.

"No, Kevin, no," said Tock shaking the knife hysterically. "That's not the way. Look at Kate. Look at Ivan." Kevin looked at his friends. They weren't crying, either of them. Their faces were blank, wide-eyed. The three of them were all still touching each other: each other's arms and hairs and faces. Kevin was afraid to stop feeling his friends, afraid he'd stop feeling. Kate put a finger on Kevin's wet face, then she put the finger in her mouth and kept it there, sucking it. Ivan stared at Tock, like he expected him to tell them something. "We're all in this together now," said Tock. "Now don't cry, Kevin. You're tougher than that. We all need to be cool so no one gets hurt." Kevin forced himself to stop, and just his breathing was jumpy now. "Good, good now," said Tock. "Now. Find the knife you tossed."

"I can't," said Kevin, not moving from his friends.

"Find it!" said Tock.

All three of them moved together, found the place where it was on the path. Kevin picked it up. "Keep it." Tock put his own back in his pocket. "Now listen, if you stay cool, you guys have nothing to be afraid of. He won't die; I just gave him a scratch. Something to remember.

"Okay," said Tock, his voice was cool, but his hand was shaking a little, "we've got to split up from here. Would've been easier if I did kill him, but I want him to remember what he's done in his life. Life is for learning, fellahs. He's afraid of you now. Alls you got to do is keep it that way."

Kate looked behind at Nick's slow progress. Kevin turned too, the thickening night erasing Nick Ford's hunched figure to shadow as it staggered away,

"Oh god. Oh ga help me someone."

"I know how to lie if I want," Kate said. Kevin felt chills all through his legs and neck. Shouldn't they help him? Mustn't they?

"I'm going," said Tock. "Don't forget. Don't ever forget anything." He kissed each one of them on the forehead. Kevin was last and Tock gave him a special look that meant Goodbye. "I'm sorry," said Tock. "Sorry for everything. Sorry I won't be around to see how you grow up."

Tock ran the opposite direction from the slow wandering shadow of Nick. He moved so quickly that both vanished completely from their senses at almost the same instant.

Kevin stood with Kate and Ivan in the dark by the tunnel that led to the empty lot, nothing to tell him it hadn't been a dream.

"Let's get out of here," said Kate and crawled into the tunnel of briars; Kevin followed on his belly, stunned that he was moving at all.

ut when he got to the empty lot, the space was too much and he ran, just ran, before Ivan was even through.

Kevin ran his breath out to keep from yelling for help. He ran and ran and still the shriek felt like it was coming, down Dearborn and into Harbor Rd. Only then he noticed Kate and Ivan still running with him, blurrily blanched faces jarred with streetlight.

It seemed like they had been running for hours. They'd already passed the harbor. But he heard the shriek coming anyway, not from himself or his friends, faint, miles ahead but growing louder.

The chainlink fences of the old amusement park were passing them by on the right. Ivan's hand lunged out for Kevin's shoulder, stopping him. Ivan's hands were on his own knees; he was gasping for breath, lifting his head to speak. Kate was there too, standing straight. "Over the fence," said Ivan, lowering his head for more air, "They found him already."

The siren was getting closer. Someone must have seen him collapse on Garden. Maybe even the Harrigans. Kevin, last over the fence, lost his footing and landed with his side on the pavement. He felt a sharp pain.

The flashing red cross of a white ambulance side wailed through the street light.

The siren shifted lower, fading with a moan down Harbor Rd. Soon dark police cars would be trolling the streets, searchlights in the maple leaves. Looking for suspects, for Tock, and them. Soon the path itself would be blocked off with orange barricades, like the Cove East was after the Shoot Out. Tomorrow, kids would come as they had for bloodstained rocks.

Kevin, scooted up one cheek of his butt to get the pearl knife away from the bruise in his side. He'd landed hard against the night-bled bright boards of the ticket taker booth. The black decaying wooden webs of rollercoaster loomed overhead. The heels of his right hand stung as he reached into his back pocket, pulling out the knife, hanging it from his fingers like a rotting fish.

The sight of it glowing gray white in the darkness.

The red smile seemed to grow out of it. Kevin shrieked.

All he could think of was hiding. They all had to find a hiding place and,

A flash of light.

"Hey. You. What're you doing? Park's closed. You're not supposed to be in here."

"Quick," whispered Kevin, scrambling to his feet, "Follow me." He dashed for the first alley off the arcade before the flashlight beam could find him. And over the turnstile and into the funhouse. The soft jiggle of bearings, twice, told him that Kate and Ivan had followed. But he couldn't see. It was pitch black and it dawned on him this might have been a stupid tactic. "We'll hold hands," he whispered, "so we don't get lost." A hand reached for his in the darkness, finding his wrist and moving down. It was Kate's, he thought, but it could have been Ivan's too.

Kevin led them past the black still objects in the maze for a few minutes before the hand in his pulled.

"Let's sit down and wait," said the even voice of Kate. "They'll find us sooner or later anyway, so let's make up some lies for when they do."

from Kate's diary,
July Eleventh, 1976:


*It was black in the funhouse and Kevin and Ivan and me were alone in the dark.*

*I remembered when I was a very little girl and the amusement park was still open and I went in there with my dad and bright lights and ugly men jumped out of the dark full of loud noises. I knew it was all turned off now but I knew there was real men now to jump out of the world like that.*

*I said Dad I don't like this it's scary make it stop.*

*He said It's a ride Kitty I can't make it stop. He said it's okay nothing will happen. He said it's okay it will be fun.*

*I said He wouldn't so I made it stop myself.*

*Ivan said What?*

*I said I hope he's dead.*

*Ivan said You saw he isn't. What are we going to do?*

*Kevin wanted to tell the truth because he still didn't understand it was me who made him stop, me and Tock did, and Ivan and Didi and Kevin too. I said They're going to believe what Nick says and he's going to lie. That's why we have to lie first. Even Tock said so remember?*

*Kevin was quiet and I felt him squeeze my hand.*

*I squeezed his hand back and felt happy even though it was black and we didn't know what would happen to us. Because I knew the shadows couldn't hurt us anymore now. And I squeezed Ivan's hand to tell him too.*

*Adults are easy to lie to if you tell them what they want to hear. And I knew Didi would help too, because she knows. And I knew that even if he wasn't dead I saw his eyes and Nick would be scared of me always like Tock said.*

*A bright light jumped out of the dark and Kevin and Ivan and me all held hands still. Then there was the big dark shape of a man.*

*He said It's all right. I'm not trying to hurt you.*

# CHAPTER TWENTY-FOUR

"We found them, sir. We found them in the amusement park; they were hiding in the fun house," said the large policeman who had first shined the flashlight on them by the train of wooden cars and told them not to worry, that he was here to protect them. "The night-watchman saw someone go in there and called us. It took a long time for us to convince them to come out."

"We were scared," said Kate.

Bill Gunn was standing there looking strangely at them, all three hip to hip on a wooden bench. He was wearing loafers with no socks. "Why didn't you go for help, Kate?"

"We thought he was still after us."

"Who, Kate?"

"The guy."

"Nick has already told me some of what happened. He's in surgery now. They say he'll pull through and be fine. Now tell me if you can what this man did to you."

Kate was silent, her face flushed.

"Can you tell me if this man was a dark man?"

Her face was nearly purple now. "He had a mask on."

"We've got a pretty good idea, anyway. You're safe now. Come on with me, we'll go and call your parents."

The policeman fascinated Kevin, how he could move around with so much weight on his broad hips, his wide black belt loaded with a black gun, shining handcuffs, a black walkie talkie, a long brown billy club, and three polished copper bullets on each side of the buckle. He was opening the frosted glass door to lead them down the hall, then out the front door of the police station.

"Are those real bullets?" said Kevin. He thought the policeman had seemed very friendly since he first talked them out of the fun-house.

"Sure are, kid." Kevin thought the policeman liked him. The name on his badge was O'Mally. Bill Gunn led them to the big next-door building, leaving the glowing globes of the police station behind; a night watchman met them. O'Mally had been opening doors for Bill Gunn all along, like he was his boss, which maybe he was. Kate and Ivan followed, and O'Mally looked down on Kevin kindly before they entered the building. "You wanna touch one?" he said, pulling a live bullet out of its little leather loop.

"Sure," said Kevin. It was cold on his finger. His other hand was in his pocket on the knife. They rode in a silver elevator, Kevin hadn't been in too many elevators, actually; there weren't too many in Port Bedford. The policeman rode in the front of the car, hands on his belt, staring at the closed door silently. Kevin could feel the elevator car moving in his belly. A sonic whir. It felt like floating in nowhere. No one said anything; the only sound was Ivan scratching his scalp beneath its thick mat of hair.

The sign in the hallway said in gold letters, District Attorney's Office of the Town of Port Bedford. They passed rows and rows of empty desks. The room they walked into at the very end of the hall was Bill Gunn's office. They had crossed from the Police Station to the big seven-story Courthouse building next to it on Harbor Rd. They were on the top floor.

The largest object in the room was a highbacked black leather swivel chair that overwhelmed the wooden desk it sat behind and, behind the chair, three big plate glass windows wrapped around the corner of the building giving Kevin's eyes the largest, highest view of Town and Commercial Harbors he'd ever seen.

Lights twinkled in two mismatched lobes, the dark jetty in between with a single red light at the end. Then the ocean, the few lonely lights of fishingboats, tankers and buoys spread out along the horizon.

"Please," said Bill Gunn to them. There was a couch and some chairs for them to sit down. "I thought this would be more comfortable than the police station. I'm sure the sooner your parents get here the safer you'll feel. Now, Kate, I've already called your mother and father, told them you were safe. They uh," here he cleared his throat uncomfortably, so Kevin felt cautious for the first time, "they, he made it to your doorway apparently." Why hadn't they gone for help? that's what Bill Gunn was asking again, looking at their faces. "Nothing here is your fault. Is that clear? Kate, honey," he said, putting his hand awkwardly on her shoulder, "your mom and dad will be here soon. They're going to Nick's house first to get Johnny, to make sure he's safe. To break the news about his father, you know," he said, still talking only to Kate, the ham-sized hand on her shoulder as he towered above them all, fat, pink, sweaty, and linked in some terrible mysterious way to Nick Ford himself. Kevin felt the knife pressing at the bruise on his butt. Kate shied her shoulder away from his fat ringed pink hand, leaned herself against Kevin. "Sensitive to touch?" He walked back to his desk and made a note on a yellow pad. "We'll get the bastard. The whole force is out right now."

"Is Johnny coming?" said Kate. Kevin felt tears swelling up inside him.

"Yes of course. He'll be staying with you again now until your uncle recovers. They're coming here first. Then you all can go to the hospital to see your uncle. He'll be in the recovery room by then. Though I must warn you, Kate, he might not be able to speak for some time. It was, a deep stroke to the throat, by a powerful left hand; we know that much already." Kevin saw Tock's big left hand, the right one holding Nick's hair.

"Now," said Bill Gunn, looking first at Kevin then at Ivan; his voice was not at all as nice sounding anymore. "We'll call your parents and then, while we're waiting, I'd like to ask a few questions."

"I'm living with my sister," muttered Kevin. Bill Gunn eyed him with a spark of recognition.

"Yes, I recall now, meeting her. Diana wasn't it?"

"Deirdre."

"Deirdre..." He scanned his yellow pad, "Hawkins. That'll do. What's the number?"

Kevin gave it to him. "Me too," said Ivan.

"In the custody of your sister?" said Gunn with raised eyebrows.

"With Didi."

"Your sister's name?"

"Deirdre," said Kevin.

"Ah," said Bill Gunn. "I'm afraid that won't do uh," (scanning) "Ivan. I can't release you into the custody of anyone who's not a family member; I'm sorry. Now..."

"My mom is out of town."

"Do you have a number?"

Ivan shook his head.

"Your father, then?"

Ivan muttered something inaudible. Bill Gunn raised his eyebrows again. "He's in jail," Ivan said.

"Ivan Otrusky, of course. Right. Well, Ivan, we may have a little problem then. We'll find you some suitable shelter for the night." Ivan looked down at the ground and Kevin looked back up into Bill Gunn's pink face when he heard a sudden sob next to him. Ivan, stonefaced a second before, was crying. Kevin put a quick arm around his shoulder.

"There's no need for that, please," said Bill Gunn quickly. Kate put her hand on Ivan's head.

"Didi will fix it when she gets here," she said.

"Didi." said Bill Gunn and went back to note it on his pad. He dialed the number Kevin had given him.

"...Miss Hawkins? This is William Gunn, District Attorney for Port Bedford...I believe we met once at one of Carol Harrigan's parties...I'm afraid there's been some trouble. Kevin...he's fine; he's here in my office, seventh floor of the court building. If you could come down, I'll explain everything. He was, kidnapped briefly, it seems. Please...Thank you...We can send a squad car if you prefer...Thank you."

"She's coming right down," said Bill Gunn to Kevin. "O'Mally, scare me up some coffee would you? And some sodas or something for the kids." O'Mally disappeared and they were alone with Bill Gunn in his office. Kevin still felt the knife.

Bill Gunn looked tired, the blue shadow of a beard. You could tell he wasn't real comfortable around kids.

"Now," he said, his small quick eyes landing unexpectedly on Kevin's. "Tell me what happened. From the beginning." The lights grew brighter in Bill Gunn's office. Kevin suddenly imagined he could smell the sweat of all the people who had sat here, Ivan's father maybe. Maybe Tock too had been here before.

"What d'ya mean?" said Kevin; he realized desperately that his sneakers were squirming and there was nothing he could do about it. "Do I have to?" He felt himself starting to cry.

"I'll tell you what happened," said Kate. "I can do it." Her voice was near to shrieking.

"You're upset," said Bill Gunn.

"He did things to me. And he still would again."

At that moment Mr. and Mrs. Harrigan walked into the office.

"Please," said Bill Gunn holding the side of his hand to his mouth towards the Harrigans. "Your daughter is upset," and in a whisper, as if Kate couldn't hear somehow, even though she was closer to him than they were. "This'll just take a minute. I don't think they'll be very coherent, but it might give us some clues. Please, Carol, Jason, be patient." Mrs. Harrigan looked very pale and shaky to begin with, but when he said that her face went completely gray.

"I am not upset," said Kate stamping her foot. Both her parents rushed up to hug her. She looked uncertainly around the room; Kevin knew who she was looking for because he was looking for him too, the only one who really mattered right now. "Where's Johnny?" she said to her mother. Then to Bill Gunn, "I thought you said he was going to be with them."

"Don't worry Kitty; he's all right," said Mr. Harrigan. "He's safe. He's right downstairs with Officer O'Mally. He's very, very upset too; that's all. That's why we're late, Bill, as a matter of fact," he said as an aside. "He flat out refused to come up when we told him Kate and his friends were here. He grabbed hold of a bench and wouldn't let go. So, in the interest of time I thought it best to leave him down there with O'Mally."

"That's fine, Jason; O'Mally's good with kids. He'll be fine."

Kevin's face felt hot. He was ashamed, but he was relieved not to see Johnny.

"Are you sure Johnny is all right?" said Kate to her father, meekly.

"He's very upset," said her father.

"Now," said Bill Gunn, "we'll try to make this as quick as possible. Please sit down," he said indicating the other couch for the Harrigans.

This was horrible. The only thing Kevin had to hang on to was the thought Deirdre would be here any minute. They'd been taken here by the policeman a little less than an hour ago and already Kate and Ivan's idea was seeming crazy. Ivan and Kate thought it best to lie and maybe they were right, but then, what would they do to Tock if they caught him? Electrocute him maybe. Then there was Nick Ford who knew the real story as well, still out there, his throat throbbing with anger and scariness. Kevin still didn't really understand why they couldn't tell what Nick had done so he could go to jail. It would never work, was what Ivan had said. "This is way better. Don't worry, Kev, we've got it all figured out."

An uncertain silence filled the room, then Deirdre bust in, flushed as if she'd run all the way, "Are you guys all right? Where the hell have you been?" She hugged Kevin and Ivan and Kate too. "I saw Johnny downstairs and he couldn't even talk to me. What's going on?"

Kate burst into tears. Bill Gunn handed her the box of tissues off his desk.

"Jesus Kate, what happened? Oh my poor girl." Mrs. Harrigan's eyes flashed up when she said that. Didi was standing to hug Kate again, but Bill Gunn checked her with his hand, "Now we're all here to get to the bottom of that. Please sit down," he said to Deirdre. "Due to the circumstances, this isn't going to make much sense from their point of view, but still, in the safety of a family setting..." He eyed Deirdre here with a laugh in his eye that infuriated Kevin. "Now I'm sure everyone is tired and frightened, but still we must try to look at this as an official proceeding. The sooner we get this done. I know we're all very concerned about Nick right now, but I'm told it will be several hours before he's out of surgery; the throat is a very delicate business."

"What?!" shouted Deirdre, "Is he...?"

"Port Bedford's finest doctors are there, I assure you. He's in no mortal danger. It's more a question at this point of damage to the vocal chords; the cut was deep, fortunately not deep enough to reach the jugular."

"You mean," said Deirdre her eyes wide, forehead wrinkled like a scared laugh, "somebody tried to slit his throat?" The force of her 's''s filled the room. Bill Gunn's eyebrows said yes.

"In a word," he said.

"Bill! For Godssake," cried Mrs. Harrigan standing up, "Must we allow this woman to sit here and..."

"Give me a break, lady," snapped Deirdre, "I'm just trying to catch up." She rubbed her forehead back and forth with her palm, massaging the information into her brain. She had on a long khaki raincoat she must've thrown over in a hurry because Kevin could see a piece of her familiar sleeping t-shirt sticking through the buttons, "Hey," she said to Gunn, "is it okay if I smoke in here?" Bill Gunn's eyes were like ice studying her. He reached into a drawer of his desk, pulled out a clean glass ashtray and slid it to her across the desktop.

"Now, because Mr. and Mrs. Harrigan had the presence of mind to call me directly after they called the ambulance, I was lucky enough to get a few words in the emergency room before he lost consciousness. Maybe he was delirious." He pulled out his note pad and read, 'Save the children,' was the first thing he said and then he said 'They're the jurors.' He was losing consciousness then; he probably meant, 'witnesses.' We got a call from the night watchman at the amusement park about three children hiding in one of the rides and I sent two of my officers and we brought them here. So here we are. He was right. You three seem to be the only witnesses. So tell us exactly what happened. Doesn't matter if it makes sense exactly; let us worry about that." Bill Gunn looked at his watch, "We have about an hour before Mr. Ford will be conscious again. We can all go see him then; I have two squad cars available to take us to the hospital. The others are out looking for the creep who did this."

"He can't talk?" said Kate.

"Not for a while dear; not until the stitches heal at least."

He opened up another drawer and pulled out a gray cassette

recorder, turned it on. "Ready?"

Kate nodded on one side of Kevin, looked at Ivan and he nodded too. Kevin looked at Deirdre; her eyes were full of love and she nodded for him, so he nodded too. "Okay then," said Bill Gunn and turned on the machine.

"Um," said Kate. "I was in the summer school on Nomans Island and I saw a man in the woods and he told me to come over, so I did. He had a ski mask on so I got afraid, but he caught me and tied something over my eyes. He said he'd hurt me if I didn't stay quiet and do what he said. I was scared. I think we rowed in a boat to another boat a motor boat for a long time, and then he put me down in the cabin I guess. And Kevin and Ivan were there and he locked the door."

Kevin couldn't believe his ears, but before he could say anything Ivan jumped in "Me and Kevin were down playing at the harbor and a guy in a ski mask, it was blue I think, with red around the eyes and mouth, told us to get into one of the boats. We were out on the water for a long time and then just sitting and then Kate got put in with us." Kevin looked at Deirdre helplessly. Her eyes said, It's okay, don't worry.

"Yeah," said Kevin, "it was a blue ski mask with red."

"That's right," said Kate, "it was. Then he came in and tied us up and put something in our mouths so we couldn't talk or move. It felt like we were there all day and it was really hot and stuffy. He didn't come back again until it was dark. He put something on our eyes and put us in a car or something and then he made us walk through some woods and then he took off the eye thing and I knew we were on the path in our neighborhood, and he hid in the bushes and told us to wait there and not say anything because he'd be watching. And we waited forever and it was scary. And then, when Nick came, he jumped out from the bushes with a big knife and grabbed him by the hair, and, and we ran."

Kevin looked at Didi in the long silence that followed. How could he not tell her what really happened? How could she not know it was Nick. She shut her eyes and opened them to him.

"Well," said Bill Gunn. "Does anyone have anything to add before I shut off the tape? Are there any identifying features at all you can tell me about this man?"

"He was big and smelly," said Kate. "The ski mask was blue with red and his lips were red."

"Blue and red," said Ivan, "you know like circles around the eye and mouth holes."

"We, um," said Kevin, not knowing what he was going to say. He looked at Mr. and Mrs. Harrigan—she was staring at Deirdre, "It was scary. I wanted to help him, um, Mr. Ford, but I was, was too scared I guess. I'm sorry." Kevin started to cry and looked at Deirdre. "I mean, I'm really really sorry I didn't."

"It's all right, son," said Bill Gunn. "You're just a little boy after all. Well. Is that it?" A moment of silence, then Bill Gunn shut of the tape with a clunk of the machine. "See what I mean, Jason. I didn't expect it to make much sense. It never does in cases like this." Mrs. Harrigan shook her head, stood up and hugged Kate, crying. She turned to Deirdre.

"Enough to give you a little higher opinion of our Judge now, I hope."

Deirdre smiled at her. "A saint," she whispered.

Bill Gunn looked at his watch. "Shall we?" he said and led them all back to the elevator. Kevin looked at Kate, then Ivan. The three of them entered together.

The elevator descended in dreadful, weightless freefall, then came to a horrible slow stop. An interminable moment before the doors slid open. There he was.

Johnny sat alone on a wooden bench in the center of the huge black-and-white tiled hallway. His knuckles were white where they gripped the edge, like they'd been holding him down with all his strength the whole time. The adults walked on ahead, leaving the children by themselves. Johnny wouldn't look at them.

"Don't say anything," he said at last, "I don't want to know what happened. That's why I didn't come up."

Kate walked up to him and carefully stroked his knotty hair.

Johnny let go of the bench and looked at her.

"I just don't want my dad to die."

She looked him back and they stood that way for a while, with Kevin and Ivan waiting to see what would happen.

"I missed you a lot," said Kate.

"Me too," said Johnny

"Guess you'll be staying with us again for a while, 'til your dad gets better?"

"'Til he gets better," said Johnny.

"Let's go see?" said Kate. Johnny got up and the four of them walked out together to the squad car.

\*\*\*\*

The hospital room was large with huge windows overlooking the harbor. Nick was the only one there. The bed was bent all the way up so he was sitting, a tube of clear fluid bubbling into his arm like a river, and another one full of blood. A white bandage glared across his neck above the thin white hospital gown where the black hairs of his body shown through like they were covered by a thin layer of snow. He was staring at nothing when they saw him; his face was pale and hollow eyed and blue shadowed and lined in the bright light. The nurse said, "Mr. Ford, you have visitors," and she left the room; Nick's eyes turned dully and then widened. They crossed Kevin's face and Ivan's, but it was Kate's face where they froze, full of fear as Kate ran up to him and kissed him on the cheek,

"Uncle Nick!" she said child sweet. "I'm so glad you're safe."

Mrs. Harrigan smiled at Deirdre, victorious.

But Deirdre smiled too.

Nick tried to smile too, but couldn't much, and his eyes were still round like a terrified kid, just like they had been on the path.

As if he had acquired x-ray vision all of a sudden, Kevin could see beneath the bandages to the real smile he had seen on Nick's throat, dripping out darkness.

"Well, Nick," said Bill Gunn, "you're a brave and foolish man. The kids told us about the kidnapping. Why the hell didn't you get some support on this, is what I'd like to know? Instead of going out there alone like some kind of super-hero. You must've known it was you he'd be after, or they? Any idea who it was Nick?"

"The kids couldn't tell us," said Deirdre, piercing his frightened eyes with her own. "Guess he had a ski mask on the whole time."

"We don't know who he was," said Kate. She was closest to Nick, over his head, speaking into his ear, looking down into his eyes, "Do you?" Nick looked quickly away from her, at Bill Gunn, shook his eyes back and forth to say he didn't know who it was.

"He had a blue and red ski mask," said Ivan, as if to be helpful.

"Dad," said Johnny; he'd been by Mrs. Harrigan's side; she had her arm around him but let him go now, next to Kate, to his father's side. Nick shut his eyes and put his hand over Johnny's on his chest. Two tears came out, stayed on his cheeks frozen there in the bright fluorescent light like two little pearls.

"We should let him rest," said Mr. Harrigan. I have some ideas, Bill. We can talk about them in the morning."

"Right," said Bill Gunn. "It's late. I'll keep two officers posted on your room, Nick, until we can get this whole thing sorted out. Jason and I'll take a look through your old court cases to see if we can find any leads there. And then, there's the harbor fire too. We're working on it Nick, don't you worry. I think we'll keep a car posted at the Harrigans too, and yours too, Miss Hawkins, if you don't mind."

"Thank you," said Deirdre. "We'd all feel much safer."

"Ivan," said Mr. Gunn; Ivan flushed up and looked at the ground. "I'm afraid I'll have to put you up in a hotel for the night. I'm sorry. We have to find a legal guardian before I can release you. Mr. Harrigan was eyeing Ivan coolly.

"He's staying with us," said Kevin. "Isn't he Didi?"

"I'm sorry, Ivan," said Bill Gunn, "but without a legal guardian or a relative, as a minor I'm afraid we have to treat you as a ward of the state."

"Uncle Nick?" said Kate and carefully lifted his hand away from Johnny's. Nick pulled the hand back and looked at her reluctantly, "Can't you do something, Uncle Nick?"

"That's right," said Deirdre, "you're the judge. Why don't you grant me temporary custody or something?"

"Well, it's a little unusual," said Bill Gunn, "but under the circumstances, if you think so Nick, I'll go along with it."

Nick grew paler and paler; his eyes lost their focus, fixed on nothing. But Kevin's own eyes were seeing clearly at last. How Nick Ford's body got stiffer and stiffer in the growing silence. Propped up in the hospital bed Nick Ford was white as salt, frozen still.

Kevin stared down into those black eyes, just this one time, without fear or confusion.

The eyes nodded mechanically, down then up. Yes.

Born in N.Y.C. in 1963, the third son of a civil engineer and a magazine editor, Erik Kongshaug grew up and was publicly educated in a New York suburb. He graduated Phi Beta Kappa from Dartmouth College with a degree in Comparative Literature—a field he would briefly pursue later in life at a graduate level—and wrote fiction  for a year in France on a post-graduate grant. He returned to the US with a scholarship to attend the Breadloaf Writer's Conference, after which he found himself, alarmingly, dishwashing in Vermont.

For the next decade-plus, he lived for the most part in small, rural communities—in West Virginia, Vermont, Maine and New Mexico—supporting himself mostly through building and woodwork, but also fishing, clerking, delivering, stocking, gas pumping and so on. At present, he is the Editor of *Random Lengths: Harbor Independent News*, in San Pedro, California—a political biweekly covering the port communities of Los Angeles and Long Beach.

Other BLINKING YELLOW BOOKS Titles:

*The Skins of Possible Lives,* by Renée Gregorio

*Shine Boys,* by Vincent Younis

*A House In Order,* by Debbie McCann

*Skeleton of a Bridge,* by Robert Mirabal

*A Little Book of Lies,* by Phyllis Hotch